SPELLBOUND

By

Jennifer Adele

For Jeff, with love.
Thank you for always being there,
for always being my very best friend and my soul mate.

Thanks to my brother, David, for the continued support,
as I took the epic journey of yet another novel.

Special thanks to Marilyn, my mother-in-law and the strong
maternal presence I cherish along this path. The support and belief
she displays for me makes a great difference.

Many thanks to my support team of dear friends for all their
technical and creative insights, which helped to make this book an
amazing reality: Alessandra, Brad, Dani, Diane, Lenora, and Lisa.

In honor of my dog, Luke, a kind and noble Great Dane who has defied the odds at every turn and taught me that there is no Fate, none but that which we make for ourselves.

"The fate of love is that it always seems too little or too much."

~ Amelia Barr ~

SPELLBOUND

Chapter 1

Everything changed the day old Mrs. Thompson died. Vera's world certainly took an irrevocable twist then and there, a twist that just kept on turning as time passed, even if that had been the only perceivable and traceable way in which the world changed. It wasn't. Vera had been so fond of Mrs. Thompson; she was fond of her old and rambling home, her well-kept yet still overflowing gardens, and all the hiding spots that could be found in both. Summering across town every year at her grandmother's was a blessing, for it meant being next door to Mrs. Thompson for three whole months.

At almost sixteen years of age, Vera hadn't really noticed the more subtle signs of aging and decay that whirled within Lillian Thompson as though she were a clock running down, rusty gears grinding towards an inevitable halt. All she saw were rose bushes gone mad with big, beautiful blossoms, lilacs becoming so fragrant that they could make one dizzy and force bees and butterflies to fall from the hazy air, and a not unpleasant encroachment of honeysuckle amid all the flowers and herbs that attempted to hold their ground with Lillian's dwindling help. All she saw was the massive oak tree at the center of the abundant grounds, an oak tree that must have sprouted long before Lillian herself had ever been born. And, it was one that seemed determined to be present even after Vera left her physical life behind. The hardy boughs and the branching leaves swayed in the hot summer breezes, and every night Vera felt closer to the heavens by staring out the open bedroom window and upwards to those leaves that appeared to be pure silver in the moonlight. The song of their rustling sang her to sleep when her mother couldn't get off work early enough to take she and her brother home for a proper bedtime. The visage of the oak did its best in its masculine appeal to replace the father that had abandoned them all so very long ago, making Vera cling too tightly to all her relationships and her brother John, who was two years younger, not able to cling tight enough.

To Vera, Mrs. Lillian Thompson was an amazing woman, someone filled with so much knowledge that she seemed like living, talking magic. And, she was always willing to share that magic with Vera in a flood of awareness mixed with an ice cream bar purchased from the truck that came through the neighborhood every afternoon. She was willing to share with John, too, on the rare occasions he appeared interested. But as a teenager, John was more concerned with school grades than sumptuous gardens ringed in by a small but steady stone wall, with the cold and calculable sciences of life than experiencing the mystery of them in personal existence, in tedious connections. John wasn't much for subjectivity, yet Vera felt in her bones that it was in that domain where every truth had its roots.

Vera's grandmother merely looked in from time to time, delighted that she could have whole hours to herself while watching her daughter's children, especially during the season in which there was no school to do the looking after. Vera's grandmother was comfortable with all of it, with her grandchildren running around the gardens and spending hours on end in the house next door, even if her more elderly neighbor had started showing the telltale signs of dementia. Lillian was a good woman, and Vera's grandmother had felt the sincerity in what was left of her more than compensated for a derailed train of thought. That, coupled with John's responsible nature, put any concerned minds well at ease.

So it was that when Mrs. Thompson died, Vera's world took on an appalling gray cast. It was as though a translucent veil had been draped over everything, and the world could only be seen afterwards with a tinge of fog; a settling that diminished the vibrancy, which had been there only hours and then days before. It took the natural bite out of life and reduced what was left of the bark to a whimper.

When she mentioned the strange fog to her brother in an ill-conceived attempt to connect more deeply with him, he merely shrugged and said, "You're upset. I've read that stress can affect all sorts of things." It was a little too pragmatic for sixteen, let alone fourteen. And, Vera didn't even bother to mention it to her mother or grandmother after that.

"Do you think she's still around?" Vera prompted further on a humid July morning, as she sat in the grass with her brother.

"What do you mean?" he replied with a question of his own.

"Do you think her spirit might still be in the house or the gardens or something?" Vera breathed a mildly ashamed sigh.

"Of course not," John snorted and began examining individual blades of grass, counting them abstractly as he did so, probably to get an idea as to how many blades were in the average square inch.

So, Vera mourned her lost and ancient friend alone. There were no more mornings spent in the lush gardens, running wild and picking flowers, or grinding herbs between one's fingertips to release their potent aromas. There were no more afternoons on Lillian's front porch waiting for the ice cream truck to roll by, and no more hour or two before dinner in which she could peek into every chest of drawers and closet in the decadent and sprawling house. It was a house that more than likely gathered dust and cobwebs as the gardens started to gather invasive, weedy interlopers.

Vera began spending a great deal of time indoors, in her grandmother's kitchen to be exact. The blonde streaks that had appeared in her hair due to summer sun faded and reduced her locks back to their regular shade of mousy brown, a color she shared with her brother. No longer subjected to the stress of humidity, her once wild and light strands lay limp around her shoulders and straight as a board. It wasn't until she sensed she was becoming as boring as John that she thought she might need to get outside again.

Maybe a month passed that way, the whole first month of summer. Or maybe it was more. But just as the gray cast, that odd mourning cloud, was starting to lift from Vera's gaze and her hair began to lighten again in the summer sun, Elizabeth appeared. And, Vera knew who she was immediately, without ever having set eyes on her before.

Elizabeth resembled her recently departed sibling so much so that Vera had thought her eyes were once again playing tricks on her. She watched intently, her tiny heart skipping beats as the old woman started moving in a couple of bags of clothes, boxes of books, and a large, dark, disturbingly ornate chest that looked like something out of a pirate movie or from a dreadful yet wondrous fairy land. Had pixies danced on it? Had satyrs cursed it? The chest would be filled with secrets. It had to be. And, Vera hoped that

Elizabeth would be the marvel her sister had been, too. But, she wasn't. Elizabeth was a unique and treacherous marvel in her own way and her own right.

Within one week of Elizabeth's arrival, a hot, dry spell settled into town. It was the hottest and driest July on record. Some people in town thought it might be the end of every garden and vegetable patch in the local area. The regional farming community began to quake with fear at what would happen when irrigation was no longer an option. The rains wouldn't come and the heat reached well into the hundreds day after merciless day. All of the grass on lawns that went unwatered turned a flaming shade of golden brown, so that it seemed heat sprang from the ground below as well as from the sun above. Insects died and fell onto hot concrete to become withered husks. Birds would not sing and parched squirrels and raccoons lapped at dripping condensation from air conditioning units. And the gardens that were well loved and well-kept year after year, the gardens that had been Lillian Thompson's pride and joy, quickly withered and turned to a maze of barren branches. The only things left to grow and hold on to any shade of green were the oak tree at the center and encroaching weeds; the unforgiving honeysuckle, dandelion leaves, and the binewood ivy. The gardens and their distinctive floral arrangements, the pragmatic herbs and their once fairly clean beds, were no more within a matter of days. It all seemed to happen so fast.

Other odd things started to happen, too, not that anyone other than Vera appeared to notice the proximity of events to the new arrival in town. The window glass of the Thompson house grew impossibly thick. Every day that Vera walked in between her grandmother's house and the Thompson home, she noticed the decreasing ability she had to be able to peek through the glass. It was as if the window glass thickened of its own accord each night while the rest of the world slept. Within the same week's timespan, the windows had grown in girth over two inches by Vera's estimation, and no one else seemed to notice. They also took on a dark emerald tint that distorted everything of once firm figure on the other side.

When Vera drug John over for a little bit of logic, he shrugged, as was his signature style and said, "I think the glass has always been thick like that." It was a curiosity to Vera how such a scrawny fourteen year old boy could impose such strong and expansive energy with his tone. When he spoke rationally, he may as well have been ten feet tall and as solid as the oak she admired, the one masculine feature in a once decidedly feminine garden that was no more, the one masculine feature that had never abandoned anyone or anything.

"Ok," Vera said, willing to let that one go on account of the fact that she had no proof, no recorded measurements or photos or anything else to back up her claims. "But, what about the tint?" she pushed. "You and I both know the windows weren't always this color?"

"It's hot," he said, as if that answered everything.

"So?" Vera pressed back against her brother, against the one person that always acted like he had the solutions to everything.

"So..." he led on, "window tint helps keep the bright light low and the house cool. All it means is that we have a smart neighbor." And with that, he went back to harassing a grasshopper he'd caught in a coffee can. Poor creature. It would have to surrender all its secrets, and perhaps even its life, in the name of science.

Vera was left to gape and gawk and feel further removed from the everyday world of everyone else. She took to wondering if she wasn't manifesting much of what had occurred, if she wasn't reading into it more than she should. Elizabeth wasn't her sister, and no one seemed to care very much whether or not Lillian was gone. There was only Vera. She was the only person left to mourn and to feel. She was the only individual that concerned herself with things that seemed so unsubstantiated, supernatural, and yet decidedly trivial while the whole town prayed for a pragmatic and life sustaining rain.

And then one day, the weeks of praying paid off. As July morphed seamlessly into the early dog days of August, one hazy evening the storm clouds rolled into town. They came in dark droves and hung ominously low, so that it appeared as if a dense blanket covered the area. Thunder rumbled and lightning flashed so bright that strange shadowy images were permanently impressed onto the sides of houses, barns, and billboards. It would be a reminder of the dreadful July they had all endured, a scar that would mock and speak to the cruel streak in nature until wise folks covered the mars over with fresh coats of paint, vowing to touch them up year after year.

Lightning split the sky in claps that caused the faint of heart to huddle in their basements. Braver souls merely held fast in their kitchens or living rooms, staying well away from the windows. It was unclear what the weather would do, what Mother Nature was capable of at that point. Would she nurture her well-meaning children? Or would she see fit to scold them for all the crimes often committed against her, well-meaning or not? Crimes like digging irrigation ditches, allowing beautiful gardens to wither, counting blades of grass, and catching innocent grasshoppers in coffee cans.

Vera's grandmother had rounded her and John up and told them to stay at the kitchen table. She wanted them away from the windows and closed in by the sheltering dining nook. It felt safe to her; it felt guarded. She paced the length of the kitchen and adjoining hall, however, suggesting that their situation was anything but secure.

"This is a good thing," she said reassuringly. Her tone was hollow though and her words fell flat upon John and Vera's keen ears. Teenagers are good at spotting a lie, probably because their rebellious lifestyles depend on telling so many. "We need the rain so badly." That part was true enough.

"Shouldn't we call mom and make sure she's ok?" John asked prudently, diligently. He was as linear and hard-lined as ever, but his voice cracked slightly. It was enough to let Vera know he was more than mildly alarmed. He was a worried youth again in an instant, and Vera felt a little larger next to him for a time.

"She's just fine, sweetie," their grandmother cooed. "She's at work, and I'm sure she'll stay there until the worst has passed us by. Besides, it's dangerous to use the phone in such weather," she pointed out.

John just nodded then as Vera touched his arm questioningly.

"Landlines," John summed for his sister. "Lightning can travel through the lines and straight into the house."

"Another reason I should have a cell phone," Vera grumbled to cover her fearful fretting.

"I'll make a note of that," John laughed dryly, and they both shared a conspiratorial smile as they thought they'd advanced a tad further in their battle towards obtaining much desired technological freedom.

As the thunder and lightning began to subside, the heavy rains finally came. They poured down after another intimidating flash cracked the sky like a hardboiled egg. The heat had cooked it a long time, and it took some serious force to peel back the shell. But, the rains within the billowy bosom at long last poured down. Vera's grandmother approached a window cautiously and looked out for several long minutes before coming back to the children at her kitchen table. "I think the worst is over. It's raining pretty good now, good and steady."

"Can we see?" John asked.

"I guess that would be all right. I don't see why not. If you two want to go into the living room, you can look out the windows and also watch some television," she said, sighing with great relief that she could go back to whatever it was she'd been doing before.

"Are you gonna call mom?" Vera inquired.

"I'll call your mom in a few minutes. Go on," she urged.

John and Vera leapt from the table and made their way to the sofa. There they proceeded to each pull back a curtain and look out the front window of the house as sheets of rain ripped apart the crusty earth, washing away with heavy tears all of the sadness and despair the lands had felt, and some of what Vera had been through.

It was just as John and Vera had settled into the sofa and some old horror movie their grandmother dug from the stash, that it happened. It was right in the middle of the phone call that had been placed to their mother that a noise so loud it shook the walls occurred. A brilliant flash from outside lit up every window and the walls vibrated so hard that unsecure plaster bits were tossed to the floors below.

Without thinking, John grabbed his sister's arm and pulled her with him into the hallway immediately off the living room. They were next to the kitchen, near their grandmother in an instant.

He moved quickly and instinctually to a sheltered spot, making Vera glad for a moment that he was so practical, so undeniable.

Vera could hear her mother's voice through the telephone receiver their grandmother clutched as she peeked around the corner at them.

"What was that?!" their mother exclaimed.

"Must've been lightning, very close by. The children are safe here and we'll go on down to the basement right away. You stay at work, dear. Everything will be fine until you get here." And with that wavering assurance, the call ended and Vera and John were destined to spend hours in the dingy, moldy basement with the washer and dryer and dirty linens for company.

When night had truly and completely fallen, and the rains had slowed to a steady drumming, a softer wash, three frightened figures emerged from the basement and went to all the windows in the house. They went to see if they could gather enough information about what it was that had been hit by the last and very close lightning bolt. Window after window, room after room, all three faces peeked out until there was nothing left to see. The windows were smudged, foggy, and the rains obscured everything. As the rains slowed even further to a fine mist, eventually, Vera and John's grandmother let them step outside to have a look around, but only as a last resort to get them calm before their mother arrived, before their inevitable and encroaching bedtime.

Begging and pleading and jumping about worked wonders on their grandmother, who never had any choice other than to finally relent. She just didn't have the stamina or the heart to wait them out, to hold fast to her position, and they knew it. They took advantage of it, as they stepped out into the night and the auspices of the backyard. In an instant they saw the damage, clear as day even with misty rain in their eyes and a shroud of nighttime over the landscape. A bolt of lightning had struck the old oak tree next door. It was the tree at the center of the Thompson gardens; it was the tree that had been the father figure and axis mundi to Vera's entire reality.

The days of summer dwindled down like the rusty innards of a decrepit clock, as did the whole withering side of a blackened oak tree, as had Lillian Thompson before she died… and autumn crept over the land. The tree at the center of the Thompson gardens had suffered such extensive damage that the entire area which had been struck inevitably and inexorably turned to rot and then to ash. Half of it fell away and then proceeded to turn to new earth, as the rest of the oak attempted to heal, to pull itself back up and together into a cohesive whole. Vera understood. It was trying desperately to become itself again after a tremendous blow.

Every day after school, Vera could be found going out to that tree, before tending to homework and until she was called in for dinner. She went out to comfort her agonizing friend and the symbol of what she'd lost in both her father and then her mystical neighbor. She wanted to be near it, to believe it still had the strength to continue. She'd sit there day after day, looking out on a world that made less and less sense while the new tenant of the neighboring house, Elizabeth, watched her.

Every so often, Vera would spy the silhouette of the removed and majestic old woman peering out a second story window. She was obviously surveying her and weighing the situation. Vera was no longer a welcome guest. By the middle of autumn she felt like a stranger, even a trespasser. But, she kept right on trespassing, doing so until she felt connected, like a partner to the healing tree and a part of the old garden space as a whole. She even got used to being looked at so disdainfully by Elizabeth. It had become part and parcel of the entire experience, the path back to a normal and rhythmic and sensible life.

And, it was right around the time that Vera was starting to believe in life and potentials again and feeling quite succinct, around the time that new leaflets were appearing in fresh fall hues on the oak, that Elizabeth hired a somewhat reputable and reasonably cheap tree removal service from two counties over.

Vera arrived at her grandmother's one early weekend morning with her brother in tow and her arms full of homework assignments due Monday, dropped off by her mother who had to pull a weekend double shift. She stepped onto the main pathway, leading to the side door to find massive and healthy branches already severed and lying in a most macabre fashion on the ground, in the abusively abandoned garden space. She could never forget it, would never forget it, for they were bleeding a thick and enveloping sap. And, the sap was everywhere. It stuck to everything: the remaining bark, the strewn and fallen leaves, the grass, the weeds, the scraps of other discarded plants, the ground, and the worker's clothes. Some of it had managed to get sprayed here and there about the gardens in a splash array and grotesque display.

"Stop! Stop it!" Vera ran towards the workers who were high up in the treetop. She ran with her arms flailing wildly, her voice drowning in the sounds of chainsaws and diesel engines. "Stop!" She screamed and yelled until someone noticed her jumping about and pointed. Suddenly the chainsaws ceased their merciless droning and the engines ground to a whining halt.

"Vera! Shit! You're gonna get us in trouble!" her brother protested from several feet away, picking up the books and papers she'd dropped in her flight without thought. As far as John was concerned though, most of what Vera did seemed to be without much rational thought.

A large man in dirty blue overalls that Vera hadn't noticed before stepped out of the cab of a truck. "It ain't safe for you here; you need to get back," he bellowed with a tinge of caution.

"What are you doing? You're gonna kill it!" Vera screamed.

"Young lady," the worker said with strained patience entering his gruff bark, "this tree is very dangerous. It's seen major damage and could fall over any day. It could fall over and take out your house or your neighbor's just like that!" he revealed with a snap. "You don't want that," he warned.

"Vera, come on, we need to get inside," her brother continued from behind her, sounding even farther away than before.

"It's healing. There are new leaves and —"

"Vera! Vera!" came the sound of her grandmother's voice approaching rapidly from behind. "Vera, what are you doing? These men have a lot of work to do."

"They're killing the tree! Mrs. Thompson's tree!" Vera insisted as she made a slight swivel to take in the form of her vigorous grandmother moving down on her. She knew even at that young and tender age how irrational she sounded. She knew she would be in for it with her grandmother if she didn't heed. And, a glance back at her brother haplessly holding her things was all it took to strike a chord in her weeping heart. He cared… maybe not about dead Mrs. Thompson, her memory, or the damaged tree… but he cared, about Vera. The trouble was Vera just didn't care anymore, not when it came to this, not when it came to something as sacred as her own personal axis mundi and maybe even the last tie she had to dear, old Mrs. Thompson.

"Mrs. Thompson?" The denim-clad bulldog of a worker looked to Vera and then her grandmother with an expression that was genuinely perplexed.

"Mrs. Thompson used to be our neighbor. She lived in the house there and that was her tree," Vera's grandmother informed with a point to the sprawling and yet disintegrating estate and then ceremoniously to the oak tree. "She passed away over the summer." And with those words, Vera received a comforting pat on the back. It wasn't that her grandmother misunderstood or lacked compassion. Vera knew then it was merely that her grandmother, Helen, was a woman who felt helpless in doing anything other than working with what was neatly ascribed to her domain.

"Is there something wrong?" A new adult voice joined the conversation. It was a lyrical, lilting, startlingly loving voice. But, there was something off about it, too. Something that felt hollow and haunted, and those were qualities Lillian's voice had never possessed. There was the underlying tone of a wounded animal crying out for freedom, an animal in an invisible trap. There was a hint of desperation and longing that was unmistakable, the same hint that was so indicative in the movements of the grasshoppers and other insects John would keep for study.

Vera peered past the grumbling worker to see Elizabeth, the sister, the one who had not been as amazing as the previous occupant of that decadent house. She was the one who had let the gardens go to seed and the weeds take over. She was not as intrinsically interesting as Vera's lost and ancient friend. Elizabeth was just as Lillian had been physically though, tall and proud and perfectly erect in stature. She commanded authority as she entered the circle and the ongoing exchange. The early morning sun set the foliage around her ablaze, and her steely gray hair stood out in a direct and startling contrast. It was daring, as daring as she was in the pristine moment of malcontent. Every whisper on the wind warned that this was not a woman to be trifled with.

"This young lady is all upset about that tree, Mrs. Drake," the blue overalled worker reported diligently.

"They're dismembering it!" Vera proclaimed as dramatically a possible, hoping for maximum effect.

Elizabeth laughed lightly and then allowed her expression to grow purposely somber as she sized up Vera in person for the first time, without a thick layer of glass between the two of them. "Oh, that's nonsense," she said with such an even tone. "Only an animal or a person can be dismembered. Look it up, my dear." She delivered her own proclamation without an audible snap, but Vera picked up on the essence of one just the same.

"That tree —" Vera started in.

"Vera…" her grandmother cautioned in the single utterance of her name. She was not pleased with this outcry or with having to be a part of it.

"That tree," Elizabeth began, taking up Vera's own words, "is very dangerous."

"That's what I told her," the worker supplied.

"It could harm people if it fell over and it needs to be removed. You understand?"

Vera said nothing. She didn't move or flinch in acknowledgement. She merely looked at Elizabeth and saw in her something cold and sad and cruel, despite the lilt her voice had managed to hang on to.

"I am sorry about this. It's a terrible way for us to get started out as neighbors," Vera's grandmother worked to make amends. "I'm Helen Caldwell, Vera and John's grandmother." She extended her hand, which Elizabeth shook cordially but coolly.

"I'm Elizabeth Drake. Lillian's sister and once nearest of kin," she responded.

"Yes, this is a small town and news of your arrival spread fast." Helen paused, uncertain if that would be received in the positive and welcoming manner intended. "The kids are here a lot because their mother works a great deal," she promptly switched topics.

"Well," Elizabeth said with something of an appraisal for all of them in her tone and in her eyes, "let's hope it goes better from here on." And with that being her instant dismissal of it, Elizabeth turned to the worker in the blue denim. "Remember to leave all the cuttings lay until tomorrow morning once you've finished taking it down."

"We can have it all out of here by end of today, ma'am. That'll save you some cash, too," the worker reported, somewhat pleased with himself.

"I didn't ask what you could do. Leave the remains lay until tomorrow. There is something I want to get from the tree." Elizabeth then turned on her heels, ignoring everyone else, and headed straight back to what Vera still considered Mrs. Thompson's house, the decadent and sprawling manor gone hard and thick and dark.

Vera wasn't able to enjoy or even be productive the whole rest of the day. Her homework sat where John had tossed it, on the far end of her grandmother's kitchen table. There the books were stacked at odd angles with papers in between and all in disarray. There was nothing that could take her mind from the muffled sounds of the chainsaws emanating through the brick walls of the house, and she sat in steadfast vigil as it went on. There was nothing that could stop her incessant wondering about what it was Elizabeth Drake wanted from the remains of that tree. Whatever it was, she would have to claim it after the workers left and before tomorrow morning's clean up. And, something deep inside Vera told her Elizabeth would not want to go get it with the possibility of prying eyes on her. She would bide her time and wait for nightfall. She would wait for the world to fall asleep.

John had lost his Saturday in studies, both assigned and unassigned. He worked away diligently in the guest bedroom that for years the two of them had staked out as their own, no matter how neutral their grandmother had tried to keep it. He was too busy to notice her sulking and planning, the mischievous and disobedient gleam creeping up over Vera's otherwise somber expression. By dinnertime, her eyes were practically glistening with the new life of a plan about to hatch.

John joined his sister at the kitchen table and glanced at her over their heaping plates of spaghetti. "Something up?" he asked just shy of a regular indoor talking voice, letting her know he was reasonably willing to keep a secret.

Vera twirled her fork around in the tomato-drenched mass of noodles. "Not right this minute," she said and gave him a little smile. "We'll talk later."

John nodded. "You get anything done today?"

"A lot of thinking," she retorted, knowing that wasn't what he meant.

"That's not going to count for much with mom or at school," he replied dryly and shoved a large forkful of pasta into his mouth.

Vera shrugged and ate a couple of bites herself. Their grandmother always made spaghetti on the weekends, and it tasted as it always did — bland, predictable, and comforting, with a pinch of basil. "I still have all day tomorrow to get my work done."

"But tonight?..." John pressed. He didn't want to wait until later to talk. That much was immediately clear.

"Tonight there are other things."

Vera and John stayed up to watch some late television in their grandmother's room, just enough programming so as to not arouse suspicion. But sooner than any other weekend night, Vera said she was tired and wanted to go to bed. John yawned almost too theatrically in great accord and trudged across the hall with her to the sound of their grandmother's rationale.

"That's good, dears. It's been quite a day," she sighed and closed her bedroom door behind them.

John joined Vera in their guest room across the hall. Once the door was shut, he was on her. "So, what's up?"

"Ok, I'll tell you, but only if you promise to put your logic brain away for a while," Vera provided a caveat.

John nodded his agreement.

"Don't you think it's odd that Mrs. Drake next door wanted those workers to leave all the dead wood just lying there until morning, when it could've been removed right away?" Vera poured out her opening line, the hook into the master plan she hoped her brother would go for.

John just looked at her blankly.

"What?" There was an awkward and heavy pause. "Aren't you going to answer me?" Vera pressed after a few moments of silence.

"You told me I had to put my logic brain away," John rebuffed with a touch of play and a mischievous grin of his own. They weren't entirely unalike, just mostly.

"Answer the damn question," she said and slugged his arm.

"Ok, ok," he relented, acting more hurt by the soft blow than was plausible. "On the surface, yeah, it's a little odd. If she just wanted a tree removed, it's odd. But, you heard her yourself. We all did. She wants something from what's left of the tree. Maybe she wants firewood for the hearth inside her new house or for some other reason. Maybe she wants to sell some of it. Maybe she does arts and crafts, like woodcarving. Who knows?" John presented the other side of the coin; he played the devil's advocate and did it very well.

Vera took it all in for a second, for cursory examination and then snorted. "Woodcarving?"

"I'm not saying it's likely. I'm saying it's possible." John defended his position. "But, that's beside the point. Just what is it you're up to?"

Vera backpedalled a bit in the face of John's improbable reasoning. "It really is no big deal. I just want to be nosey. I want to wait her out and see what she does."

"Who? Mrs. Drake?"

Vera nodded.

"And, when you say wait her out…" John led in.

"I mean sit outside all night and see what she does with what's left of that tree," Vera clarified, but then suddenly wished she hadn't. Even to her own ears, her words and her half-baked scheme sounded dramatic and ridiculous. It was a behavior that appeared to be becoming a habit.

John cocked his head and looked at his sister sideways, a look that held haughty derision. "If it makes you feel better," he sighed, sounding all too grown up again, old beyond his years and a touch stodgy. "But, how do you know she hasn't already gotten what she wants while we were watching television?"

Vera didn't waste another minute after that possibility hit the reverberating air. After clicking out the light and carefully creeping down the hallway to the kitchen, John and Vera made their way out the side door to sit in near silence and enveloping darkness, to sit within a comfortably embracing shadow that fell halfway across their grandmother's back lawn. And, they waited….

It seemed as though they waited hours for something to happen, for Mrs. Drake to appear. It was as though the movement of the night ground to a standstill and the moon refused to budge from its perfect placement in the sky. They waited so long that John finally fell asleep under the auspices of near silence and shadow. The crickets had chirped him a lullaby he couldn't resist, and when Vera found him snoozing so peacefully, she didn't have the heart to wake him. She also didn't want a witness in the event that nothing occurred. She didn't want to have to hear all the logical outpourings that would follow if it were something simple and harmless either. Vera actually found she was more content to be in this endeavor alone.

It was about the time that Vera found herself dozing off as well that the rustling of dry and brittle leaves pricked up her ears and re-engaged her senses. She went from barely conscious to high alert in a flash, her heart beating madly in her chest like some sort of fidgety bird anxious to get out of its cage. She felt fluttery all over and crouched low to the ground to peer forward, preferably without ever being seen.

Soon enough, the silhouette of a tall and proud woman emerged from the clinging shadows and low light that were the hallmarks of the gardens at night. Elizabeth was moving swiftly and with very little sound among the leaves and the weeds and the darkness. She was revealed only in glimpses of pale moonlight, and every once in a while the crickets would hear her footfalls on the dead leaves and go still themselves, as if afraid. And as Elizabeth approached the remains of the tree, she stopped and bent low. She stayed there for some time, doubled over and hardly visible unless one knew exactly where to look, unless one had been stalking her movements from the very beginning, and Vera had.

It took a great deal of time before the obvious scavenging behavior revealed itself in what Elizabeth was doing. She started carefully moving branches in her wake and in her search, making more and more noise, as the crickets grew increasingly silent for longer and longer stretches. She moved about in concentric circles until at long last she stopped and stood stock-still. She stayed that way in the milky moonlight until the night regained its composure, its normal rhythm and balance, until the crickets sang and a light breeze felt confident in its return to the area.

Vera watched with baited breath as Elizabeth bent low to the ground one last time and retrieved an item, a fragment, a portion of the tree. It was a piece retrieved from part of the trunk. Vera couldn't help herself. She was obsessed now, compelled to take the chance and inch closer. She couldn't help but wonder what was so special about that particular piece of wood.

Vera stopped when she was close enough to hear Elizabeth take in a long breath and then sigh.

"The heart piece," Elizabeth breathed with something of awe and rapture and sadness. It was so important that she felt compelled to give a verbal acknowledgement.

Vera watched as the wood in Elizabeth's hand began to beat with an impossible pulse all its own. It beat to a dying rhythm, steady and then faulty and then attempting to be steady once more. It pulsed, it vibrated, and then it bled the signature sap from earlier that day, a sap that ran down Elizabeth's arm and began tainting her soft, white nightgown and robe. On and on it beat with a diminishing tenacity, until Elizabeth quite suddenly squeezed it and all the sap ran out in a horrid gush. The wooden heart, the fragmented center, then turned hard and black and shiny. It was so sleek and shiny that it practically shimmered in the moonlight. It twinkled and caught the gleam of a tear in Vera's eye.

Vera gasped and then clapped her hands quickly over her mouth. But, it was too late. Elizabeth spun on her heels in the direction of the sound and in an instant spotted Vera's slight form in the scratchy yet sublime autumn grass. Their eyes locked. They held each other there in a moment that felt of forever, and neither one it seemed could turn away. They were sharing this together, all of it, whether either of them wanted to or not. Fate had sealed them in with the last heartbeat of the momentarily revivified axis mundi and the silvery white moonlight.

Chapter 2

Vera started to have dreams. Not normal, mixed up, making no sense at all in a waking framework style of dreams. They were not nightmares that any person might occasionally succumb to from too much spicy food or a late night binge. No. She started to have dreams that were not like any she'd ever experienced before; they were not the sorts of dreams she'd ever heard anyone talk about either. And, these nighttime abominations were not something she wanted to tell others about. In fact, she didn't even tell John. Vera was inclined to keep all the weirdness of Elizabeth's retrieval of the tree heart and the dreams that followed a secret. John hadn't seen it, and it was too far-fetched for the one person who had. Her mother and grandmother would have dismissed her outright or sent her to counseling to deal with the disturbances, and Vera wasn't partial to either outcome. She was determined instead to ride out the rough patch on her own.

To make matters all the more interesting and startling, Vera noticed after several nights in a row of disenchanted autumnal sleep, journeys into the Land of Nod, that all her dreams included Elizabeth in some form or fashion. Some nights her nocturnal visions would show her the heart of the Thompson oak tree, beating out its last. Sometimes a tidal wave of blood would erupt from it and swallow Vera whole in a warm sappy mess of drowning liquid. But no matter the scenery or outcome, Elizabeth was in every single one. She even saw Elizabeth chopping down the tree herself, and no matter how many times Vera would stand in the way and even lose appendages that suddenly grew back, Elizabeth, or the visage that appeared to be her, would not stop. She awoke the morning after that terrifying dream to find herself flailing against her brother who was trying to snap her out of the night terror's firm hold.

"Geez!" was all he could exclaim as she was finally catapulted into a waking awareness. John helped his sister untangle herself from her sweaty mass of bed linens. "That must've been one freaky nightmare."

Vera's head was swimming and she couldn't manage to respond right away. By the time they stumbled out into the hall in their pajamas, well on the way to a Sunday morning breakfast of their grandmother's scrambled eggs, she spoke. "Too much late night television." She met her brother's gaze cautiously.

"I'll say," was what he replied and then gave a shrug. It was as good an explanation as any, she supposed. It was good enough for John. It made rational sense.

It made so much sense that Vera started to believe her own stories, her own reasonings, her feeble attempts at dismissal. When she woke in the mornings, she would say things to herself like dinner the night before had sat too heavy, too many sweets before bedtime, the coffee she was allowed to have was very strong, or the horror movie on television must've really bothered her. But she knew in her heart, and somewhere deep in the recesses of her soul, that all those excuses were not the case.

It wasn't until Vera had a dream one night that involved Lillian, a dream that was the epitome of graphic, that she knew she was in trouble. She knew the matter was far too big and dangerous to ever be overlooked again. In that crazy and undeniable dream turned nightmare turned waking vision, Vera saw Elizabeth as she always appeared, in her soft white nightgown and robe, chopping down the tree. The oak tree became a man on this night and then became a tree and then became a man once again. He had a face and a voice and a vicious sappy blood splatter every time the axe hit him and dug out a little more of his wooden flesh.

"Stop!" Vera screamed. But, her declaration morphed at the last minute, right as it left her throat, making her sound only like a hoot owl giving a call.

Elizabeth turned and looked at her, and then behind Elizabeth's imposing figure emerged her sister, Lillian. It was dear, old Mrs. Thompson. She looked just as she had most of Vera's life, aged but regal, tall and proud and wise. She resembled her sister so very much that Vera found herself liking the both of them as she drew nearer to her lost and ancient friend. She wasn't as afraid of Elizabeth with Lillian there, even if she had been chopping down the tree man but mere seconds ago. And, there is rarely any logic to dreams anyway.

Vera made her way straight to Lillian and threw her arms about her friend. Lillian hugged her back and there was a genuine connection of welcoming and gratitude that flowed between them.

The energy was so strong that for a moment Vera thought everything was going to be all right. And, then Elizabeth spoke.

"I broke her heart," Elizabeth intoned and nodded towards her sister. "And, now she will break mine." And with that being her final decree, Elizabeth's long, strong, and boney fingers tore through her soft gown and aging flesh, they tore straight through to the rib cage and then sank in until she pulled the sternum to one side. Elizabeth revealed a cracked and bleeding and broken wooden heart. It had only a flutter left and not a true beat. It was the heart of a walking shell, a ghost of flesh.

It was after that dream Vera began trying in earnest not to sleep, but she quickly found she couldn't keep that up indefinitely. And, no matter how long she went without a nap or a night's rest, the dreams came back. There was no length of time that could separate her from them. She also started to attract unwanted attention, first at school and then at home. It was a little disappointing to Vera that a couple of her teachers should be the first to notice, but she had to admit her family unit was far from ideal and always had been. Her grades began to slip during the winter of her junior year and not only had the teachers voiced their concerns, but it wasn't long after that the main guidance counselor decided to get involved. The prospect of college was on the horizon and Mr. Martin was taking quite an interest in Vera's sudden slide down a slippery academic slope.

Vera did the best she could to keep up appearances after one trip to Mr. Martin's office. She went so far as to talk to John, getting him to help her through the roughest patch she'd ever experienced. And, Vera was pleasantly and deliriously surprised at his willingness to assist that went along with his further willingness to let the matter remain between the two of them, and the school, for the time being.

"Mom's stressed," John said to justify his behavior and his sworn oath to secrecy. "She's going through a lot at work and doesn't need to know if we can get a handle on this ourselves."

"And, what about grandma?" Vera checked.

John looked at her with a tinge of worry he'd never confess, and that emotion was mixed with a sympathy Vera could barely stand to see from her younger brother. "She'd just tell mom. I agree with you on this. We should try to get through it together.

Besides, it might not be that big a deal in the long run. Lots of people have sleep problems a time or two in their lives."

Vera had wanted to hug her brother then and say thank you. She wanted to declare her undying loyalty to him from then on. But, she hadn't been able to do either of those things. It would've been like admitting to a far graver situation. It would have been admitting the truth… and it would've just been too awkward given the natural state of their relationship.

Vera and John struggled along for weeks that way, without anyone at home knowing that to which the school staff was privy. Vera kept on alluding sleep only to inevitably be captured in the vortex of some somnambular attack, and John kept trying to help her fit all the life pieces back together during her waking hours. But, her days grew consistently more dull and gray with exhaustion.

It was right around the turn of the seasons, as winter morphed into a fluctuating green and brown springtime backdrop, that the school called Vera's mother and had her come down for an afternoon discussion about the deteriorating situation. Apparently, John could only do so much, and secrets can only be kept for so long.

Vera hated it. There was so much to detest about it, but the very worst thing that occurred during every one of her mother's rare and forced visits to the school was the way all the staff members called her 'Mrs. Norton.' It was bad enough that her mother had never bothered to change their last names after their father left them, but she then allowed everyone to continue to refer to her in that consistently erroneous married term. It made Vera nauseous; it felt like so much pretense.

"Mrs. Norton, we've been working very hard with Vera for some time now, trying to get her grades back up. And for a while there, she was improving, but we find ourselves unable to make any sort of noticeable long term difference at this juncture," Mr. Martin stated in a reasonable tone and with heavy coffee breath, as he sat on the front edge of his desk, appearing casual.

Vera's mother shook her head as though she had water in her ears, mousy brown hair flying from side to side. "I don't understand. Why wasn't I called sooner? Why wasn't I notified when her grades started to drop in the fall?"

Vera cringed. She knew what was coming next.

Mr. Martin looked at Vera's mother, Marilyn, in that key overly perplexed away. "Mrs. Norton, we did notify you. We sent home numerous notifications about study halls and rigorous academic plans designed to get Vera back on track for college, notifications that you signed." He produced from his top desk drawer a flourish of paperwork, all sheets bearing forged signatures. It was over.

Marilyn reached out an exasperated and unsteady hand to clutch the papers being thrust at her. She was missing a much needed work shift to deal with this mess. Vera watched with great resignation as her mother's eyes roamed over the incriminating documents. "I can't believe this," her mother whispered. And, for Vera there was no escape beyond that moment.

With the soft suppleness of springtime, came regular school counseling sessions, increased study halls, and even therapy with a trained psychologist who visited the school and was paid by the state to do so. John backed away from his sister slowly, so as to not be caught up in the maelstrom that seemed to have ahold of her. And, Vera couldn't blame him one bit. What else had there been for him to do, really? He'd just turned fifteen and had his own concerns; he had done all that was reasonable and then some. It was no surprise to Vera that he should feel helpless. Vera herself felt helpless, too, and especially so when she had to think of ways to dodge the artful questions of the therapist that saw her every Friday afternoon. She figured if he knew the full extent of the truth, he'd have no choice but to have her committed, or some equally awful outcome.

It wasn't until the heat of impending summer bore down on the town that Vera felt the strange sensation inside herself of something going snap. A portion of her own psyche had fractured under the immense strain of haunted sleep and subsequent bouts of sleeplessness, and with the fear of summer school looming and of possibly being held back a grade and forsaking her college dreams, Vera confessed to her therapist. She confessed that she was having difficulty sleeping. She omitted the nightmares from her revelation, omitted the sensations of waking visions, and forsook details of the graphic natures of her dreams and her own self. But, she did cop to not being able to sleep regularly, sometimes hardly at all. She also told her therapist about her growing fear of falling asleep, which he said could readily be induced just by the sheer lack of proper circadian rhythms.

"It may not be rational at all, this fear of sleep when you need it so much, but it is quite simply a very common defect in our brains." And, he said that medical mouthful with great authority and as if it were actually no big deal.

Vera thought then of how much John would've liked the man. Perhaps he would've gotten more out of those therapy sessions than she did. At least it would've been an educational endeavor for John, a chance at further analysis towards life and its mysteries.

Not long after that conversation came the pills. And, not long after the pills, school let out. But the dreams continued. They went on and on and on, in spite of the medications, until one night the madness ground itself to a horrendously lucid halt.

One night, Vera woke to a call on the summer winds. The guest bedroom window had been left open by their grandmother to keep the air circulating, without the need for expensive air conditioning. The ceiling fan whirred faintly, moving the delicate breezes. There was no other sound though. No crickets chirped, no frogs croaked, and there were no distant sounds of cars passing by the town on the highway that was less than half a mile distant. There was just the whir of the ceiling fan, the fan that was saving them money until the heat got to be too much.

The strange call on the winds was akin to a whisper. It was saying something; it was speaking to Vera. She knew that much intrinsically, instinctually, even though the words spoken weren't clear and distinct. Vera sat up in bed and strained to hear above the soft concentric rhythms of the fan overhead. The whispers were simply too faint with any background noise present. Perhaps that was why the animals and insects had gone so still; perhaps they were listening, too.

"John," Vera called out into the fuzzy charcoal darkness of the room. "John, are you awake?"

After several seconds there was still no response.

Vera pulled herself up and went to her brother's bedside, planning to give him a good shake so he could hear it for himself and know there was something more to her dreams and restless sleep episodes than just bad brain chemistry. But when she got there, the bed was perfectly made, as if it had never been slept in, and John was gone.

"John?" she said his name a little louder and with the hint of a question.

No response.

Vera went to the open window and peered out at the vacant back lawn. She saw stars and moonlight and shimmering blades of moist, emerald summer grass... but that was it. There was no one. There was no person waiting there in quiet refuge. The winds continued to whisper, and there was no one but her to hear them.

"John!" she practically shouted out the window, hoping not to rouse her grandmother if he had decided to sneak out and investigate the odd phenomena on his own.

But, silence fell upon her ears again and was then dissipated by the ceiling fan's perpetual spin. Then came the return of insistent, whipping whispers on stronger breezes.

Vera moved away from the window and searched along the wall for two switches she knew were there, they had to be there — one for the lights and one for the ceiling fan. She found them and felt for the switch that was flipped up. With great ease, her fingers ran over the top of it and shut the fan off... and she listened.

The syllables the winds were speaking became more distinct. There was a phantom's muffled enunciation to them. She could almost make out words from the very far end of her bedroom. So, Vera went back to the window hoping for even better luck. She thought it might have been John, involved in some sort of investigation outside and not wanting their grandmother to know about it. She thought he might have been trying to call for her, too.

"John," she tried again, giving a good amount of breath to her inquiry.

Silence. She waited.

"John?..."

More silence.

With the fan off and the whispers suddenly refusing to communicate now that they could, Vera felt a new sensation creep up on her. It was the feeling of eyes gazing back from the murky summer darkness. She felt as though Fate were staring her down, looking straight at her, and then through her with glowing ethereal eyes that she was not attuned to see but could sense nonetheless. They felt like red-hot embers throwing heat from a distance.

Vera didn't call out for John again. In only her pajamas, which were basically a tank top shirt and pair of boxer shorts, emblazoned with the faces of some random cartoon characters, she left the perceived safety of her overly warm bedroom and made her way out to the hall. It was vacant. Only a small nightlight showed the way to the kitchen and also straight across to the room where her grandmother Helen slept.

Vera decided to crack the door, to check in and make sure everything was all right across the hall. But as the small golden glow from the nightlight illuminated her grandmother's room, Vera made another terrible and mystifying discovery. Helen was gone, too.

"John!" Vera didn't bother holding back. She called out so loud that her voice made the air ring throughout the house. Her shouts bounced off the walls. "Grandma! Where are you?" She made her way down the hall to the kitchen, where she yelled again.

No response.

"John! Grandma! Please, answer me! Please!" she practically screeched as she arrived in the living room to once more be met by no one.

No one answered. She called and called. She pleaded and circled. But, no one answered.

Vera fled the living room, shot through the kitchen and out the side door of the vacant home to the backyard. They had to be there. They had to be. She was almost certain she'd find them in the shadows somewhere, equally disturbed by the near silent night and drone of windy whisperings.

"John," she said a little softer and into the shadows. "Grandma," she tried again… for what else was there to do?

The quiet and the absolute stillness only served to punctuate her growing fears. The winds didn't move and the animals didn't cry. There were no traffic sounds or human voices or barely audible breezes. There was only Vera, locked under the merciless glare of Fate and the abandoned house looming over an empty grass lot.

Vera wanted to cry but was too frozen to do so, gone stiff with fright. She was left to wonder over and over in her mind if there was nothing and no one left anywhere in the whole town or on the entire planet. There was too much nothingness present with Fate.

Eventually, she found herself able to melt down into the dewy and cool summer grass. The earth still smelled alive and there was a thrum that emanated up from the ground. She took solace in that without even knowing if she should. It seemed enough merely to be assured that something else was alive and sensed her, some being aside from the Fate that would not show itself and the whispers that had abandoned her, too. She curled up on the ground and ran her hands through the blades of grass that John, on occasion, liked to count. And as minutes merged into what felt like hours, she thawed to the point where she could finally cry, sobbing into the welcoming soil. She thought she'd cry forever; she was sure she'd cry a river.

Then there was a sound, a very familiar sound. It was a rustling that she never thought she'd hear again. It was so distinct in its pattern and placement that Vera knew before she even looked up to confirm it. It was the oak tree. Its leaves were rustling in the returning winds that whipped up all around her. The silver slivers of leaves that were now easily spotted in the moonlight swayed back and forth, and they made a reassuring rustling noise that staunched the flow of her tears. Vera got to her knees and peered up longingly at the tree, at her axis mundi that had come back from beyond a wood chipper's final veil.

Vera blinked in rapid succession to clear her vision of the remnants of tears, and every time she did so she feared opening her eyes to no tree at all, but the tree remained. It stood tall and enlivened in the moon's incredible glow.

And, the winds whispered their message to her once again, only this time she could make it out. She understood every word. "We always think we will have more time…"

"What? Time for what?" Vera said to anyone and anything that might answer.

Nothing did.

The winds then took refuge in the treetop of the mighty oak until the snap of a twig sent them off and the night fell dead silent again. The moon darted back behind a cloud and the oak tree was cloaked in shadows and hidden from sight.

"Who's there?" Vera said with a tremble. It could be anyone or anything.

When the moon made its way back out again, bringing with it a pure beam of light that was almost as bright as noonday, it fell to where the tree had been, but was no more. Instead, there was Elizabeth. She was crouched low and almost hidden amid the overgrowth that had once been the gardens.

Vera took a few unsteady steps forward. It wasn't that she was happy or even relieved to see Elizabeth; it was more that she seemed to be the only other person in the entire world.

As Vera made her way slowly but surely to the edge of the hedge line, and the tiny stone wall that separated her grandmother's backyard from the neighboring property, the wall that ringed in the garden space, she saw Elizabeth was not only crouched low to the ground but also diligently working. There was noise and movement. There were rhythmic strokes. There was also this air of determination spiraling up from Elizabeth, and it was so potent the weeds started to unwind from dead bushes and back away. Vera wondered if she shouldn't take the hint and do the same. But, where would she go? Back into a vacant house and an empty life?

Vera glanced behind her to see if anything had changed in an instant and it hadn't, so she decided to move forward, to speak with the old woman who had wrecked what happiness Vera enjoyed before her arrival. But, even that decision had taken too long, had been a mistake, and Elizabeth was to be found missing in the amount of time it took to make the judgment call.

Vera was alone again.

"Hello?" she spoke to the gardens and the oak tree she couldn't see and the weeds and the moonlight and maybe even Elizabeth.

No one answered, and Vera was starting to wonder whether anyone ever would again. Had anything been there in the first place? Or had she imagined it?

She stepped firmly into the gardens that had gone to seed and approached the spot where Elizabeth had bent so low. She stood in the foreboding shaft of pure and cool moonlight and scanned the area for signs, for clues, for a signature of individual life or affirmation. She discovered one. A sigh much like the coo of a dove escaped her lips as she retrieved what looked like a little dark doll lying in a patch of barren dirt. As she picked it up in her trembling hands, she realized that the color of the doll was nearly the same as the shade of dark brown to almost black that matched the disturbingly ornate chest Elizabeth had brought with her. She'd brought it when she first moved into the Thompson house. It was a chest that looked like something out of a pirate movie or from a dreadful yet wondrous fairy land, and Vera had been so certain then that the chest would be filled with secrets. Had this doll come from inside it?

Vera held the little wooden thing up to the moonlight for closer examination, and it was then she took note of how shiny and black the wood actually was and how warm. It felt as though it might come to life at any moment and beat, much like the heart of the tree had beat and vibrated its very last. Had this doll been forged out of the wooden heart of her beloved axis mundi? Vera started to suspect the latter more and more during her rudimentary exam.

The little doll, so intricately carved and well-polished, had no eyes — it could not see, not even the stark and naked truth. It had no arms — it could not hold on to anything, not even love. It was both beautiful craftsmanship and tragically sad in its final expression, in its twisted artistic message.

The snap of a twig again caught her ear and the rustling of invisible birds' wings or maybe even those of bats, but something moved and then slithered. Were those shadowy creatures alive or dead? Vera could not be certain of much at that point. She turned and caught sight of Elizabeth peeking through shafts of moonlight as she drew near, returning from goodness knows where. As she stepped in to share the bright beam Vera occupied, a range of emotions flashed across her face, and all of them served to make Vera deeply uncomfortable.

"I-I'm sorry," Vera stammered and held out the doll for Elizabeth to take.

But, Elizabeth didn't touch it.

"Really, I know I shouldn't be out here, but I can't find anyone. My brother and my grandma are both gone," Vera explained and pliantly set the little figure back onto the bare patch of earth.

Elizabeth watched her curiously, like one of the ghostly birds Vera had heard taking flight. She said nothing but just took it all in. She didn't even offer an explanation of such strange goings on or suggest that she would help the girl find her lost loved ones who had mysteriously vanished. Elizabeth seemed far more concerned with the little doll lying in the dirt.

Vera felt confident of only one thing, that Elizabeth was not going to be helpful. "Again, I'm sorry," Vera said softly and started to traipse back to her own yard and maybe even the house. She had to go somewhere, she supposed.

"Wait," Elizabeth commanded in a quiet voice filled with tremendous authority.

Vera turned to take in the specter dressed in white, standing in the moonlight.

"The doll is you," Elizabeth said with such determination that Vera instantly knew her to be mad. And, Vera had also begun thinking of herself that way, so it seemed a reasonable match, an honest attraction and repulsion, ebb and flow.

"What?" Vera came in closer, drawn by the concept of any sort of explanation of the oddities that had befallen her life since Lillian died. She stepped back over the tiny stone wall and through the segmented hedge line. "What are you saying to me?"

"The doll is you, but it is more," Elizabeth waved for Vera to come and stand beside her, to contemplate the wooden handiwork at their feet.

Vera complied.

"One day this doll will come to you. It will come for you," Elizabeth went on, talking more to the doll than to Vera.

"What? Why?" It was all such a riddle wrapped in the greatest riddle of all, Vera's deteriorating life. And, it was the very last thing she needed.

There was a pregnant pause filled with possible answers hanging between them; it was growing, pulsating.

The ancient Elizabeth who so resembled her deceased sister finally locked eyes with Vera. "Because you touched it."

Vera shook her head to try to snap out of it. And when that didn't work, she pinched her skin hard and over and over again to try to wake up, to try to be jolted back into some semblance of a recognizable reality. But, it was all to no avail.

"I'm going crazy," she resigned at long last and squatted down into the dirt, where Elizabeth inevitably joined her.

In a move that was more human and even maternal, Elizabeth draped a slender arm around Vera's hunched shoulders and held her in perfect union for minutes upon minutes. They compounded to the point that Vera began to distort Elizabeth back into her sister. But, she was most certainly Elizabeth.

"One day that doll will be as much yours as it is now mine… for what I have done, dear girl," she said to Vera with a wistfulness that revealed she did indeed have feelings, an opening chasm in her heart space of emotions.

Vera let her slowly steadying hand run along the smooth surface of the warm and sleek doll. "What have you done?" she asked, uncertain if she was now speaking to the little figure or her unwilling human companion. They felt like the last two people on earth.

It was Elizabeth's turn to sigh, and she was growing more relatable with every passing moment. She was becoming more of a real person to Vera, and less of a stoic and unmovable force to be reckoned with… or not.

"I denied my sister all those years, so many years. I let her go. I cut her out and set her apart from my life," Elizabeth poured forth from an internal damn that was surely breaking. "I denied a whole love, a true love… and I can't even remember why, not now. It was so many years ago." Her speckled and veiny hand joined Vera's in caressing the shiny black and brown doll as it started to shimmer in the moon's quickly cooling glow.

Vera started to shiver and shake, she trembled hard with a pressure inside raging against the cold that was compressing from the outside. Elizabeth loved and she hurt to the point that she grew cold and harsh and determined. Everything started to grow hazy and blurry. Elizabeth moved away from Vera as strong and demanding winds whipped up and whirled across her small frame.

"Wake up!" the wild winds insisted. "Wake up!" They prodded her with a familiar voice.

"Wake up!" It was her mother. She was standing over her bed, in work clothes, and giving her a good and proper shake.

Vera sat bolt upright to take in the comfortable surroundings of her grandmother's guest bedroom, and what was quickly becoming her main resting place over the years. A window was open, bringing in fresh and slightly chilled summer morning air. John's bed beside her own was made already and she could hear the faint noises of activity from the kitchen.

"You can't sleep all day," her mother chided. "You need to get up and dressed and started on your studies before I go to work today." Marilyn didn't trust Vera's keep to hardly anyone anymore. She knew her own mother could be easily swayed to let the kids do what they wanted, especially in the laid-back summer months. "You have to keep up or you'll be put in all-day summer school, maybe even held back a year. Is that what you want?" she went on.

Vera rubbed the sleep from her eyes and shook her head. "No," she said with half-hearted surrender.

"Then get up and get dressed. We only have four weeks to resolve your grades. Have breakfast and then start on the studies Mr. Martin sent home for you. I need head in to work," she insisted. "It's going to be a long summer," her mother said wearily as she pulled back the covers Vera had been wrapped up in.

"For the both of us," Vera agreed, giving her words more gusto this time. And, she suspected in her heart that her own summer would prove to be far longer than anyone else's.

❖

From that point on, from the night of the dream about the little doll and Fate, Fate who had invisible yet glowing ethereal eyes that felt like red-hot embers, the sleep attacks and upsetting episodes stopped. In fact, Vera stopped dreaming altogether. At first the only thing she noticed was that there were no more nightmares and she slept straight through. This then gave her much needed and long overdue clarity of thought and vision, and she was well equipped to catch up on her studies and right the wrong that had thrown her academics so far off course. Her mother was pleased. The school staff, and especially Mr. Martin, were also greatly relieved to find Vera passing on to her senior year unimpeded and preparing for college. It looked good on such a small school not to have any children falling behind, and it kept tax dollars flowing. Vera's therapist was also happy with her turn around, and by the time her studies were completed and the heat of July was gripping the town, he removed the sleeping aids from her regimen. She was pill-free and deemed to be all better; as far as everyone else was concerned, the evidence was conclusive that she had merely been the victim of a random sleep disorder, a freak abnormality that had run its natural course.

"It feels so strange how I got better all at once, you know, just like that," Vera said with a snap, confiding in John a week or so after seeing her therapist for the last time. The two of them sat on their grandmother's front stoop, waiting for the afternoon run of the ice cream truck, and Vera occasionally caught herself peeking over her shoulder to the front porch of the Thompson house. She would've rather been waiting over there.

"That's probably because you were getting used to it," John said with instant dismissal.

"Hmm…" was all Vera had to come back with, and she must've done it with a gloomy expression because after a minute or so her brother elbowed her in the ribs, playfully pulling her out of it.

John smiled at her then in a goofy sideways fashion. "You know, you were becoming well-adjusted to being crazy."

Vera lightly slapped the back of his head. "Crazy my ass," she retorted when she couldn't find a more witty rejoinder.

"I think more of you is crazy than just your ass," John went on, causing Vera to roll her eyes.

"What person goes from sleep walking, talking, and nightmares, to suddenly and completely normal?" To Vera's mind that was a more than fair question.

"A crazy one," John said and gave her another shove.

Vera rolled her eyes at him again and with more flare, knowing he meant well, he meant to be funny. "And, I'd been on those pills for a while. They weren't doing anything," she persisted.

John interlaced his fingers and leaned forward over his lap then, as if he were very tired, tired of her or waiting for the ice cream truck or both. "Some medicines take a while to build up in your system before they have an effect," he argued back. He just couldn't help it; it was his nature, the very core of who he was and how he worked. Deep down, John liked to disprove things, especially irrational and incomprehensible things. He liked to organize, catalog, and strategically place everything where it should be in his environment. Vera guessed that it gave him a sense of control, a sense she always saw right through as never actually being real. To Vera control was an illusion, and a dangerous one. It could lull a person into an insidiously false sense of security, and that was when bad things happened.

Vera sighed. What had she expected from John anyway?

"Also, didn't the therapist say what you had was self-limiting? That it ran its course?" he prodded on.

"Yes," she said reluctantly.

"Well, there you go," he sewed it all up nice and neat. Case closed.

But to Vera, it didn't feel so nice and neat and over with. When catching up with schoolwork had possessed her mind, along with appeasing her mother and getting off the medications, she hadn't really thought about it or felt about it. But now that the idleness of summer was trickling down upon her, a new feeling emerged, a sensation that all was not better, all was not right. She felt like she was sitting smack in the middle of the deceitful eye of a hurricane. It was the calm before another bout of storms.

The jingle of bells and a merry little tune yanked her from fretting.

"What you need is ice cream," John said and pulled her by the arm to the curb for cool refreshments under the hot and hazy sun.

Unlike the summer before, there were heat waves balanced by refreshing rains. No droughts took hold of the town and no monster storms lashed out at ancient and important trees. John had his pursuits and Vera decided to lose herself in them as well. She helped him catch all sorts of insects and shoved aside her revulsion at what was to become of them. To her, time with her brother and a distraction from the brooding was more important. She was determined not to go back to how it had been before. It seemed to her that the best way to avoid a possible relapse was to emulate John as closely as possible. Her brother never once in his life suffered from sleep disorders or obsessive worrying or irrational flights of fancy. John may not have had the control he believed, but he had an air of normalcy. And, Vera was drawn to it more and more.

In the harsh light of day and under the fine levels of vision of John's microscope, it felt as though nothing out of the ordinary could touch her. Nothing unexplainable could happen. And, every night Vera drifted into a sea of black, into a visionless void. She was no longer troubled by nightmares or terrors or attacks or episodes. But, nothing lasts forever…

Right around the time school started again, as the leaves on the trees began to show the first hints of golds and reds and browns, Vera felt a rift. John started having even more afterschool programs and commitments. Her moving into her senior year meant he was a sophomore, and he had to prepare for life after high school. He had to start thinking about it and building up his own portfolio of accomplishments. During the day there was school and then in the late afternoons John was involved with things like science club, math tutoring, drama, shop class projects, and even baseball. It never seemed to stop with John. And because of all his budding extracurricular activities, he had gained a myriad of friends who occupied the bulk of his weekends. Their grandmother, Helen, was, of course, quite pleased. It was far less looking after that she had to do. But, the entire situation left Vera feeling very much alone.

Vera couldn't bring herself to branch out into her own extracurricular pursuits, not that she'd done much of it at any point in school, ever. And, too many of her classmates had come to think of her as an outsider after the bout of bad dreams and sleeplessness she suffered the previous school year forced her to pull back and away. So after school each day, Vera took to traipsing around in the Thompson gardens, or what was left of them, while Elizabeth peered out from various windows now and again. She looked on disapprovingly, but Vera hardened her heart to it. She thickened her skin so that Elizabeth's cold stares were a source of curiosity and contemplation, and nothing more. She was somewhat surprised that her neighbor didn't complain or threaten to have her arrested for trespassing. No, she simply stared. Perhaps she was pondering Vera just as much as Vera was contemplating her.

There was so very little left of what the gardens had been. They had become mostly patches of binewood ivy and long trailing vines of creeping honeysuckle. Crabgrass and dandelions sprouted up here and there, but there were no definitive beds and no living shrubbery left under all the encroaching vines.

One blissful autumn night when it was too warm to close up the house but too cool to throw open every window and whirl the fans, Vera fell into a state of deep and dreamless sleep such as she'd never had before. She could have been dead for as gone as she was. She never would've known about it. The day had been hot and humid, but the night was cool and clear. There hadn't been a cloud in the sky or the slightest chance for more rain the rest of the week. All seemed right with the world as crickets sang, frogs croaked, and the occasional glide of some creature slithering in the grass or swooping through the air reached the ears of those delicate enough to hear them.

And, it was that night Vera was shot out of the void of slumber by the intense brightness of what appeared to be a flash of lightning, followed by an incredible roar of thunder. She sat up in bed so fast it made her dizzy, and it took her several minutes just to get her bearings in the heavy dark. Once her head finally stopped spinning and her eyes adjusted, she looked about the room to see John sleeping peacefully in the twin bed next to hers. Nothing was out of place. Their bedroom window had been left open half way to let in the crisp, clean night air and outside all the stars twinkled in a perfectly clear sky. There had been neither lightning nor thunder. There wasn't even a cloud from what Vera could see from the confines of her bed. However, something awakened her abruptly. Something had snapped her out of her blissful coma; something had appeared as lightning and thunder.

She quickly and quietly got up and made her way to the window, careful not to disturb her brother. Vera gazed up at the sky and saw only a flawless night. There must've been hundreds of stars visible, and the sound of all the nocturnal animals stirring was reassuring in a primordial way. She took in a deep breath and let it out to slightly fog the window. She did it again and again until the whole surface fogged and then laughed lightly at herself for being a bit rattled by what she assumed to be the very first approach of a dream into her life again. The lightning and the thunder, it had to have been part of a dream. Vera let out another long breath and then wiped her hand across the window glass to clear it, but as she did so a figure emerged. There was someone in her grandmother's backyard. There was someone out there looking in.

Once Vera got over the initial jolt of a specter appearing in the backyard, she looked further. She squinted and made out the undeniable outline of Elizabeth Drake in her signature robe and nightgown. She was standing on her family's property now, peering in at her. And, the irony was not lost on Vera. Turn-about was fair play, she supposed. What disturbed her most was when Elizabeth began to wave, beckoning her to come out.

Vera didn't know what to do, and for quite some time she stayed locked in place and only watched in a frightened and surreal suspense. But, there was also an alluring element about the way Elizabeth wanted Vera to join her. She didn't seem as intimidating as before, as she always had, and eventually Vera's curiosity got the best of her and she slipped a pair of house shoes on with a bathrobe and headed out to the dewy lawn. Deep down she wanted to see what would come from their strange interaction. There was that powerful draw and the realization that she still missed Lillian dreadfully.

A couple of feet away under a crescent moon that kept the inky swirl fairly dark, Vera came to a standstill. She wasn't ready to get any closer, at least not yet. Lillian was gone and Elizabeth held some sort of awful secret. That much Vera had come to believe from the dreams that had mentally raped and scarred her. The oak tree was gone, and that was Elizabeth's fault, just as the gardens going to seed was her doing. And the house, the grand and illustrious and decadently mysterious Thompson home, had grown dark and started to turn to shambles from neglect. Vera found all these things to be unforgivable. But still, Elizabeth resembled her long dead sister so much.

"Why are you doing all these terrible things?" Vera shocked herself by finding a voice.

"Because I am a terrible person," came Elizabeth's retort. It was meant to be candid and witty and horrible all at the same time, and the reply hit its marks. Then Elizabeth went completely cold, inside and out.

Vera cocked her head at that revelation. She'd never met anyone as simultaneously cruel, fascinating, alluring, and straightforward in her life. And, cold. "What do you want?"

"Too many things. I want all the things I can no longer have, what life and time and tide have taken from me. They will take from you, too, my dear. That I can promise you." Elizabeth held an expression on her face that was both sad and reproachful. She was harmful.

Vera drew back as though she were about to be slapped. "Why would you say these things to me? What have I ever done to you but wander around in what used to be your sister's gardens, gardens you've let go to waste?" Vera was exhausted from it all. And, what else could Elizabeth possibly do to her anyway?

Elizabeth clucked her tongue at Vera's words as though she were no more than a foolish child. "I don't want to say these things to you. I don't even want to talk to you, but I have to. You see, I am a terrible person, young lady. I treated my own sister, my very own flesh and blood, with no regard all those years. So much is lost to me now over a petty squabble I can no longer remember. I have been cruel and callus, and I misused all I'd been given. I am a person who deserves to be punished, who deserves to be cursed."

Vera held her own tongue. She wasn't about to argue with any of that.

"And, I suspect you and I are a lot alike," Elizabeth came right around to it, to her ultimate point, or the beginnings of making it.

"I'm nothing like you, just as you are nothing like your sister," Vera spat in defiance, pushed to a brink she hadn't seen coming.

The old woman who had grown pale in the slight streak of moonlight also became somber and grim. "Oh, you are. There's no doubt about it… or the doll wouldn't have summoned you."

"What the hell?! That was all a dream! I was only dreaming!" Vera began to come unhinged and drone on and on, saying those same words in a fast chant. It didn't alter a single facet of the moment though.

Elizabeth was wise enough, if not kind or maybe even unkind, to let her ramble until she had exhausted herself, run dry of words. "If it was only a dream, then how could I have known about it?"

Vera absolutely hated how in that instant that woman could sound so pragmatic and rational, so much like John.

"And, I suspect you have many of the same hidden traits I display now. You have the same sorts of issues in relationships. Too much closeness or not enough."

Vera glanced at Elizabeth quizzically.

"It's all the same issue, really," she dismissed with a wave of her hand as though that were beside the point. "There is no one in your life that you feel is close enough to you, is there?"

Vera found she couldn't answer. Her throat had gone completely dry. It was as if the truth had parched her.

"And you want them all to be closer, so much closer. In fact, too close," the old woman went on. "There is no untainted, pure, true, fearless love in you, is there?..." The question reflected back. "It's not there anywhere," she finally answered. "And, it is what you value most, what I valued most… and now you are cursed and I am cursed. I bathe in the curse, in my condition, in what I have become. And, that love will elude us both. This will be yours," came the irrevocable decree.

Elizabeth shoved the little eyeless, armless doll that she had carved and she had cursed into Vera's unwilling and trembling hands.

"It's yours…" she leaned in to whisper into Vera's ear, much like the winds had whispered.

Vera recalled the words of the winds as she closed her eyes tight and felt breezy arms wrap around her — "We always think we will have more time…"

She felt glowing red eyes from somewhere, those ethereal embers of Fate, glaring. It was reminding them both of its immovable presence as Vera then opened her tear-glazed orbs wide; she woke up.

She was beneath the covers and in her bed. John was sleeping only a few feet away, like before. And, like all the other times before, she would've been able to convince herself that this was just another dream, a return to dreaming, had their not been blades of grass from the yard between her toes, along with bits of honeysuckle and binewood ivy, to suggest otherwise.

Chapter 3

Vera didn't have a single dream after she left town for college. She didn't dream, not even one single solitary time, in the whole four years she was away. In fact, the nightmare or whatever it was about the eyeless, armless doll was the last she was to experience, and then came the big move. Vera thought for sure if anything were to induce more odd night terrors or waking dreams it would be the stress of going off to college; it would be all the major changes that manifested along the way, but she stayed blissfully dream free. Nothing strange or curious happened to her after that horribly evocative autumn night, and Vera dove head long into creating a vibrational pattern of normalcy for herself. It was only prudent. She thought it would be her only salvation.

She not only indulged in a rather pedestrian and well-worn routine, but also immersed herself so fully that it seemed no remnant of her old world or her old self survived the plunge. To anyone looking in from the outside, it would appear as though Vera had been reborn, a delicate but tenacious phoenix bird arising completely new from a fiery womb of late high school destruction. She built what felt like a solid structure out of mundane habits for her own soul and psyche to live in all the time. And, it felt so incredibly safe, despite the still small voice nagging at the back of her head time and again. That voice knew it was a grand illusion, but its warnings went largely ignored. And the less she listened, the less it talked.

Not only did that life feel so very safe, but it also attracted the right people, or folks Vera considered to be the right and best kind: high achieving artists and artisans, business owners and aspirers, writers, founders, community organizers, charity workers, educational consultants, and full-time teachers. They were people who were all too busy to get caught up in a trick of the mind or a far-fetched fantasy. There was no time for daydreams or night terrors. Even the artists were lucid, for they were the people in the creative world making money, not the ones starving on behalf of this vision or that one. Vera had even managed to snag herself a dependable boyfriend, Lance. He was someone, it seemed, who certainly knew how to keep a proper place, too.

It seemed perfectly clear that moving away from her small hometown had been good for Vera. She felt she'd escaped the invisible but palpable confines where boredom and personal pressures allowed her imagination to run wild. She was prone to flights of fancy, and was eventually able to admit that painful fact to herself at some point during her second year of college. The epiphany happened while she was contemplating her future. And on the heels of that realization, Vera then had the bold emotional surge that told her she didn't want her future to be anything like her past. Where she lived during her formative years and how unsupervised she'd been had made for a slipped focus, and that wasn't helpful for someone as vivid as she could be. It wasn't the best atmosphere for her development. It was what had been though, but it didn't have to be the focus, the center point, what she'd become, or she didn't think so.

Time away from John had also been beneficial, surprisingly enough. It let her see just how right he was from an empirical standpoint, or what passed for it. After four years away, Vera was absolutely convinced he'd been consistently right in his approach to life, even if he hadn't chosen the most prudent course and gone off to college, too. All the work during high school on his end to make himself college ready and institutionally desirable went down the tubes, from Vera's perspective. That was her prevailing opinion. But, no, John felt it was better all the way around if he went straight into the actual workaday world and made some money; he strove to move forward in a stable field, maintaining all the while in his own unique way that the best and most accurate answers were the logical ones. He found his place among numbers and structures and physical efforts as a carpenter enmeshed in historic home and commercial remodels.

It was so simple then, for Vera and John. The imposed order of the external grown-up society functioned more as a crutch for them both, and also as a framework. Their own frequencies had harmonized by the time Vera came back home. They were in accord and moved in what looked like tandem. Both newly minted adults were of the mindset that the best people were the ones you could pin down and easily categorize, people that kept their proper place. If they couldn't be pegged, then they ought not be liked, and definitely not trusted. And the best college degree in John's mind, and Vera's, was the one that focused on the money producing minefields of business. Vera got her business degree after a tiny bit of nudging from her brother in that direction early on. And, her studies remained math and social science heavy while she was away. She stuck to her plan instead of responding to the innate and therefore totally wrong, albeit alluring calls, of literature, art, and philosophy.

Everything lined up for Vera from that standpoint, too, and she was starting to feel strong enough, sturdy enough, to finally come home to an adult life. She thought she could face the town and her past without it affecting the days ahead. It all began with John's phone call before her last semester at school. The ball was rolling.

"I've got this great little shop lined up for you in the antique district, and the remodel is almost complete," he started in immediately as she answered her cell phone's upbeat techno-toned ring.

"Hello to you, too," Vera said sarcastically.

"Yeah, hey," John acknowledged his lack of manners unnecessarily. There was no formality at play when it came to siblings, no matter how far away or how long it has been since the two have seen each other. "Listen to me," he went on. "You wanted a great storefront for your bakery and coffeehouse concept, and I've got one. It just fell into my lap as a remodeling project from the bank, and they want to move it quick once it's done. You wanna take a look?" he pressured good-naturedly.

"Can it wait until the end of the semester? I'll be coming home for sure then," Vera asked, already sensing the answer to that pointless question. John made important decisions quickly, and if he was in the driver's seat on it, she would have to go at his pace or eat proverbial dust.

"No. It'll be gone by then. Come home this weekend," he instructed.

Vera sighed. "It's a long drive and I've got a lot —"

"Are you serious about this or what? You're gonna be done with school in a matter of months and will need a source of income. Now is the time. You can rest and recover later, when it's convenient," he pointed out the obvious.

"Oh, ok," Vera moaned. And, she went home that weekend to see the totally adorable little shop John's small and budding company had all but completely redone. There was very little left to do to it by the time she got there, which led her to believe it had good bones underneath the new and tempting outer layers.

The shop was positively exquisite and in an instant Vera knew she would gamble her whole professional career plan on it. Not only did the place speak to the romantic in her, to the tendency she had for those flights of fancy whether they were shoved aside or not, but it also spoke to her newly developed pragmatic side. And, it didn't hurt to have John's abiding approval either.

The storefront was immaculate and welcoming and bursting with fine 1920's detailing. John and the couple of workers he kept on as regular contractors, along with a hired architect, had done an incredible job at pulling in new materials that were in accordance with the originals used by the designer. If Vera had been a gambling woman, she would've gone so far as to bet what good and little money she had on the chance that the recently completed design of the place was exactly what the original architect had intended. It might have been a perfect echo of what had come before, of what had been there, then wasn't, and now was again. John was skilled at bringing forth the facts and facets with no personal interpretations or creative slants added. He would re-envision it only to the point that it had been a vision the first time, and the only substantial differences to be found would be in the age of the building materials.

Brand new mosaic tile flooring in octagonal blues and whites made for a heavenly walkway throughout the main room of the storefront. Coved ceilings with sturdy metal beams shaped like columns here and there set up the authentic tone of the main room and gave a feeling of airy lift coupled with earthy support. Their metallic blue color was only a shade or two off from what could be found on the floor. There was room for a bakery case on the left side of the great room and for a coffee bar on the right. And then there was the benefit of plenty of space for tables and chairs practically everywhere. Customers could relax while being served. Vera could see it, and it all made sense.

"There's a fully functional kitchen in back ready for appliance hook ups, so you would only need to get the equipment delivered to be operational. Add in some wi-fi, and this will be a kickass place," John said with strength in his voice and a sturdy nod. If he had been confident as a boy, he was absolutely domineering and charismatic as a man. And that made Vera comfortable, in a weird way. John was never wrong. He couldn't be. It wasn't in his character.

"You really think so? You think this can work?" Vera checked. She wanted to hear his decree again.

"Sure. Don't you?" he shot back.

She did. In one fell swoop Vera helped herself, her brother, and her new but as yet unrevealed business partner with the stroke of a pen. John would like her partner in this entrepreneurial endeavor, her current college roommate who was native to their region of the state and only hailed from one county over. He would have to. Odds were good he'd also get along with Lance, when and if the two ever met. And with some insistence and a lot of encouragement, Vera Norton became the newest business owner in her own hometown, the town that had been the setting for the early shambles of her life.

Vera was correct in her assumption that John would like Misty, her ex-college roommate and brand new business partner by summertime. And, what wasn't to like?... Misty was the pinnacle of easy-going and good-spirited people. She always meant well and even though she may not have been the brightest or best equipped for studies and business arrangements, she was creative and classy and ethereal. She was warm and fun to be around, and those qualities were what drew Vera in as a close friend and confidant. And as it turned out, those characteristics drew John in as well.

It happened suddenly when Vera went with her brother and Misty to once again tour the shop space in the antique district. Misty hadn't seen it yet and was relying on Vera's decision alone, but as a partial owner Misty had every right to see and to judge.

And, Vera had every reason to insist she do so before appliances and bakery cases arrived.

Vera watched as her friend took in the grand layout with the same rapture that had overtaken Vera the first time she'd laid eyes on it. She could tell in a blink that Misty was hooked, and it only took her a little longer to realize the same emotion subtly brewing in John.

"Well, I'm glad you girls are happy with it," John concluded as they stepped out the front door and Vera locked it behind them. "When are appliances being delivered?"

"Next week," Vera said dutifully.

"And the bakery cases and tables and chairs, et cetera?" he inquired further.

"Already on the way," Vera beamed. "In fact, Misty picked them out, along with some artwork and durable tableware for serving. She's far more artsy than I'll ever hope to be."

John smiled at Misty in a way Vera had never seen him do before. It was a long, soft, inviting smile; it was one that Vera wished she could receive some day from a man so taken with her.

"Is she?" John asked of Vera but directed towards Misty.

Misty smiled back as her cheeks simultaneously flushed. She was good at that, of cuing up reactions that should have been involuntary, and on her it looked natural even when summoned. "The only proof I have of that right now would be my barely achieved art degree," she chimed in with a slight coyness.

"And your clothes," Vera added for good measure.

Misty was the offspring of hippies who had let her run wild and free for all her days. But instead of tending towards the other end of the spectrum as she grew up, Misty embraced the energetic inheritance she'd been given by her parents and had gone with a touch of classy Bohemian swirled into the earthy mix. It was her own signature to the metaphysical family crest. She consistently donned soft, flowing skirts and layered tops of bright colors and rich fabrics. Exotic prints and risqué cuts never frightened her away either. And, her illustrious blonde ringlets that cascaded down her back whispered evocatively at the waistline of treasures to be found further below.

In the right lights, especially at the golden hours of dawn and dusk, Vera had taken note of how her friend could appear positively magical and not quite of this world, and she secretly envied that strange and innate ability, that gift of nature, which had been given to Misty and not to her. No, Vera was plain to the point of being mousy, and she'd grown more lack-luster with every passing year. Vera was a drab dreamer hiding in a businesswoman's stuffy attire. She figured it was the best she could do, the most she could hope for in the physique she occupied, and the life she'd both inherited and then continued to build.

"You do look very nice," John confirmed for Misty unnecessarily, giving her outfit and fine figure the once over. "Listen, I know you are inundated with a lot of new. I mean, you just moved into town and now the shop, but would you be open to grabbing a cup of coffee sometime?" John never wasted a single moment. It was the obvious and rational next step towards his latest goal.

Misty giggled in her intoxicating way. "A cup of coffee?"

"I'll be in the car," Vera said, excusing herself. She quickly made her way to the vehicle and shut the door. She even kept the windows rolled up for their privacy and the protection of her own memory, no matter that there was a relentless summer heat ruthlessly gripping the day.

"Yeah, coffee," John kept on. "Is that not okay for me to ask?"

Misty gave him a bright smile and touched his arm reassuringly. "No, it's okay to ask. It just seems a little odd with me opening a coffee shop or coffeehouse, or whatever Vera is calling it. That's all," she pointed out the irony.

John gave a hearty chuckle then. "I guess pretty soon the last thing you'll want is coffee."

"Not at all. I love a good, strong, hot cup," Misty said a touch slower then, to display her growing involvement with the idea.

John brightened at her response. "That's great! We have a diner here in town that serves a decent cup and pretty good burgers. Would you be up for that?"

"Sure. It'll be a nice way to get to know more about the town. I've only been here a few times as a kid for the state fairs and occasional shows, even though I'm only from a county over. I just never had any other reason to come here," Misty acknowledged.

"No one does," John said with a wink. "But, your shop will get lots of local business, and the folks here will love it. You'll see. It's not a bad spot to call home," John encouraged. "So, I can call you and make arrangements?"

Misty gave her newest suitor a phone number, a sexy sideways smile, and a couple of blinks of her daring aqua eyes. They were a sultry reprieve in the heat of the day, like two limpid pools of refreshing water. "Absolutely."

John had been just as busy as Vera during the four years she spent at college. He'd managed to start a thriving business of his own on the offshoots of a dying one, previously owned by a dying man. He'd managed to scrounge up and then provide a new workspace for Vera and Misty, and also remodeled their grandmother's old house. He hadn't suffered from idle hands through the years, and he hadn't grown lazy or complacent with the passage of time either. Even with things going reasonably well, John stayed busy and on top of his life. He kept his grandmother's house, that was now his own, in order.

Vera's grandmother, Helen, had passed while she was away, and coming back for the funeral had been a tough time. It had been even tougher for her keeping Lance at bay when she went home for services; he strongly felt the need to be there, the manly urge to support. In his eyes, it was a boyfriend's duty.

Lance was also something new and thriving in Vera's life, and he would soon encroach on sacred ground, on her home turf, and there was no keeping everything nice and neat and compartmentalized anymore. No, Vera sensed it was becoming more a matter when than if. College had helped Vera do that, compartmentalize. It helped her have decent relationships while also keeping folks from getting too close. But, that was ending now and Lance only lived a town over and less than an hour's drive away. As a teacher, he had nights and weekends pretty much free, aside from grading papers, and he was already making plans as to how they would start to spend that time together.

John was bound to meet him soon; it was inevitable. And, he would give his approval or disapproval and then leave Vera hanging with it, and truth be told, she didn't know which was worse. Ever since that terrible autumn and that wretched dream that might not have been with Elizabeth and the doll, she had corrected herself from clinging too tightly to people, to relationships, to emotions… even though not being able to cling tightly enough might turn out to be just as bad, the exact same problem. It just felt better, safer.

John immediately invited Vera to stay with him in their grandmother's house, giving her one bedroom rent free for as long as she wanted it, for as long as it took her to get established and generate what amounted to a paycheck. It was generous and not entirely unlike John, but Vera suspected there were other motivating factors spurring on his offer. With Vera living there, it meant that Misty would be by a lot… and she was, for either one or both of them.

"I'm really glad you're going to do this. I think it's a smart move and will let you save some money," John had said as he helped haul in boxes full of Vera's personal things. "And, I'm not home as often as I'd like to be, which is hard on Frank," he suddenly admitted a secret of his own, letting it slip on purpose to cause her natural inquiry.

"Frank?" Vera played the game.

"Yeah, once we get all this inside, you'll have to meet him. He lives here, too," John drew out his mystery, savoring it, and gave her a small grin to say it was all in good fun.

And once she was moved in to the old guest bedroom she and John had shared during their childhoods, she joined him in the kitchen for the big reveal. She stood next to the dining nook where they had consumed so many meals as kids, served up by Helen mostly, by their grandmother's hands.

"So… Frank…" she led her brother on.

"Yeah," he said and opened the door that led not only to the side walkway and backyard, but also to the basement.

Frank charged up the steps, all one hundred and forty pounds of him. He was a horse-like dog, and a bundle of furry fun on four legs. Vera was instantly greeted by the love and affection of a mantle-marked Great Dane, full of youth and vigor.

"Oh my god!" she squealed. "You got a dog!" Vera threw her arms around his gigantic neck and hugged him tight, feeling instantly drawn in by his joyous company.

Frank loved it. He slobbered everywhere.

"Stating the obvious," John picked at her.

Vera rolled her eyes at her brother and continued to fawn over the huge beast that looked like it was wearing a tuxedo with all his black and white fur, his very distinctive markings. "When did you get him?"

"Only a couple of weeks ago. One of my workers found him roaming the streets. We tried to find out whom he belonged to, but never did. So, he lives here now," came John's pristine summation, a quick string of facts.

"Oh, Frank, you are such a good boy," Vera crooned, watching the dog's tongue loll happily out the side of his mouth. She then looked back to her brother. "Why Frank?"

"Why not? It's as good a name as any," he replied.

Vera tilted her head to one side like a curious bird. "True…"

John sighed and gave in to his sister. "Frank Lloyd Wright. He's named after the architect."

"That makes perfect sense," she finally gave her own form of not so weighty judgment to his choice. And, it did. It made crystal clear sense. As a matter of fact, it was so very telling that Vera felt she knew for the first time what it was John dreamed of being but feared he would never become. She knew whom John admired and what his standards were for greatness. She knew he had dreams, even if she had run dry of them. Vera started to feel a long lost sense of closeness again, and it was sprouting inside her belly from a seed long denied nourishment. Now that she had come home, she was transfixed by her old ways, and maybe that was what had prompted her to ask a very hard question on that roller coaster of a day. "Have you heard from mom?"

Vera hadn't.

"Not since she ran off," John snorted and turned his back to head over to the refrigerator. He threw the doors on it wide open and stared into its brightly lit and gaping maw. "You hungry?"

Vera patted Frank's head as she sat down at the kitchen table and he obediently lay down at her feet. "I could eat."

Their mother was a sore spot for John as much as she was for Vera. The only mental injury that might be worse was their completely absent father. At least their mother, Marilyn, had been there somewhat during the course of their childhood. However, her running away with the first man that became interested and had a small bankroll left a bad imprint on John and Vera. Marilyn had moved several states over and into a life of luxury, by comparison, with a man who could give her material belongings along with the exclusive beats of his own heart. Vera understood why it had been so easy for their mother to pull up stakes; she didn't like it, didn't approve of it, but she understood.

"You know, just because mom wasn't very happy here doesn't mean we can't be," Vera offered a gentle and more positive means at reframing.

John shut the refrigerator doors with his foot while transferring an armload of food to the counter near the stove. "I know," he said a bit too sullenly.

Vera decided not to pursue discussing the issue further. It was time to change topics. "So, do we still have the same neighbor?" Vera wasn't even sure where that question had come from.

"What neighbor?" John asked absently, as he began washing vegetables.

"You know, Mrs. Thompson's sister…" she led on for him.

"Oh…" He let his mind wander. "I think so. I haven't seen much movement from over there lately. Everything's been pretty quiet, up until you and Misty got here."

"Are you saying we're trouble makers?" Vera joked.

"I know *you* are," John eyed his sister cautiously, as though she might start up with her vivid imaginings any minute. "I don't know about Misty yet."

❖

John took Misty out for coffee as offered and planned. John took Misty out for many coffees, even after the shop she shared with his sister opened up and found itself well under way with a burgeoning clientele. Misty may have served coffees and pastries all day, but John was determined to take her out for them anyway, although they were often decaf, sugar-free, and in the evening hours. He paid for meals and went with her on long walks about town to take in what little sights there were to see on balmy summer nights, when the crickets sang and cicada thrummed through the trees.

He let Misty tell him about her childhood over in the next county, growing up with lax and loose parents, running the fields and chasing wild animals, laying out under the moon and stars to wake bright-eyed and bug bitten in the dewy grass. John listened when she spoke, but he also watched. He was enamored with her hair of spun gold and her supple, sun-kissed skin. He adored the way her clothes twirled loosely with each movement as her facial expressions did the same, morphing seamlessly one into the other. He could listen to her without having to talk much, and he liked that. There was very little of himself that he had to put out there to get close to Misty, and he could get as close as he liked and then go no further. Misty didn't seem to want for much, or if she did she kept her desires well hidden, maybe even better hidden than John's.

"So, you've really lived here your whole life and never had any desire to leave?" Misty asked one day as they trespassed on the grounds of an old, abandoned rock quarry that was never monitored. Limestone piles were everywhere as they wound their way up trails to then go through the shells of lifeless buildings with vacant window eyes. There were ghosts in this place. Misty could feel it. She sensed the energy patterns of what once was, but she was smart enough not to say so to John. She sensed that he didn't care for such things, just as she could tell his sister kept her interests in them safely tucked away.

"None at all," he said back, as they took the path towards the immense pit. It was a hole that yawned from the nearly empty earth, an earthen hole filled only with rainwater, and just barely at that. It wasn't enough. It never could be.

"Why? Aren't you curious? Don't you want to see something new, something you've never seen before?" she pressed on as the trail started to slant downwards and the tree lines thinned.

John just shrugged and peered down at his feet. "There's nothing out there that's going to be any different from what we have here."

Misty laughed. "There's a lot that's different out there," she dismissed. "You mean you don't want to see anything new?"

They stopped but a few inches away from the water line, the very lip of the quarry. "I'm seeing something new, something wonderful, and I didn't have to go anywhere for that to happen."

John felt like the quarry then, as he spoke those words. He understood it. He suddenly knew why the open, fractured, and gaping abyss moaned like it did in high winds and why it craved something more substantial than fickle and evaporating rain water. He knew what it was like to become aware of a hole inside you that seemed impossible to fill, and yet he longed for something to fill it, for someone to do so. For the first time in his life, he thought maybe one person could act as all the mud and plants and rock that would eventually fill even the quarry's incredible depths, if given the opportunity, if given the time.

Vera watched her brother falling in love, and she watched her friend Misty doing the same. Day after day, Misty would burn biscuits, scorch bagels, and create cookies that more closely resembled charcoal briquettes. She was a woman in love, and a woman in love always burns things in the kitchen. It was as though all the heat and passion from the person got the stove extra hot. Or, it could've been that all the longing and desiring and daydreaming allowed for the baked goods to sit too long amid the flames, much like the chef. A woman not in love simply forgets to turn the oven on. And, Vera never cooked, not even for Lance, who probably deserved better.

Vera watched her new business start to build, despite singed pastries. The coffee was good, the wi-fi was better, and the entire shop was one of art and atmosphere. It was very different from anything the town had offered to them before, and surprisingly enough the locals took to it. Misty had done a tremendous job in picking out prints and canvas reproductions to go on the exposed brick walls. She had a tendency towards impressionistic landscapes, including open fields and broad lakes. She liked whites and blues and greens, and her tastes went perfectly with the main colors already provided by the structure they occupied. The floors and the columns matched exactly to the works placed on the walls, tying the vibration of the massive room together. It was all coming together, and Vera thought for sure by the end of the year she would be drawing close to a low-end paycheck for herself. Misty was already taking home some small amounts of cash.

Ashamedly, Vera also started to watch the house next door to her living space again; the house next door to what had once been her grandmother's home. Vera began watching the Thompson house, as she would always think of it no matter who lived there, and the grounds that had once been the sumptuous gardens around it. Lillian may have passed long ago, and her grandmother may have passed more recently, but Elizabeth was still alive. Vera caught sight of her one day, out on the back steps. Elizabeth was gazing aimlessly out into the old garden space as though interesting things were happening there, as though she could see the weeds' spiraling growth from millisecond to millisecond. Perhaps she even heard the minimal movement of the invasive interlopers that were now dominant life forms. Vera couldn't be sure what she was doing, and she was afraid to say hello, let alone inquire. No, Vera just watched for over an hour and then finally gave up on trying to solve the riddle of her old specter of a neighbor. Elizabeth had never been kind to her, so Vera figured there was no use in trying to send a little compassion her way either.

Life went on, as it should. Life went on for some of them, most of them, and Lance started to become a pragmatic and reoccurring driving force in Vera's, whether she wanted him to be or not. He had quickly discovered that it only took forty-five minutes with no traffic to arrive at Vera's doorstep from his place. It would've taken even less time on those windy roads if Lance had been the type to ignore speed limits and safety protocols, but he wasn't. He was a teacher and liked to both create and follow rules. What had once been an endearing quality was starting to become an irritant. And, he went from being close but not too close, to too close. He was over every weekend and had started suggesting that he stop by an evening or two during the week for dinner. He was leaning into her space so much that she knew eventually John would meet him, despite all the time he spent out and about with Misty. And one day, Lance showed up around sunset unannounced to find Vera in the backyard staring at her neighbor's property.

"What are you doing?" he asked with a casual smile as he arrived at the end of the side walkway, which emptied unceremoniously into the yard.

Vera turned with a start to see him staring at her as though she were odd and still adorable somehow. "What are you doing?!" she snapped back. "What the hell are you doing here? And, why are you creeping around and spying on me?"

Lance lost his smile and all the luster that went with it. He brushed back his thick blonde mane and stared at her, contemplating. "I'm not spying on you. I rang the doorbell several times, but no one answered. I was only coming around to try the back door when I saw you out here," he explained as though he had to, and maybe he did.

"What are you doing here anyway? I wasn't expecting you," Vera went on, calming down a little.

"That's the beauty of it. I thought I'd be a good boyfriend and swing by, pick you up, and take you out somewhere nice," he said, a brief smile returning. Lance was everything that little girls dreamed of marrying someday. He looked and acted so much like the mythical Prince Charming.

Vera sighed. He also wasn't a quitter, she had to give him that. "Lance, you should've called."

"It's only dinner," he said and came over to her. "Why don't we go out and enjoy tonight?" He slid his arms around her waist and drew her in close, so close that his breath tickled her cheek. "You've been working an awful lot lately."

Vera pressed back against his chest with both hands, but he was reluctant to loosen his grip. "That's what it takes to start up your own business," came her reply.

"One night out won't derail your plans," he insisted.

Vera continued to press and press hard until he let go. "Actually, it will. I have to meet someone at the coffeehouse this evening for an interview."

"What interview?" Lance said as though she might be lying.

"We've gotten busy and I need to hire some help. I'm interviewing someone for a clerk position to help run the cash register, keep the place tidy, and fill supply orders… you know, all the day to day stuff that starts to overflow."

"And you have to meet this person tonight?" Lance grew even more suspicious.

"Yes," Vera put her foot down. "We have an appointment, and Misty and I really need the help. Why do I have to keep explaining myself?"

Lance reached out and rubbed her shoulders reassuringly. "You don't. I'm sorry. What time is the appointment?"

"Why?" Now Vera was the one getting suspicious.

Lance sighed gently. "Just tell me."

"Seven o-clock," Vera reported.

"How about if I swing by afterwards and we grab a quick meal? Have you eaten yet?" he suggested.

Vera would've said yes and been content with the lie, but right at that exact moment her stomach growled, betraying her. "No," she said with the hint of a sulk.

"Good. So, eight o'clock I'll pick you up at the coffeehouse and we'll share a quick meal. Ok?" he arranged.

Vera just looked at him.

"Ok?" he asked again.

"Ok," she resigned, feeling all the more that Lance really did deserve better. But for some reason, she just couldn't give it to him.

Lance followed Vera back into the house where she got ready for her interview and subsequent date night. He talked about his work and his week while she primped and prepped, and all the while she couldn't stop thinking about what she saw in the Thompson garden space. The scar of where the massive oak had once stood was still visible on the ground if one knew where to look, if one could see through the ivy that was trying desperately to fill in a spot once occupied by an encompassing axis mundi. Vera had wanted to get closer and examine what was left after the years had gone by, but she'd been interrupted and sidetracked. So, Vera acted as normal as she could and got ready for the evening instead. She went out and met Keith, who had to be the most overqualified clerk in the world.

Misty and Vera could hardly believe their good fortune in having someone of Keith's caliber apply for the job. Both women had been resigned to the probability of having to accept a local high school student who wouldn't even be able to spell the word 'responsible,' let alone grasp the implications. But, instead they were sitting down with Keith. He was ex-military, honorably discharged, and had seen a wide variety of expanses and experiences in the few years he'd been in the service. Afterwards, he'd gone off to college for a couple of classes only to then inherit his grandfather's farm on the outskirts of town — the Simms Farm. He'd decided then and there, at the moment of that fortuitous inheritance, to drop school and dive straight into life. It had been a bold move and perhaps even a wise one in the long run, only time would tell. However and for the time being, the farm wasn't fully operational and he needed additional income to make ends meet. Vera was intrigued by Keith's background, but also by his new property. It had been years since she'd seen or even thought about the old Simms Farm.

"Well, you certainly seem qualified and ready to go," Vera said, looking into steel gray eyes that held a tinge of hazel softness around the edges. "To be quite frank though, we were expecting to hire a local student or something, you know, a teenager not looking for a full time job or very high wage."

Vera felt Misty holding her breath as she revealed the downfalls of the opening to their prospect.

"It doesn't have to be full time," Keith met her head on. "Even if it was, odds are that when next spring gets here I'd have to drop to part time anyway. I'm interested because it's supplemental."

Vera nodded. He was interested because it wasn't too much of a commitment. She liked that. She then looked to her partner, Misty, who was nodding in agreement. Apparently, she liked that, too.

"Well," Vera said after a long pause, looking Keith over and seeing a man in his prime, well-heeled and well rounded, with all the discipline she could ever hope for, "what do you think?" She turned to Misty, putting her on the spot.

Misty fidgeted a little, as she was never very confident in business relations. "I feel good about it," was what she came back with, giving Vera a shaky smile.

Vera then met Keith's gaze and gave him a grin of her own. "I do, too. Ok, plan to start on Monday morning. We get here early, at four-thirty."

"A.M.?" Keith checked back.

Vera just gaped at him. "This is a bakery and coffeehouse…"

Keith laughed at her then, a hearty and embracing chuckle. "I know. I'm just teasing you. What's work without a little humor," he said with a wink and a nod.

Misty nudged Vera in the ribs and the two of them shared a glance. It was all going to work out just fine; the feeling was mutual.

Life trudged along as the summer season wore its way from the bright and early days into the aptly named dog days, and August heat hugged the town and glazed the fields with a wilting golden brown hue. And, it was during those dog days that John worked more and Frank went outside less. Vera's household had all but ground to a total halt. The days were deliriously similar and the nights were dreamless and deep. The coffeehouse was on its feet though, despite the fact that it would likely still be months before Vera could safely draw a paycheck. But, Keith had been a good addition, after all. His presence meant that Vera and Misty could take a few more breaths, have a bit more of their lives back.

Misty spent what time she could with John, and Vera did everything she could to stay inside the house with Frank. Vera actually enjoyed it, except when Lance popped by. And, if having Keith there at the coffee house meant Vera would have to wait even longer for take home pay, she felt it was worth it in the end.

And, Vera definitely didn't mind watching Keith's fine and fit form hustling and bustling about the place. He bussed tables, hauled heavy loads of dishes, pulled baker's racks, and brought in supplies. Vera was also intrigued by the fact that he kept his head shaved even after the military released him, and the chosen look had made him stand out. He appeared about a foot taller than everyone else, even when he wasn't. It was sort of an optical illusion, and something of an alluring one. He gave all indications of being a strong and tolerant leader, too, of being solid and dependable. But, Vera chose to ignore the budding attraction. She already had a man in her life, and that one was proving to be one too many. The last thing she felt she needed was another one, even one as good-natured and hard working as Keith.

Within a span of three months, Lance had gone from seeing Vera mostly on weekends with the occasional weekday surprise visit to being in town four nights a week and staying over at the local motel for the entire length of the weekends. He just couldn't get enough of her, and Vera had a difficult time doing and saying things to make him mad. Even when her actions should have caused some sort of tension between the two of them, it seemed to slide off, and Lance's response was simply to get closer. It was becoming a mount of madness, and one she didn't understand. How could a woman as mousy and dry as herself provoke such a fuss and fervent flurry of interest?...

Lance was around the house and shop so much that he and John started to form their own sort of male bonding pattern and loosely corded relationship. They made small talk when they happened to see each other, and Vera came home to find them in the kitchen one day, having a beer and kicking back while Lance waited for her after work. John took to Lance. They were both practical, reasonable, logical, rule-abiding men. Neither had unrealistically high ambitions even if they dreamed big, and both were steady in their lifestyles. And, it wasn't until Vera walked in on their manly moment together that she realized exactly how much they had in common, and then she started to wonder if that was what had drawn her to Lance in the first place. She was fascinated and repulsed by the proposition stemming from within her own psyche, and it set all kinds of issues awhirl.

Vera found herself starting to scheme, to concoct notions of how she could excuse more of her absences from their date life. It was happening so fast, going too well, and she needed it to slow down. If she could've, she'd have brought it to an immediate stop, but that would've caused more drama than it was worth. Then one day, the answer just presented itself, or at least the start of an answer, one piece to a hopefully higher hurdle.

"I'm going to be having a drum circle out at my place once a week or so," Keith told her casually, as they both cleaned up after a morning breakfast rush.

Vera looked at him over a bus tub they shared, as she wiped down the last of the tables. "Really?" she asked in passing.

"Yeah. It's going to be very casual. Folks will be out in the evening time, drumming up good music. I'll have a fire going and some artists coming in to sketch, maybe some dancers, too," Keith informed her of his personal plans.

Vera laughed at the thought of it, a light lilt that was more dismissive than she'd meant for it to be. "In this town?" she questioned and cocked her head to the side to see if he was serious.

He was. "Yes, in this town. Lots of people would be willing to come in one night a week for something like that."

"People you know?" she continued with her inquisition, and it was certainly beginning to feel like one.

Keith's jaw twitched and it was a reaction Vera hadn't seen before. When he got a little agitated he actually looked devilishly sexy. "Yes," he spoke slowly, "people I know. A lot of my friends would enjoy the open space of the farm for an event like that."

"But, drummers and artists?... You're a military man."

Keith narrowed his eyes and touch at that, seeming slightly offended.

"Ok," Vera conceded. "Sounds great," she said and headed back behind the bakery case. "So, why are you telling me this?"

Keith picked up the bus tub and began making his way to the kitchen in the back. "Because I thought maybe you and Misty would like to join us sometime, that's all," he explained and then promptly disappeared to get on with his work.

The gears in Vera's shrewd and vivid mind clicked into place. One night a week of frivolity… Lance would take no part in it, and Vera would have a whole evening liberated. Yes, she was interested, so interested that she instantly went back and told Keith as much and that made him light up. He was looking for connections in his new hometown and she was looking to sever some of hers. Misty was for it and piped right up to say so, and the entire atmosphere of the coffeehouse coalesced then into something more cohesive. But, was it only an illusion of control in her life that Vera was seeing, or was she exerting some sort of control over the grander illusion they all agreed was the shared reality of life? Vera couldn't be sure.

She went home that night feeling as though a portion of her load had been lifted. She thought surely her mood would be contagious and a great night lay ahead as she rounded the corner to step onto the street where she lived. The sun had dipped below the horizon, setting the sky on fire, and a sliver of a moon peeked out from behind tall trees. And, on a stretcher that crossed her path, along with the haphazard and disjointed sidewalk, rolled a full body bag. Elizabeth had died.

Chapter 4

Elizabeth's passing away was not the quiet, draining, madly life-altering affair that Lillian' death had been, not for Vera at least. It did not protract itself out over months, making it difficult to breathe, let alone think. Every day did not go gray with a death pall's coloring, making one wonder if anything was worth it in the greater and grander scheme. The retrieval of the body from out in the once-lush garden area gone weedy had set the town abuzz though, also unlike Lillian. When Lillian passed almost no one seemed to notice or care, and everything was swift and silent and gentle. It was as though Lillian left their realm of existence in a quiet and breathy rush and dispersed like smoke on the wind. Graceful. But, Elizabeth's death was forceful in its elegance and had repercussions, whether folks wanted it to, and were consciously privy to them, or not.

Vera herself couldn't get over where the body had been found, in the scar left by the oak Elizabeth herself had destroyed. It went beyond the ironic and had a sick sense of justice. The entire scene that played out in her mind from details spoken of by her brother, the one who actually found Elizabeth lying there like a large and shriveled up leaf, set Vera shivering. It may have even set the town on edge, and who knew why? After all, what was so unusual about an old woman dying, dropping over on the lawn in the summer heat? Everyone just seemed to be talking about it, giving it a lot of attention, the kind Lillian had never received because the attention itself was not kind. In all those years, no one in the town had really gotten to know Elizabeth and so rumors had been spread, stories had gotten started, and after her death Elizabeth became something of a town legend, and a dark one at that. People started to say they'd seen her prowling the grounds and even the streets on moonlit nights, a specter in white that if vexed could turn one into wood or stone or something equally insane.

"People can't be turned to stone," John snorted the one time Vera caught him listening in on the nonsense that often got spewed around the coffeehouse while people ate their pastries. "Ridiculous. I lived right next door to that old woman all those years, and I'm telling you, nothing happened," John assured his sister. And, that left Vera wondering why he'd felt she needed reassuring. She'd never told him about the content of any of her dreams. All he'd known about from that time in her life was the tree episode. That he knew in detail. That was probably a blemish to both their memories. Vera did secretly wonder if she would start to dream again with Elizabeth dead and buried. She thought she might, but she was mistaken. Whatever Elizabeth had done to her, whatever had broken inside Vera all those years ago remained that way.

Some of the townsfolk started to claim that Elizabeth had kept to herself so much and for all those years because she was a witch and had a house full of spell bottles and sacred herbs and secret potions. They said she kept toads and snakes and bats under lock and key. Perhaps she had killed her own sister to take on that rambling old house, some said. Perhaps she had murdered her husband long ago and moved to get away from where she'd originally come from, away from people who already knew the truth about her. Perhaps she wasn't really gone, not even in death.

Vera couldn't help but overhear most of what was being said, as she worked day in and day out at the coffeehouse. She was sure Misty and Keith were hearing a lot of it, too, and that made Vera slightly ashamed of the place she'd grown up in. And, she didn't have the guts to ask John any questions. She didn't really want to know what he was thinking from the one tidbit of conversation he'd caught in her establishment.

Then to top it off, there was Derrick's arrival… Derrick blew into town on the heels of the turmoil. It was just as things started to settle down again and life began returning to its mundane drone that he burst in like a whirlwind that could not be stopped, and he whipped the town, and Vera, into a heady froth. It was as she was finding peace in the routine of work and the promise of drum circles soon to come, that the disruption that was Derrick stirred her to the point of having an internal cyclone. There was nothing anyone could do to hide or deny or even look the other way when it came to Derrick, women especially. There was nothing Vera could do to help or save herself either. It was a lost cause when she caught sight of him parking his motorbike along the curb and heading up the steps of the Thompson house's front porch. The poor place seemed as though it were one strong wind away from falling apart completely.

She'd been arriving home from a long day, and as she passed by Derrick gave her a cool, casual wave and then smiled. But, it was the way he smiled that stopped her. It was a long, soft, inviting smile; it was the exact same way John had smiled at Misty the first time he'd met her… or so Vera presumed to think. Derrick grinned at Vera in that unmistakable manner, and in that moment she came undone on the invisible hook that held her. Snagged. Unraveled.

Vera stopped dead in her tracks on the unhinged sidewalk; tree roots twisted up under her feet. She did her best to wave back in a polite fashion. She tried hard not to stare, but he was so unlike everyone else. He was positively unique, one in a million and beyond, one of a kind with his long, dark hair and his purposefully tattered up clothing. She's never seen anyone care so little and affect so much. Vera felt a panic boiling up inside her for no external reason that she could deduce, and she found herself wanting to run away and hide in her house, in John's house, but that seemed dramatic and uncalled for given the circumstances. There was no way to explain such behavior later.

Derrick came down off the porch to join her on the sidewalk.

"Hey," he said, as if the world weren't coming apart.

"Hello," Vera replied as best she could, given the fact that her throat was going dry.

The sun was straddling the horizon behind his back and it set his dark locks ablaze with a tinge of fiery red. The russet tones almost looked like a halo. Vera studied his face quickly for her own pleasure and to see if he resembled anyone in his family. All Vera could really tell was that he had the greenest eyes in the world, so bright and lush and vivid. "I'm Derrick Drake," he offered and extended his hand.

Vera just looked at it placed there between them so precariously. She wanted to shake his hand. Vera knew she should, but she wasn't really confident that she could do so and not feel as if she'd just made a pact with the devil. The entire and sudden experience was too surreal. It was too dreamlike to be trusted. Dreams and the promise of dreams were never to be trusted.

Derrick finally pulled his hand back. "I should've started with the information that I'm Elizabeth's grandson," he tried again, but not too hard. He didn't have to put much effort out there to get his way.

Vera shook her head a little and gave a light laugh. "Right, right," she acknowledged and put her own hand out. "It's been a long day. I'm not usually this rude or clueless, I swear. I'm Vera Norton. I live right next door."

Derrick took her hand in his and gave it a firm and decisive shake, but then he didn't let go. The two of them just stood there, holding hands for what felt like forever and then an instantaneous blink separated them. And, the world went back to moving as it always did and as it should.

"Listen," Derrick dared to speak again, and somehow it felt profane for him to do so, "I've been going through the house, cleaning it out, getting rid of some stuff, and putting other things into boxes for storage, you know…"

"Yes, and I'm sorry for your loss," Vera said more appropriately, trying to find what would be commonplace in an otherwise otherworldly encounter. She doubted that Derrick felt that way.

Derrick smiled again in a manner that demonstrated tenacity mixed with longing, only the smile went deeper this time and Vera felt something tug beneath her ribs. "Thanks. I hadn't seen her in years. My grandmother was sort of a black sheep in my family."

"Like you?" the question left Vera's lips before she'd even had time to think about what she was saying. She didn't know why she'd said it, and there was no way to call those words back, to retract her inquiry and substitute a better reply.

Derrick merely smiled again, slyly beaming as if that in and of itself absolved her of her faux pas. "You're really observant," was what he came back with.

"Maybe too much so. I don't know," she returned with a grin of her own. It wasn't such a far reach. He dared to have his appearance diverge so much. It was probably his chosen look that had triggered Vera's assumption.

"Come over to the house when you have some time," Derrick sprang on her. It felt quick and determined and made Vera cringe with a mixture of fear and desire. It felt like she had stepped into a dream all over again, from what she could remember of somnambular wanderings all those years ago. It felt twisted and disjointed and the moment didn't seem to connect with all the others around it.

"Why?" That question was all she had as an oar to hopefully steer her back to pragmatic, logical, and linear reality.

"I've been going through a lot of items and I found an old chest in an upstairs closet. The chest is locked and has your name on it," he informed her.

The winds picked up all around them then and brushed Vera's hair over her ears, as if they had something to say and her limp locks might be in the way, a secret to whisper to her that they then never told. The strong breezes pushed Derrick's hair over his eyes, as if he shouldn't see what might transpire between them and Vera. But, the late summer winds also felt too delightful to really be threatening or mysterious, and it brought them in a touch closer to continue talking.

"My name?" Vera was astounded, and she was pretty sure she knew the chest he was speaking of without ever having to go inside the house and see it.

"Yeah. I talked to your brother earlier today and he said you'd be by after the coffeehouse closed. I was keeping an eye out for you. I figured you'd have the key," he went on, brushing his hair back from his eyes.

Vera shook her head. "I don't," she said a little sadly, sort of wishing she actually did.

"Ok, well, come over when you can anyway and we'll find the key together. The chest is obviously yours or she meant for you to have it, so you should pick it up," he said plainly and with a simple but effective lure, as he turned to head back to the house.

"Wait," Vera called to him softly.

Derrick turned to take in her form again, what she was sure was a drab silhouette in the low light. There was nothing subtle about the man. "Yeah?"

"Why don't you bring the chest over to my place? My brother can probably find a way to open it," she offered another option, and one that seemed safer, for some unknown reason.

"It's really heavy. It would be better to open it first and take stuff out. Besides, my grandmother would've wanted you to come over, to go through and have some of her things," he said a little forlornly, and that shook Vera. It instantly rocked her to a depth of her core she hadn't known was there. It also made her feel obliged.

She couldn't deny him. "I doubt she'd have wanted that," she said honestly enough, "but I'll come over," she caved and found herself happy to be doing so.

"Great. When can I expect you?"

Vera shrugged. Her schedule was quite full. There was work during the day and Lance planned on being by the next two nights, despite her whining that she was tired and needed some space. Suddenly, the thought occurred to her that if she was occupied with helping the town's newest arrival clear out the house next door, that would be yet one more hurdle to slow things down with Lance, a great big and immediate speed bump.

"Tomorrow? After work?"

"See you then," Derrick said, his plan in place, and went inside the Thompson house.

Vera let out a breath she hadn't even realized she'd been holding. "See you then."

Vera stayed outside, basking in the dying sunlight and shivering in the fervent heat, for longer than she'd intended. Something was causing her to quiver from the inside out, and she despised her body for its own small betrayals. She stayed on the sidewalk and gazed longingly at the Thompson house, while the remains of the day passed slowly before her. It had been so very long since anyone had invited her within the auspices of that house. It was a place she used to think of as her own magical abode, a sphere guarded by Lillian, maybe even a kingdom. Lillian had given her free reign during the summers, and Vera had relished exploring the twists and turns and hidden secrets that had always been waiting there. She feared there would be new secrets, and then she feared there would be none at all. It was a gigantic leap in emotions, and they played themselves out beneath a placid surface where no one else could see. Would all the secrets be gone now that both Lillian and Elizabeth were dead?... No, Vera knew in a split second they would not be, when her haphazard brain recalled the fact that there was a dark and ornate chest waiting with her name on it. Whatever was in that chest had waited years for her.

It was as the sun dipped completely below the horizon and Vera caught scent of the very first hints of autumn on a late summer air current, that she went inside her own home. She found John there, cooking something that smelled exquisite for dinner, and Frank was to be found not too far away from all the action. The large dog sat patiently near his master, hoping for a morsel, or maybe many morsels. Misty was at the table in the nook, the table where Vera and John had shared many a childhood meal, watching him absentmindedly and carrying on relaxed bits of conversation. Misty lit up as her friend entered the room. "We were starting to wonder if you'd ever show up," she said and patted the seat of a chair next to her, indicating that Vera should take a load off.

"I got sidetracked by a conversation with our new neighbor," Vera replied and plopped down in the chair, letting it bear her weight and her burden, momentarily. It certainly did feel good to sit.

John glanced at her from his place in front of the stove, as he stirred whatever was searing in a pan. "New neighbor?"

"Derrick Drake, Elizabeth's grandson," Vera clarified. "He said you spoke to him."

"Oh," John said and gave the sizzling items more attention. "He's not a neighbor. He's just clearing the place out, from what I understand. He'll be here and gone before we know it."

Vera's heart sank, and her expression must've dropped with it, for Misty suddenly reached out and placed a warm and steady hand on her forearm. The move was done gingerly and with great caring, causing the two women to lock eyes.

During college, Vera had told Misty everything, or almost everything. She never shared much of the past with anyone, only the present and plans for a pristine future. She had shared all that with Misty, and Misty had been gracious enough to not only accept her for who she was trying to be, planning to be, pretending to be… but also for who she really was and chose to hide. Vera was aware of all that Misty gave to her. She could sense what Misty knew and yet chose not to say out loud.

"You ok?" Misty asked softly, keeping her voice below the hissing sizzle from the stove.

"Yeah," Vera lied. "Yes," she said more firmly, "I'm ok. I think I'm just worn out from the day."

Misty tossed her blonde curls over her shoulders, sending them spiraling in luscious waves down her back. "It has been a full one. You should've let Keith shut the place down by himself this evening. He wanted to."

Vera shrugged, not giving a hair toss of her own. Her drab and limp locks barely reached her collarbones. "I'd hate to start relying on him too much. He may not be there by spring, depending on how busy he gets with the farm."

"I think he'll still be there," Misty said in casual contradiction, as John shoved a plate of piping hot food in front of each of them. Dinner was a delectable stir-fry.

"Dig in, ladies. Bon appetite!" he said with a hint of flare that was unusual for John. Vera thought for sure Misty must be rubbing off on him a little, and there was no harm in that.

John joined them at the table with a plate of his own, and Frank settled in at his feet, and every so often throughout the mellow mixture of idle conversations that would start and stop, Vera would see her brother glance at Misty. Sometimes their eyes would meet and create a practically palpable connection. Something would flutter. It would be brief, fleeting, but it was there. Sometimes John would merely look at her friend in a way that said she was all he wanted, in the moment, in his life. Vera understood that. She could tell what it was he wanted, just as surely as she knew on some primal level she yearned for it, too. He wanted someone to cling to, to bond with. John wanted someone who would come into his life and stay. He wanted the house and a wife and some measure of worldly success. He wanted to find his place and have it all. John desired the dream that was captured by what he'd named his dog, or at least he longed for a portion of that dream. Vera felt herself slipping into a brooding melancholy at that realization. They were so much alike, equally damaged. Or were they? They may have had many of the same issues, but upon deeper inspection, Vera started to wonder if she wasn't in a far worse state, and college along with the start of a new business had only masked it for an extended period of time. But, masks can't be worn forever.

John could sit comfortably at a table with Misty. He could open his home and his life and create for her a meal of his own making. He could change, or try to change. He was willing to take her out, show her off, and spend precious amounts of time and energy on a person who appeared to be just as committed to the process of adoration that was unfolding. Vera was not so capable. Lance offered her as much, if not more, and yet there was something gnawing in Vera. She had an urge to push him away. And, every day she wanted to shove harder, force him back, back behind an invisible line she'd drawn since she'd come home. At first, she thought it was the encroachment after college and the sudden interweaving of life paths that was setting her off. But day after day, back in her grandmother's house with all those memories, memories tied to the house next door and the gardens and the dreams, she began to suspect there was something else afoot. There was something amiss, unnerving. It was unsettling her life all over again.

And, then her mind went back to Derrick.

"He's very attractive," Misty said out of the blue, pulling Vera from her moody ruminations that sprang from the silence that naturally descended after dinner.

Vera looked up to see John had cleared the table and was busying himself with dishes. And, Frank was nowhere to be seen. "Who? My brother?" Vera inquired.

Misty laughed at her and gave a shove. "Well, yes, he is… but I was talking about Derrick. He's got a mysterious edge to him, that one," Misty sized up. "And, there's quite a buzz going around town about him already."

Vera would've felt threatened by Misty's interest in her latest and worst infatuation, if Misty hadn't already been dating her brother. No, Vera could tell that Misty was talking to arrive at a different goal. "People talk. That's all they have to do in this tiny town. Imaginations run wild. Just ask John and I'm sure he'll tell you stories."

Misty cracked a wickedly crooked smile. "About you." It wasn't a question. Misty was calling her out, beckoning to a piece of Vera's past tucked away deep inside her. She spoke to a facet kept beneath a tight lid.

Vera gazed at her friend, eyes wide.

"Relax," Misty said with a sigh. "It's not like I'm blind. You think I can't see what's been going on ever since we got here."

Vera interlaced her fingers and leaned forward as though the discussion were a business deal. "What do you think has been going on?" Vera challenged.

"You've been reverting to form," Misty said and her well-chosen words were the clincher.

Vera wasn't sure how to respond, so she probed lightly. "What are you talking about?"

Misty leaned in closer to be friendly, to suggest there was nothing to fear from her. She was not a threat. "Look, you're good at business, great at negotiations. You're smart and strong and I trust your judgment. You don't ever have to doubt that," Misty eased.

"Thank you," Vera sat back a little.

"But, that's not all you are. Those qualities and the person you were when we were away from here is obviously not all that you are," Misty continued, leading somewhere. "Did you go away to college only to achieve a dream?"

Vera had gone away to college to escape the lingering memories of them. And now with that reminiscence at the forefront of her mind, she simply couldn't see where Misty was leading. "So what are you saying? What are you driving at?" Vera glanced at the kitchen, making sure John was still occupied.

"I'm saying you can't escape yourself and you should be all that you are and to hell with the consequences," came Misty's bold advice, and she served it up with a smile as sweet as her pastries. "I can tell you're fascinated with Derrick. It was obvious given your intense expression at the thought of him leaving so soon. And, I can tell you're less than thrilled with Lance, although the gods know why… he's perfect."

"Well, if you like him so much…" Vera extended.

"Spoken for," Misty overrode and gave a nod towards John.

Both women shared a laugh then, and their merriment acted as a release. All the pent up tensions from work and relationships and life came spilling out of them at the table, and it got loud for no other reason. Eventually, John grabbed a beer from the refrigerator and beat a hasty retreat, merely stating that he would "leave them to it."

"So, what's really going on?" Misty finally sobered up from her fit of giggling. "Are you ending things with Lance, or what? And, no, I cannot take him off your hands."

Vera stared at her blankly.

"Oh, come on! We used to talk about this kind of stuff all the time!" Misty nudged.

"No, we used to talk about all the good stuff all the time. We talked about starting new relationships and new business endeavors and moving into new places. We never talk about ending things, about hard things," Vera said, and she was aware of how petty it sounded.

"Fair enough," Misty let her be. "Let's talk about new relationships. Are you thinking about ending your relationship with Lance so you can start something new with Derrick?"

"Why are you so interested?" Vera returned with a question of her own.

"Who wouldn't be interested in you?" was Misty's odd rhetorical response.

"What?" Vera was blindsided by such a strange and seemingly empty answer wrapped in a question. As far as Vera was concerned, there was nothing redemptive about her other than the knowledge that had been implanted during her educational pursuits.

Misty sat back luxuriously and unfurled all her charm so Vera wouldn't be too upset. "I'm keeping secrets, too," she said with a winsome wink. "Somebody likes you…" she regaled in a sing-song voice.

"Cut it out," Vera blurted. "I'm in no mood and we have an early day tomorrow. It's getting late," and Vera wanted to be done with their unusual exchange. "Shouldn't you be getting home?"

"I'm sleeping over," Misty informed Vera as she rose from the table to stretch.

"Huh?"

"Yeah, I think your brother hates it when I leave right after…" Misty blushed, but Vera knew her friend well enough to realize it was mostly for show, a cued reaction.

"Got it," Vera said with a hint of dismissal and got to her feet.

"You going to drum circle at Keith's on Friday?"

"I was planning to. Are you?" Vera asked, making small talk as she headed slowly down the hall towards her room.

"Yes, I'm really looking forward to it, and I know Keith's excited," Misty reported.

Vera narrowed her gaze. "You talk to him a lot, huh…"

Misty smiled. "We talk. But, you have nothing to worry about. I won't break your little brother's heart." With that promise hanging in the air, both women went their separate ways at the end of the hall for the night, shutting the doors tightly behind them.

❖

"I don't think we should do this again," Misty said to John, as she rolled off him and to her side of the bed, her slender form golden in the glow provided by the bedside lamps.

John was still panting a bit and sweating profusely, but he turned to her with a faltering expression already taking hold. "What the hell do you mean we shouldn't do this again?! We are most certainly doing this again."

Misty patted his chest. "I'm not talking about this," she said and gestured to the bed and both of them lying there. "I'm talking about me sleeping over. I don't think we should do it again after tonight," Misty clarified.

John brushed his thin brown bangs off of his sweaty forehead. "And why not?"

Misty ran her hand up and down his arm lovingly, with the lightest touch, with the most delicate caress. "It probably makes Vera uncomfortable. It's bad enough that she knows we sometimes talk about her, but when I stay over I bet she wonders what we're saying while she's asleep right across the hall."

"That's ridiculous," John dismissed. "First of all, we don't really talk about her. Sure, her name comes up sometimes. She's my sister and a part of my life, and, well, you're in my life, now, too. You're a big part of my life, to tell ya the truth," John propped himself up on one elbow and leaned in to look at her more closely as he went out on a limb. He wanted to gauge her reaction in case he needed to brace himself for a fall.

Misty leaned in and kissed him tenderly, letting her lips linger for a good while before pulling back. "That's so sweet," she sighed. "And, it means a lot to me."

"Good," John gave a firm nod. "That's the kind of response I was hoping for." He grinned at her in that boyish fashion that she'd come to adore, to cherish and hold close to her heart. Misty loved it when something she did or said made John happy like that.

"It's just that her and Lance may be breaking up soon, and here we are, a happy couple while she's going through… whatever it is she's going through," Misty spoke with a hint of sadness.

John didn't like hearing it, not even for a second. "Ok, now we're talking about her. Let's not. It's obviously upsetting you."

"Maybe it would be best though if we stayed at my place more," Misty offered a solution that bordered on a compromise.

John placed a warm hand over hers. "If it'll make you more comfortable, we can do that. We can switch it up a bit. But, I want you to be at ease here, too. And believe me, if Vera is uncomfortable or acting out of sorts, I'm sure it has nothing to do with us. Vera's always been kind of…"

"Introspective? Hyper-aware?" Misty suggested.

"I was going to say peculiar, but those work," John gave in and let the discussion die there. He wrapped Misty up in his arms as tightly as was practical, and they both relaxed back into the bosom of sleep, letting the night consume their time together.

❖

Lance wasn't happy to hear about Vera's plans for the next two nights. He wasn't happy that she was opting to help out a neighbor as opposed to spending time with him. And, Vera felt even more guilty that what she'd told Lance wasn't the exact truth. She'd made loose plans with Derrick to stop by for one evening, not two. And, she wasn't sure there would be a second night. And, why would there be? The blow was softened, however, by the fact that the neighbor was someone who had recently experienced a death in the family, and Lance had known enough about Vera's feelings towards the Thompson house and one of its previous occupants to be gracious. He didn't like it, but he understood. He let Vera go without much of an argument at all, merely an exasperated and let down sigh, and his lack of fight, lack of coercion, made her feel even worse. Lance had longed for time with her on both nights, and would've settled for one, even if it was the one getting cut in half by festivities at the farm.

Vera had felt further irritated but also guilt stricken in the moment and extended an invitation she'd never entirely meant to. It was guilt-lined and pity-driven, and Vera knew in her heart that Misty had been right. Lance was perfect; he just wasn't perfect for her because Vera wasn't good enough. "Do you want to come with me to drum circle on Friday night?"

A baited silence was at the other end of the phone call, as Vera awaited Lance's reply. She felt a breath rustle and then Fate drummed its fingernails on a metaphorical surface that might be a well-marred oak, with the effects of life lived and pathways trodden readily readable in its surface, massive and deeply substantial.

"That's the thing out at the farm?" Lance inquired after some time, attempting to put all the pieces of her twisted up and feverishly full life together in his head.

"Yes, it's out at Keith's farm, the Simms Farm. There'll be drumming and dancing, and I think he said some artists would be coming in to do sketches. I also know he's planning a bonfire," she reported.

"What's the farm like?"

"I haven't been out there since I was a kid, so I don't really know what the farm's like now. I know it's big, a great deal of land," she said, almost wearily. "Do you wanna go?"

The drumming of fingernails and the twisting of the fabric of Fate. It felt like a simple but serious twist was happening in her life all of a sudden. Lance had never been prone to bouts of silence. He always knew what to say. He had constantly been eager to rush in there with the right words, to do the right things. Now he seemed stalled, and that set Vera on edge. She didn't want to keep him, but she hated the thought of being rejected by him before she could do it herself.

"I think I'll pass on this one. It doesn't really sound like my kind of thing," Lance admitted. He was a man made more for intimate dinners by candlelight and romantic moonlit walks. That's what he had desired for himself with Vera. He preferred small family gatherings and lazy Sunday afternoons spent in contemplation. He was a safe and superior man who would never stray, at least not without good reason, and Vera felt as though she were tossing away a flawless pearl of a person, giving him that good reason.

Vera felt the gap she had been nurturing finally grow between them. The void that she had started with as a small ethereal seed was starting to sprout into a bittersweet divide. She'd known it wasn't his sort of venture. She'd been aware of it from the very start, when she had first accepted Keith's invite. It was one more thing placed in her schedule to keep them apart, to keep Lance at bay.

"Ok," Vera accepted. "Then I guess I'll see you this weekend."

"It's probably for the best," Lance echoed some form of sadness of his own. It hugged every word he spoke. "I have a lot of papers to grade, and I've been falling behind in my work recently."

And, Vera knew that was because he'd been very busy chasing around after her, trying to make their relationship work. He'd been desperate to save it. On some level, maybe they both were now that they stood at a precipice neither wanted to acknowledge. It was as though they'd been walking along, side by side, knowing they were headed for the edge of a cliff, taking solace in the inevitable jump and yet all the while thinking they'd never really get there. The simple questions nagged quietly at them both… Were they close? Were they almost there?...

After the hard realities of that phone call, Vera busied her mind with thoughts about the Thompson house. It was easier that way, and more intriguing. She thought about Lillian and the days during her rampant youth when she used to run around over there, exploring every nook and cranny. She'd peer into closets and sort through chests of drawers. She'd dashed about in the gardens and rub herbs between her fingers to release their aromas. She'd even find the time to sit contentedly under the noonday sun. Vera understood now that she had been most herself there, in that place, and at those moments. But, those moments were gone and that place wasn't what it used to be. There was no going back. All she had left were memories of what once was, of who she had been and longed to be again, but she knew it wasn't safe to be that person. Better to merely remember, she thought. She reminisced all morning long as she poured coffees and cleared tables, until Keith came out to help her after the breakfast rush, and he roused her from her reverie.

"What are you thinking about so hard?" he asked easily enough. His regimented manner had an edge of carefree expression that balanced him out nicely. Vera felt very comfortable around him. Keith was contained.

Vera looked to Keith and thought again about how lucky she was to have him as the first hire at the coffeehouse. He was dependable and safe. His personal life and his own guarded goals were never an intrusion. "Oh, I was just remembering some of the activities I enjoyed as a child here in this town," she reported vaguely. "Not sure why," she lied with a shrug, "I just happened to be thinking about it." She made it sound way more superficial than it was, and her words came across as slightly forced to her own ears.

Keith looked deep into her eyes, as though there was something mysterious to be uncovered or solved there. Vera gazed back and found herself enchanted with the delightful swirl of gray bordered by a ring of hazel she found in his irises. Had she ever noticed the color of his eyes before? Yes, yes, she recalled that she had when he'd been hired. But, Vera had quickly forgotten, being too taken with the safety and security that surrounded the man, along with his very vigorous build and alluringly shaved head. Vera wanted to reach out and rub it.

"I bet it's good to be back," Keith nodded.

"In some ways, yes," she said and let a sideways smile play upon her lips. It was the best she could do.

"When was the last time you came out to the Simms Farm?" Keith kept the conversation going as they got the main room back into shape for the lunchtime spike that was right around the corner.

Vera gave a hearty snort, a well-meaning one. "It's been years. I don't even remember that much about it. I know my mom used to pick up some fresh produce there on the rare mornings she didn't have to work. The prices were really good. Cheap. Sometimes my brother and I would tag along when we were little, but most of the time we were at my grandmother's," Vera said with a hint of regret about her childhood, about her mother. She bore the woman no ill will. There was no malice anywhere in her body, not even hidden down in the marrow of her bones. Vera was sure in her own mind that her mother had done the best she could; the only trouble was that her best hadn't been nearly good enough.

"Your brother stopped by to see it the other day," Keith revealed, causing Vera to cease her perpetual cleaning.

"What? Why?" Vera was alarmed and she didn't even know what was to blame for the sudden spike in adrenaline that coursed through her veins. There was just this feeling of all the loose ends of her life being tied up. They were being brought too close together, and that bothered her greatly. The borders of every area were being stitched and it made her nervous, nervous that if one unraveled they would all start to come apart. She also thought that perhaps she feared being found out. If one person got to see too many portions of her life, they would figure her out, see her for who she really was, see too much of her and she would be unmasked and then consequently discarded. Vera had learned after her last two summers spent in town before college not to trust who she was at the core. It was the Fate of all frauds.

"The place needs some work and I thought it would be a good fit to hire your brother. He did a great job with this place," Keith explained and glanced around the shop for added effect.

"Yes, he's very good at what he does. John is good with anything he sets his mind to," Vera conveyed about her brother.

"That's great to hear. So, when he was out the other day he noticed something on the farm that he said you'd really like," Keith went on.

"Oh?" Vera's curiosity was piqued.

"I can't wait for you to see it," Keith grinned. "You and Misty are still coming on Friday night, right?..."

Vera nodded her head. Keith was keeping secrets. Maybe he wasn't as safe as she'd like to think. Maybe she was pleased to find that out, and surprised at herself for feeling that way. It was then Misty's words from the night before ran through her head at lightning speed — "Somebody likes you…"

Vera wondered if that somebody was Keith. "Yes, we'll be there."

"Terrific," he said and left her to tend to his own list of duties that just kept growing.

Against her own better judgment, Vera allowed Misty to keep adding to Keith's responsibilities. Against her own prudent advice, Vera found herself relying on him more and more, despite the fact that his role was meant to be part time and more than likely temporary. Keith had all but said so in those words when they'd hired him. The farm was his first priority, and yet they kept on evolving his position and he let it evolve. Where were things going with Keith? Where would it end?

Vera had more questions by the end of that one day than she thought she'd have in her whole lifetime. But, the night would bring even more to her than she could ever dream, which then spawned yet another question… would she ever dream again?... Being back home had caused her to miss the ability to fall haplessly and hazily into another realm, free of the framework that came with waking hours. Elizabeth's death had made her increasingly curious about her inability. Dreaming was becoming an elusive and evocative desire. She hadn't pined for it so much in college, when her days were slammed with classes and her nights busy with studies and dates and friends. Her world had appeared full to overflowing, and she was so ready to black out at night that falling into a dreamless abyss had been blissful. But, now it was starting to wear on her, tell on her. She so desired to dream once more, to have one more chance to walk in a realm where she might feel like her truest self. And with Elizabeth dead and buried, it might be possible to have sweet dreams again, if they would ever come at all. Would they return to her? A month from now? A year? At the end of her life? With Derrick she thought they might come quickly. With Derrick everything felt like a dream.

Vera went straight from work to Derrick's house, pausing only to touch herself up in the bathroom at the coffeehouse. She applied some shimmering face powder to even out her complexion and then a slick surface of lip gloss. She also attempted to plump up her limp, mousy brown locks. She'd put more effort into her appearance that evening than she had at any point in time during college or before. She couldn't ever remember caring so much. She also decided to spice up her wardrobe a bit and dug out a soft summer dress that she let Misty buy her on a random shopping excursion when they'd both initially became roommates at school. The price tag was still on it, that's how much action it had seen. None. The little white cotton dress sat in a drawer then in a box and then a drawer for all that time. It had been waiting for an occasion, a reason to be put to good use. Maybe it wanted to been seen as much as Vera secretly and shamefully did. It was a desire that woke from a level that betrayed all the others in her pent up psyche.

Vera caught sight of her own full-length reflection in the bathroom mirror as she headed for the door and was about to hit the light switch. A slender, sleek female with simple brown hair that framed a moderately freckled face, that was her own generous assessment. The soft white cotton of the summer frock barely hugged any of her subtle curves; it only whispered at what might be underneath. Vera was draped in delicacies. It was as good as she was ever going to get, or that was her assumption, at any rate.

Vera turned out the lights, locked up the shop, and began the short walk to Derrick's, to the Thompson house. Her grandmother's home, and now John's, was only a few blocks away, and therefore so was her destination. She had to head out of the antique and business districts into the residential areas. But, their street wasn't that far in. It flirted with the edges of the bustling busy places, if anything in their small town could be said to bustle. The sun was working its way towards the horizon slowly, inexorably, and a light breeze pushed at her back, egging her on. It felt as though the winds wanted her to continue along the path she was choosing for the night. She turned a corner and the winds shifted to press again. They changed direction as she altered her course. Before she knew it, she stood at the foot of the stair steps that led up to the Thompson house, and on the slowly rotting porch was Derrick.

He was reclining in a whitewashed wooden chair when she spotted him, half draped in shadows and looking as deliciously tattered as she recalled from yesterday evening.

"Hello," Vera said and waited at the bottom of the steps, suddenly unsure if she should proceed any further. Her new home, and the safety of her bedroom, was right next door. She could dash inside and never have to face any of this. She could spend the rest of her life safely wondering while amid the routines she'd built. But, she didn't move a muscle in that direction.

"Wow," Derrick said, just short of a true exclamation. "You look beautiful!" And then he arrived at one, as he got to his feet.

Vera turned her head away, not wanting to meet his gaze as he appraised her. "Thanks," she managed to say without a tremor to her voice, although one did work its way up and down her spine.

When she finally did look back to him, he was still eyeing her and not being subtle about it. He was contemplating the very lines and curves of her. He seemed fascinated and pleased.

"Come on in," Derrick invited and stepped inside the house, leaving her there to make her own decision about whether or not to follow.

Vera darted up the creaking steps and went inside, letting the screen door bang shut behind her.

The house was exactly as she remembered it, down to the last tiny detail. The structure may have had the appearance of dilapidation on the outside, but it was perfectly preserved within. Looks were deceiving. It was as though Vera had stepped back in time and was sixteen all over again. She could've walked the house blindfolded, it was so exact. It was as if Elizabeth had never lived there, had never been, and Lillian might be in the kitchen now cooking something delicious or out in the gardens tending to her beloved plants. The decorative maroon and mahogany sofa and chairs with the claw feet, the oblong coffee table, the matching end tables, the paintings on the walls, the floral draperies, and the plush sand-colored carpeting were all the same as before. It was all still there and in immaculate condition. Even the grandfather clock on the far end of the left wall, out of which a staircase grew, remained seated in its original position. It kept guard over every single second.

Derrick finally broke the silence between them. "You ok?"

"It's just like I remember," Vera told him. It was just like a dream.

"How long has it been since you were in here?" Derrick inquired and slowly started to lead her through the living room to the stairway at the start of the adjoining dining area. A crystal chandelier winked at her as she went by.

"Years. I haven't been in here since Lillian passed," Vera revealed as she moved by the shining silver and gold face of the old grandfather clock. "It looks untouched," she said and then glanced at Derrick. "I thought you were packing things up and clearing stuff out."

Derrick stopped quickly, so quickly that Vera almost crashed into the back of him. "It's going to take time," he said and placed a hand in hers, interlocking their fingers. "Come on," he insisted as he began ascending the steps. "The chest is upstairs."

Vera longed to see more of the house, the dining room and the hearth of the kitchen, but didn't protest. First of all, she figured she had no right to protest as a mere guest, and a transient one at that. And secondly, his hand in hers felt too good for her to want to complain.

Derrick took Vera down the long upstairs hallway that was lined with small and well-polished tables, the wooden surfaces had been buffed to a high sheen and they were decorated in a wide variety of knick-knacks, objects from all over the world. Robust chairs were situated between rooms for casual seating, and elegant paintings of people from times long past hung on the walls that were covered with a brocade pattern. The people in the painted pictures had more than likely been forgotten, except in the maintenance of a regular dusting. The house could've been a historic shrine based on its condition.

All the doors to the rooms coming off the hallway were closed, save but one, the one at the very end. It was to that room Derrick was taking Vera. It was the master bedroom of the house where Lillian had slept and dreamed and kept all of her most prized possessions and precious secrets. She had shared many with Vera, but chances were good that there were still some to be found.

That room went untouched as well, except for what must've been a thorough cleaning, and Vera had to check in with her sanity, wondering if Elizabeth ever existed. The place felt like Lillian's house, hers and hers alone.

"I can hardly believe Elizabeth Drake lived here, slept here. This room is just as I remember it, too," Vera confessed as she took in the sight of the large cherry wood wardrobe, matching chest of drawers with tilted vanity mirror, antique rocking chair draped with a crocheted afghan, and large master bed with the hand carved evergreen art in the headboard. The feathery white and opaque drapes beckoned from each window as a delicate breeze touched them, causing them to dance a few flirty steps. Derrick had opened the house up, but barely.

"The chest I was telling you about is in the closet here," Derrick went on, practically ignoring Vera's ruminations and giving her arm a tug. He then let go of her entirely and brushed aside the clothing that hung on a bar above, meant to display it.

It was the chest from Vera's memory; the chest Elizabeth brought with her when she moved in over six years ago. Vera wondered if that and a few other personal items, books and clothes, were all Elizabeth had ever contributed to the abode. She stepped forward to gaze at it, to take in all the fine detailing. It was certainly a large, dark, disturbingly ornate chest. Vera affirmed silently to herself that she'd been right to initially think it looked like something out of a pirate movie or from a dreadful yet wondrous fairy land. Those had been her thoughts from years ago, and they felt well suited in the present space. She stared at the exquisite thing that now held secrets locked up tight. Vera felt her old questions surfacing around it… Had pixies danced on it? Had satyrs cursed it?... Did it matter? She looked closer, squatted down to join Derrick on the floor. The two were so near one another that she could hear him inhale and exhale rhythmically, soothingly. The dark chest did indeed have her name on it, placed there by a marker on a piece of masking tape. Her ownership of it felt as frail as the labeling.

"We'll have to start searching for a key that looks like it'll fit this," Derrick said, but his voice had changed slightly, and it sounded huskier now, lower, and a touch sinister.

Vera ran her hands along the top of the chest and felt the lid wiggle. She glanced to Derrick and their eyes locked. The top of the chest had moved. Vera brought her hands back around to the front and lifted. The lid came open with ease. "I thought you said it was locked."

"It was locked," he said sternly, "or at least, I thought it was…" Derrick said and peered inside. He then sat back on his haunches. "Huh."

"Huh?" she echoed quizzically and peeked in herself with what little light came in through the bedroom windows. It took a few seconds for her eyes to adjust to the level of darkness within, but as they did so an outline emerged. It was familiar, but at first Vera had a hard time placing it. She squinted and then squinted tighter. She brought her face in ever so carefully until she was mere inches away. And, then it hit her. The faint outline that grew stronger with each passing second was the shape of the eyeless and armless doll from all those years ago. It was the doll Elizabeth had painstakingly carved, the doll from her hurtful past, the doll from her dreams… and from her nightmares.

"It wasn't what I was expecting," Derrick said candidly enough.

Vera didn't want to touch it. She preferred to focus on something else, something logical and distracting, like a discrepancy that needed explaining. She shut the lid. "I thought you said this thing was too heavy to move and we'd have to take stuff out. It's practically empty." Her tone became very accusing, very frustrated, very quickly.

Derrick looked a little embarrassed. He gave her a devilishly sexy smile to allay any growing feelings of anger or annoyance. "I said that to get you over here," he explained, as if that answered any of the thousands of questions simultaneously forming in Vera's brain. Her mind was running wild with all sorts of theories, and bringing her sweet relief as he went on. "I knew you'd have me haul this thing over to your brother's, if it were feasible."

"Well, yeah…" she said and then had nothing more to contribute, aside from a puff of air.

"I gave you a reason to come over," he said and leaned in so he was barely a hair's length away. His nose was almost touching the tip of hers. "I gave you a reason to be with me, alone." The revelation sounded ominous; it sounded dangerous.

Vera knew she should be scared, a small and fragile female alone in an old house with a stranger, and by all appearances a large and very capable stranger. Vera knew she should be angry and insulted. She knew the proper reaction was to shoot to her feet and storm out, leaving him and the hideous doll full of so much perversion behind. But, she didn't. Vera found that she couldn't. In a flash, she discovered her arms looped wantonly around Derrick's neck, and her lips pressed firmly into his. The sweet slipperiness of her lip gloss was a delight to them both and drove the kiss further and deeper with a honeyed aftertaste. Vera gave herself over to the pull that brought her there, that told her she could do better by herself if she put in the effort. And, Derrick made her want to put in the time and the energy. She made the effort — for him. She wanted to be more for him because she feared she'd never be enough anyway, and he drove that fear and that desire until they were both on the bedroom floor, clothes coming off in a feverish frenzy and carpet burning bare skin.

Derrick fit inside Vera like an ancient key in a highly specific lock. But, were the clicking of tumblers in her only a prelude to the opening of her own Pandora's box? Derrick was not a man to be taken lightly, and she sensed in his passionate and sudden intensity about her that he never took things lightly either. Was the chest yet another box that should not have been opened? It was hard to think and even harder to talk with body and soul occupied as they were in a room that had once belonged to a magical and mystical woman, a woman who had devotedly cared for Vera.

The only witness to that mad ecstasy was one that could not see. The eyeless and armless doll lay in the chest where it had been placed long ago, as winds outside picked up and then whipped throughout the room, as words filled Vera's ears and mind just as sure as Derrick filled her in every other way — "There is no untainted, pure, true, fearless love in you, is there?... It's not there anywhere." The breezes brought Elizabeth's words back to her in a breathy rush. So, it had been Elizabeth's house, too. "And, it is what you value most, what I valued most… and now you are cursed and I am cursed. That love will elude us both. This will be yours," Elizabeth had said. The winds did say, and red-hot ember eyes threw heat at her from a distance. Did they stem from Fate, a being who would not show itself?... "It's yours…" came the whisper, the decree.

Chapter 5

Vera had plenty of reasons to be distracted, and at the top of the list was Derrick. She'd left what was now his house without taking the trunk or the doll inside it. She'd beat a rather hasty retreat after their amorous encounter, not wanting him to have too much time to really look at her with clothes off and makeup mussed. The low light of the setting sun had been perfect for her exit, and she left the Thompson house to slip into her own through the side door, after creeping quietly across the backyard.

John hadn't seen her come in, but he'd heard her. He called her name and she'd been forced to emerge from her room right after getting in there.

Vera smoothed her haphazard mane and wiped at the smeared lip gloss before throwing open the bedroom door. "Yes? Just what is so important?" she said a little more sharply than intended.

"I thought I heard you come in and wanted to see if I should grab you dinner. I'm making a food run for burgers and Misty will be over soon," he informed, taken back a bit, but not enough to be put off. Brothers were often like that. They just ignored whatever obvious signs their sisters sent in deference to their own agendas, helpful or not. And, Vera was often grateful for that. It was usually helpful.

"Oh," she said blankly, "I... um... well, sure. That would be great. Thank you," she finally got around to managing her tongue and the words her brain threw at it.

"All right then. I'll be back shortly," John said and trudged out of the house with a singular sense of purpose — snagging food.

Vera sighed and leaned against the doorframe. What had she been thinking? She wasn't usually this way. She wasn't this type of person at all... the type to sleep with a man she'd only just met. She didn't take risks and she certainly wasn't prone to living in the moment, at least not anymore. She'd left her flights of fancy and her sneaking around days behind her. The only problem was that quite suddenly they seemed to be right behind her. Who she'd been was catching up with who she was trying so desperately to become.

It was as Vera began to drift off into her own thoughts and most recent memories that she heard the sound of a key fitting in the lock of the front door. She heard the loud tumblers of the deadbolt click and then the door give way with a weary creak. Their grandmother's house may have had some remodels, but it was still old.

"Hello? John?" came a familiar voice. Misty.

"He went to pick up dinner," Vera called to her friend. "I'm going to change clothes and be right out. Make yourself at home," she instructed and then pondered how it was Misty had a key in the first place.

Vera shut the door to her room and slid out of the dress her friend had rightfully talked her into years ago. She washed up as best she could in the adjoining bathroom's antique basin sink, with the new plumbing John must've put in before she'd taken up residence. She felt fairly confident in her near normal appearance. Vera had also donned some relaxed pajama bottoms and a t-shirt before stepping out to greet her friend.

Misty was waiting patiently at the table in the kitchen. "Hey! How's your evening been so far?" she said in her typically chipper tone, as she ran hands over the smooth surface of the historically significant table. It was significant to Vera's mind at least. So many meals had been served up there; so many memories lived there still.

Vera eyed her friend cautiously. Did she know about her evening? What all did Misty know? Vera had found that over the years Misty often knew far more than she initially let on. "Fine. I just got home a few minutes ago and John said he was going to get dinner. Eating kind of late," Vera pointed out to throw her friend off track, if she was on one. Better to nitpick at their discrepancies, their idiosyncrasies.

"Yeah. I had some things to finish up at my apartment, so our routine got pushed back a couple of hours. Did you go next door?" Misty asked innocently, sweetly, and Vera couldn't tell if it was on purpose or not.

"Yes, I met with Derrick and we got the chest open," Vera replied. Had she told Misty about the chest, about the main reason she supposedly went over there in the first place? She couldn't be sure. They'd all been so busy lately, had so much going on. It was getting harder and harder to keep up.

Misty nodded. "And?..."

Vera sighed. "And… there was nothing in it worth having. Just junk," Vera lied. Vera hid. She hid the truth and her supposed Fate.

"I see," Misty let it go. She looked Vera over, caught a twinkle in her quickly darkening irises and let it remain unfettered.

Vera stared back at her friend for some time, locking eyes, assessing, allowing Misty the advantage of looking through the windows to her soul until she couldn't keep it bottled within her another second. "Oh god, Misty! I fucked up!" she proclaimed and buried her face in her palms. The tears were starting to flow, and they may have been tears of joy for all she could tell, but an edge of sadness salted them as well.

"I guess so, since you're upset," Misty said, giving Vera's feelings room to breathe and space to be just as they were. She placed a hand on her friend's back and let it sit there, slightly heavy and comforting.

"I cheated on Lance," Vera confessed in a hushed tone that was even further muffled by the downward angle of her face.

"Yeah," she sighed, "technically you did, since you haven't broken up with him yet." Misty acknowledged the assessment without ascribing judgment. She merely moved into rubbing Vera's back gently and with a genuine compassion that flowed off her fingertips.

Vera sucked it up like a sponge. She couldn't help herself, as she was torn between horror and delight at what had transpired less than half an hour ago. "What do I do?" she finally asked, as she raised her head to see Misty's kind and lovely face once more. It dawned on Vera then that it might have been her kindness that had given her such enchanted beauty. Yes, Misty would have been pretty either way, cruel or kind, but Vera suspected her innate caring had tipped the scale. It had taken Misty beyond simply pretty into a realm of exquisiteness.

Misty joined hands with Vera, interlacing fingers in a way that said their bond went beyond any surface friendship. She tilted her head in a mirroring gesture of Vera's own body language and met her head on. "You do what you were going to do anyway."

❖

Vera left a voice message the next morning telling Lance that it was over between them, purposely calling when she figured he'd be teaching class, and when she should've been at work. She knew how cold it would seem if others knew her chosen delivery method, but that didn't really matter since she'd vowed to her own self to keep it a secret. And, Lance most certainly wouldn't be telling anyone in her sphere, since there'd be no reason for him to come around anymore. Her secret was safe. Vera also assuaged her twinge of guilt with the knowledge that more than likely Lance would've preferred it that way, and she would soon be headed out the door for the coffeehouse, as she should be. Better late than never.

Vera had all night to think on it and felt Lance would be grateful on some level for the voice mail, for her choice. It made things less awkward; there was less chance of a scene, of real and uncomfortable emotions bubbling up to the surface. Lance had been a lot like her own brother John in that respect, and powerful emotions for all three of them were best left below the surface, buried beneath the façade of everyday living. John and Lance were doing admirably with the management of their feelings, from what Vera could tell. Vera was failing miserably. She wasn't prone to deluding herself and could sense the crack in her own outer walls.

As Vera ended the call, she felt simultaneously relieved and saddened. Something had ended, and she sensed that an amazing chance had just passed her by. It was the death of a possible future. There was a road now that would never be travelled, never be taken. Destination unknown. Vera would never get to know the outcome of a life lived with Lance as her companion. Over and over again, she thought about how Misty had been right. Lance was perfect. He'd been perfect for her in college, and he was perfect even now. They'd had a good amount of distance between them, and Lance never fought back against her whims, at least not her strong ones. He might have kept her secure her whole life. He might have allowed her to keep her well-hidden goal of personal seclusion. Vera wondered if she'd ever find another man like him, or if she would find another person so pliable, so willing to let her feel safe. Deep in the pit of her stomach, a knot started to grow. She doubted it.

Whatever might have been with Lance was well and truly over. It was over with the push of a button on her mobile phone, with the ringing of the doorbell at the house she shared with her brother, and with the bark of a Great Dane as he burst down the hall and through the living room in anticipation of greeting a visitor.

Vera gave a nudge to Frank's muzzle with her hip, as she joined him at the wooden barrier and pushed the large dog out of the way so that she could crack the door open. On the other side was Derrick.

"You forgot this," he stated simply and shoved the monstrous wooden doll into Vera's empty hands. "Guess you must've had a lot on your mind," he said with a mischievous grin.

Vera stared at the disgusting thing and only came back around to her visitor when she heard the throaty growl of her canine protector. "Oh, Frank! Stop that!" she corrected the usually good-natured beast, uncertain who or what he was stirring over.

"Nice dog," Derrick said half-heartedly, and with the hint of an icy edge.

"How did you know I'd be here?" Vera asked, still focusing on discrepancies.

"You live here," Derrick replied easily enough.

Vera snorted. "Yeah, but I should be at work."

Derrick nodded. "Ah. And, that's where I was going next, if I didn't find you here," he informed her.

Vera gave a courteous nod of her own. "I see." There was nothing so mysterious or wondrous there for her to find. "You know, it could have waited," she went on, as her eyes beheld the hand-carved figure and she attempted to quell a quick wave of disgust. The doll was real. That meant her dreams, her nightmares from all those years ago, they could be real. That meant her curse could be real. Her curse; Elizabeth's curse. Vera felt the need to talk to John immediately and have him snap her out of this craziness.

"I didn't want to go through the trouble of getting everything in order and then forget to give it to you," Derrick told her and took a step back, and then another.

"Are you in a hurry to go somewhere? Or would you like to come in for a cup of coffee?" Vera nudged the door open further to indicate that Derrick could walk on in and past the furry guardian at her side. Frank gave a little moan of derision, a huff that flared his large lips, and then scampered off to another room.

"No. I've gotta go," Derrick said and took another step towards the sidewalk.

Vera came all the way outside to join him, letting the door remain slightly ajar behind her. "Where are you headed?" She couldn't contain herself. Being near Derrick was just too intoxicating, too addicting. It felt like an eternity since she'd seen him and not last night.

"For a ride… around. I've got plans, stuff to do," he answered vaguely. It wasn't even subtle. He didn't want to share all his information with her.

"Ok," Vera said softly and looked to the eyeless, armless figure she held. It was both a curse from Elizabeth and a gift from Derrick. Now what would she do with it?

"Come over tonight," Derrick instructed.

Vera glanced up and perked. "What?"

"Come over tonight, after you get off work," he clarified for her.

Vera beamed. "I will," she agreed.

Derrick took on a sly smile at her obedience and headed down the sidewalk for his bike.

"Hey!" she shouted before he could pull away, zip out of her life for hours on end. "I have a drum circle tonight, too. Later. Wanna go?" She wanted tonight, all of it. She wanted tomorrow and the night after that. She wanted the morning, the afternoon, the evening, and everything that naturally followed. She wanted it all, and she wanted it from Derrick, a man who seemed far too removed and tattered to ever be tamed.

Derrick revved his motor. "Maybe." He kept her dangling on his hook.

He left Vera there in a plume of exhaust and dust, curious as to why it was that forty-five minutes away was too close for

Lance, but right next door yet out of sight was too far for her to be from Derrick. Vera was definitely unraveling, losing everything she'd worked so hard for, strove to build, desired to become. She took the doll inside her brother's house and placed it carefully on top of her chest of drawers for consideration. Perhaps being alone was her one true Fate.

Vera didn't want to think about it. She went to work and threw herself headlong into it; she lost herself in it, in the business and the routine and the rightness of it. Misty and Keith both took a cue from her and got busy as well, baking and ordering and cleaning and serving. Everything went off like clockwork and before Vera realized it, the time had come to close. The sun was setting and Keith was getting antsy about heading home to set up for visitors, to prep the farm for the very first of what he envisioned would be many drum circles and gatherings to come.

"So, you'll be there?" he checked as they all gathered on the front step to lock up.

"Yes," Vera affirmed.

"Of course," Misty replied warmly.

And with that guarantee, Keith was off. He waved goodbye as he headed another direction, as he headed away from town, leaving the two friends to walk together to Vera and John's home. They had to get ready for the night ahead.

"Are you excited?" Misty inquired as they turned the corner and the Thompson house came into view.

There was no motorbike out front at the curb, and all the windows were dark. Vera watched intently for flickers of movement, but there were none visible. The house was vacant. Derrick could be anywhere… and with anyone.

"Should I be?" Vera asked with a hint of melancholy. She was supposed to come over, to meet with him before drum circle.

"You act like you're marching to the gallows," Misty criticized and slung her purse off of one shoulder and onto another. She seemed unusually weighted down by it as they strode along.

"This event might be the most fun thing to happen since I got here." She was trying to pull Vera out of the slumps, and maybe even more for her sake than Vera's. Misty wanted to let loose and to have a good time. She wanted to unwind from the natural stressors that had been placed upon her, and she desired the same for Vera, too. "And if it goes well, Keith could have it every week," she went on.

"Every week," Vera echoed. It didn't mean so much now that she didn't need it strategically placed in her schedule to keep Lance at bay.

Misty slid her hand in Vera's and dragged her the rest of the way to the front door. "Come on," she said and used her own key to open it. "Let's get you ready!"

John fed the dog and played a quick game of fetch in the backyard as an early autumn chill hit the air. This went on while Misty coaxed Vera into clothes that were not her own. She pulled a bright blue peasant skirt and white cotton top trimmed in lace from her bag and shoved them at Vera.

"Put these on," she instructed with a smile. "And after you're in them, I have a wrap to give you in case it gets too cold for that shirt tonight."

"What the hell for? I have clothes," Vera barely objected as she gathered the items from Misty.

"Yeah, you do," Misty smirked and gave Vera a shove towards the bathroom.

The clothes were Misty's so they naturally fit a little differently on Vera, but as Vera slid into them before the bathroom basin mirror, she was surprised to see how well the top fit. It wasn't as tight or as seductive as it might've been on Misty, but it hung delicately well on Vera. It gave to her a refined gentleness and an alluring fragility that she hadn't realized she possessed. The blue skirt hung low on her hips and just barely stayed on. Another fraction of an inch in the waistline and it might have fallen completely off, but it didn't. It rested on the crests of her hipbones and swished like a fickle little fairy bell as she moved. Glimmers of fine silver threads shimmered in the fabric, causing Vera to feel a hesitant glee as she emerged from the bathroom.

Misty looked her over from head to toe, smiling and nodding the whole time. "That's just amazing," she said without a tell as to what she truly meant.

"What? What is?" Vera portrayed more excitement and nervousness than she ever had in front of Misty.

"How you seem out of your business clothes. You are an adorable woman on your own, Vera, don't get me wrong, but you dress so… so… plain all the time," she did her best to phrase it sweetly.

"It's how I'm comfortable," Vera defended.

Misty met her friend's gaze. "It's like you wear armor every day."

Vera swallowed hard and was curious if she and Misty were now getting too close. She had destroyed her relationship with Lance over that issue, and another. Would she eventually severe her ties to Misty, too, if nearness became a problem?

"You look more natural like this," Misty went on.

Vera lowered her head, not sure what emotions might be playing out through her facial expressions. "I'll wear it if it'll make you happy."

"Great!" Misty chirped and wrapped an arm about her slender shoulders. "Does that mean I can do your hair and makeup, too?"

"What?!"

"Oh, please! Pretty please!" Misty chimed on in playful begging that Vera found hard to resist. Misty knew full well that deep down Vera was a people pleaser. She never wanted to hurt anyone's feelings or make a scene or get overly involved. She never chose to fight. And to Misty's credit, she very rarely used that trait against her.

Vera let out a tense puff of air. "All right."

Misty drug her friend into the bathroom, produced a small case of cosmetics and tools, and set to work. It was as though Vera were an art project, a lump of nondescript clay that could possibly be worked into a masterpiece, Misty's version of a masterpiece.

Mascara, eyeliner, and shimmering shadows. Sheer face powders, a hint of blush, and a tinted lip gloss. A handful of gel, a comb, and a curling iron. Those were the sculptor's tools, and Vera shut her eyes as the makeover master set to work on her. She didn't want to see. She didn't want to know how it was going, how much work needed to be done, how bad off she really was, or if they were anywhere near being finished.

A spritz of perfume hit her square in the chest.

"Voila!" Misty declared, as if she were at an unveiling.

Vera opened her eyes gingerly and glanced at her friend with great caution.

"Aren't you gonna get up and take a peek in the mirror?" Misty prodded.

"Can I have a moment?" Vera asked, wanting to be alone the first time she saw herself as the product of another person's vision.

Misty softened her gaze. "Sure. I'll be right outside the door… listening," she said, half-serious. "Bellow if you need me." She shut the door tight behind her.

Vera had been holding her breath on and off throughout the entire process. Her hands were sweaty and her legs were fidgety. She simultaneously wanted to see and didn't want to see. She had both high hopes and severe doubts. What if all of Misty's handiwork wasn't good enough? What is she would never live up to the kinds of potentials a person like Misty had? But, there was only so much time she could delay. She eventually had to look. Vera had to see herself and what she'd become through the eyes and ministrations of another.

Vera stood up and approached the bathroom mirror a little at a time, with true baby steps. She saw the generality of herself from the waist up first. The familiar outline of the white cotton top she was wearing and then the soft bounce of sumptuous golden brown curls that hung all about the edges of her face. The curls softened her further. They made her seem full and generous, not perfect but knowable. They took any hint of harshness out even from a distance. Next she saw supple and shiny lips paired with easy smoky eyes outlined in a blue-gray hue, the kind of eyes that came with a person who would listen without judgment, a person of great subjectivity and sensitivity. And at long last, Vera got up very close to the mirror and examined her face. Her freckles were still there, only lessened slightly under a subtle sparkle of mineral powder and blush. She had become closer to Misty, more like Misty but not as good or as glamorous. She had become closer to and more like herself. The woman in the reflective pool on the wall resembled the adult that her childhood being could've easily grown into… and she had chosen a friend who inevitably brought that out. Vera had come full circle, despite some obvious signs of lack, and there was no hiding it anymore.

Misty was draped in light and loose fabrics that both complimented and directly opposed Vera's for the evening out at the Simms Farm. The dazzling blonde that Vera felt positive she could hardly hold a candle to was dressed in flaming oranges and reds, bold and daring colors that would draw the eye of every onlooker straight to her. Vera was dressed in whites and blues for the night, colors that would most certainly appear drab and dingy by moonbeam, or so she had led herself to believe. And, that got her to feeling a little resentful instead of grateful for all Misty had done. John went along for the festivities, too, deciding to join them for the gathering at the last minute. But, Vera suspected it was more to be with Misty than to enjoy a new and culturally diverse experience. Vera thought about Derrick and their missed rendezvous the whole way to their destination.

Vera could hardly believe her eyes as they rolled up the old gravel road towards the main house on the rambling farm property. The place was alive with flittering visitors moving here and there about the fields that were barely lit up by flame or by moonlight. As they came nearer still, and closer to the big bonfire in front of the large red barn, the number of people swelled and the brightness grew to that of midday. It snapped her from her sad ruminations about Derrick. Floodlights from the house were on, and the entire place looked like something out of a movie. It resembled a wild fraternity party from all surface indicators. Keith knew a lot of people; he knew a lot of different kinds of people, people Vera had never, ever seen before. They were not from town. No, the folks roaming about the house and grounds were from somewhere else, and they seemed exotic and strange and intriguing. Keith was not as plain and safe and easy to understand as Vera had hoped, as she had led herself to believe. When her brother stopped the truck, she stopped her diverging train of thought at one final station — Keith was not at all who she envisioned him to be.

"Ok, so now what?" John asked as they piled out of his pick-up and shut the doors behind them.

Misty darted off towards the fire and sounds of idle chatter intermingled with random drum beats. Vera figured that response must've been instinctual given her upbringing. She was answering the call of her people.

John just looked at his sister with a perplexed expression on his face.

"Maybe you should go with Misty. She seems very comfortable in these situations. It's natural for her and she'll know what to do. I'll try to find Keith and let him know we're here," she said in a practical tone of voice, in John's native tongue. Vera spoke as though there were nothing to be nervous about, but she felt completely out of her element and plenty jumpy.

"All right," John agreed. "I guess I'll see you by the fire in a while."

"Yeah, sure," Vera said and headed for the house.

In the nighttime and amid the bathing fire glow, the farm and farmhouse looked nothing much like what she remembered from the infrequent visits during her childhood. This place was completely foreign to her now and teaming with natives of another societal circle. Women dressed in all forms and styles of lavish and trendy clothing wandered here and there with friends or dates, mysterious and colorful beverages in hand. There were people reclined on the wooden slats of the porch and standing in the doorway that led inside the home. Vera did her best to squeeze past. And as she made every small move, she was also well aware of the sensation of eyes on her, stares following her. People were looking at her as she attempted to take in her surroundings and find the one person Vera felt she would recognize. She couldn't be sure if the visitors were staring because she was new to them and seemed out of her natural habitat, or if it was because she seemed so exposed, so vulnerable, so herself now. She was very unusual and complete.

Inside the farmhouse was a massive throng. It was packed tight, and the further in Vera went, the harder it became to maneuver. There was very old furniture and decorations littered about everywhere, from what Vera could tell through the sea of people that ebbed and flowed chaotically. The entire house appeared unsettled, and not just by the company. It was mostly left as Keith had probably found it and had not yet taken on the characteristics of its new owner. The house and grounds were still Keith's grandfather's, in spirit and tone and texture anyway. The people and the gathering were Keith's contributions.

"Vera!" came a shout above the relentless drone of idle conversations.

Vera whipped her head this way and that to try to pinpoint who was calling to her.

"Vera!" the voice was growing nearer. "Over here!"

Vera turned and turned again, but couldn't find the source. Then, finally, a random guest, a man dressed in acid-washed blue jeans and a vibrantly striped shirt with hair that looked like a parrot's crest, tapped her shoulder and gave a nod towards the person seeking her company.

It was Keith. Of course, it was Keith. He was headed her way, slowly but surely. "It's crazy in here," he said needlessly, as he reached her side. He looked freshly shaved and smelled of soap and beer.

"Yeah," she replied and heard a jittery edge enter her intonation. She tried to swallow it down.

"It'll ease up some when the drumming starts and more people move outside," he told her and began to lead her back the way she came. "Let's step out there now. There's something I've been dying to show you." It was when they got on the porch and found a small open area that he stopped. "You look amazing!" Keith said to her out of the blue as they both enjoyed a breath of fresh air and a little elbowroom.

Vera simply smiled and cast her eyes downward towards her feet that were clad in white ballet flats. She pulled the bright blue wrap Misty had loaned her tight about her shoulders. She didn't know what to say; she only knew to brace herself.

"I've never actually seen you like this before," Keith went on, carefully, giving her appearance a mild examination.

"These are Misty's clothes," she confessed.

"Well, they look perfect on you. I really like the way you're dressed tonight," Keith persisted and then waited for her eyes to meet his again. He waited for her to grow comfortable with the words he was saying, with the ideas behind them. "I really like the way you are tonight."

"Thanks," she said and allowed herself to glance up at him again. And she had to admit, she liked the way he was dressed, too, and the way he seemed. Keith was more open and primal outside of the confines of work. Vera could tell that in an instant. He appeared very at home in relaxed blue jeans and a plain white t-shirt. The shirt was well fitted across the chest and made his shoulders seem immense when compared to his waist. He looked very broad and very capable.

"So, does the farm look like you remember it?" Keith asked innocently enough.

Vera gave a snort. "It's hard to tell. I've never seen this many people here… or anywhere else in town before, and I don't recognize anyone. Who are all these people?" Vera got around to inquiring.

"Friends mostly. Friends and friends of friends," Keith began explaining. "A lot of them are from one or two counties over. I just happened to meet quite a few while travelling. Some are people I met while in the military. And, you know how it is… people bring their own guests with them to a party."

Vera nodded silently as she attempted to unwind a bit and take it all in. "It's impressive that you're able to draw a crowd like this," she eventually said what she was actually thinking.

"I'm glad I'm able to impress you. You know, there's more to me than just my military background and what I do around the coffeehouse," he told her rather candidly but with not a hint of discontent. "There's also more to me than the family farm and what you think you already know."

"Of course," Vera readily agreed and allowed her eyes to linger with his for an extended moment.

Keith grinned at her. "I like you better this way, softened up and making honest and unguarded eye contact. I like you better as yourself."

Vera's eyes darted away instantly and she engaged herself with peering out at the bonfire. "What do you mean?"

"Don't be embarrassed," he told her and placed a firm hand in hers. "I meant that as a total compliment. It's nice that you're here and I'm getting to see you this way."

"It feels strange. I mean, we work together and I'm your boss. It's weird," she insisted.

"It doesn't have to be," Keith told her.

Vera didn't know what to do or say next, not in response to that quick comeback. The situation was becoming very awkward for her, but she didn't pull away.

"Excuse me," came the sound of a deep and almost booming baritone voice. But, there was something elegant and trickling in the tone that kept it from coming across as intimidating.

Vera whirled around to see a total stranger standing mere inches from her and also looking past her, above her head to Keith.

The stranger then took a moment to peer down at Vera. "I'm sorry to interrupt. Just wanted to say a quick hello to my friend there," the man explained.

And, what a man!

Vera had never seen anyone or anything like him before. He was tall to the point of her needing to strain her neck to see his face properly. He was dark skinned and of obvious African heritage with amazing dreadlocks that reached down to his waist. Interwoven throughout his hair were strands of braided fabrics and cords and silver clips, exotic beads and bones and bird feathers. He even had metal leaf impressions tied by leather straps to dreadlocks here and there. His clothes were average enough though, creating a sort of unhinged dichotomy, a bizarre alchemy of new and old, ancient and modern. He presented in what appeared to be well tailored and lightly starched jeans, along with a button down polo shirt in yellow. His top was the color of the sun at noon.

"Isaac. It's good to see you, man," Keith said with great affection as he moved past Vera. The two shared a brief embrace.

"Good to see you, too. Thanks for the invite," Isaac replied in kind.

"Oh, I'd like you to meet my friend, Vera. I work at her coffeehouse in town," Keith introduced.

Isaac held out a hand for her to shake.

For some unknown reason, she more than gladly accepted. Vera ached to touch him, and she was embarrassed by herself.

"So, you're Vera," Isaac meditated, as if there were a backstory hanging around that went with the introduction. "It's a real pleasure." Isaac's eyes were as dark and as daring as his dreadlocks, and Vera quickly found herself lost in them, catching flickers of flame reflected in his irises from the fire not too far away. She had the strangest feeling, too. It was a sensation that sent a message about the man holding her hand. She felt that if he looked at her long enough, gazed at her deeply enough, he would be able to crack her soul open. He would crack it swiftly and sweetly as if it were contained in no more than an eggshell, and all her internal workings, her very essence would come spilling out as a multi-tonal and raw yoke.

"Likewise," Vera said a tad hoarsely.

"Well, I'll let you two get back to your conversation," Isaac broke off their exchange graciously. "I'll see you later, Keith. And, Vera, I look forward to many happy encounters in the future." Isaac gave her a sincere smile and then walked on to become seamlessly swallowed up by the crowd. He simply moved away until he disappeared.

"Are you ready for your surprise?" Keith asked her.

"What?" she tugged her attention away from trying to spot Isaac again.

"There's something I've been wanting to show you," Keith reminded her.

"Oh, yes. Of course. Lead the way," she said in a more upbeat manner and followed Keith down the steps of the porch.

They went across the front lawn and behind the barn, moving quickly and quietly past all the others until they were standing alone in a moonlit field that was obviously in need of a good plowing. Vera had been so concerned about watching where she stepped to avoid twisting an ankle on all the loose dirt and sprouting weeds that she didn't see the surprise until the two of them were practically right up on it.

It was an oak; it was a massive, sprawling, branches reaching to the heavens oak. It was the largest oak tree she'd ever seen, other than the one that had resided in the Thompson gardens. And, Vera was held in awe. She was enraptured. This oak tree did have one startling and alluring difference from her old axis mundi though, and she couldn't help feeling enthralled by it. The trunk of the tree was spiraled. It had grown so that it wrapped its own self into a perfect spiral from the very base all the way up to the beckoning branches. The oak had chosen for some unknown reason to contort its own being.

"Oh!" it was a whispered exclamation that escaped Vera's trembling lips.

Keith circled around the gigantic tree and then came over to her side. "This tree was the deciding factor in my move here and taking over the farm," Keith revealed to her as they both stood before the majestic being of bark and branches.

"Oh?" Vera formed her single syllable into a question.

"I didn't want to ever see anything happen to a tree like this. When I saw it, I knew my grandfather and my father must've loved it as much as I do now. So, I came here to protect it, to see that nothing ever happened to it, ever," Keith continued. His hand once more found its way inside of Vera's, as they both stood there in reverent contemplation.

A shaft of moonlight dappled the leaves until they were as silver and all the branches started to sway proudly in the light autumn breezes.

"And, I was right to come here, meant to do it. And, I'd like to protect you, too… if you'll let me," Keith said low, so low in fact that Vera wasn't sure he'd spoken at all. Had she heard those words on the winds or as a voice inside her own head? "Vera, I really like you. I'd really like to start seeing more of you, outside of work, and here on the farm."

"Oh-oh, Keith," Vera began snapping out of the spell the oak apparently had her under, and so quickly. She tore her eyes away from the spiraling trunk and placed them on the face of the man at her side. "I'm not sure that's such a good idea, us dating." Vera pulled her hand back.

"Why not?" Keith asked gently.

"We work together," she stated to the sound of sudden drumbeats growing more and more rhythmic, more and more insistent.

Keith came in closer to her, as close as she let him. "It's ok, Vera. I'm not dependent on that income. There doesn't have to be a power differential. Is there something more? Something personal about me you don't like?" He was digging for and with a truth even Vera herself didn't know about. She wasn't sure why she was saying no to him, why she was putting a hurdle up between them when she didn't have to.

"No, not at all. I like you just fine, Keith. I really do like you a lot…"

The drumming just kept on getting louder, raising its energy, pressing its call, demanding that they come in to it, return to the source, come close to the fire.

Vera began walking back towards the festivities, with Keith following at her heels.

"Will you come back out to the farm to see me?" he pressed.

After seeing the oak, she knew she would. "Yes."

"Can we at least spend some time together and see where things go?"

There always appeared to be no harm in a thing like that, but Vera knew well and good that there could be. Still she answered, "Yes."

The two of them emerged at the edge of the drummer's circle, and inside of it the flames of the bonfire were leaping high. They were growing and dancing and delighting… delighting to Misty's enchanting and timeless dance.

Inside the circle was Misty, twirling and swaying and moving in time to the beat. Her orange and red skirt swirled and licked at her legs as though the layers were flames themselves and the fire responded in kind. There was a sort of hypnotic quality to her every gesture and the drummers beat on and on and on. Furiously fast artists' hands attempted to sketch what they saw, to capture what could not be contained. Keith walked with Vera and they took their place among the others and for the first time in Vera couldn't remember how long, she let herself go. She shut her eyes tight and felt the music and the heat from the fire. She let herself feel as free as her friend looked in that sacred and primal dance that needed not word or song. At some point, Vera leaned back to find the firm wall of a chest and a steady heartbeat. Arms wrapped around her and Vera could feel the acceptance that came with being so near to Keith, so natural and so much a part of his world.

When Vera opened her eyes, she saw her brother only a few feet away, and he was watching Misty, who had been joined by other dancers as she continued to spin about. John watched her and her alone, and Vera longed for someone to see her that way, especially now that Lance was gone from her life. She longed for someone to see the real and complete her that way, and that was something Lance had never seen… but Keith had in a fleeting encounter, in a brief reveal.

Vera continued to look around the circle at strangers who all moved and beat and gyrated in tandem, who sketched and clapped and held hands to become as one. There was an embracive and primitive and correct quality about it all, and she could see now why Keith had associated himself with these folks. She could see why he wanted the farm and was drawn to the oak tree, and why he was drawn to her and she liked it. She thought she was starting to understand a great deal, but there was always more to learn, a mystery at nearly every turn.

Vera's eyes stopped scanning the circle when she caught sight of Isaac again. He was keeping beat on a drum made of animal skins and an ebony wood. There were fur clumps and charms hanging off the thing and brightly painted symbols all about the base. He moved back and forth as though he were stepping between realms, and there was something otherworldly about his appearance beyond what the naked eye could see. He seemed to be not one man but two, and he sensed Vera's gaze. His eyes locked with hers and he seemed to be trying to lead her, lead her away from another disturbance that had entered the circle's envelopment. There was a strong wind gust, quick and furious autumn air currents that slapped at Vera with her own hair, soft curls going straight from the force. There was something pulling at her, telling her to step away from Keith as much as Isaac was silently telling her to stay put. Vera felt as though she were instantaneously going insane, sensing all these things that were not verifiable on any tangible level. She was slipping, slipping back into who she was through what she allowed herself to sense, to possibly become.

She followed the winds, followed the pull, as she moved away from Keith. She moved out of his embrace and a bit more into the open, where she could be viewed on the sidelines thanks to the firelight. And, it was there that she at long last saw a figure emerge from the shadows. It was the figure of a man, and she immediately recognized him.

It was Derrick.

He had come. He had accepted her invitation and joined them at the drum circle. He had come to the gathering and was looking for her, seeking her out. But as the drummers played on, something started to happen. Derrick was shifting between the worlds, too, moving from one side of a ghostly veil to another, and he both did and did not have red-hot ember eyes.

Chapter 6

There was very little beyond that surreal moment with Derrick that Vera remembered before they arrived back at the Thompson house, Derrick's house. Vera recalled her movement away from the blaze of the fire and the temporary heat she shared with Keith. She could still recall clutching Derrick tightly, arms wound about his waist as he whisked her away into the night on the back of his motorbike, cool winds fanning flames she inwardly brought with her. But, those same winds seemed to have chilled Derrick. It was true that he still fit inside her, with her, in a way no other man had ever done or ever could. He opened her in a manner that was impossible to understand, and yet when he made love to her that night, under Lillian's roof, under Elizabeth's roof, under his roof, it felt less than it had been the time before but more important. Urgent. He had gone a touch cooler than the time before, as though the night breezes had brought down a temperature that was no mere matter of degrees Fahrenheit. No, it was more of a draining of warmth from Vera's vital center, and she let him have it. For just as before, there was no denying Derrick. He may have been colder to the touch, but her torch for him glowed insanely bright.

Vera lay in bed with him afterwards, not so eager to run away and be in her own home. She let the early dawn move her in random waves between sleep and wakefulness, but without dreaming. There was no dreaming. While half-conscious, Vera basked in the glow of pride that she was the one in Derrick's bed. No other woman in town had managed to snag him the way she'd done, at least not to her knowledge.

Inevitably, birds began their chirping as the early dawn approached.

"Why are you here?" Vera found herself asking Derrick, whether he was awake or not. "Why did you come here? And, why do you stay?"

He didn't answer her for the longest time, so long that she assumed he was asleep. And then quite suddenly, he spoke. "It's all a matter of time."

"Hmmm…" Vera murmured, as if that answered anything. It didn't, but she couldn't bring herself to care. She also didn't care that she couldn't dream, for being in Derrick's intoxicating presence eased that. Being around him was good enough. It almost felt like he created his own dreamscape, like a web constantly woven and rewoven about him. She and Derrick hadn't really spoken much, and any response from him also felt like heaven. It felt even more powerful than that. It was as though it fed some sort of sick and demanding addiction within her, and she was sated with every syllable… but not for long. She craved more. She wanted to be eternally found in the spotlight of his attentions.

Derrick let out a long breath. ""We always think we will have more time…"

Vera rolled over, those words stirring her to a sober wakefulness, and for a span of time she wasn't sure why. She gazed through thin lashes on heavy eyelids at Derrick. His eyes were closed as his head reclined back on a satiny white pillow. Derrick's brown hair tinged with fiery red was scattered this way and that, and his tousled appearance only served to make him incredibly gorgeous in the golden hour of dawn, in the most early light. He wore nothing more than a bed sheet about his lower half and a small chain around his neck. Vera couldn't see what charm the chain supported, for it had fallen back and behind his body. "Are you sad?" Vera inquired tenderly.

Derrick didn't speak. No. He held his tongue.

"You miss your grandmother," Vera surmised for him, but that didn't appear to be the whole of it.

There was a simple, soft whisper that whipped about the bedchamber. It echoed Derrick's words. "We always think we will have more time…" Derrick had echoed the whisper's words. And, Vera then knew that the whisper merely repeated some portion of Elizabeth; it was a thought, a revelation, a summoning. It could have been anything. But with that quick recollection, Vera was unnerved and coincidentally frozen in place.

And then Derrick replied. "I will always miss her," he said.

Vera both wanted and didn't want to touch him. Derrick and the room and the air and the moment became disjointed to her. If she touched him, would she shatter? It might be worth it for the chance to comfort him, to feel that kind of intimate connection.

The two lovers stayed still next to each other until Vera noticed a detail that roused her from her frigid condition and minor preponderance on his chain. Tears. The slightest evidence of moisture slowly made its way in chaotic trails down Derrick's face.

Vera placed a hand on his chest. "We should make the most of the time we have," she offered.

"We always think we will have more time," he repeated, "and then it runs out."

Vera drew her hand back in swift reaction to the iciness of his words and lay back on her own pillow. She shut her eyes tight and began to wonder just who it was she kept company with last night and into the morning hours. Who was this man that she allowed him to take her right to bed? Who was he that she could not resist? At some point in her frightful musings, she must've drifted off to sleep. And when she at long last opened her eyes again, bright daylight was streaming into the bedroom. Derrick was gone.

Vera was wounded more gravely than she'd ever admit to by Derrick's leaving her there. She shamefully retrieved her clothes, which had been tossed all about the room, and made her way out into the hall in a sullen slump, not to mention rumpled attire. She really should've taken better care of the finery her friend loaned her, but Misty was a forgiving sort. And, it did quite a bit to ease Vera's guilty conscious when she decided in a snap to have everything dry-cleaned.

"Derrick?" Vera called out in question, as she peered down the long upstairs hallway. "Derrick, are you there?" she tried again and took a few steps.

There was no reply. Odds were good she was alone in the house.

Vera considered picking up and heading straight home, to the safety of her own room and the comforts of her own shower and bed, when some strange sensation stopped her.

She was alone in the house. She was alone in the Thompson house. She was back inside Lillian's home with nothing to hinder her, no one to pull and push and persuade. She had the entire place to herself and could explore it, just as she had done all those years ago. The gleam of the woodwork and the details of the paintings, the suppleness of the carpet and the possibilities of closed doors beckoned to her. And in a single suspended moment, as she shut her eyes and breathed deeply, she thought she smelled the scent of the herbs in the Thompson gardens, a signature aroma that often clung to Lillian's clothes and hair. She thought she heard the padding of great and graceful footsteps. She thought she felt the touch of a familiar hand on her shoulder, a touch of gentility that said 'welcome back' and 'stay a while.'

Vera decided to remain, despite her responsibilities in the outside world. She made up her mind to explore. She moved to the first door on the right and turned the knob. Hinges creaked from being still for years. They had grown dry and rusty from disuse. Vera peeked in to see that it was the old sewing room where Lillian had created many of her own dresses and shawls, not to mention a skirt here and a costume there. There had even been one Halloween when her brother John and she both dressed up as alien invaders, and Lillian had created the costumes from scrapes and from scratch, but no one would've ever thought so. The detailing and the decadence on both outfits that night had been exquisite and very extraterrestrial. John paraded around in his getup long after trick-or-treat ended. Vera recalled sleeping in hers. She wondered whatever happened to those costumes, and had her mother or grandmother taken pictures that night. Vera figured there probably were no pictures and the costumes had surely been discarded a short time after the holiday. Vera shut the door. It was but a single memory encapsulated in an old and all but abandoned room, neat and tidy though it might be.

She made her way to the next door to find a reading room piled high to the rafters with books along every wall. It was also untouched and very clean. Then the next door revealed a guest bedroom, arranged and presentable; it was ready to receive. There was very little to be found inside of it, and that, too was much like Lillian had left it. She always liked to make her guests, and especially her relatives, feel at home. She always left that one room ready to take on the characteristics of the occupant. It was quaint and charming and open to impressions. There was space for personal items and room for individual interpretations. Inside such a tiny room was the vibration of a great and nonjudgmental expanse. A visitor could be exactly who they were in there, no questions asked or aspersions cast. Vera shut that door with a touch of compassion. As an adult, she could now fully appreciate what it meant for someone to offer up a space like that. In all the years she'd been away and in all the years Lillian had been gone, no one had ever come along that could measure up. Elizabeth may have been impressive in her own right, a force to be reckoned with, but Lillian had been a beacon and a haven and a heaven and a home. Vera felt positive now that no matter where Lillian would've lived in her life, she'd have made it a home.

There was one more door left to open; it was the door that overlooked the staircase down. And if Vera remembered correctly, it was the Treasure Room. Well, Vera had called it the Treasure Room. Lillian and John both referred to it as the Junk Room. Lillian had done so with a gleam in her eye and the occasional whisper about how one man's trash was another man's treasure. John just said it was junk and left it at that.

Vera tentatively opened the door.

It was the Treasure Room all right, precisely as it had been laid out years ago. It was a room full of stuff. Dressmaker's dummies in all sorts of fabric wraps, half done projects that would forever remain that way, abused books, baskets, crafty items, threads and ribbons in every color imaginable, seasonal decorations for each holiday, old jewelry in even older and half opened jewelry boxes, large chests, small chests, but no chests as ornately impressive as the one Elizabeth had brought with her. Vera let that thought, the idea of the dark pirate chest that had once held the grotesque little doll inside, slip past her, go right through her. There was not a place for it in Lillian's greatest space, in Lillian's grand harvest of fine arts and frivolous findings. Vera moved throughout the room, weaving in and out of structures, as if she were in a museum. Each and every item seemed to have various and random interpretations, stories to tell and secrets to keep. There were clues to be ferreted out. There were mysteries to solve.

It was as Vera arrived at the very back of the room that she caught sight of a dominating figure, an incredibly imposing specter merely standing there and eyeing her. She jumped back with a start at seeing the ghost of a great woman holding her ground. Do ghosts hold ground? It was a weird question to have conjured up. Her first thought after that had been about how John was wrong all those years ago. He was wrong when he cast aside her idea about Lillian still being around after she was dead. He had dismissed the concept of those who were well loved remaining present, of life after death in general, with a simple, "Of course not." That had forced Vera to abandon her hopes. But, now stood the visage of Lillian directly in front of her, only she wasn't old and speckled and withering, despite her otherwise regal stature, as she had been in her final days. No, she was in her prime. Death had been good to her. Fate must've kissed her a thousand times over and then over again.

"Oh my god," Vera sighed and took a couple of steps forward and once more towards the back of the room, towards the image that had suddenly appeared. But as she did so, she realized with horror and then shock that it wasn't Lillian at all. In a couple more steps, the figure began to resemble someone else. In a blink, Vera saw Elizabeth staring back at her. "Oh my god!"

It was Elizabeth who had been resurrected and unfairly rejuvenated. It was Elizabeth who had clawed and crawled her way back from the depths of the grave, who had defied death, and Vera felt silly for supposing death could keep its icy grips on a woman like her. It was Elizabeth appearing as tall and proud and dominating as ever, only now she had the strength of vibrant youth in her bones and in her sinews. She looked majestic and beautiful… and cold. Vera darted away. Moving fast without looking where she was going. Vera ran smack into a dressmaker's dummy, turning it over and falling herself. Both her and the framework landed in a jumbled heap. When she glanced back over her shoulder to see if Elizabeth followed, if the cruel undead were almost upon her, she saw an awful display, a hideous realization. She'd been looking into a full-length mirror.

It was her own reflection that had startled her, terrified her. Nothing more.

She let loose a few pressurized tears as she got to her feet. She felt both foolish and alarmed. In fact, beyond those two initial sensations, she didn't know what to feel. She set the dummy

upright once more and straightened the haphazard fabric. Then she
did her best to straighten her mussed attire, too. It was time to go.
She didn't want to see anymore. But, that didn't mean there wasn't
more for her to see. For as she was exiting the room, a glint of
morning sunlight caught the gleam of a metal latch. Vera looked to
a small table that sat off to the right hand side of the doorway. It
happened just as she was about to leave and shut the rest of her
memories away. The gleam came from a small but impressively
thick book. It sat on the table as if it had been there forever, and
maybe it had, but Vera didn't recall seeing it in her childhood or in
her morning wanderings that drew her to this room. And, the book
was dreadfully familiar. The outer bindings and the dark color had
been made to resemble something else, something horrible and
mysterious. It was not unlike a dark and disturbingly ornate chest,
the very chest Elizabeth brought into the house. Vera couldn't help
herself any longer and picked the book up in her trembling hands.
Gold letters were painted on the cover in exceedingly fine script:
'EMD'. E and D could have easily been for Elizabeth Drake.
Surely they were. Vera was curious what Elizabeth's middle name
was as she tried to open it, only to find the metal latch kept it
securely locked and required the tiniest key. Vera ripped and
pulled and then resolved to find a letter open later that would help
her pry it open. She brought the book that was so obviously a
journal, a diary, with her as she left the Treasure Room.

      Vera then left the house without further exploration. She
got herself better situated and went out via the back door. She
crossed the lawn and entered the back side door of her own home,
moved through the kitchen swiftly, only to find a lonely Frank on
her heels, and quietly she went straight to her room. She did have
Frank in tow. She didn't catch sight of her brother or Misty though.
They might have been in the house or not, for all she knew. She
leaned on the locked bedroom door and took a few deep, soothing
breaths as she stared at the friendly beast of a dog that demanded
petting. A locked door and the calming company of a pet. It was
the best plan she had for the undead, both in that house and
apparently within her own flesh. But the longer she stood there
coming to terms, the more time she took taking each breath and
then counting them, the more she felt something else moving
through her room. It was like an invisible animal skulking about,

sizing her up, making decisions. She sensed it come to a stop near her dresser. And, in a flash the little hand-carved doll both did and did not have red-hot ember eyes.

Frank growled in protest and then whined with worry. Then Vera knew beyond the shadow of a doubt that it wasn't just her imagination and it never had been. The dog sensed it, too.

Life settled down. Everything became eerily normal, strangely quiet again as one day flipped like a switch quietly into another. There were times throughout Vera's life where a calm would come, where Fate would take a break and let her think things were capable of being normal, and it was happening again. Derrick disappeared for several days after that, and it was as if the whole town let loose a breath they'd all been holding. The day-to-day routine was working its way back for everyone. John took on a new project only a block away from home, restoring a kitchen of the most minute and thoughtful details, a kitchen that had an original open hearth. He began making a regular habit of coming home midday for lunch and a romp in the yard with Frank. The Thompson house was quiet and when Vera went home from work all throughout the first half of the week she almost thought the entire episode with Derrick might've been a dream, maybe a delightful somnambular episode. And, that would've meant she was suddenly and miraculously cured of whatever flaw had ailed her, denying her a proper sleep cycle for years. Obviously, with any sort of surface examination it was clear it wasn't all a dream, but it felt so much like it… from what Vera remembered. It felt so very far away with the house still and vacant again.

Work was mundane and fairly easy, too. There were regular hours, consistent chitchat with Misty and Keith, and plenty of townsfolk wandering in and out for refreshments, along with the use of their wireless internet. Misty was becoming so happy in her new and stable life, her relationship with John, and the hours and pay at the coffeehouse. Vera went into the kitchen of the shop one day to find her humming and swaying as she placed puff pastries onto baking trays. Misty resembled a happy and hippie version of a fantasy domestic. Her long blonde hair swung about her back in tandem with the folds of her bronze-toned skirt. She occasionally wiped her hands on the dusty rose apron she'd tied loosely about her waist.

"Someone's in a good mood," Vera noted.

Misty perked up and smiled at her friend with a quick glance over her shoulder. "Why shouldn't I be? I think I have everything I want right now. And, it's such a crisp, beautiful autumn day outside," she reported.

Vera cocked her head. "Really? I hadn't noticed."

"You've been inside too long. Why don't you step out for a bit? It's slow right now and Keith and I can handle it," Misty urged.

Vera smiled back. "Maybe I will. I think I've been caught up in the routine these past couple of days."

"And, in your own head," Misty added and went back to paying attention to her precious pastries.

Vera shrugged and left the kitchen without another word. After all, what was there to say in her own defense? She had been in her own head quite a lot. She'd gone home after work every night and half-heartedly attempted to pry open the diary she'd found. The days may have been routine, but the evenings weren't, at least not exactly.

Vera had no success getting the diary open, so it wasn't like any newfound evidence or special information had fallen into her lap. And, some nights she'd merely contemplate the book she discovered, going over it as though it were a trinket to be admired, an antique, unique and original artwork. There were nights when she'd think a great life's story might be in there, and that made every facet about the book seem less sinister. Then there were nights when she'd think dark and evil secrets might reside within those pages. Would those revelations be inked in human blood? Vera shivered whenever her imagination ran wild like that. She wanted to open it… but she didn't. Plus, she had the added albeit mildly worrying train of thought that ran multiple tracks about where Derrick had gone off to.

The Thompson house was still stuffed full of all its contents, and the place hadn't even been locked up. Anyone could wander in, not that Vera didn't keep a watchful eye on the place and pop by a time of two. For Lillian's sake… wherever she was now. But, after her last fright in the Treasure Room, she was steering clear for a while and working back up to it gradually. Vera figured Derrick would be back. The house was full of stuff and Derrick would be back to claim it. She thought maybe he was having a hard time processing his grandmother's passing, the new town, and their raucous relationship. He didn't seem like the type to talk about those things either. Vera felt in her bones that he would return.

She stepped out the front door and off to the side of the walkway, leaning back against the brick building and taking comfort in the rays of a sun beginning its late afternoon descent. Misty had been right. It was indeed a crisp day, a fresh day, one in which anything could happen and it just hadn't done so yet. There was routine and balance to be found for everyone. There was routine and intrigue and imaginings for Vera. She didn't know what would happen next, but she liked to imagine, especially if she kept it light and harmless.

Vera could see up the whole rest of the street from her position on the corner, about five blocks or so. The storefronts were decked out in illustrious fall hues and many of the boutiques and dry goods stores had started putting out festive Halloween displays. There was a penny candy store diagonal to Vera's shop that had placed bright orange pumpkin buckets made out of cheap plastic, with black jack-o-lantern faces, in the windows. The buckets were stuffed with any number of treats, all looking delightfully enticing. Halloween had been a fun time for her and John in years past, and for the second time in less than a week she thought back to those alien costumes Lillian had made for she and her brother years ago.

Vera expanded her lungs to their fullest capacity and exhaled slowly, watching a puff of smoke leave her lips when warm moist breath came into contact with chilled autumn air. It was subtle and barely noticeable, but it was there. The seasons were most definitely changing, and it wouldn't be long before the vibrancy that seemed so joyous began to die. Sap would seek the center of trees and leaves would fall off to the grave of the ground. Grasses now golden would become a somber brown and then with enough snows whole patches of earth would go muddy and barren and bleak. There would be gray clouds and early darkness and a long, hard winter ahead that drove many indoors. There was sunshine and some measure of warmth and color for Vera now, but those things never lasted.

She sighed.

"Deep in thought again?" Keith asked as he joined her alongside the sturdy brick wall.

"Oh," she peeped. "You startled me." Vera slid down a ways to make room for Keith.

"I thought you heard me come out." He found his place against the building and leaned back, following her line of sight.

"No, no. As you said, I was deep in thought again," Vera confessed playfully and considered Keith in profile. He was even more stunning that way, for only seeing half of him made her want to see more.

"Where do you go when you're thinking like that? Do you remember the past or contemplate the future?" Keith went on with the same line of conversation.

Vera gave a little snort. "Serious questions? Really?"

Keith nodded his head once. "Why not? We haven't had a decent conversation since drum circle."

"What does that mean?" Vera asked, caught off guard entirely. When Keith didn't give a reply, she nudged him in the ribs gently but hard enough to be more demanding. "Hey, what does that mean?"

Keith looked at her with his voracious steel gray and hazel eyes. They seemed to be eating her up. "I think you know what that means."

"We've been talking on and off every day so far this week," Vera defended her position.

Keith gave in, but only enough to portray a simple smile. He drew up the corners of his mouth with gentility, and it was the first time Vera noticed the faint smile lines about his mouth and eyes. Keith wasn't perfect either, just like Vera. He was subject to the forces of nature and the time and tides, just like Vera. Some folks, like Misty, like Derrick, might have been given a kinder lot by Fate, slower aging and deeper beauty to draw on… but not Keith. Not entirely. And, not Vera. By her own estimation, she'd been given scant resources with which to work. She smoothed the outline of her navy blue suit and tugged her overcoat tight to brace against a fall chill and Keith's pending response.

"We've been talking to help us pass the days. We've been keeping our discussions on the surface. That's not really talking," Keith explained. "That's occupying time."

"So, what do you want to talk about?" Vera questioned him and had the sudden sensation that she was drowning, going under in response to his hungry depths and his diving for answers in her layers. She felt like she was completely submerged when he looked at her so keenly.

"Are you seeing that guy you left with the night of drum circle?" he asked straight out.

"Derrick?" Who else?

"Yes," Keith replied. "Derrick. Are you seeing him?"

Vera scrunched up her mouth and looked away. "Maybe. Sort of."

"Come on," Keith pressed.

But, it was sincerely the best answer she could give. Derrick had made her no promises and had provided no labels or outlines for what they shared. He hadn't even told her he was taking off for days on end. There was no communication with Derrick until he determined there would be; there was no intimacy with Derrick until he felt the need for it. And, then it was all over with as quickly as it had begun, at least for Derrick. Vera seemed to be carrying around a great blazing torch within her that only dimmed slightly when her motorcycle riding phantom was away and became nothing less than a raging inferno when he was present.

"It's complicated," Vera said helplessly, and that had been enough to get a head tilt from Keith and buy her a moment or two of silence.

"Is it serious?"

"I don't know."

Keith drew in a breath. "Does it feel serious to you?" He was nitpicking and he knew it. He also knew Vera knew it but was too polite and proper in the broad light of a business day to say so.

Vera wasn't sure how to answer, mostly because she wasn't sure how she felt. When she was with Derrick it felt incredible and insane and like all there was to living. When Derrick wrapped her in his arms and focused solely on her, Vera felt like the most important woman in the entire world, and she enjoyed that, she craved more of it. Yet, when she was away from her mysterious lover he seemed far less substantial and life altering and much more like a dream and even a bad idea… which made it no less alluring. The situation was severely jacked up.

"I don't know," Vera finally gave over. "And, I'm not trying to frustrate you," she went on. "I just really don't know."

Keith sighed and weighed the possibilities in his mind, and as he flirted with each potential outcome of every path that might be trod he eventually arrived at a suggested destination for the moment, a place to rest before the proverbial fork split. There was no way decisions and determinations could be put off forever. "How about a meal?" he asked.

"What?" Vera sought clarification.

"Come back out to the farm this Sunday, a couple days after the next drum circle and things have settled down from the bonfire. I'll make up a meal," Keith offered.

"Oh…. I don't know…" Vera vacillated.

"You're saying that a lot today," Keith pointed out and gave her a nudge.

Vera grinned at him. "I guess I am."

"I'll make something simple," Keith went on, trying to persuade her.

It was difficult for Vera to decline because Keith was so good-natured and extremely attractive, and there was the undeniable pleasure in being out on the farm. Plus, Vera found herself thinking back to that spiraled oak he'd shown her. She certainly wanted to see that again, to draw nearer to it, to touch it and see if it would feel anything like her old axis mundi. She had been adrift all those years without her anchor. She'd been lost, a connection had been severed, and Vera longed to realign herself.

"Isaac will be there," Keith baited. "I know you two hit it off. How about sharing a meal this Sunday evening with me and Isaac?"

Vera felt giddy about it and gave a rapid nod. "Ok."

❖

When Derrick still hadn't returned by late afternoon on Friday, Vera thought he might be gone for good, despite the nagging in her gut, and she decided to head home from work early to tour the Thompson house. She wanted to start picking through the items there, salvaging whatever she fancied for herself. She still hadn't gotten the diary open, and to a certain extent she'd given up trying. There was work and Keith and thoughts of Sunday's dinner to keep her mind occupied. There were even random musings about the upcoming drum circle and what to wear that night.

All of those subjects were whizzing through her brain in no particular order as she walked up the steps to the porch of the Thompson house and opened the unlocked door.

"Hello?" she gave an obligatory shout out. "Derrick, are you here?"

Only silence met her ears; silence in the form of a steady thrum so common of places alive with energy. Vera found it impossible to set foot inside the house and not think of all the memories contained therein. She had memories there, as did her brother, as did Lillian and Elizabeth and now even Derrick. Many of Lillian's relatives and even Vera's own grandmother had memories held inside the home, and the place was alive with them.

Vera gleefully shut the door tight behind her and threw the lock into place. She didn't want to be disturbed. Not for any reason. There were still a few hours before drum circle and the house was hers until then to do with as she pleased. Vera stood dead center in the living room and once more admired the claw-footed furniture draped in tones of heavy maroon, but none of the fabrics went so far as to become a true and tawdry burgundy. The soft sandy carpet and the luscious floral draperies wrapped her in an ambiance of decadence. She breathed it in and was thankful for it. Preservation had been so important. As she stood in the heart of the house, with no distractions, Vera felt like she'd finally come home.

Sometime later, Vera moved on and passed the shiny metal face of her old friend, the grandfather clock. "Continuing to watch over every single second?" she asked him and took in the vision of the sun giving way to the moon, and moments that ticked on by. That massive clock didn't have to say anything. He didn't have to speak to answer her. He was still a fine keeper of time.

The crystal chandelier winked at Vera from the dining room beyond, just as it had the first time Derrick invited her in, only this time she could choose whether or not to respond. Vera glided past the staircase and went straight into the dining room. She peered upwards at the exquisitely detailed chandelier made of fine crystals. As she walked full circle around the long dining room table that seated eight comfortably, every little facet of the hanging artwork overhead got the chance to glisten and gleam. Every tiny gem face got the opportunity to say hello.

After peeking at plates and cups and saucers in an offset curio, Vera made her way out of the dining room and back into the kitchen. Other than in the sewing room, it was here that Lillian had done her best and most appreciated works. Homemade soups and chilies, stews and sumptuous roasts, less involving but still delicious sandwiches and pies, jams and preserves, syrups and sauces. Lillian had also made Vera and John homemade ice cream in the churn sporadically, and there were times when she'd let John and Vera contribute some effort to the mix and churn it themselves. Vera took in a deep breath and smelled the remnants of sumptuous meals long over. There must've been a residue of old foodstuffs, for the aromas lingered in the walls and clung to the stove. Vera also thought she caught a whiff of the easy to identify herbal scent that came from Lillian drying whole plants provided by the garden every autumn season. She'd hang them upside down from the kitchen rafters with twine. There were a few scant herbs hanging there even now, but they were far too old for use or to give off any scent.

From where Vera was positioned in the kitchen, she could see straight out the back windows above the sink and into the gardens that were no more. The entire back lot was full of bed upon bed of weeds, and the invasive pests had gone so far as to start destroying the delicate concrete outlines that had demarcated where those beds once rested. Another year to two and it would appear as nothing more than an overgrown backyard, as if nothing else had ever been there in the first place. The vines may eventually envelope the small stone wall that separated the Thompson lot from her brother's.

Vera didn't want to think about it. Perhaps Derrick would move in. Maybe he would sell the house to someone determined to restore it to its former glory, someone kind and sweet and caring who would be a good friend and neighbor. Perhaps a demolition crew would be paid to take it down and bulldoze the property under. Maybe a million things and then a million more. It mattered a great deal and it mattered very little.

Vera sighed, if only to hear her voice bounce off the walls, and then she headed for the upstairs.

The long hallway looked even longer after a hard day's work. The walls seemed thicker, as though they had moved in closer or simply grown in girth like the windows when Elizabeth had taken up residence, not that there was anything simple or normal about it if they had. Vera moved past the Treasure Room, still not eager to go in there again. There was no telling what might happen or what she'd find. She far preferred to have her discoveries be under control, if such a thing as control could ever be more than an illusion. She'd reverted to form in thinking control to be a case of smoke and mirrors. It felt good, but it was a grand deception played upon oneself. Instead she went straight to the sparsely decorated guest bedroom.

She went through a practically empty chest of drawers and a totally empty closet. There were a couple of oddities on the night table by the bed, a cozy little twin mattress covered in yellow sheets placed upon a black steel frame. Vera fondled the porcelain statue of a squirrel holding a gigantic acorn and then set it down to pick up the smooth likeness of a lanky black and white dog. Vera turned the dog over and over in her hands. She studied every facet and small detail. She scrutinized it for discrepancies. It was when she found none that she realized the small canine decoration was identical to Frank. It was Frank. It could be no other dog. The figurine was too exact. Vera put it down, feeling more alarmed than she had reason to be, and she had every reason. Someone was playing tricks. Vera shut the door to the guest bedroom.

Vera thought for a few minutes more before she dared to walk through the next doorway; the precipice to the library or reading room or whatever it was she and Lillian had felt like calling it. Books were everywhere, along each wall, shelf after overflowing shelf. There were also some tomes stacked up in the couple of plush chairs the space held. Vera decided it would be most prudent to go through the books, to at least skim the titles and see if there were any works she'd like to take home. Her eyes scanned cookbooks, travel guides, herbal references, exotic and native plant manuals, wild animal picture books, art history and art appreciation hardbacks, various genres in paperback fiction, and last but not least were the volumes upon volumes of short stories. Lillian loved to read; she was a woman of vivid imagination. In many ways, Vera came to realize they had been much alike. They had been more alike than any two people could ever hope to become. Vera missed Lillian so badly because she had been a beacon of hope and a proud example of what Vera herself could develop into naturally, effortlessly. Lillian had been there to assure her that it was all going to be just fine.

Vera plucked an armful of books off the shelves, not bothering to look at the titles or subject matter. What was in the books wasn't the important part. Having a sampling from Lillian's vast library was what counted. She then left the library and passed by the sewing room for the master bedroom.

Once inside, she set her burden of books down on the cherry wood chest of drawers and took in the sights and smells of the chamber. Derrick had left the windows cracked open again, and Vera could hear the winds picking up outside. She could smell the fragrance of decaying leaves and moist, rich earth; the aromas of autumn carried on the backs of chilly breezes. She closed her eyes as she had done downstairs and drew in deep breaths. It felt so good. It was absolutely invigorating. But no matter how deeply Vera sucked air, she could not discern Derrick's scent or Elizabeth's presence. She couldn't find anything alien or amiss. She breathed in Lillian's signature scent alone. And, somewhere within the span of an hour or merely a minute she heard it, distinctly — the rustling of dense and dappled leaves.

Vera opened her eyes. She continued to hear it. The sound of leaves swaying and slapping in the winds. Back and forth she took in the melodic whirl, the musical drone. Hearing the sound alone allowed her to envision in her mind's eye a mighty oak, its top branches bending ever so gracefully as it danced to the song of the air currents. Vera went to the back bedroom window and stepped behind the billowy white curtains, and that was when she saw it. There was a large oak growing dead center in the back lot, defying logic and reality and all sorts of weeds. It stood there so proud and bold, even though it was impossible. It stood there, as one of a kind. There was no other oak tree like it. Vera knew because years ago she had memorized every line and curve and groove in the bark. She knew this tree. Her axis mundi had returned from the dead.

Vera gaped and gawked and stared through the tears that threatened to stream down her face. She would've stood there forever, never daring to take her eyes off that beloved tree, were it not for a peculiar sensation creeping along her back and decidedly up her spine. Someone was watching her. She sensed eyes that were hot and penetrating and yet did not burn. Vera understood those eyes to be lingering on her, smoldering with an ember's surreal glow. She turned and saw nothing, but that didn't mean there was nothing there, nothing to see beyond simple vision. As she continued to look around, as she let herself adjust to what was actually taking place, shadows shifted right in front of her and the eyes that had played and preyed upon Vera remained, ethereally. The shadows shifted until they became a swirling and embracing vortex of Fate. It was Fate in that bedchamber with her, cloaked in the illusion as though it were royal raiment. And, Fate nudged her in one direction, back towards the chest of drawers.

Vera didn't fight it, mostly because she didn't want to. She went along with the shadows and made her way over to where she'd set the books down. She then had the compulsive urge to open wide the drawers and expeditiously did so. Inside she found fineries she couldn't believe were real. The clothes were so elegant and subtle, so fine and also dramatic. They were items that belonged to a greater wardrobe filled with flair, and there condition was good as new. The fabrics smelled of lavender and distant dreams as Vera pulled a white satin top trimmed in lace about the neck and open arms. She then reached into the next drawer and retrieved a purple and peach skirt that looked like a bundle of scarves but felt like it had the weight of a winter coat. Vera stripped down, tossing her workday clothes aside and slid into the amazing apparel. She then dug around some more to pull to the surface a cabled peach sweater jacket with bell sleeves. Vera slipped it on and appraised her appearance in the mirror.

This was who Lillian had been in her prime. This was who Lillian had been before Vera ever met her.

This was who Vera was meant to be.

Vera began emptying drawers in a frenzied flash and threw all the clothes she could fit into the trunk that lay abandoned in the closet, the chest that Elizabeth had brought with her, the dark and disturbingly ornate thing that felt less ghastly when filled with Lillian's belongings and given a purpose. Vera tossed the books in on top, latched the chest tight and then paused to catch sight of herself again in the mirror.

The winds were picking up outside as she contemplated her choices. They were moving about the bedroom now, activated by an outside force larger than the basic nature Vera was privy to understanding.

A whisper greeted Vera's ears. "We always think we will have more time…"

Was her time up?... Vera made a frantic search for shoes in the closet. She found a pair of purple suede boots and put them on. She then grabbed up the few other pairs hidden in there and brought the handfuls with her as she clumsily half-drug and half-hauled the dark pirate and fairy chest out of the house, across the back lawn, and into the home she shared with her brother, and Frank.

Frank made a quick attempt to love on her at the back side door when she came bursting in, but he got out of the way instantly when he saw the mess she was dragging.

Vera didn't call out to see if her brother was home. She didn't wonder if Misty was around. She didn't stop to pet Frank. Vera was obsessed with getting her new possessions into her room and properly put away. She had a drum circle and bonfire to get ready for, and it was a whole new outlook she was bringing with her to this one. Fate was driving her crazy. Was it also setting her free?

❖

"John has to work late. I guess his project isn't going as smoothly as he thought it would," Misty's voice relayed the update through Vera's cell phone, "so I'll be by to pick you up." Misty hadn't driven her own car in quite a while, not even once since she'd moved into town. There was no reason to, as practically everything seemed to be within walking distance, and when it wasn't John was driving her around in his truck. Misty kind of welcomed getting her small economy vehicle back on the streets.

"Oh, ok," Vera agreed with little input and less interest. She was in the bathroom, occupied with creative and slightly vain endeavors when her friend called.

"I just have a few things left to do here and then I'm going to run by my apartment and slip into fresh clothes," Misty went on. "I shouldn't be too long."

"All right," Vera replied. "I'm finishing up myself. See you in a bit,"
she dismissed.

And, the phone call ended. It was informational and short and kind of unusual for the two women, but both of them were preoccupied, both of them were busy. That's how Vera figured it. Vera also assumed she should feel bad for not working as hard as Misty at the shop lately, but Misty was getting paid, as was Keith. Vera was yet to draw any take home pay. And that was fine, so long as she could focus on other things, too… things that gave her a great deal of pleasure, like shelving Lillian's books, wearing Lillian's clothes, and putting on a fresh coat of rather alluring cosmetics.

When Vera was done making herself up for the night and she stepped out of the bathroom to contemplate her form in the bedroom mirror, she felt like a goddess draped is supple peaches and purples. The clothing appeared tailor made for her. She had never known such beauty about herself. She softened her hair and gave it lift with a slight wave, a tender curl. She'd added sheer powder and silky shimmering eye paints to the point where she appeared downright exotic and much more daring than Misty had envisioned during the previous makeover. This was who she wanted to be. This was how she'd always dreamed she'd turn out, before she had stopped dreaming entirely.

Vera stepped over to the dresser to consider adding a couple of pieces of the scant amounts of jewelry she owned, when her eyes caught sight of the glint of the metal latch on the diary again, the metal lock that required the tiniest of keys to open. She hadn't taken a letter opener to the book marked 'EMD.' She thought she would right off the bat when she first brought it home, but other than half-heartedly tearing at the thing, she hadn't really forced the issue. Vera began to think she'd rather open it with a key instead. She'd rather take her time and invest some effort and find the key that fit what may have been the world's smallest lock. She might do serious damage to a book that old if she really tore into it. Vera then let her eyes roam over to the doll Elizabeth had carved years ago and Derrick had given to her recently, and she got a bad feeling. It was that same swirled, animalistic, hot embers feeling. Whatever was in the house next door was also in her room, also in or around the doll.

Vera forgot about the jewelry then and left her bedroom before matters could go any further. So far it had been a reasonably good day, minus Derrick still being away. No need to let issues get out of hand and spoil what remained of it.

She met Frank at the kitchen table and lavished love on the dog, who had also obviously had a full and vigorous day by the looks of him. His tongue was lolling out the side of his mouth and he seemed contented to do nothing more than lay at her feet, head in Vera's lap, and be petted.

"You are such a handsome boy," Vera crooned as she stroked his gigantic head and strong neck. "I feel so safe with you around," she confessed to a being that would no doubt keep her secrets. Vera was growing incredibly fond of Frank. They may not have spent large quantities of time together, but the time they did spend was of high quality. Frank was impressive and easily impressed. Vera adored both of those characteristics, and she went on with her attentiveness until Misty let herself in and roused Frank from the hypnotic ensnarement of constant strokes.

Misty entered the kitchen and bent down a tad to greet Frank, as per usual, but it was when she raised her head that it seemed the world had changed. She initially wondered whom the woman was sitting at the table in such fine dress and with such regal poise. It took but a moment or two to come to the realization that it was her dear friend Vera, but it was Vera dramatically changed, remarkably different. And, Misty was simultaneously stunned, magnetized, and threatened. Much to her dismay, her hackles went up. She literally could not take her eyes from Vera, and she knew no one else would be able to either. Misty understood the gravity of the development as it applied to her instantaneously. Vera had the potential to overshadow her in an area of her life where no one else had ever done so. Misty was so used to being the pretty one in whatever social circle she chose that she'd never had to contend with such a situation before, and certainly not from a friend she'd picked out for herself and grown so close to. How would she compete, and could she? What would it mean to her if she got eclipsed in that arena? What would it be like to become Vera's mildly charming friend, a friend posed simply for contrast next to a natural siren?

"Want to relax for a few minutes before we press on?" Vera asked and signaled to an open chair for Misty to be seated.

"Ummm…" Misty was at a loss for words, and that had never happened to her before. Another terrible first.

Vera titled her head a fraction of degree, causing a whisper of a golden brown wave to fall over one eye. It was devastating. "Are you feeling ok? You look pale," Vera informed her.

"I'm-I'm fine. Really." Misty had to find her voice. She dug down deep and frantically. She had to. She had to reassess and find her sense of self. "Let's just go," she suggested with what small pieces of dominance remained within her. Misty suddenly felt far from cohesive.

The two women left the house for the night, with Vera locking the door with the click of a bolt behind them. Vera stepped forward into the many years she figured she had stretching out in succession. She was stepping out as herself, and she felt so good about it. Vera figured it meant one day she'd be as influential to others as Lillian had been to her. She'd come back into her own skin and zipped it up tightly, and everything was falling so synchronistically into place that it appeared as if the world was right and nothing could possibly go wrong ever again. But as Misty started the engine and began to pull away from the curb, Vera saw it. The motorcycle was back in front of the Thompson house.

Chapter 7

Vera sat in Misty's car with the passenger side window cracked, letting in the tiniest bit of cold night air. She glanced out at the stars overhead and then to the silhouette of leaves holding fast to trembling trees. Winter was really coming on. In the past few days a front had rolled into town and the temperatures were dropping, and it was most noticeable at night. It was still possible for the temperatures to climb back up again, but before long everyone would have to commit to bundling up. And, it was looking to be a cold Halloween they had in store.

Misty and Vera rode in predominant silence the whole way to the farm, not that it was a long drive, but the two friends typically chattered like magpies. Not tonight. Vera thought about the strange behavior for a few seconds, but then concluded that if it had anything to do with her Misty would eventually come right out and say so. In the meantime, Vera amused herself with other mindful meanderings. When the car turned onto the long gravel drive that led up to the farmhouse, Vera saw the top of the gigantic oak tree Keith was graced with on this property. She saw its uppermost branches peeking out above the big barn's pitched roof. That structure stood in front like a guardian. The tree reached ever upward and embraced the heavens. It seemed reverent, as though it were wrapping all of the skies in a single, silent, simple prayer. Vera noticed stars glimmering through the black branches and wisps of smoke trails from the newly lit fire below were drawn to the big, wooden being. As she continued to contemplate the magnificence of her friend's property, she saw a shift and it appeared as though the treetop shivered against an onslaught of quick and determined cold, a biting wind that caused Vera to roll her window up the rest of the way. Winter. It was coming for them. Soon the trees would be bare; soon they would go to sleep and not hear her when she spoke or sense her when she touched. The trees would withdraw themselves as they had to do. Many animals would go into hibernation or torpor. Many beings would pull back and away, leaving Vera to gauge everything against a stark and practically empty backdrop.

There were fewer people at this gathering than there had been at the last one, at the first one Keith had thrown. It was the initial aspect of the evening that caught Vera's attention when she stepped out of the car. Where there had been upwards of maybe forty or fifty people at the original circle, there were now right around twenty or so. It was less like a fraternity bash and more like a subdued harvest party. The atmosphere was totally changed, and Vera found she was grateful and relaxed the tension from her shoulders.

"Thanks for driving," Vera said to break the ice with Misty, and maybe to regain some state of normalcy between them.

Misty made eye contact with Vera over the top of her car. "Yeah, it's no problem," she replied and scanned the area, keeping the mental boundary between them.

Vera contemplated letting the entire matter go and moving away, but then figured she and Misty deserved better, deserved more. There were many times that Misty pulled the troubles out of her, troubles that Vera had been determined to keep buried. Misty prodded and poked and dug at her on several occasions to get to the truth, to get whatever Vera was holding back into the open so it couldn't grow bigger teeth and sharper claws and eat Vera alive from the inside. "Hey, are you upset with me? Did I do something wrong?" She laid it on the line.

Misty met Vera's heady gaze once again and wished she didn't have to. Not only did Vera appear even more enchanting by a starry glow and flickering firelight, but it made Misty face how awful she was feeling and subsequently behaving about it. She knew she should be happy for her friend, a woman now unchained. Misty saw plainly enough that Vera had taken a bold and giant step forward in her life, and she wanted to be happy for her, but she was truly unable to make it so. The issue was she couldn't seem to get herself to stop feeling combative. The feeling grew and with it her behavior worsened. "No, I'm not upset with you," she assured as best she knew how, under the circumstances. She lied. She lied to Vera, her very best friend for the very first time.

"Then what is it?" Vera pushed. "Something is obviously bothering you and I'd like to know what it is. I've never seen you this way before."

"And, I've never seen *you* this way before!" Misty shot back without thinking. She wasn't used to filtering her thoughts or her words.

Vera looked at her as though she'd been slapped and a wave of guilt came crashing over Misty. It was a miserable exchange with which to start the night's festivities.

"Oh… that's not really what I meant…" Misty began to backpedal.

"What the hell is it? What's wrong?" Vera demanded, and she did so with such force that Misty felt compelled to respond and let it all out, to tell the truth whether she really wanted to or not, whether she was ashamed and horrified or not. But right at the moment she would've done so, Keith joined them.

Keith brought the gift of beer and goodwill, and spared Misty further embarrassment. "Good evening, ladies! Welcome back!" he said and shoved a bottle towards Misty and then joined Vera on the other side of the car. "Enjoy," he said as he gave Vera a beer that was warm to the touch. "It's home brewed."

Vera shook her head, a cascade of waves and subtle curls dancing about her high cheekbones. "Is there no end to your talents?"

Keith gave her a wicked smile. "None at all," he answered with a wink.

Misty took her beer and with an acknowledging 'thank you' beat a hasty retreat up the steps to engage with others on the porch. She preferred the company of strangers to what was happening in her friendship. Vera's eyes followed her a ways, until Keith brought her back to the man standing right in front of her.

"Every time you come here I am so amazed," he told her, and Vera heard the catch of surprisingly strong emotions creeping into his voice. Firelight danced across Keith's handsome face and Vera found she was drawn in by the warmth there and the kindness. She was pulled by the undeniable sense of safety.

"Really? How so?" she asked of someone who was no longer merely a handsome and reliable coworker. No, he was becoming a friend, which was good because Vera wasn't sure what was going on with Misty. She had this uneasy sensation creeping up into her intestines regarding the unknown issue there. What had gotten into her friend? And, for that matter, Vera had to wonder what had really gotten into her own mind, as she'd so rapidly grew into her own skin; it was new skin, supple skin.

"You always have the guts to show me who you really are when you come out here. I get to know you, and I think it's pretty amazing," he said and took a step in, closing what little gap there was between them.

Vera was happy he did so. It was cold outside and Keith was so warm and inviting. She'd have been more than willing to snuggle up against him, to have him put an arm about her and lead her to the fire or the tree or any place where a blanket and more of their nurtured bond was waiting to grow.

"Well, thank you," she spoke sincerely. "It may have started with me coming here. I don't know for sure. But, I do know it won't end here." Vera had no intention of letting it end ever, now that her decision was made. She leaned in close and breathed, "I want to be me all the time… everywhere."

Keith had a somber expression when she pulled back again and glanced up at him. "I'll drink to that," he said and raised his bottle.

Vera clinked her bottle against his and they shared a mutual sip, eyes locked.

"You know, I knew this was who you really were, right from the start. From the moment I met you, I saw through those stuffy suits to this person. Every time we were around each other and working together, no matter what you said or did or wore, I saw this person," he spoke slowly and carefully, as though he were confessing a dark and horrible secret… it was anything but.

"Oh, you did, did you?" Vera playfully challenged.

"I did," Keith affirmed. "Others might not have, but I did. And, I guess that makes me smarter than the average bear."

Vera responded with a burst of laughter. "Aren't you pleased with yourself?…"

"Most of the time," Keith quipped. "Let's just say I'm more aware then. Is that more humble?"

"Pardon me," came a luscious baritone voice that Vera recognized in a heartbeat.

She turned around. "Isaac!" she sounded more excited than she'd meant to, but Vera couldn't help it. Her gaiety had slipped its leash. There was an indefinable quality about the man that made her happy and indescribably comfortable. No person other than Lillian had evoked in her such a feeling of home… well, maybe her axis mundi, but trees weren't people, even if they appeared as such in twisted dreams, disturbed apparitions. "It's good to see you again. Keith tells me we'll be having dinner together this Sunday. I'm really looking forward to it," Vera rambled on until she finally shoved the beer bottle back into her mouth to force a cessation.

Isaac put an arm around Vera as though they'd known each other forever, just like old friends. He was contented with her presence, too. "It'll be a pleasure to break bread with you," he responded most graciously. "And, I didn't mean to interrupt, but I wanted to catch you prior to the night's activities getting seriously underway."

"Ok, sure," Vera said with a nod and listened intently.

"I have a gift for you," Isaac revealed, and with that he held a hand out in front of Vera, palm side up. In his loose grip sat the most exquisite item Vera had ever seen; it was more magical than a house full of Lillian's things or Elizabeth's ensnaring pirate-fairy chest. Isaac held in front of her a brilliant and bold, glimmering and gold acorn.

Vera didn't say a word. She stood there and stared.

"It's a white gold acorn. I came across it when I was looking for items to add to my drums. There's an actual acorn preserved inside the gold," Isaac told her, as if he was unraveling the plot to some awesome tale. "Hold out your hand," he instructed.

Vera did so and was rewarded as the trinket transferred to her.

"It's yours," Isaac said with great finality.

"I-I don't know what to say," Vera stammered as she looked up at the tall, dark man with the beautifully decked out dreadlocks and exotic eyes. "It's the most thoughtful gift anyone has ever given me."

Isaac beamed a dazzling smile at her then. "I'm thrilled you like it, and I have a feeling it will mean a lot more to you than it would've ever meant to me. So, for you, my dear," he concluded with a gentile half-bow and closed her hand around the gleaming little gift. "And, I'll let you two get back to your conversation." Isaac excused himself and wandered off towards the fire, smoke enveloping him.

Vera continued to inspect with great reverence the gift of tiny size and enormous potentials in her hand, and finally returned her gaze to Keith. "Wow!" was what she had to say. "Is he always like that?"

Keith nodded his affirmation and took a healthy swig of beer. "Yeah, pretty much. I've known Isaac a long time and he's full of surprises."

"I'll say," Vera sighed.

"It's actually one of my favorite things about him," Keith went on. "That and his uncanny ability to judge a person based on character first. With Isaac it's like he doesn't even see the surface, the clothes or the hair or the posture or presentation. He doesn't get confused by any of that. He goes straight to the heart of it."

"Of a person?" Vera attempted to clarify.

"Of everything. He would've been great in the military," Keith was rambling some now.

"I suppose that is an impressive trait," Vera agreed.

"Come on, let's go in the house and see if we can find a chain to fit that little charm," Keith led.

The farmhouse was dramatically different when it wasn't crammed wall to wall with people. It held a loose, airy, significantly open feeling as Vera stepped over the threshold and into the great room. Everything looked old and worn and well loved in there, even if it was a tad disjointed. But, she knew none of that was Keith's doing, other than maybe keeping the place tidied up and adding to the feeling of an off-centeredness. It wasn't his house, yet. No, the furnishings were more than likely the remnants of his grandparent's life together, his grandfather's most of all. Keith let her wander around and examine as much as she liked before he suggested a detour upstairs.

"My grandparents shared the master bedroom for over forty years, and most of my grandmother's belongings are still in there. I guess my grandfather never had the inclination to get rid of them…" he said as they ascended to the second level in the house.

Vera admired the vaulted ceiling as they made the short walk to the master bedroom that was down the hall and on the right. As she stepped inside the chamber, Vera noticed that the room must've gone unaltered for many, many years. It resembled every woman's vintage boudoir she'd ever seen represented in old movies and magazines. The place was a haven, a miniature palace, and a blatant declaration of ardent and fervent love.

"Oh my!" Vera breathed as she joined Keith in the embracing suite. "Your grandfather, he —"

"He loved my grandmother very, very much," Keith finished for her and went to a nightstand on the far side of the bed where a small box laid waiting. Keith opened it and the tinkling of a musical box's signature tones filled the space they shared. This place, too, was alive with memories — strong ones, eternal ones, and friendly ones.

"Are you still planning work for this place? I know you and my brother had conferred," Vera poked.

"Yeah," Keith said casually as he withdrew a short and shiny chain from the box. The lid closed. The music stopped. "I've got plans, but I'm holding off on some stuff," he said rather vaguely.

"And, why is that? Doesn't your boss pay you enough?" Vera teased as Keith took a few steps in towards her.

"I'm holding off because the timing isn't quite right. I'm waiting on some other things to fall into place. And, they will," he said with great assurance and handed her the chain.

"I feel weird taking this," Vera admitted while she slipped the acorn charm onto the necklace. It fit.

"Don't," was Keith's only reply to that, and he took the chain and charm from her and then dutifully helped put it on. He placed it gently about her neck and fastened the clasp. "I was very close to both my grandparents. They raised me for years after my parents died, and I know both of them would want someone like you to have it. My grandmother would've approved, I promise. There's a mirror on the bureau."

Vera took her time digesting all the personal information from Keith that came out in a flood, and she approached her reflection in the glass slowly, following Keith's suggestion. She was now prone to approaching any looking glass slowly, thanks to the fright in the Treasure Room. Who knows what one might see? It was best to proceed with caution.

The tiny acorn glimmered and danced about Vera's neck, accentuating her collarbones. It belonged there. It belonged on the chain. Some things were just meant to be together.

Vera turned to Keith. "Thank you so much."

Keith walked over to her, joining her on the far side of the bedroom. "Thank you for letting me into your life," he returned. "Vera?"

"Yes?"

Keith placed his hands on Vera's shoulders gingerly. She was so slender and delicate next to his looming frame. "I know relationships are complicated for you right now, but I want to kiss you," he confessed.

Vera swallowed a large and sudden lump that swelled in her throat, but it was for naught. All the swallowing in the world wouldn't have made a dent. The lump would not be moved. "Keith, I-I'm not sure —"

"It's ok. You don't have to kiss me back. The blame is on me," he said. He spoke all the right words in exactly the right way. "I want to kiss you, at least once." It was a hard reality that this opportunity might never come again. The thought that this was their only chance in a lifetime to do so made Vera shiver.

Vera said nothing. She didn't move a muscle. In fact, she wasn't sure she was breathing anymore. She stood there. Silently waiting. Vera was not one to let such an opportunity pass her by… not anymore.

Keith brought his face in close to hers and stilled himself as their foreheads touched, giving her a chance to pull back, to pull away, to run away if Vera so chose. She had to have the choice. She didn't do any of that. She let her forehead rest against his. They shared a few inhales and exhales. They shared the sensation of compression and of closeness, a frightful closeness, for a while before Keith tilted his head and then pressed his lips into hers. It was like a flutter, the landing of a butterfly, and then more significant, as Vera kissed him back. And, that blame was squarely on her.

Keith kissed her; Vera kissed him back. She wrapped her arms around his neck as he hugged her about the waist and brought her to him. It went on and on and on that way, with neither of them wanting to end it. But, the drums started. Reality came crashing in and Vera and Keith found themselves thinking about the other guests and the night ahead. They both thought about where they were and who they were and the obligations they had. It was as if the drums insisted it was enough for now. The rhythm of the guests demanded that they join them, and even though there were fewer people on this night than the one last week, the drums were louder, more in sync, and highly communicative.

Keith took Vera's hand in his and led her outside. It was enough for now.

There was no one in the house or on the porch anymore. Everyone was around the bonfire when they came back downstairs and then stepped out into the cold night air. A few folks were banging their drums and some were hanging about absorbing the vibrations, the heat from the fire, and the openness of the farmland. There was one sketcher in their midst, too. Isaac approached with his charm-laden djembe covered in symbols. He'd yet to join the circle. Instead, it appeared as though he were waiting for Keith. Maybe he was waiting for Vera.

"There are a lot less people here than there were last time," Vera finally remarked.

"It's all right," Isaac said as he followed her gaze and eyed the group around the fire. "That's how it should be. You don't keep all of the grain you harvest. You have to separate the chaff from the wheat," he told her simply.

Vera cocked her head curiously. "Is that so?"

Isaac gave her a brilliant smile. "Yes, that's so. You know it's so," he called her out. "Come, Vera. There are a couple of ladies I'd like for you to meet." Isaac used a strap to sling his drum over one shoulder and then extended an arm to Vera.

Vera happily accepted Isaac's offer and let herself be led away from Keith. She thought it a fine idea to take some time away to process what had happened between them only moments ago. After all, those types of scenarios are hard to gauge for what they truly are when one's heart remains all aflutter.

Isaac took Vera to the far side of the circle where two women about her own age stood arm in arm. But other than having their age in common, the two women couldn't have been more opposite. They were like personal representations of bright, beautiful noonday and dark, mysterious midnight. "This is Casey and Magdalena," Isaac introduced, as the two women looked to him and then Vera. "Ladies," Isaac addressed them, "this is my friend, Vera. I thought it best if the three of you met," he explained and uncurled Vera's arm from around his own, graciously leaving her there to interact with such intriguing strangers.

"Hello," Vera finally said with a nervous smile.

"Hi," Casey of the midday sun returned.

"Hello," said the dark and seductive Magdalena.

There was a pregnant pause, Vera's favorite and most intimidating kind, for it was filled with all sorts of possibilities.

"Isaac's told us a bit about you," Magdalena started off. "He thinks we will get along famously." Vera detected the trace of an accent she could not place. "You are good friends with Keith?"

Vera glanced over her shoulder and back in Keith's general direction. She then turned towards Magdalena with a grin. "I tend to think so."

"He's a very good man," Magdalena confirmed and smiled at Vera. "We've known him for a couple of years now. We met him and each other through Isaac," she got the ball rolling on a very connective conversation. Vera liked that. "How did you come to know Keith?"

"He applied for a job at the coffeehouse I run in town, and I hired him," Vera summed up.

"He applied for a job?" Casey chimed in with a question of her own.

"Yes," Vera answered and watched as the two women exchanged looks of mild disbelief. "Why is that so odd?"

"I guess it doesn't have to be," Casey said, letting the real answer slip past Vera's probe. "We're really glad to meet you, by the way," Casey chirped. "We've been looking for a third."

"A third what?" Vera quizzed.

Magdalena then took over. "Two people only have each other. Three people always have the ability to find support. It has always been that way, at least for us. And, it has been hard finding a friend worthy of such trust and investment of self. It can be a challenge to learn whom you can really trust in life. It can be difficult to find exactly what you are seeking. Don't you agree?"

The entire encounter with the two women seemed to be more questions than answers to Vera. It was almost like introspection, except this process obviously involved outside people, external communication.

Vera thought about it. "Yes," she said, as her mind wandered to Misty's curious behavior from earlier that evening. "Yes, I do agree."

"People come and go, and that's to be expected from most. Very few stay for the whole path of your life. But, when you find someone not only willing to stay, but someone who fights for their position next to yours, that is a person to invest yourself in. That is a person to cherish and to love," Magdalena told her as the drumbeats around them changed and the volume softened. Each individual player attempted to sync up with the drummer next to them, and then on and on about the circle.

"Magdalena and I only live one county over. It's not far. Just under an hour," Casey added a random tidbit of information.

"You live together?" Vera pried, sensing that she'd be allowed to do so. She also thought they probably lived very close to Lance. They might even know Misty if they were from one county over. More edges of Vera's life might be knit together. She shuddered.

"We are sisters," Magdalena explained, disrupting Vera's tempestuous thoughts.

Vera gave a light laugh. "You certainly don't look like sisters."

"Looks can be deceiving," Magdalena said.

"And, sisters can be found at any time in your life," Casey rallied in agreement. "Do you feel you have one... or more?"

Vera thought to Misty and she almost said she did have one, but something inside stopped her. She felt an energetic hook sink into the base of her tongue and pull it down to her jawbone.

Magdalena caught the flash of activity on the surface of Vera's rapidly changing expressions. "You thought you had one, but now you are not so sure."

Vera locked eyes with Magdalena; Magdalena had amazing eyes, as black as a crow's feathers. Vera tore her gaze away after a couple of minutes and looked around for Misty, but she was nowhere to be seen. "No, I'm not so sure... all of a sudden."

Magdalena placed a hand on Vera's arm. "At least you were not too quick to speak then."

"Why don't the three of us have coffee or tea sometime?" Casey attempted to lighten the mood.

"At my place?" Vera inquired.

"It doesn't have to be, but I'd love to see your shop," Casey said.

"Oh, yeah, sure. I'd love to have the two of you come over," Vera extended.

Magdalena and Casey nodded in unison. "We will come by," they said in tandem.

Vera gave a lilting laugh again. "Great. Great. I look forward to it." She glanced around once more to try and spot Misty. "I think I should go. I haven't seen my ride in a while."

"We can get any information we need from Keith or Isaac," Casey said easily enough.

"It was a delight," Magdalena assured her and swept Vera into a caring embrace. "We will see you soon."

Vera was let loose then into the stirring rhythm of the drumbeats and the heat of the fire. She walked carefully and casually about the circle, taking in the faces of visitors. She now felt the group was a bit more cohesive and even more manageable to be around. There was less interference, less chaos. She now knew a fair amount of people out of the entire pack. She saw Isaac near the barn, keeping time and pace on his large drum covered in symbols, dripping with charms. He seemed to be keeping them all together; he appeared to be talking without saying a word, speaking with his hands on the skin of an animal, beat after beat after beat. No one seemed to mind Vera wandering. No one questioned it and no one allowed or disallowed it. She did as she pleased and it was accepted. Vera made her way around the entirety of the circle, and Misty was nowhere within it.

Vera stepped away from the warmth and the music. She stepped outside the circle and looked over to where the cars were parked. Misty's was gone.

Vera made her way out behind the barn. She made a beeline for the tree, for the great spiraling oak.

❖

"Thief!" The word was spit at Vera containing a tremendous amount of venom.

There was nothing she could do to deny it. She was lit up for all the world to see under the glowing orb of the moon, standing there in Lillian's old clothes. For a night that had gone so well, minus the mishaps with Misty, it had taken a quick and terrible turn. Derrick may have been undeniable in any casual set of circumstances, but he was downright uncontainable and inescapable when angry. Vera almost wished Isaac had stayed for a decaf coffee or a late evening into early morning tea when he dropped her off... almost. Derrick may have been severely mad, but at least he was so near and focused on her.

"I'm sorry," Vera began, hanging her head low with a remorse she really didn't feel. "I'm sorry. I know I shouldn't have," she bumbled on, trying to maneuver through whatever the situation was, whatever predicament she was in.

"You're damn right you shouldn't have!" he bellowed at her. From where the two of them stood, on the cracked and dislodging sidewalk in front of the Thompson house, Vera feared if the dialogue got any louder they'd wake the block. "Thief!" Derrick declared again and pounded a fist against his own leg. "You went into my house — my house and stole!"

"I did," she said softly, praying that if she were gentle enough and kind enough and sorrowful enough he would ease up on the verbal attack. "There's no excuse," Vera agreed. She was a thief, plain and simple. She had no right to assume he wouldn't come back. She had no authority to claim any aspect or portion of the property. She'd made a unilateral decision and it was turning out badly. What had felt so right was going horribly wrong.

"Where the fuck is it?!" Derrick demanded answers.

Vera carefully let her eyes meet his for the first time in the short span of the tirade. "I-I... I'm wearing some of it," she stammered. She thought that was obvious.

Derrick brought his face in close to hers and finally lowered his voice, but that only made the intensity more severe. "I don't give a shit what you're wearing," he growled.

It was when Derrick came close and bent low that Vera saw an object on a chain slip out of the top of his shirt. The little thing caught a glint in the moonlight and an awkward gleam of recognition in Vera's reddened eyes. It was a key, the world's tiniest key. But, Vera couldn't do this now and turned away.

"Where is the book? Where is my grandmother's book?" he pressed her.

Vera looked nowhere else other than at her own feet. She'd tore her eyes off that key. She'd forced herself. "It's inside… in my house. I'm sorry. I didn't mean to take it. I didn't mean to take all that stuff. I thought maybe you weren't coming back…" None of her explanations seemed to matter.

Derrick backed away a couple of paces and stood to full height, ramrod straight. "You thought wrong, and you don't know anything about me," he warned.

Vera knew she didn't. She knew he was altogether accurate in that assessment. She thought she knew him because she knew she loved him and had experienced sex with him, but she honestly had no idea what was coming next or what he was capable of doing. He was a raving, ravishing mystery. What may have been a surface glimpse of his daily presentations to the world was no indication of the totality of his being. Vera acknowledged to herself right then and there that she didn't know this man. And crazy or not, she wanted to.

"I want that book," he insisted, "and I want it now."

"Ok," Vera conceded. "Of course. If you'll just come inside —"

"Did you open it?" he asked, the thread of anger tightly weaving his words.

Vera dared to glance at him then. He was tremendous with the broadness of his shoulders and the hard set of his chiseled jaw roughened by beard stubble. He was beyond handsome in his fury, and Vera wanted to drop to her knees and beg his forgiveness and hope that he would then sweep her up and take her inside and make violent, passionate, insane love to her. It made no sense, but it was what she craved the most in the moment. "No. No, I didn't open it."

Derrick gave a single jut of his chin and indicated that she should take him inside the house and straight to the book he sought. So, Vera headed for the front door obediently. Pliantly.

"I'll give back everything I took, I swear," she said as the key entered the lock. "Just please, please don't be angry with me."

Vera could no longer contain the trembling in her voice. She was not the woman she'd been less than an hour ago. Where was all that new skin of hers? Had it been ripped to shreds before Derrick's piercing stare?

Derrick said nothing, and the silence sliced her heart as she swung wide the door and allowed Derrick to enter the residence before her.

The familiar click of toenails happened right as Vera switched on the living room lights, and by the time she'd done so Frank was standing in the hallway and peering into the living room. The dog gave a low growl, raising his floppy lips enough to show the sharp edge of teeth underneath, and he dared Derrick to come but one step further.

"Do something with that dog," Derrick instructed, clearly out of patience… as if he'd had any to begin with.

"Frank, no," Vera timidly corrected the animal and made her way to the hall. She gripped Frank's collar and led him through the kitchen and to her brother's bedroom in the back, regretting that she felt forced to do so. Vera understood the dog's position. She grappled with the fact that Frank was only trying to protect her, that he had her best interests and the interests of the household at heart, but she ended up taking him away despite his noble nature.

The door was shut to John's room. Vera wondered if her brother was asleep in there, and if he was with Misty, too. It was easy enough to suppose Misty would seek John out after drum circle, especially with some issue Vera wasn't privy to clearly upsetting her. She thought about giving a light rap to alert them of the visitor in the house and Frank's need for a separate space of his own, but then she decided to crack the door instead and take a peek inside. John wasn't there. A delicate shaft of amber light from the hall revealed his bed was vacant and also neatly made.

"Get in there," Vera told Frank and nudged the rear end of the dog forward so that he moved smoothly into John's room. She quickly shut the door behind him. "It's ok," she called to Derrick and he emerged slowly from the shadows that speckled the hallway. "The book's in my room," she told him. "I'll just go get it now… along with all the other things…"

Derrick's bright, mossy green orbs met her strained and practically tearful gaze, causing Vera's breath to catch. He looked at her with longing, lashing, and a vitreous blend of love and hate and life and death. Vera wanted to capture the image of him in that instant because she felt quite certain that no one and no thing would ever come close to portraying that heinous level of aliveness ever again. He was everything and he was dangerous and he was standing but a few feet away.

Vera dutifully turned the knob and went into her room to get the ancient book, but she surprisingly found she didn't have to turn on the lights in there to see. A combination of glow from the hallway mixed with a curious luminescence coming from inside the room brought the space to a perfect light level, good enough for reading. If she had been able to open that diary, that incredibly old journal, she'd have been able to make out every last word. Vera hadn't initially realized where the illumination was coming from when she stepped inside the bedroom, for if she had she would've darted straight out and made for the front door. She might've turned Frank loose, consequences be damned. But, Vera got distracted from thinking about it, from having a basic awareness, because in a flash Derrick was on her.

Derrick's hands were heavy on her shoulders, and his chest and abdomen were pressed flat up against her back, smashing her into the front surface of the dresser. His breath tickled her ear while his weight caused her a minor degree of delightful discomfort and shallow inhalations of her own. She could hardly draw a decent breath.

"If you're going to be in my life, you have to respect me and do things my way," Derrick placed the caveat.

Vera tried to whip her head around to see him but couldn't. He was at an impossible angle for eye contact.

"You can never betray me," he said in a sharp and husky voice. "I've been betrayed so many times. You can never betray me."

"Derrick, Derrick, I —"

He cut her off. "Few women can handle this, can handle me." Derrick was determined to reveal whatever was gnawing at his soul. He'd rather it eat hers whole than have one more bite of his. "Can you?" He put it to her.

Vera wasn't sure. She was about to answer yes and find out along the way when her general awareness started kicking back in. She caught sight of the little doll on the dresser. It was alight; it was aflame. It had the brightest pair of glowing red eyes Vera had ever seen or even imagined. It was no longer a trick of the mind or an ethereal representation of deeper issues. The doll itself, carved from her axis mundi that had perished years ago, was lit up in her room like some demonic apparition. It was on vivid display for her to see, for Derrick to see. The doll, too, was aware. And, whatever Elizabeth had given to the wooden figure moved about the room. Yes, Vera could feel it now, that prowling animal she and every other person she'd ever known tried to avoid day after day, and year after year. Fate stalked them and pushed them and stared at them with a glee that meant it was meeting its own agenda, its own inevitable end. And, it spoke to her in a deathly whisper… "There is no untainted, pure, true, fearless love in you, is there?" The question was horribly rhetorical. "It's not there anywhere," Fate exhaled in an icy equivalent to a breath.

"No!" Vera cried out to what haunted her.

But, it was Derrick who responded. "No?! How dare you tell me no?! I let you into my life!" he frothed and grabbed her wrists, slamming her hands on top of the dresser, causing the dark doll with ember eyes to rock from side to side, but it refused to fall over.

"Please, don't do this," Vera whimpered to any being in the room willing to listen. How many were there?

It was Fate who replied. "And, now you are cursed. This will be yours."

Vera prayed she was going mad, despite all the evidence suggesting otherwise. The farther along this personal path she went the less able she was becoming in convincing herself. She hoped Derrick would slap her silly, knock some sense into her that she lacked, get so close that not even a wisp of air could slip between them. For as close as he was, as on her as he was, he was not close enough. Vera wanted him to be nearer… in fact, too near. For what she had done to him thorough stealing his things, for what she had done to Misty and to Keith, for neglecting her work and her friends and her own brother in all that swirled about her life. For Lance and for hiding and for lying and for opportunities missed.

"Can you?! Can you handle this?! Can you handle me?!" Derrick roared. He went on because he could not stop. He was bringing her back to him, around to only a flicker of the all-consuming fire that had ahold of them. It was eating him and it was haunting her. She never should have come back to her hometown. Maybe she never should have left either.

"Yes!" Vera shouted back. "Yes!" She dug down to find the strength to fling him off and whip around. She confronted the man that stood before her. She accepted the Fate she felt she could not escape. "You leave for days at a time. You leave me alone with no explanations. You are not close enough to be trusted, but I... I can be loyal! I can be faithful to you, but what the fuck does it matter?!" she demanded an answer to a question that had none. Tears found their flow, a dam in her ruptured and salt water spilled down her fevered cheeks freely. "I'm a person who deserves to be punished, deserves to be cursed..." Vera wept; she gasped for air. Her father had left and then her mother. Lillian was gone and Keith was too good to be true. And, she had spurned Lance. Her hands clutched at Derrick's shirt and she brought her face into him. The wild male scent that was characteristic filled her nostrils. She clung tightly so that he could not force her away. He could not escape her clutches again.

At long last, and as Vera's weeping eased to small shudders that wracked her body, Derrick brought his arms about her and cradled her to him. He had no choice. He had to do something. He had to take it further. "I suspect you and I are a lot alike."

Derrick listened to Vera's low sobs and sad moans and outside he heard the wash of a late season rain tapping against the window glass. He listened intently until he thought he was surely sobered by it. Vera cried in remorse and in surrender and the skies cried with her. He wondered if they cried the day his grandmother had died. No one else had. No one but him. Everyone else in the family had let go a sigh of relief that day and again when he'd left to attend to the estate. His parents sighed the loudest and plainest of all. Derrick continued to hold Vera until the rains upped their pace, increased their severity, and it sounded like the storm was trying to rip the house apart, tear the fabric of the world asunder.

A bold flash of lightning snapped Derrick out of enamored listening and pointless pondering. It brought him to the edge of the dresser where he'd held Vera captive only minutes ago. He let Vera stand alone in the middle of the room as a thunderclap shook the very foundation of the house. The walls rattled and the air sizzled. Derrick snatched the beloved book up in his hands. He knew what he had to do.

Vera watched Derrick's movements amid the unusually violent autumn storm. Everything he did was so odd and perfect. Everything about such a turbulent storm so far into autumn was odd and perfect. It fit. It reminded her of the summer storm that had taken place when Elizabeth moved into town, after the drought had all but strangled the town into submission. The sky had burst then, as it was doing now. Lightning struck and took down the only beloved paternal emblem Vera had ever known, the oak tree, her axis mundi. She frightfully admired Derrick's smooth determination, his fearlessness inside such a majestic and awful torrent of nature. The glow of the doll's impossible eyes was no deterrent either. Derrick loomed large. He was an entire cosmos worth of power, to Vera's estimation.

"Come with me," he instructed her.

"Where are you going?" Vera asked.

"Next door."

Vera advanced towards him. He didn't step back, but he didn't meet her in the middle either. Vera went the whole distance and stopped once her fingertips were able to reach and rest in the center of his chest. She wanted to feel his heartbeat. "The… uh… the storm. It's storming out."

It hadn't stormed in such a way since the night the oak tree in the Thompson gardens was hit by lightning…. Vera couldn't let that memory go. And, that may have been because that was the night which kick started it all. Vera couldn't determine for sure though; she didn't know with any plausible certainty. Perhaps Lillian's death had done it, or Elizabeth's arrival. It might have been the drought or the lightning strike or one too many grasshoppers sentenced to torture and death in a coffee can. Vera tried hard to figure out right then and there what had been the tipping point or the fork in the road for her to inherit such a Fate, such a miserable and ghostly companion. When and where had the veer in her personal path happened to bring her here to this moment, and what had caused it? What was the catalyst? Was there one thing? Or did Fate like to hide in many, many twists and turns, in tiny nooks and crannies?

"Come with me," Derrick said again as he brought a hand up behind her head and threaded his fingers through her hair. He gripped her like a chalice and was about to take a healthy mouthful of her potent blend.

Vera shut her eyes tight and savored the sensation of his lips locked madly against hers. Derrick's tongue swirled in an evocative dance and she was helpless and hopeless. Vera was bashed about by his emotions and the intensity of the storm that pounded outside. There was no serenity left for Vera. Whatever she'd had ahold of earlier in the night was gone now, ripped to shreds. There was nothing worth having in life if it didn't come with a dollop of Derrick's approval. She was positive that if he were to turn away from her at any point, if he withdrew his affections ever, she would simply cease to be. Vera felt she'd dry up into dust and blow away or melt into the earth in an oddity of a storm that should not be happening.

Vera went with him. The two of them dashed across the backyard and up over the small stone wall, into the weedy lot of one time gardens that had been sumptuous ages ago. By the time they entered the kitchen through the back door, they were soaked through. Derrick shed his garments in no time flat, in two or three slick moves. It was hypnotic, like watching a snake slither out of old and unusable skin. He stood bare before her and let the raindrops and low glow that emanated from somewhere in the center of the house bathe him in a sensational golden hue. He was surreal. He was fantastic. He was tall and lean and powerful. He was hot and dripping wet with a storm's sweet current. He was hard and virile and waiting to claim her, to mark her, to brand her. Derrick was well aware of his effects on Vera, on most women. Those effects were an asset he'd used before to get his way, to achieve what he wanted, to reach a goal when nothing else would get him there. He targeted Vera with his salacious mixture of emotions and wide range of responses, all playing out across his wickedly brooding expression.

Intrigued. Undone. Vera hadn't found the will to move. She wanted to stare at Derrick forever and say over and over again in her head that he was hers, and no other woman in town had possession of him. He was wild and demanding and freaky beautiful. She was ensnared, and when too much time had passed, when she had stood still as prey too long, the predator moved in. Derrick swooped down upon her and ripped Lillian's clothes, her clothes, wet clothes, herb heavy clothes from her trembling body. He worked on her until they were both nude and writhing on the cold kitchen floor, until no fire in any hearth anywhere could rival the heat that Derrick could make Vera feel… whether he remained cold inwardly or not.

Chapter 8

Days can get away from a person. Time can pass one by with great ease, such a slippery thing, and that was what happened to Vera in the throes of a frozen, white-hot passion. When Misty was falling in love with John, she hummed incessantly and burnt the pastries she whipped up at the coffeehouse. When Vera began falling head over heels for Derrick, down a rabbit hole and then into a snake's den, she lost all sense of time and to some degree place. She trembled and shivered as she spanned a spectrum of emotions throughout a single day. Friday shed hours into Saturday and then morphed into early Sunday morning.

A late morning light cast its   filtered rays through bedroom curtains at the Thompson house and reality slapped Vera in the face — hard. She sat bolt upright in bed, in a panic. She shot up so fast she roused her lover from what appeared to be a deep and peaceful sleep.

"What? What is it?" Derrick asked, as he hauled himself to a sitting position.

"Oh no!" Vera said and threw the sheets and blankets off of her. "Oh, shit! What day is it?"

"It doesn't matter," Derrick answered and plopped back down on his pillow.

"How long have I been here?" she went on as she scurried about the room retrieving clothes to wear, clothes that were still damp with rain from the storm on the night he'd brought her to the house.

"Not long enough," he said with a gravelly tone that was far too seductive. "Come back to bed."

Vera slid on the cold and clammy fabric of a heavy skirt and then a soft, supple top. The clothes may have been damp and wrinkled, also tattered and torn, but they still felt comfortable against her skin. "I can't. I have a business to run, and I haven't been there in god knows how long! Oh my god! How could I've let this happen?!"

Derrick propped himself up on one elbow and looked at Vera as though she were being ridiculous, as if her absenteeism were of no consequence. "You've only been gone since Friday night. What? You've missed one day? Big deal. There are other people who can handle it, so let them."

"It's Sunday?" she inquired.

Derrick nodded. "Yeah. It's Sunday."

"Well, that's a busy day at the shop. I have to go," she replied and slipped on boots.

Derrick stopped her before she could reach the door, however. He got out of bed and stood there, naked in the late morning light. The only thing he had on was the chain about his neck that bore the ever so tiny key, which looked ridiculous in contrast to his massive form, like it should quake with fear and then wither away, but it did neither one. He put firm hands on her shoulders and then brought her body into his, letting her feel just how much he wanted her, desired her, hungered for her.

Vera moaned. "I really have to go."

"You come straight back here after work," he told her.

Vera glanced up at him and then looked to the little key that was right about eye level for her. She let her fingers play over its smooth surface. "What's this?" she asked carefully.

Derrick took a moment to think about his response and then prefaced with a sexy sideways smile. "The key to my heart."

Vera felt her breath catch.

"Your undergarments are on my side of the bed," he whispered into her ear.

"Geez!" she said and shot out of his embrace. Vera snatched up what was left of the outfit she wore, some of it ripped beyond repair, and as she did so, she noticed a strange shape protruding ever so slightly from under Derrick's pillow. Vera stayed half bent for a moment or two longer and squinted to try to make out whatever it was. The metal binding and the dark exterior tugged at snippets of more recent memory… it was the edge of that book, that diary, that journal so precious to Derrick.

Vera stood up and tried to act normal, like she'd been doing nothing more than retrieving remnants of her ensemble. She wasn't sure why, but she had a suspicion she shouldn't mention seeing it. Vera made for the door once again.

And once again, Derrick stopped her just shy of it. "You'll be here right after work," he reminded her, as though she needed it.

Vera nodded. "Yes, yes, of course." It was somewhat flattering to see him want to be with her so much, to express it in what she was sure was the only way he knew how. Vera wanted to make allowances for Derrick. It felt caring.

Derrick opened the bedroom door and watched as Vera dashed the length of the hall. He listened as she made her way down the stairs, and he didn't climb back into bed until the sound of the back door slamming rang throughout the house. He had a lot of work ahead of him, too. He sighed heavily as he thought about it.

Vera streaked across the backyard and entered her brother's house through the back side door, as quickly and quietly as possible. She'd given up assuming she'd know what or who to expect anywhere or at any time. It seemed as though the house was empty. No one called out to her as she came in, and no one banged on her bedroom door once it was shut. Somewhat confident that she was alone in her own room, Vera stripped off her tattered clothes from two days ago and made her way to the bath. A quick shower and she was back in the main space of her boudoir to don fresh garments. But as she threw open her drawers and then the door on the closet, she was stymied. What to wear? Before her hung many of the over utilized but ever so protective business suits, along with the alluring fabrics of items that had belonged to Lillian and now her. Derrick didn't want them back, but he hadn't readily approved of the fashion choice either, of the outlandish and extraordinary change.

Vera decided to play it safe and chose one of the more somber skirts Lillian had left and a button down silk top that had originally been made to go with a more proper suit. Together the two items created a sort of hedged blend. Vera didn't know who she was dressed in such a manner, and that seemed an accurate reflection of her inner turmoil. She gave a worried glance back at her alarm clock. It was already after nine a.m. She'd have to hope against hope that Misty and Keith were there; that they were picking up the ball she'd so selfishly dropped in order to further her relationship with Derrick, in order to stay in his bed and in his sphere.

Vera dashed back to the bathroom for light cosmetics and was getting ready to bolt out of the bedroom door when she caught a flicker of movement. She spotted it out of the corner of her eye and instinctually turned to see what had shifted.

To her left, the side from whence the motion had come, sat the dresser with a few fineries on top: some loose jewelry, a small figurine, and the wooden doll. Vera knew if anything had changed position, it was the doll, it had to be. The doll Elizabeth had carved and Derrick bestowed, the doll that had red ember eyes, whether physically present or not. Those eyes were always there; sometimes they were visible and open, and other times Vera could only feel them.

Vera looked at the doll. She studied it hard. Every hideously chiseled line and every lacking feature. It had no eyes — it could not see, not even the stark and naked truth. It had no arms — it could not hold on to anything, not even love.

But it had eyes, despite the fact Elizabeth had given it none.

Vera looked at the doll. The doll looked back.

Vera blinked in rapid succession, but it appeared the doll did not. In the stark and raw and sober light of day, the doll stared at her with unblinking, unwavering, and physically present red eyes.

Vera backed up slowly, making for the door once more, feeling for the knob and not daring to turn away from the heinously twisted rendering that worked at staring her down, at sending a very strong and foreboding message. Without a word, it reminded her of the Fate that waited on swift and silent haunches. The doll gave a sudden lunge and twisted itself round until a dark, sappy red liquid oozed from the cracks and crevices.

Vera screamed and bolted out of the room, slamming the door shut and clinging tightly to the knob to hold it in place. She feared the freakish figure would be hot on her heels, following right behind her and readying itself to do something terrible, like chew her legs off. However, in the hallway, Vera was greeted by a mournful howl, a saddened beast's call echoing throughout the house, and Vera almost resigned herself to going mad. Was there any escape? If that was what Fate had in store for her, why not get it over with? Vera laughed at that. When was it ever that simple? She should be so lucky…

The howling went on. It repeated for several minutes until Vera regained enough presence of mind to realize the sounds were coming from directly behind her, from her brother's room.

"Frank?" Vera called, fully expecting the dog to answer somehow. What would be so strange in that, given everything else that had gone on? "Frank?" she called again in question and put her ear to the grainy surface of her brother's door.

The dog woofed a couple of times in anxious response.

Vera exhaled slowly and opened the door to allow the gentle giant to join her in the hall. He pranced about a bit and then darted off to the kitchen. Vera followed. He then made a hasty jaunt to the back door and demanded to be let out, with a not so subtle pleading in his eyes. The poor creature had to relieve himself after being shut up in that room all night… or longer. Vera let the dog into the yard and then checked her brother's room straight away for a mess, but there was none. Frank had most certainly not spent two days in there, which meant John had been home sometime after Vera went to Derrick's. Frank and the house had both been tended to. But, Frank had been shut up in that room again, and Vera wondered why.

When Frank came back in, Vera promptly fed him, feeling guilty for how she'd treated him when Derrick was over. The dog only wanted what was best for her, and she'd shoved him aside. It was a terrible thing to do, and Vera knew in the pit of her soul that she'd betrayed him. She understood full well what kind of person that made her out to be. Was there any way to make amends? Vera decided to let him have the run of the house, too, as she slid on her overcoat and then beat feet down to the coffeehouse. She didn't want to dwell on it anymore and was horribly late. Plus, she had no idea what she'd be walking into.

❖

Vera arrived in the middle of what was the Sunday breakfast into lunch rush. Sundays were by far the busiest days at the shop, and she wandered smack into the center of the fray. It worked out well though, given that both Keith and supposedly

Misty were too occupied to indulge in a third degree. Vera got behind the bakery case and counter, tied on an apron, and got down to brass tacks. Coffee drinks, pastries, and some sort of soufflé that Misty obviously made special for the day passed from hand to hand. Vera served and rang up indulgences on the register while Keith bussed tables and helped in the kitchen. Misty was yet to reveal herself, but Vera had a strong suspicion she was in the back, immersed in her domain and deliciously creative work.

The satisfying lull of a hectic but routine pace gave Vera a false sense of security, and when the fever pitch finally died around two o'clock in the afternoon, she was unprepared for what awaited her.

Misty burst from the kitchen the moment the dining area was free of visitors. "Do you know how upset your brother is?" she put it to her. Misty was flush with ferocity.

"Misty," Keith cautioned as he joined them near the counter. "Take it easy."

Vera was glad that at least there was the counter and bakery case between them. She and Misty had never fought, ever. Vera had no idea what to expect.

"No, no. Something has to be said," Misty shot back at Keith and then turned her attention once more to Vera, blonde ringlets flying every time she turned her head with such force. "Do you have any idea what your brother and I've been through looking for you, waiting for you, hoping you'd come home safely?! He even shut Frank up in the bedroom, thinking something had gone wrong with you and the dog when he'd found him there, like that!" Misty challenged.

Vera surprised her own self by accepting the challenge, despite her remorse over Frank's unfortunate situation. The sounds of throaty laughter reverberated through the shop, and it took Vera some time to realize she was the one doing the laughing.

"What is so funny?!" Misty pressed, now madder than before.

"If you were so worried about me getting home safe, then why the hell did you ditch me at Keith's?" Vera had a razor sharp edge of her own. She may not ever be able to use such a thing with Derrick, but she could certainly wield it with practically everyone else, if necessary.

"Hey," Keith prepared his objection.

"Oh, this has nothing to do with you," Vera said and waved him off. "This has to do with my friend and my ride leaving me past the outskirts of town, at night, in the dark, in the cold, with no way home," Vera presented her side of the argument diligently, point after painful point. Truth be told though, Keith's farm wasn't so far away she couldn't have walked if need be.

Misty softened her stance; a half step back was all it took to convey the message that she was unprepared for where the conversation was going. "I knew you'd get a ride back," she said, attempting to hold what ground she still had.

"And, I did. But, why did you leave me there in the first place?" Vera asked, matching the dwindling level of intensity her possible friend displayed. She had no concept of where she stood in Misty's world or what place she might continue to hold in Misty's pantheon of affection.

Keith also looked to Misty for the answer to that question. No doubt he'd heard plenty of scathing comments about Vera during the course of the weekend, but now it was Vera's turn to balance it all back out, if she could.

"Look, I just didn't want to stay Friday night, that's all. I was uncomfortable. I wasn't having a good time," she tried to explain and then met Keith's gaze. "Sorry," she said to him. "It wasn't anything you did or that there was anything wrong at the farm. I was just in a different place that night and my happiness wasn't organic. I didn't want to affect the festivities with my mood, so I left," she vaguely summed, giving a few quick bats of her beautiful blue eyes complete with feathery angel lashes. Then she turned to Vera. "And, I left you there because you were having a great time, and you should be allowed to continue having it for as long as possible, despite my feelings."

It wasn't personal, and yet it was. Misty was saying a lot, revealing a great deal, and yet she wasn't saying or revealing much of anything. She'd also fallen back on using cued up body language to sway those around her. That style of dancing around the truth was highly unusual for the typically straightforward albeit seductive Misty, and too much and simultaneously too little for Vera to truly accept.

"Fine," Vera told her. "Fine." If that's how Misty wanted it.

"Vera, where have you been for the past day and a half? You didn't go home, except to lock up your brother's dog, and you definitely didn't come to work. We needed you here," Keith informed her.

And just as she had felt towards Frank, Vera knew then in her soul she'd betrayed Keith, too. He was good-natured and wanted only the best for her, just like Frank. And, she'd trounced all over his kindness because she could. There was no forgetting what had passed between them in the bedroom suite at the farmhouse. There was no losing that sense of connection, of intimacy, that interwove itself with a new palpation of hurt and denial. She was forgoing what Keith offered her, and she really didn't want to. She wanted to be accepting for his sake as well as her own, but there was a very big consideration smack in the middle of the ability to do so — Derrick.

"Yes, yes, you did. I let you down. I let you both down here at the shop, and I'm sorry. I had personal issues to tend to and I guess I trusted the two of you to handle the business needs. I didn't even give it much thought," Vera shrugged. "I guess I just knew the two of you would pick up the slack, and you did. But, I had no right to place that burden on you, especially without asking, and I'm sorry for that. And, I'm sorry I shut Frank up in a room without explanation. There was no real reason for him to be left like that," Vera owned up to the two parts of the entire botched episode that were without any excuse. She could live with vocalizing and admitting to them. She could not handle her sordid feelings toward Keith or her strained relationship with Misty, at least not directly and not at the present moment. And, it was anyone's guess how her brother would react when she found herself in his sight for the first time since her little disappearing act. If she thought about it for too long, she'd have to consider the distinct possibility that she was treating John badly, too. She was behaving disgracefully towards her own brother, her own flesh and blood, and the person who had taken her in and helped her get started when she'd had nowhere else to go. Vera wasn't even sure what type of person she was becoming, treating Frank and Keith and John so poorly, and deciding in a split second not to pursue any inquiry that might lead to a healing with Misty.

"Call your brother," Misty told her and twirled on her heels as she made for the sacred space of her kitchen. The raucous sounds of the swinging door portrayed in no uncertain terms Misty's continued discontent.

Vera took in Keith's visage, standing on the other side of the counter but coming in close enough that she could touch him easily across the expanse. "I'm sorry. I really didn't mean to dump so much on you."

"It's ok," he said and patted the backs of her hands.

Vera let her fingers weave in and out of his and eventually their hands were locked together, loosely but definitely. "Keith, I don't know why I'm having such a hard time balancing everything all of a sudden. I was so excited when I first moved back home and got the ball rolling on my business and… and… I just don't know."

Keith gave a gentle smile to her, a gracious and accepting grin. "We can work it out. There's no problem that doesn't come with a solution."

"God, I hope that's true," Vera sighed and let her head loll forward for a bit before tossing her hair away and considering Keith from an accentuated upwards angle. He was a tall man, a proud man, and a good man. That much was evident merely from glancing at him. Vera found renewed interest every time they were together.

"It is. If you believe in the problem, then for sake of balance you have to believe in the solution. Think of it as a very uplifting cause and effect," he consoled.

"I'll try," she affirmed.

Keith gave her a decisive and agreeable nod. "Good. Now let's talk about better things. You're still planning to come out to the farm for dinner tonight, right? Because I've got a great meal planned and Isaac is thinking about bringing some of his elderberry wine and —"

"Oh, shit!" Vera exclaimed and slammed her head into her palms.

"What? What?" Keith pressed her and placed his hands on her arms, rubbing up and down, trying to stimulate further response.

When Vera finally looked up at him again, dared to make eye contact, she was beyond guilt ridden. "Keith, Keith, I can't… Something's come up and —"

Keith didn't make her finish. It was tearing him apart to watch her try. "Listen," he opened firmly but softly, "I know people have probably been counting on you your whole life… you and your brother, too. I'm sure the two of you have carried a lot from a very early age. I can see it clearly in your behaviors and from bits of conversations here and there. And, I understand that you've probably never gotten to do the selfish thing, and you've never taken any real time for yourself to explore and to go wild and to make mistakes and messes, at least not lately. I get that," he explained and perhaps even made excuses for her. "But, while you're doing all of this, and wherever it leads you, just remember there are people who care about you along the way. Your decisions don't just affect you. They affect us."

It was painful for Vera to see Keith care so deeply and completely and to know that he wanted the same towards him from her. She so desired to give that to him with careless abandon, but the breaks were on, a hook was in her mouth holding her tongue still, a heaviness was keeping her from doing and saying those types of things. There was a palpable weight about her neck, not an anchor; no, it was more like a millstone.

"And, it's not the tangibles in life that'll give you true comfort throughout the years, Vera," Keith went on and placed a hand under her chin to force their eyes to meet. Her irises appeared exotic when coated with tears that were yet to fall. He wanted her to see what his held at bay inside of him, held in proper place for her. "Houses, clothes, good looks, hot sex… motorcycles…" he stopped there. He needed a moment.

Vera tried to turn away. She was hurting him, doing considerable damage and she was afraid there was no stopping it. How could so many aspects change during the turn of one season into another?

Keith kept her gaze with his. "It's the intangibles. Those are the things that never perish. Those are the only things worth having in the end." Keith let her go. He retracted his hand and gave her a few seconds to decide if she should come to him.

She didn't. She stood there and pondered. She hesitated and stammered but never spoke a cohesive sentence. Vera wanted to go with Keith but knew it was a blatant betrayal of the promise she'd made to Derrick only that morning. She could not tamper with that. She dared not.

Keith went back to work.

And, once Vera had inwardly composed herself, she found her phone and called John for an unpleasant but not unredeemable conversation.

Halloween rolled around and John's life was unsettled for the very first time. Since the moment he'd bought his own business from the clutches of the estate of a dying man and then grown it, he'd never instituted another massive change. Now something new was working its way into the picture, into the plan. He'd thought Misty was all the newness he'd need, but on the heels of their budding relationship came the dramatic revelation that the only means to continued growth for his venture was to infuse it with energy from the outside, a spark and then a roaring fire of something entirely different and immediately lucrative. A merger. John hadn't said anything to anyone since the paperwork was not finalized yet, but a significant merger was indeed underway. It would bring in a lot of capital and a much needed leveling up. Although John thought it a more than prudent idea, the process was a disruption to daily life, positive or not.

Vera came and went erratically, which didn't help stabilize John's home life, and Misty both did and then did not go to the drum circles Keith held every week at the Simms Farm. John had no idea if his sister went. He also had no idea how things were going at the shop. He started to adjust by assuming if Misty was in a good mood, work went as it was structured to do. If she came home in a bad mood, somewhat sullen and unnerved, he knew there had been upheaval and it was his job to lighten the load. John found it best and easiest to simply adjust his tactics around Misty.

He didn't want to take any risks. He didn't want to lose her — ever.

As he and Misty sat out on the front stoop of the house, bundled up in coats with a big bowl of candy as they waited for each new batch of trick-or-treater's, John found himself thinking back to the day he took her to the quarry. John had always enjoyed the quarry, ever since he was a kid. So much to see and explore and study there. He'd never taken anyone else out to see it until Misty came into his world. And, he'd never self-identified with it on such a personal level until that day either.

John remembered the feeling as it washed over him anew, triggered by Misty being so close, or by the cycles of quiet and sound, or by nothing whatsoever. John felt like the quarry once again, as he thought about Misty and his future and all he'd hoped to achieve. He understood the abandoned pit. He knew internally why the open, fractured, and gaping abyss moaned like it did in high winds and why it craved something more substantial than fickle and evaporating rainwater. John was once more fully and keenly aware of the hole inside himself that seemed impossible to fill… until that moment when it was possible, when an opportunity presented itself. For the first time in his life, he thought maybe one person could act as all the mud and plants and rock that would eventually fill even the quarry's incredible depths.

"Hey," he broke the silence that had settled in between he and Misty, between waves of kids that ran up and down the block, their costumes covered by heavy coats. The weather had gone bitterly cold so fast.

Misty turned and gave him her full attention, as she always did, with those brilliant blue eyes peering into his soul. "Yeah," she opened.

John stalled. He wanted to ask something specific, but then he stalled. "So, what's on your mind?" Better to work his way up to it.

Misty let out a lovely little sigh in a puff of smoke. "Everything's changed," she finally said with a distinct note of melancholy.

It made John's heart ache. "What? What's changed?" He needed to know the exact problem in order to begin fixing it.

"Me. I've changed even though I didn't want to. I never planned to. And, Vera... Vera's changed the most of all. I don't know why this is happening and I don't know what to expect on any given day." Misty looked down at her fingernails as though the solutions to her vague dilemmas might be hidden underneath, in the nail beds.

It was vague, but somehow John found himself understanding the gist of it. "If you're waiting for Vera to be a rational, normal person, you're in for a long wait. I've known Vera for most of her life, and I can tell you that even though she seems pragmatic a majority of the time, she's anything but when she doesn't have to be," John informed her.

"But that pragmatic person, that business person, that's the Vera I initially met. That's the person I became friends with," Misty practically whined. Deep down she longed for Vera to become that mousy and strategically placed person once more in her sphere.

"I know," John sympathized. "But, that's not who Vera really is... that's only who Vera has to be from time to time."

Misty kept her eyes on her fingernails.

John placed a hand over hers, shifting the candy bowl to a step below their feet. He noticed a light suddenly turn on in a second story window of the Thompson house. The yellow glow pierced the darkness only a tiny bit. Vera was probably there. John estimated that she was there a lot now, and the visitor who was supposed to be so temporary, who was supposed to be cleaning up and clearing out the estate, had done next to nothing with the endeavor. Derrick looked to be an almost permanent resident from what John could surmise.

"I feel like I'm becoming less than what I used to be," Misty confessed in a tone barely louder than a whisper.

"What do you mean?" John inquired further.

"I used to be this wild person, this carefree woman who did whatever she wanted whenever she wanted, you know?" Misty poured forth and looked to John carefully. She saw that he met her with interest but not with judgment. She went on. "I was so spontaneous and free and... and... desirable," she paused and swallowed her emotions. They could erupt and then flow freely later. Misty had to let it out carefully, cohesively. She had to say what it was that ate at her and be understood in the process. As she and John sat under the brilliance of a full moon, she was inspired to come clean, to speak her newfound and horrible truth. "I'm none of those things now. I'm settling. My life is settling. I have an apartment and rent to pay. I have a job and a business to run. I'm in a committed relationship —"

"And, that bothers you?" John had to know. It was selfish to hone in on the singular point that pertained to him directly, but he really had to know.

Misty brought a hand to the side of John's face and touched him lovingly. "No. It's been wonderful," she assured and then slowly retracted. "It's just that with all of these situations occurring at the same time, I feel like I'm becoming tame, domestic… boring by comparison!" There it was, the ugly truth sitting in between them and under the sterling silver rays of the gibbous moon.

"By comparison to what?" John hit on it. Smart. Deductive. Detailed.

Misty couldn't say. She couldn't bring herself to speak it out loud and merely gazed at John, hoping he would understand, somehow read her mind if that's what it took.

"Vera?" he questioned after a couple of minutes had ticked past.

"She wasn't this person when I first met her and now she's this wild, mysterious, edgy…" Misty had to stop herself. It went beyond petty and jealous.

John got it. He understood in an instant what it was like to not measure up to a standard one set for oneself. Even if the whole rest of the world never judged you like that, it was awful when you did it anyway. "Are you happy at your apartment?" John diverted the conversation. He had to stop Misty from torturing herself any further. There was no more need to vocalize those wretched feelings.

"Huh?" Misty said as she wiped at an escaping tear, one little glistening tear. "What to do you mean?"

"Do you want to be strapped to renting an apartment? Are you happy there?" he clarified in one question broken symmetrically into two.

Misty shrugged. "Oh, I don't know. It's all right. It's a nice space." She retrieved the bowl of candy at her feet to have something else to do, to focus on.

"Move in with me," John threw it out there.

"What?" Misty checked.

"Move in with me, Misty. I want you to move in here, into my house, and live with me," he told her.

"Stop it," she said as though he were joking and tossed her ringlets back over one shoulder to denote a carelessness she really didn't feel. A cued reaction.

But, just as Misty had needed to be heard only moments ago, now John needed to speak his truth and be heard. "I'm serious. I want you here as often as possible. Stop paying rent and stop shackling yourself to commitments that don't matter. Move in with me. Please."

Misty set the big bowl of assorted and colorful candies back down on the step. She leaned in and kissed John firmly, longingly, sweetly. "Ok."

Autumn ended before the calendar officially declared it to be so. It ended badly and harshly, with sleet cascading down on All Saints' Day. The sleet tore away any leaves that dared remain on the tree branches and it strained the lands, the locals, and a few friendships. All Souls' Day, which followed, took on a sharp mourning pallor with gray skies, black tree limbs, and muddy earth.

The coffeehouse, along with most of the other local businesses, was closed for a few days in a row due to the inclement weather. But, it really didn't matter. Vera had a new but already well-trending pattern of coming in to work late and then leaving early. The passion she'd once had for the place was waning quickly, and no matter what she tried to tell herself, no matter how persuasive the internal dialogue, there were no words or thoughts she could conjure that would create a fresh infusion. Vera had thought that by winter's onset she'd be drawing at least a small paycheck from her endeavor, but there was no money to pull, nothing to take for herself. A loss of focus had plateaued or perhaps stagnated the business growth. The surge that had been ongoing in the first couple of months was tapering off. The townsfolk had acclimated to the shop and there was nothing so new or grand about it anymore. It was just another business in a district brimming with them, on a street that had a lot of other options. The heart and soul of the venture had been ripped out quickly and easily when Vera stepped back, and she wasn't sure she'd be able to step up to the plate again, as she'd done at the start. Vera tried every morning to care, but she simply didn't.

If she were being perfectly honest with herself, Vera would have to admit to being gravely distracted. And, it wasn't just Derrick and the all-consuming, albeit frightening, love affair they were sharing… his ever heightening and dramatically cool intensity about her… although that was certainly part of it. No, it was more than that. Vera was starting to see things, things she could not shove aside. Thinking the dead might somehow remain in the places they occupied while alive was one thing. Thinking it as a young girl made it all the more excusable and viable. Thinking it and even feeling it as an adult while all alone in the evocative Thompson house was understandable and manageable, too. It could be contained. It could all be labeled and boxed and set aside to peer at when the hour was more convenient. Even a doll with glowing eyes and surreal abilities could be shoved aside and not looked upon until one was ready, or so Vera assumed. But in addition to all of that, in addition to all Vera was able to take on and handle and categorize and set aside, she was at a loss when the latest wave of insanity hit her. What does one do when faced with immoveable specters of the dead? Not mistaken reflections in an oblong mirror glass in an enchanted Treasure Room… Lillian had paid Vera an undeniable visit.

Lillian appeared to Vera first. It was an early morning visit when Vera rose as she did, before Derrick, and dutifully marched herself downstairs to start the coffee. Derrick slept so soundly these days, as though his plans had not been disrupted at all and everything was proceeding as he'd intended. It was the exact opposite from Vera's experiences and feelings. Vera had been ruminating on how deeply Derrick slept and that it might still be possible to slip that precious, priceless, ancient book out from under his pillow and even make use of the key without his knowledge. She was pondering the possibility when Lillian stepped gracefully in front of her.

Vera was just passing the grandfather clock when a quick sidestep brought her face to face with Lillian. The long dead and impressively tall Lillian, with her gentle demeanor and wizened expression, blocked her path to the kitchen.

Vera's jaw dropped.

"Don't scream," Lillian brought a warm and solid hand to Vera's lips and laid it over them lightly. "Don't scream, child."

The two of them stood that way, lovingly locked together, until some aspect of Vera's posture changed and assured Lillian she would not give out a terrified shout. Lillian removed her hand then and the two women were left at the base of that clock, with only the paltry years and fast flying time situated between them.

Vera couldn't help but notice that Lillian looked and felt exactly as she remembered; it was as if not a moment had ticked by, she was so beautifully preserved and draped in sumptuous fabrics that hung off her frame like a bundle of cascading and exotically colorful scarves.

Lillian smiled. "What did the digital clock say to the grandfather clock?" She cocked her head and blinked at Vera, awaiting a response. "Look grandpa, no hands," came the punch line. A joke. She'd made a joke. Unbelievable. "It's not easy to see me before coffee. Am I right?"

Vera never thought of the dead as having a sense of humor. But, before she realized it, Vera was smiling back. "That was awful," Vera referred to the quip.

"I'm rusty," Lillian justified. She reached out and turned the white gold acorn Vera wore around her neck over and over between her fingers, admiring it. "This is a very nice piece."

"It was a gift. You like it?" Vera asked.

"Very much," Lillian told her, causing Vera to automatically beam with great pride. "Did you see my little squirrel figurine upstairs?"

"In the guest bedroom?"

Lillian nodded.

"Yes. I love it," Vera replied.

"Good," Lillian approved of her preferences. "Me, too."

"It's been a while," Vera made her own version of a segue into a more purposeful conversation.

"Not for me," Lillian revealed. "I get to see you all the time."

Vera wanted to shout 'aha!' and 'I knew it!'… but stopped herself. Instead she went with, "Why didn't you say anything until now? Were you too busy thinking up a joke to tell?"

"It's a matter of timing, isn't it? And, I'm not here to disrupt your life, while you still happen to have one," Lillian told her with a bittersweet edge of kindness.

Vera wondered though if she was being vague on purpose. "Ok, I'm sorry, but what the hell is that supposed to mean?"

"We always think we will have more time, my dear. We think we will have time to right our wrongs or get things together or set things right. The truth is much less appealing though. The truth is that we never have the time we think we do, we suppose we will. Time always runs out and options go along with it. Your time is running out. The window that is open to the life you want, the life you should have is slowly closing and you don't even see it. I had to speak up, all kidding aside," Lillian explained and took up Vera's hands in hers. "This house, it's not everything. The furnishings and the art and the books, those aren't everything. The gardens that I once loved and the memories contained in all these places, they aren't everything. Can't you let go, Vera? Please, let go, Vera." It was practically piteous begging and too much to take from a proud and regal woman like Lillian. She was so strong in death that her spirit was like flesh and blood. So incredibly real.

"I-I don't want to," Vera confessed. "It's all I have left. It's all I have left of you and of me, of who I used to be, Lillian. I can't let go of it."

"Do you really think he's going to let you keep any of it?" Lillian challenged, gripping Vera's hands a little tighter. "The more you cling, the more it hurts when it is ripped away."

"What?" Who was she referring to? Derrick? Keith?... Fate? Someone Vera hadn't even met yet?

"He will take and take and take from you until it is all gone. And when you have nothing and there is nothing in you that's left to give either, you will know. You will sit with the painful knowledge that I do now. Don't let that happen," Lillian pleaded. "I had a good life, Vera, when I see the sum of it. The bulk was wonderful. There were great years, amazing spans. We had good times together, you and I, and great memories. Those memories that we share in our hearts and in our souls after our hearts are gone, they keep us together, no matter what, my dear."

"I miss you," was all Vera had to come back with, but the words poured forth from a scar in her heart center that was tearing open again. Vera closed her eyes to fight back teardrops. "I don't understand what's happening to me. All I know is that I miss you…" her voice trailed off and when she blinked her moist eyes open once more, Lillian was gone. All that was left from Vera's encounter with her deceased friend was the signature scent of herbs on a breeze that should not be rustling the draperies.

Vera went and made the coffee.

Vera's second encounter with an immovable, undeniable, and untenable specter was not as affectionate or affirming. It was not with Lillian. Vera's second encounter was with Elizabeth. But, Elizabeth had been up to other things and interacting with other people before she got around to messing with Vera. Not only could the dead be humorous, but they could be busy. Despite what many people often presuppose, the dead do not gain enlightenment after the shift across the veil. No, the same issues and petty desires that were theirs in life are theirs in death as well. Those issues don't burn off as though the soul is passed through some primordial furnace. They remain and sometimes become even more magnified, even more twisted and turned.

Elizabeth went straight to Derrick, but she hadn't gotten the initial reactions she'd been hoping for that way. Perhaps Derrick wasn't naturally inclined to give them to her because he'd been seeing her all along, seeing and saying nothing. In this way, he was a lot like his own grandmother. There were many days and nights in times past when she'd watch silently from the windows of the house; she'd watch Vera and the weeds and the moon and the life she'd created unfurling. Now it was upon another to create her will for her.

Derrick lay in bed alone, an icy morning gripping the external world and acting as a perfect representation of what beat on in his chest. He drifted between dream-filled sleep and dreary wakefulness, back and forth.

"Time is running out," Elizabeth's imposing voice rocked the room, shattering what little serenity there might have been, yet she spoke barely a notch above a whisper.

Derrick opened his eyes and beheld his grandmother in her milky white moonlit gown, moonlit despite the dawning day. He blinked once or twice and then decided to prop himself up for the exchange.

"The window of opportunity you have, it's closing," she warned.

"I'm doing all I can," he told her. "You should know these things take time, like slowly adjusting the water temperature to cook a frog in a pot. What more do you want from me?" They'd been so close and shared so much; the last thing he'd ever wanted during the course of her life was to disappoint her. He wanted it even less after her death, if such a thing were possible. But, certain goals take time to properly manifest.

"Whatever it takes," she insisted. "You will do whatever it takes." Elizabeth pointed to the tiny key that dangled about his neck. "You know what this means to me. You know full well what it's going to take. Do it."

Derrick glanced down at the key and to her dark, beloved, and equally abhorred book. He did know what it meant. He understood what had to be meted out. It was transfer and conclusion and the easing of a painful burden by projection onto another. Derrick comprehended that. He even wanted it for himself as much as for his grandmother. "You got it," he swore an oath he'd already taken in his soul with three simple words.

And, it was on the same day that Elizabeth manifested before Vera, just as midday was turning to evening and the land fell betwixt and between to match the natural state of the Thompson house. Derrick had stepped outside for some unknown reason. He may have even stepped outside and away. His phone had gone off and it was immediately following that he grabbed his coat and strode purposefully out the door. It could've been anything, that's how little Vera knew him. She didn't pry, that's how much she loved him. She'd have done anything and everything to keep him happy, to assure a contented state. She didn't speak of anything outside their relationship anymore, and the sleet and subsequent icy road conditions had chilled his fiery rage against her constant work shifts at the coffeehouse. It was no longer enough to come in late and leave early. Vera sensed that when the ice melted and the rest of the world returned to normal, she'd be facing a problem, perhaps the problem Lillian had been attempting to both warn and advise her on.

It was just as midday was turning to evening that Vera found herself antsy to take a chance and head back upstairs to the master bedroom. The book was there, although the key had gone with Derrick. There might be another way to open it. Vera was becoming more and more obsessed with the concept, so much so that it completely overwhelmed her rationale of what Derrick might do if he found the journal, the dark diary, ripped into. The book was forbidden and attractive and could hold any number of tellings. Vera had even convinced herself that it might hold the key to her ability to dream again, something she'd lost so long ago, something she felt sure Elizabeth had taken from her.

Vera slowly climbed the stairs and with precision steps walked the length of the well-lined hallway. She'd only made it to the bedroom door, hand on the metal knob, when the sound of someone clearing their throat reached her ears. Someone immediately to her left. Vera turned, half-expecting to see Lillian. Instead, Elizabeth sat in one of the chairs, legs crossed, back straight, and decadently draped in her impossibly white nightgown.

"I really don't think that's a good idea. Do you?" She stared with horribly intense eyes.

Vera stepped away as far as she could from her otherworldly visitor, pressing her back in against the solid surface of the door. Her instinct was to run, but some force stopped her, held her in place. It may have been her own fear or something external, a power more sinister.

"Well, do you?" Elizabeth's question was not rhetorical, and she demanded an answer.

"It seems better and better to me all the time," Vera gave a haughty response, which would have been more intimidating had her voice not trembled, were her body not quaking.

"Oh, I can assure you now, there is nothing that can be undone," Elizabeth said. "There is nothing about any of this that will go away… save the aspects that you'd like to have stay," she informed her with a wicked grin. It was devilishly effective at breaking Vera down.

"Why are you doing this?" Vera brought the conversation back around.

"Same old question… why?... Was the answer I gave you the first time not good enough? You think back. Think on it," she instructed harshly, as if she were exhausted from having to speak to a total dolt.

Vera was about to do as told, to actually think back, when a shift happened. It was as though some other entity had joined them in the hall. Initially, this made Vera more alert and even a bit upbeat as she thought now it might be Lillian, but it wasn't. No such luck. Whatever had entered the hallway, still entirely unseen, was keeping low and was animalistic in tone. There was this sensation of a slow prowling to the point where it was almost more true to a slithering. Vera had felt it before, most recently in her brother's house, in her room. Fate crept about the hallway with the two of them, and it seemed to be siding with Elizabeth. The old and imposing woman became even more self-assured, more grounded and centered and determined.

Elizabeth stood to full height, stick straight and as mighty as any tree Vera had ever seen. She took a couple of steps until she was standing right in front of Vera, less than an arm's length away. "And, don't think because you shut something up in a room, block it off from sight and from thought, that it's gone. It is never going to work that way. Never."

Vera reached her hand back and tried the knob, she twisted and pushed, but the door to the chamber at her back would not open. She was trapped in the hall with Elizabeth and awaiting whatever Fate had in store. "Please," Vera began pleading, "please, don't do this. You don't have to do this."

"Oh, but I do. You see," and with a great flourish came Elizabeth's big reveal, "for this doll is you," she said and produced the ugly little figure she had carved out one night, under a full moon, in a weedy garden, from the remains of a sacred tree brutally slaughtered. "The doll is you, but it is more."

The eyeless, armless thing twisted and turned this way and that as though it were taking in information, making decisions, sensing and being sensed. Then the eyes it didn't have, shouldn't have had, opened and took in the sight of Vera's quivering form. Red ember eyes peered into her soul. What did they see there?

"It has come for you. The time has come," Elizabeth said, almost sweetly.

"Why? Why?!" The same old why. Vera was losing it. Her nerves were fraying, her concept of identity and reality were shattering. Her insanity was eclipsing what might have remained sane under different circumstances.

"Because you touched it!" Elizabeth thrust the doll onto Vera and a red, sappy liquid spurted out, coating them both from head to toe. Vera couldn't see. She couldn't touch. She couldn't breathe.

Chapter 9

Vera found herself sitting peacefully on the sofa downstairs when she came to; she was serene only because she was completely out of it, detached from what was happening around her. She had no recollection of exiting the upstairs hallway and no memory of cleaning up, changing clothes, or finding Derrick. In fact, as Derrick sat across from her, spewing words that made no rational sense to her mind, she wasn't even able to bring into the forefront of her thoughts the conversation they appeared to be having.

"You have no idea what the fuck I just said, do you?" Derrick put it to her. He leaned forward in one of the armchairs and positioned his body rather precariously on the edge. There was a dark shadow about him and Vera wasn't sure what an anti-inflammatory response might be, for she truly had no idea what he'd said. "Are you listening to me?" He gave the glossy coffee table a shove and sent it slamming into the far wall, just below the windows. The glass rattled and Vera remembered how thick and dark it had been when she was a teenager, when Elizabeth moved in. Now, however, the glass was tinted and of average, expected thickness. The Thompson house could've been normal, if glass measurements were any estimate. They weren't.

Vera jerked in automatic response to the table's bang, if a little late. "I'm sorry. I don't know what's happening!" She burst into tears. There was no other alternative inside her. She went from numb and unresponsive to hyper reactive in a sudden internal swing.

"I think you can't wait to get out of here. You want to leave me, like everyone else!" Derrick accused and got to his feet. He was formidable; he was intoxicating.

Vera shrunk back into the sofa's plush upholstery, keenly aware there was nowhere else for her to go. She'd never make it to the front door before getting nabbed, and there was no way around him to get to the back exit. And, did she want to go? Or was she simply afraid, experiencing a flicker of fear in a fleeting moment before he would take her in his arms again?

"Your work is all you care about," he said with great distain. Then a flash came over him, changing his expression like a light bulb clicking on. "Or is it?"

Vera wiped at her puffy eyes piteously and tried to keep tabs on Derrick as he started pacing before her, small and tight trails emerging in a pattern made over and over again. "Derrick, please... I can't seem to remember... what's going on?"

"That's a great fucking question. Just what the hell is going on? Are you so anxious to get back to your little shop? Or are you anxious to get back to your special hired hand?" Derrick stopped his back and forth motions and stood directly over her.

Keith?... He was referring to Keith. But, why? Vera wondered what she possibly could've said or done while in a stupor to make him think such a thing. Whether it was secretly true to some degree or not was beside the point. She kept that secret well hidden below her super-conductive surface, the expressive surface she kept running on high for Derrick. Derrick was the one who made her feel alive. Derrick was the one who had made her entire life seem like a dream world. He gave her the tantalizing dream-like quality in her waking moments, a gift so precious, considering she never got that during sleep.

Vera wasn't sure that bringing Keith up, and asking further questions, would calm the situation. Her memories of minutes or hours or perhaps days were gone. Maybe they would come back, maybe not. But in the meantime, she had no idea what she was blundering into with Derrick. No, it was better to listen and speak only when spoken to. That's the advice John would've given her, hypothetically, if she'd ever had the occasion to ask about such a scenario. She knew her brother so well, or so she supposed. Her mind went to him in that instant. It went to a safe person and a safe place. She thought on the house next door and the people that might be there... and Frank, the protector she'd shut up in a room for his valiant efforts.

"I don't have any idea what you're talking about," Vera admitted weakly when the silence bore down upon her and Derrick awaited some sort of reply. She tried to curl up into a ball, bringing her knees to her chest. Her limp brown hair falling forward, shrouding her face.

But, that was a mistake.

"Don't you dare shut me out!" Derrick roared and grabbed her by the arms. He hoisted her to her feet, strong fingers biting into her tender flesh, and brought her up next to the coffee table. The same table he'd recently sent skidding across the carpeted floor, causing an electric wave of friction that seemed to remain, hovering all around them. He shoved the table back to where it had come from and out of his way. Derrick brought Vera over to the window and drew back the curtain. "You think I didn't notice it, too?" he asked.

Vera peered out but wasn't sure what she was looking for in the frenzied scan her eyes made of the landscape. She took in the tree-lined street and the muddy ground, the dead patches of grass and the sun streaked sky, as it was right about sunset. The scene was beautiful really, in harsh contrast to what was going on inside the Thompson house.

"I don't look forward to it the same as you," Derrick sneered. "I look out there and see the ice melting, and I know we'll have to be apart again."

Vera's heart leapt and cried and danced and then went motionless for a second or two. The cardiac pump sat like a cool stone in her ribcage. The admission should have been oh so terribly romantic, and in a certain sense it was. Derrick longed to have her all to himself. He wanted her near, desired to extend the time they had together, get the most out of it and the most out of her. The idea that she could drive such an exquisite man to such emotional extremes was intoxicating. Vera had never felt more validated in her entire life. She'd also never felt more terrified. The admission should have been purely romantic, but it was more than that. The growing bud of a fevered fear eclipsed it. Vera wanted to both embrace him and get as far away as possible. What was it about this town, this house, and her life that caused the wonderful and the awful to intersect so often?

Vera kept staring out the window. She now saw with new eyes and rapt attention. The ice was melting. The streets and sidewalks were growing dark with moisture and the ground was eagerly sucking it up. The roadways would be passable by morning, and whatever the next day was and whatever it brought, Vera was determined to do what needed to be done, and find a way to make Derrick content with it. There had to be a balance, if she could only find it. There had to be reasons, and a way to bring harmony and stability into an area that had never known it prior. She would go to work at the coffeehouse, even if it was a case of better late than never.

Ice doesn't last forever. Nothing lasts forever. Vera emerged from the cocoon of the Thompson house alone. Derrick had left her sometime during the night, as Vera existed in unconscious limbo, sleeping but not dreaming, never dreaming. She crossed a black abyss and came back again. A journey that seemed to be her perpetual destiny. That was all sleeping was to her. It was not the chance to have nocturnal visions, and it hadn't been in years. It was the chance to rest as best she could.

The chilled call of a few birds woke her around dawn and Vera found a note on the pillow beside her own: 'I have plans for us —alone. Come back right after work.' She took the note in hand and meandered about the house until finally gliding across the frost-laden lawns to pop into her brother's home. The residence was quiet, but Vera heard breathing from her brother's room as she made her way down the hall. It was the cadent inhale and exhale of sleep. Frank was nowhere to be seen. And, Vera couldn't discern much other than what she already knew to be there in the drowsy dark. Had she bothered to flip on a switch and take the chance of rousing the household, she would've seen the latest developments; a few random pieces of Misty's clothes were scattered here and hung up there, and there were boxes stacked at the farthest corner of the hallway where shadows stretched low. Misty had all but completely moved in and Vera saw nothing of it, not yet.

Vera went into her own room, tossed the crumpled note on the currently doll-less dresser, showered, and donned another mixed outfit from the offerings of her blended wardrobe. A sweeping yet heavier crimson skirt and a conservative black sweater top. Black boots, a checkered scarf, and then on with her coat once more. It was fairly early but still probable that Misty and Keith were already there, getting the coffeehouse ready for the first run of customers for the day. The breakfast rush would be on them in no time.

Vera put on her heaviest coat, grabbed up her purse, and walked the few blocks to the shop. She noticed the lights on as she turned a corner to the main street of the antique district. Someone was there already. Not only were the lights on, but also the window glass of the storefront was fogged from heat inside. Whoever was there had already kicked on the furnace, if not the ovens, too. Vera braced herself against the scattered wind gusts and hurried along the sidewalk at a more than brisk pace. She reached inside her coat pocket for her keychain, found her work key with ease, and let herself in. It was the earliest she'd shown up in quite a while, and it was still later than what would be considered optimal.

A blissful wave of warmth hit her as she entered. Vera turned the bolt and locked the world outside. She left the cold at her back. The streets weren't crowded yet, but she didn't want a local wandering in and catching them unprepared. The very last thing Vera needed in her life at the moment was another surprise, another situation in which she was caught with her guard down.

The distinct aromas of cinnamon and praline filled her nostrils and she took a good, long whiff. Vera whisked off her coat and checkered scarf and chucked them on a rack in the far back corner of the main room, her purse tucked away underneath. It felt good to be at work again. It felt great to have the perception of normalcy. The sensation felt far better than it should have, so much so that Vera caught herself relaxing a tension in her shoulders. It was a burden she didn't know she was carrying. Vera let loose a heavy sigh and rolled her neck around, allowing her head to also move in slow circles to release the tightness. Vera luxuriated in the extra layer of heat that radiated from the kitchen, creeping along from the small gap that ran the length of the swinging door. The ovens were on and something marvelous was baking inside them, that was guaranteed. It made Vera deliriously happy. Cinnamon rolls perhaps, praline pecan rolls were a better bet. Maybe cookies or delicate pastry puffs of some kind. Curious about the source of the smell and also fairly eager to find out the tone she'd share with Misty for the day, Vera headed into the kitchen. As anticipated, she found Misty there, well occupied.

Misty wore warm stretch leggings in a beautiful shade of turquois and brown, and she wore beige fur-lined boots that matched her swirling sweater top. It all went so perfectly with her blonde hair and azure eyes. She was pure summer delight in the middle of a frigid wintery blast. Misty glanced up as Vera sauntered in quasi-casually and then returned her gaze to a tray of pecan rolls. "Keith went to do a supply run," she reported dutifully.

"What day is it?" Vera asked her. It wasn't how she'd planned to start the conversation, but up until that point there'd been no one else to tell Vera. There'd been no one else Vera felt safe asking.

"What?" Misty looked up again and considered the absurd question, tilting her heard slightly so that curls cascaded down over one eye. She was so very beautiful, and yet not as lovely as she used to be. Something was off with her, too, and had been for a while. Misty was suffering from an untold issue; she had that in common with Vera and might not know it.

"What day is it?" Vera asked again and swallowed hard against a fast growing catch in her throat. It was tragic she even had to ask with such earnest searching. She'd lost track of time with Derrick, and had he been at the house when she woke she'd have been afraid to inquire, worried it might set him off and he'd give up on her. She wasn't exactly sure what it was that tied him to her and she was taking no chances. It was as if she were waiting for the other shoe to drop, for him to tell her no to some issue she found important. She thought for sure one day he'd get on his bike and never come back, and that fear tore at her with steely claws and sharp fangs.

"Are you all right?" Misty finally eased her frigid demeanor and sought out an answer with a tone akin to true caring.

"Yeah…" Vera cleared her throat. "Yes. I'm just having a rough morning. Plus, the ice and everything being closed for a few days…" Vera said and silently pleaded with Misty to let it go and give her the information.

"It's Friday. Keith makes the supply runs on Friday," Misty reminded her. "Goodness. Why don't you just check your cell phone?"

A wave of nervousness hit Vera. How had she forgotten about her phone? Had it been on her the whole time she was at

Derrick's? Was it still in her coat? Her purse? She resolved to check. Vera also found herself nodding at Misty's suggestion as she simultaneously felt close to crying, without a solid reason as to why. Perhaps that was because there were too many reasons for her brain to choose from. It would be the second time in two days that she'd cry, if only she'd let herself. But, work was no place for it. "Oh, of course. You did say that."

"Yes, I did," Misty agreed awkwardly.

The two women stood there for the longest time and stared at each other. They considered one another and what it would mean to both of them if they kept going the way they were, kept letting an invisible wedge come between them, grow between them. Vera had done it on purpose with Lance. Was she doing it again with Misty? Was she building what would turn out to be an insurmountable hurdle? Was Misty aiding in the cause?

"You look nice today," Misty extended an olive branch. "Those clothes look very warm and seasonal." Misty was a bit more comfortable with the mildly muted down versions of outfits Vera chose to wear to work. They were nothing quite so intimidating as what Vera wore to the last drum circle she'd attended.

Vera peeked at her garments for a second and smoothed the front of the skirt, the more daring piece. "Thanks. Yeah, they are nice and warm. A good thing, too, because it's really cold outside."

Misty nodded politely. "The temperature is up enough for the ice to melt though," she pointed out. "Did you stop by your brother's this morning?" A swift change in the conversation.

"I did… to grab more clothes. You know…" But she doubted highly if Misty did. Misty knew nothing of what Vera had been experiencing lately, which was fair. Vera knew next to nothing about what was going on with Misty.

"Was he still sleeping?"

"I think so," Vera did her best.

Misty nodded again and wiped her hands on a towel. "I better give him a call. He wanted to be up early so that he'd get everything together before his afternoon meeting."

"What meeting?" Vera was so far out of the loop she couldn't even see it anymore, and that hurt when it came to matters concerning John.

"He has a meeting with an investor," Misty explained and then gauged Vera's pained expression as too much. "Don't look that way. I only found out about it yesterday myself. John plays things close to the vest. You of all people should know that. He's taking conservative but significant steps to grow his business."

Vera kept on staring at Misty in that strained and stunned manner.

Misty touched her arm as she moved past. "I'll be sure to let you know how it goes," she promised.

"Ok," Vera said somberly. "Thanks."

Vera followed Misty out of the kitchen just in time to see Keith coming in the front door with boxes and bags. He was loaded down with so much stuff that Vera experienced a mild wave of panic. How much had he spent on this week's run? And, given the slower rate of business recently, could they really afford it? Were the purchases wise? Time with the accounts would be well spent later in the day. Vera resolved to make it happen.

"Oh my god! What did you get?" Vera inquired as she crossed the room to help him drag it all in.

"Everything we needed… and then some," he added with a wink and a smile. "You're here earlier than usual," he commented.

Vera smiled back. "But not as early as I'd like, or as I should be, but I'm working on it. I've gotten into some bad habits," she admitted and locked the door once more.

Keith shrugged and stood up a little taller then. "Yeah, well, it can happen to the best of us. And since you're admitting that you're not entirely professional, I'd like to ask a favor right now," Keith led in.

Vera met his glance straight on. She was impressed that he managed to still treat her like a reasonably competent boss. "Ok, go ahead."

"I'd like to take a long lunch this afternoon," Keith said.

"What time?" Vera inquired, not that it mattered. She knew she was going to say yes. It was only a formality to ask, due diligence.

"I plan to head out around one o'clock and I'll be back as soon as I can," he told her.

"Everything all right?" Vera checked. Keith was usually more forthcoming with details, at least with her.

Keith smiled at her obvious caring. "Definitely."

"You're keeping secrets," Vera softly accused and gave him a playful nudge in the ribs. "They're good ones, I hope."

"Great ones," he assured.

Vera let him have his edge of mystery and began snooping through the bags brimming with a wide assortment of items. She saw bright colors and all sorts of shapes. She reached a hand gingerly into one, grabbed, and then pulled at what was obviously a strand of artificial autumn leaves. "What is all this?" She brought the topic of conversation back around to supplies.

"Harvest decorations for the main room and front windows. I thought it would be a good idea, especially since other stores along this street have displays up, and we missed doing it for Halloween," Keith said plainly, for good ideas never need much defending.

Vera snooped through a couple more bags filled with stick-on art and wreaths and table toppers. "I love it! I think that's a really terrific concept. We could use a boost around here."

"Glad you approve. I'll take some of these boxes around back and shelve, and then afterwards we can start placing the decorations," he suggested as he slipped out of his coat. There was something so undeniably sexy in the methodical way he did it. Vera knew he would be as thorough with every other aspect of his life. He'd already shown her that in the way he worked and the way he arranged private gatherings at his residence. It was in the diligence with which he still seemed to be kindly and respectfully caring for her, maybe even pursuing her. And, a portion of her heart managed to continue to hope that was the case. She didn't want him to give up on her either.

Vera sighed as Keith left the room with the first load of boxes. Maybe she didn't exactly know what she wanted. All she could be sure of in that singular moment was that there seemed to be a new and small infusion of energy coming into her veins. She was getting easily wrapped up in the thought of hanging decorations and putting her attention back where it belonged. Serving coffee and pastries with a smile to the people she'd grown up around sounded quite suddenly like heaven. She was ready, eager, to get right down to it. This was still her goal, still her plan, still her waking dream. She had that to cling to, no matter that the sleeping variety had abandoned her.

Vera took a box or two back herself as Keith finished up with the rest; and after the shelving, it was time to open the doors. It was time to serve coffee and simple, sugary sorts of breakfast foods. It was time to become immersed in glorious everyday living and the drone of routine. There was work to be done and friendships to mend, even if only ever so slightly from a short strain.

The hustle and bustle of the morning rush brought a surge to Vera's weary soul and a flush to her cheeks. By the time it was over, she had more energy than what she'd started with and was chomping at the bit to put out the decorations Keith had unilaterally decided to purchase. There was no reason to reprimand him for his unauthorized actions, or to deny him the long lunch that had him back at the shop in surprisingly short order. Though it did cross Vera's mind briefly to say something about the purchases, to mark her territory and her role. It felt as if words should be said, but then a wiser part of her personality spoke up. Keith had made smart decisions in her absence, and he had treated her like a competent boss upon her return, whether she deserved it or not. Keith and Misty had both kept the place going, kept her dream alive, saved the opportunity for her to come back. There was no benefit to asserting a hierarchy in an environment like that.

When there were only a couple of people left scattered about the main room, sipping coffee and surfing the internet on their wi-fi, Keith brought the bags out from behind the counter, the bags stuffed with fun and festivity.

"Let's do this," he said to her.

Vera whipped her apron off and came from behind the counter. "Let's," she said and took one of the bags from him.

The two of them began laying out items on a couple of empty tables. It was far easier to see and plan that way, and both of them seemed to have the same method for sorting and arranging.

Vera found she didn't have to say a word to Keith; he picked up on her flow and patterns and made his fit into hers by default.

Once the bags were emptied, before them sat an arrangement of autumn wheat and leaf wreaths, long strands of artificial autumn leaves and berries of deep scarlet and bright golden hues, braided sweet grasses, purple and yellow mum table toppers in bubble glass bowls, and a wide variety of stick-on harvest art to place directly onto transparent surfaces. Keith had also gotten a full cornucopia display that Vera immediately knew she was setting by the cash register. Everything would be easy to hang, easy to remove, and full of the abundance of the harvest season… despite the fact that nature blew right through it to a winter's bleak backdrop. Perhaps the new artworks would bring abundance back into her coffeehouse, like attracting like.

"Where to begin?..." Vera said and then snatched up the cornucopia bursting with fake fleshy fruits, wild herbs, grains, and goodness. She walked it over to the counter and placed it strategically so that it accented the register. Orders would be placed, monies received, and happiness a natural by-product. That was her original goal when she'd signed the lease, when she and Misty had taken on this shop and embarked on their business adventure. It was possible to bring that back, and in doing so perhaps the situation with Misty would heal.

Keith grinned at her. "Very nice. You're a natural at this. But, of course, I knew that already," he boasted.

"Oh, you did, did you?" Vera challenged as she came over to the tables.

"Certainly. When you first hired me and this place opened, the wall art and everything else was nicely arranged," he complimented, but Keith's aim was off, unbeknownst to him.

"That wasn't me," Vera told him and picked up a dazzling leaf wreath. "That was Misty. All the artwork and interior decorating was done by Misty."

Keith didn't let his mistake affect him for too long. "Yeah, but… you had to approve it," he pointed out. It wasn't much, but it was a small comeback. He was lifting Vera's spirits. His might have been low after not seeing or hearing from her for days, but he could tell the minute he'd laid eyes on her, it was nothing compared to whatever turmoil she had raging beneath the surface and behind closed doors. He found it within himself to attempt to buoy her. It didn't hurt his efforts that the lunchtime appointment had gone so quickly and so well.

Vera shook her head and smiled at him. "Wrong again. She and I are partners. She can pretty much do whatever she wants, so long as it doesn't hurt the business."

"Well, the vibe in here is you. That's definitely all you," he kept on. He was not a quitter by any stretch of the imagination, and he wasn't prone to distractions.

"And, the shop is falling behind. It's failing." Touché! Vera went to the front door with a stylized hanger and took her time putting up the most attractive wreath Keith had bought. It was of sturdy and welcoming design, not unlike the man who had brought it back for her, for the shop, for a person and place he had no real vested interest in, at least not logically or linearly. It was not a vested interest that Vera could discern.

Suddenly, Vera felt warm, strong hands caressing her arms and body heat radiating along her back. The mood was cautious and courteous and well aware. They were not alone in the shop. A couple of straggling customers and Misty remained. This was not the master bedroom suite out at the farm. This was a public place where anyone walking by or coming in might see, might judge, might whisper about goings on. The heat from Keith's nearness cut right through the wool of her heavy black sweater top. His proximity wasn't fair. It made Vera want to do and say things she knew would only bring trouble.

"It's not failing," Keith corrected her assessment. "Things have slowed down, sure. We can't be positive where it's headed, but the window of opportunity isn't closed, Vera."

His words were so like Lillian's that Vera was instantly and genuinely comforted by them. How had he done that? How had he known what to say? Vera thought the only one so gloriously gifted like that around women was Derrick. Derrick could undo her with a look or a word or a single stride in her direction. Derrick could make her feel elevated or flattened by only the extent of his attention. He could drive her to the highest heaven or the lowest hell. The things Derrick could do were exquisite torture. With Keith it wasn't like that at all… but maybe it was better. Vera sensed a slow burn and another topic riding below the surface of the conversation they were having. "Are you still talking about the shop?" she checked in. It seemed as though he was doing so for her sake, for formality, but in reality he wasn't doing so at the same time, and for his own sake.

"Yes and no," he said and tenderly kissed the back of her head.

Vera let him and didn't peep. She stood there at the front door for a minute or two, glancing out at the moderately bustling street, while also listening to Keith walk about the room, placing more autumn finery. He went straight back to work. He knew the boundaries and how she'd feel. He understood how far was far enough in any given situation.

Vera thought. She thought about a lot of stuff then. She considered what would happen after the sun went down and the shop closed around dinnertime. It wouldn't be long now. Vera knew she'd return to the Thompson house and her memories and the specters that wandered there. She'd cohabitate with the Fate that stalked the home and the grounds, the weedy gardens and the weathered walls. Fate was growing stronger, getting bolder, forcing himself upon her and there may be no stopping it. Elizabeth was probably right in that, that there was no stopping it, and her determination after death could prove it so. Whether the little hand-carved doll was shoved away in her bedroom at John's or appearing in horrid encounters at Derrick's, there seemed to be no stopping it. It was as Elizabeth had told her during the terrible episode from which she'd no recall of escaping — there is no good thinking that because you shut something up in a room, block it off from sight and from thought, that it's gone. That was dangerous. It made one feel in control, and control was an illusion that led to poor outcomes. Vera chastised herself silently. She should've known better by now.

Vera considered these musings as they echoed in her mind, and she stared outside until her breath had fogged up the glass entirely. And, that was how her life felt — foggy. Unclear. Uncertain. Tumultuous. She breathed and breathed. Heavy exhales. She decided to fog up the transparent surface and obscure the rest of the world. There were no answers for her out there. Every time she left the shop to go home, to go back to a world constantly spinning in one dominant direction, she got lost; Vera had a tendency to fall down a proverbial rabbit hole and became this wild, hypersensitive creature no one understood. It was like that, too, when she'd first returned home from college. When she left the sane structure and sanctuary of school; it was then she appeared to be doomed. But, her answers weren't found in the fog either or in the normalcy of the work that continued to reassuringly call her name. Work was at her back; it was tapping her shoulder. It was dangling the promise of productivity. She wanted to bite the lure and preserve bits of sanity a while longer. It was time to check on the account ledgers and know the true state of her coffeehouse, of her joint venture with Misty. What if they couldn't even afford to keep Keith anymore?... Vera's heart sank at the thought. She needed clarity, not this murky abyss.

Vera took a firm hand and swiped at the condensation she'd created, and in doing so revealed a face. It was staring back at her from the other side of the dripping wet glass. It was a smooth, dark, handsome face; it was a smiling face with features as decadent and captivating as the springtime sun. But most of all, it was a familiar face, which therefore made it all the more attractive. It was Isaac.

Isaac waved to her cheerfully and then playfully mimicked her body posture until Vera snapped out of her surprise. She stepped back so he could open the door. Isaac strode into the room with two women right alongside. "I got off work early and decided to swing by. I hope we're not catching you at a bad time," he said politely as he began removing his coat. "Hey, Keith!" Isaac greeted with enthusiasm and a rich timbre that was elevated but not too loud.

"Hey!" Keith shouted jovially to him from across the room, where he was setting down the last table topper. The timing was perfect. The main room looked sensational in all its festive fall finery, a few dirty dishes aside. "Glad you finally made it over here," he said as he joined them.

"It's been on my mind. Casey and Magdalena happened to have the entire day free, so we thought we'd get a jump on the evening. It all came together as it should," Isaac told his friend.

"It's still afternoon, my friend," Keith pointed out.

"Late afternoon," Isaac teasingly amended. "And, it's our early start to the evening."

Vera took Isaac all in, as he was conversing with Keith. She also heard the melodious sounds of two feminine voices entering the conversation and then managed to see that the women he'd brought were familiar, too. Magdalena and Casey. Yes, Isaac had spoken their names, but it had taken Vera several minutes to really recognize them. She was coming back into the outside world slowly, but at least it appeared to be surely. The two women were equally stunning in the sober light of day, but a little less exotic than by the light of the fire. Magdalena held more of an edge in these new surroundings than Casey did, with her dark wavy hair and piercing black eyes.

"Is this a bad time?" Isaac asked Vera directly when she hadn't yet responded to anything being said around her.

"No, no, not at all. It's great to see you," she assured and found her manners rising to the surface of their own accord. Happiness soon followed and she pointed the three visitors to the coat rack as Keith made his way about the room, removing dishes and wiping down what was left of the tables to be bussed. "Please, come in and make yourselves at home. Can I get you anything? It's on the house," Vera offered graciously, without knowing if she could actually afford it. Commonplace worry was settling in alongside her supernatural stressors.

Isaac gave her a quick study, as though it were no big deal to glean massive amounts of information from her in a second and without any further questions. "I'd enjoy a simple coffee, if that isn't too much," he replied and led Casey and Magdalena to the nearest table, drawing out their chairs before being seated himself.

"Cream and sugar?" Vera prompted further.

"Neither, thank you," he said and casually stretched his long, muscular legs. Vera could tell how strong he was, even clad in demin and a substantial sweater. He was strong in body, mind, and presence. And clad in fiery shades of yellow, orange, and red, he visually dominated the room. His large stature and awesome dreadlocks aided in that, too.

"Ladies?" Vera turned to the two women she'd met at the last drum circle she'd attended. How long ago had that been? It felt simultaneously recent and also far too long. She missed it. Vera hadn't been aware of how much she'd missed it until laying eyes on the people involved, the little community that had formed around the weekly event. She'd been too busy pleasing Derrick, and being pleased and harassed by Derrick, to really notice. She rode the private waves of pleasure and terror out to sea and had no idea how far away land was becoming.

"Mocha latte and whatever it is that smells so sweetly of cinnamon," Magdalena said, not shy about her desires. Her accent filled the room, making it an incredibly inviting place, more so than it had been in weeks.

Vera nodded. "That's Misty's pecan rolls. They're delicious." She then turned to Casey.

"Do you have any teas?" Casey asked.

"A wide assortment. If you want to pop up to the counter and pick out one you like, I'll get the hot water and bring it to the table," Vera instructed kindly and watched as Casey dashed over to the counter. She was a live wire, that one. She always seemed to be switched on and moving fast. Her bright blonde hair was a couple shades lighter than Misty's, and her porcelain skin seemed to have an internal glow of its own. As it was, Casey reminded Vera a great deal of Misty, and even more of how Misty used to be before whatever burden had arrived and dimmed her luminescence, flattened the spring in her step.

Vera turned her attention back to the two remaining parties at the table. "Anything else?" she checked.

"I think you're giving us more than enough for this little impromptu visit," Isaac told her.

Vera waved his words off. "Nonsense. I'll be right back." She darted into the kitchen to retrieve the pastry and encountered Misty there, already putting a roll on a plate.

Misty handed it to her. "Here you go."

Vera accepted. "Thanks." It was as she turned to head out into the dining area that the question occurred to her. "Why don't you come on out and join us? I think the day has pretty much tapered off."

"Oh," Misty hedged, "I don't think so. They're really more your friends than mine," she said. It was the first real instance of Misty cracking the wall that had started to build between them.

Vera sensed the fragility immediately and extended again. "Actually, they're Keith's friends and folks we both know from drum circle. You've probably seen them more than I have; I've been such an odd recluse lately. Come on out," Vera encouraged.

Misty shook her head. "I'd rather not."

Vera held out a hand, an empty hand, a hand not holding a culinary masterpiece. "Come on," she said, hoping they were still close enough Misty would take her up on it. "I need help gathering the hot water and coffee drinks," she pressed.

Misty took hold of Vera, of the woman she'd once been very, very close to. They'd shared many a good time, many a fond memory. What was happening to them now? Whatever it was, it came from inside Misty and she could hardly get a grip on it. The issue was slippery inside her, despite having vocalized it to John some time ago. Words hadn't cured it; they had complicated it. She looked at Vera in the strong lighting of the kitchen before they proceeded out and realized then and there the transformation hadn't mattered so much as the reality of the whole person. Misty hadn't really seen Vera out of her shell before moving into town and taking up the coffeehouse venture. She hadn't seen her friend for all she could be until whatever it was about being home and going to drum circle had dragged it out of her. Maybe it was Vera living in what had been her grandmother's house that brought her back to self. Maybe it was whatever so possessed her about the house next door. It might have been Keith or Derrick or her brand new friends that sparked it. Whatever the causative factor, Misty knew one thing for sure; it wasn't anything about her that made Vera into the marvel she was naturally, and that compounded Misty's agitation even more.

The two women set to work behind the counter, gathering hot water, whipping up Magdalena's mocha latte, and pouring a quick cup of the house brew for Isaac. Misty arranged everything while her mental gears were grinding, including the pecan roll with plate on a tray, and then she gave a quick 'hello' out to the visitors before sending Vera to the table with everything.

Misty preferred to stay behind the counter… and watch. She had a lot to process due to her fluctuating feelings and thought patterns. She couldn't afford to force them upon Vera again.

Vera didn't press her friend and business partner any harder. She went about her work and set everything down on the table for their guests.

"Please," Isaac said as he got to his feet, "have a seat, Vera." He pulled over an extra chair for her.

No one looked to Misty. Not a single person in the room invited her over, causing Vera to feel the edge of pity rubbing up against her stomach.

Vera glanced about the room and noticed that the other customers had already left and there was no one in there but her acquaintances from drum circle, Keith's friends. Keith himself had already taken a seat and brought over a cup of coffee.

Vera shrugged. "Ok. Why not?..." She relaxed in the chair next to Isaac, putting Misty from her mind with a quick pang of guilt. Time to be cordial.

"So, what has happened to all the beautiful clothes and hair and makeup that I remember you having?" Magdalena put it to her, as she bit off a piece of the pecan delight.

"Magda, she's working. It's obvious those are her work clothes," Casey chirped as she dipped a tea bag about a dozen times in rapid succession.

"Ahhh…" Magdalena said and gave a long pause. "Are they? You do not seem comfortable in them," she noted with her lovely accent and tilted her face downward, but only so she could peer up over the edge of her latte mug with friendly, well-meaning suspicion.

Vera laughed nervously. "I grabbed the first clothes I could find when I bolted out of the house this morning," she confessed. "You know how it is when you try to get a jump on the day…"

"Are you planning to change into another ensemble, something more you, before we see you at drum circle tonight?" Isaac asked, taking a short sip from his coffee cup.

"You are coming tonight, right, Vera? I messaged you about it days ago," Keith informed her.

"You did?" Vera inquired, relaying a great deal of surprise in her tone. "I didn't see a message come through."

"I sent you a text," he added.

"I'm sorry. I must've missed it. I'll check my phone before I go home today," Vera promised. She wondered who else might have called or texted her. She'd never heard her phone go off. What else had she missed? What else did she not know about? What was is about the Thompson house that made the entire world outside of it seem so far away? It had always been that way though. That place made the rest of the world seem practically impossible to touch.

"Will you be there?" Isaac gently lured her to answer his question about later that evening, about drum circle.

"It'll be in the barn, so no fire but lots of fun anyway," Casey chimed in and gave Vera a sweet little smile. "Keith lights all the lanterns. It's really something!"

"It's a lot of little contained fires," Keith jested and winked at Casey.

Vera couldn't understand for the life of her why these people should take such an interest. They barely knew her. Why should it matter so much if she went to Keith's circle? What Vera had shared with Isaac the few times she'd seen him had been special and very unique, but it wasn't life altering. Magdalena and Casey were even newer in her sphere, as she was in theirs. Why should it be so important? Vera couldn't deduce an answer. She was lacking in clues. Either that or there was no logic about it at all, which bothered and intrigued her.

"I don't know if I can go," Vera replied hesitantly. She hated disappointing people, but it wasn't until just this morning that she'd found out it was Friday. She was totally unprepared, and she knew Derrick would expect her to spend the evening with him.

"Oh, why not?" Magdalena queried, as she polished off her pecan roll in two more large bites. She was quite the voracious woman. "Is it not your life?"

No, it wasn't. Vera could see that now. It had become Derrick's and so fast. It was Derrick's life. He was expecting her to come to him after work, and that was what she intended to do. She would walk over to the house as soon as the shop closed. She would go there straight away, no questions asked and no thought towards her own needs. It was as if she were a homing pigeon flying right into the gaping maw of the most hypnotic snake. Even if Derrick decided not to be home himself, she knew she would go there. She would go there and wait for him. After all, he'd said he had plans, plans for them alone. The note in his scribbled scrawl was on her dresser to prove it. Black and white evidence of promises made, vows to be fulfilled. Vera couldn't resist the possibilities, the attention, the carnivorous desire.

"I guess Fate is just set down against me being able to go to these things lately," Vera replied rather haphazardly. Her words seemed to spill everywhere, carelessly, as they came tumbling half solid with determination out of her mouth. Derrick had plans for them. There was no way she could go.

Isaac sighed and stretched the slightest bit before leaning in to speak with Vera. He leaned in as though he were telling her a secret, but spoke loud enough for everyone at the table to hear. "It's only when an inner situation is not made fully conscious that it appears outside of you… as a sort of Fate."

The rest of the workday was a strange whirl of delightful and insightful conversation, and it eventually drew to a natural end at closing time. The sun had set by then; the days were short as leaves disintegrated on the ground and a few flurries floated about the air. Goodbyes were exchanged as Misty made her way back to the kitchen to clean up and shut down. Vera got up to retrieve her coat and purse and check messages. Keith had his own last minute dialogues with members of the group.

Vera pulled her phone out of her coat pocket to find it had a decent charge left, and that she did indeed have several messages and a few missed calls. She'd never heard her phone ring, not once. Granted, she hadn't always been nearby, but she found it hard to believe that all those texts and calls went unnoticed. Vera also found it unusual that the phone, although infrequently used, held the charge for so long. Days had gone by at Derrick's and she hadn't plugged her phone in once. It wasn't possible, for time didn't stand still at the Thompson house. On the contrary, it ticked by in measured increments, each second well known and accounted for, slippery or not.

Vera went to the texts on her phone first and saw one was a drum circle reminder from Keith and three were ice warnings and no show updates, one from Misty and two more from Keith. She hadn't missed anything really pressing, but she'd missed communications that should've been snagged. They deserved a bare minimum response from her, and she'd neglected to send any. There were also the voicemails. And as it turned out, they were all from Keith. Vera hit play on the first one eagerly. What had he called to tell her?...

Keith was concerned about her. That had been the gist of the first message. He was checking in to make sure she was all right, since he hadn't heard back about the ice or the status of the shop. It was touching. It was responsible and sweet, like the source. Vera looked over her shoulder at him. She examined the back of him, the line of him. He was even more delectable than when she'd first laid eyes on him, first held hands with him, first kissed him. He was tall and broad about the shoulders, but lean and lanky and fluid in his movements. He was self-assured and carried the burden of others well.

Vera heard herself sigh and then turned attention back to her phone. The second and third messages went beyond touching; they were downright stirring. Keith spoke of how he cared about her and hoped she wasn't out in the weather, trying to get to the coffeehouse. He also hoped she was safe and sound at home and everything was going ok. He asked about Misty and her brother. And, there were instructions to call him if she needed anything, if she needed food or water or if the furnace went out. He would do whatever he had to; he would get to her. He was sure that if needs be, his truck would be able to make it through. Vera played them all and then she played them all through again. She listened until she heard the distinct sound of footsteps coming up behind her.

Vera whirled around to see Keith only a few feet away and the rest of the people milling about the dining area, more than likely waiting for him. They acted as though they were interested in the artworks on the walls and the types of tea on display, but Vera suspected they were more curious about what would happen next. There was an electric current of excitement sizzling about the space.

Vera smiled as he reached less than an arm's length away. She gazed into his gray and hazel eyes and saw gentility there. For a man who had been in the military, for a man that had seen the rough underbelly of life, who may have seen war, he was always startlingly gentle. Maybe the stress of holding the horrors of humanity back and fighting off death, destruction, and Fate had been the cause of the faint lines around his mouth and eyes. The lines were what he had to show for his efforts; they showed he was not naïve. His kindness was most certainly not born out of weakness.

Vera held up her phone. "I finally got around to checking messages," she said, a tad embarrassed. "I'm sorry I missed your calls."

"I'm sorry, too. I would've preferred hearing from you," he replied.

"The weather was severe and it was thoughtless of me not to assume people would check in," she went on. But, then her brain spawned a couple questions from the soil of that rich logic. Why had her brother not called? Didn't he care where she was and if she was all right?

Sadness flashed across Vera's delicate features and Keith instinctively reached out for her.

"Yes, but I forgive you," he said and took her hands.

"Keith, I —"

"Enough," he said in a whisper and brought his face in close to hers. If she listened to the messages all the way through, then she knew. He knew that she knew, and it shouldn't shock her what was coming next. Keith felt it had all been enough, and he feared ever since the ice initially set in that if he didn't make a firm and bold move at the next organic opportunity, then he'd never would. He'd never get the chance again, not in this lifetime. It would surely pass him by.

Vera was right. The air was electrified. Something profound was about to happen. She felt as though the earth should tremble below her feet. It should open wide and swallow them both. A lightning bolt should rip the sky in two and come crashing into the coffeehouse. The bolt should charge them with massive amounts of energy and let parts of them shrivel into ash and die. The old needed to burn away and be done so that they could get around to the business of healing, the work of pulling themselves together into something completely whole.

Keith wrapped Vera in his arms and brought her in close. He held her as tight as he could and also allow her room to breathe. He wanted to feel her soft and pliant self pressed against the length of his body. He wanted her to have no one else on her mind and nowhere else to go. And, when he was satisfied that she wasn't speaking and fairly positive she wasn't thinking, he kissed her. He kissed her long and hard and deep. He kissed her in the way that every little girl dreams a man will kiss her one day, with all that he is, telling her that she alone can make him everything that he might be.

Vera was shaking as she kissed him back. She was so voracious and so overcome that she didn't know how she was standing on her own two feet. Was Keith helping to hold her up? The world burned away in a lightning flash that wasn't really there. No one else saw it and no thunder followed to verify.

Only a single word was spoken to break the spell Keith had her under, the spell she had him bound by. An utterance from Magdalena brought Keith and Vera around to the shared and hard reality.

"Wow!" Magdalena exclaimed. She truly had no shame. With eyes as black as crow feathers she looked at the hunk of man that was Derrick. He was insatiable and impressive. And, Vera ashamedly experienced a surge of jealousy; it rose up fast and unbidden within her, a furious possessiveness.

Casey stared at Derrick, too. Riveted.

But, Derrick didn't take in anything other than Vera, Vera and the man who had ahold of her. He charged across the room before Isaac could intercept or Keith could properly react. "What the hell?!" he boomed and ripped Keith from Vera's clutches.

Keith was thrown off balance but only for a split second before Vera saw him charging back, ready to take on the one person who stood in his way. Enough.

Vera could still hear the word the way Keith said it to her, in a whisper. Enough.

Time seemed to slow down. Isaac emerged in the center of the scuffle and pushed the two men apart. But, he seemed not like one man; he appeared to Vera again as two, as he had during circle.

"Enough!" Isaac proclaimed and Keith stepped away.

"I'll end you!" Derrick raged on as Isaac gripped him. Derrick was a large and powerful man, but next to Isaac he was nothing. Not because Isaac was that much bigger in physical space, but because he was that much more in all the other planes of existence. Vera could see it now as she'd seen it then, in the firelight and the moon glow. Isaac was far more than anyone could ever hope to comprehend.

Vera stood transfixed until she heard a small tinkling, a musical clatter. Some object had dropped. Something had fallen to the floor and no one else noticed. Magdalena and Casey stood transfixed by the violent outburst. No one realized it except her.

Isaac's gaze met her own. Except Isaac. He looked at Vera and then down to the floor.

The tiny key gleamed in the bright light of the shop. It was still attached to the chain Derrick constantly wore around his neck. It was the key to that ancient diary, that sacred journal marked 'EMD.'

"What's going on out here?" Misty demanded as she came barging out of the kitchen.

Derrick peeled Isaac off him with an irritated chant. "All right, all right, all right!"

Isaac let him go but kept a close and wary eye.

Derrick slicked his long hair back and away from his face. He rolled his shoulders and puffed some air in and out of his lungs. He glanced at Vera and then looked to Keith. "You touch her again —"

"And, what?" Keith tested. "What will you do?"

Baited like a wild beast, Derrick rushed his competition again, to have Isaac intervene once more. Only this time, Derrick stepped away and paced about the room, trying to cool off, attempting to plan in the heat of the moment. He didn't want to contend with Isaac. Blinded by his anger and mounting frustrations, he didn't see Vera retrieve the key from the floor. He didn't notice her shoving it in her coat pocket and then sharing a long moment locked in the depths of Isaac's dark irises.

Vera knew what she had to do. She went to Derrick's side. "Please, please, take me home."

Chapter 10

Vera rode behind Derrick on his bike, partially shielded from the freezing winds and biting snowflakes that tended to hit the skin like small shards of glass. The sun had gone down completely and the fiery rays that remained after were disappearing fast. Derrick rode out of town instead of taking her home. He drove along the highway and into the night. He took her away from the place she knew and the people she loved. He took her from friends and family and her most prized possessions. He totally uprooted her and didn't stop driving until an internal sensor went off and he pulled the motorcycle over, finding a nook of gravel nestled up against a barren tree line.

Derrick dismounted and resumed pacing. Vera was starting to suspect that was the only outlet he had, the only coping strategy he knew, other than attacking whatever set him off, verbally or otherwise.

Vera continued to sit on the bike and positioned herself sideways so she could watch him, gauge him, and decide on the next best move. She didn't speak. She was too cold. She was so cold she could barely shiver anymore and had lost most of the sensation in her hands and feet. There was no running from what came next. Derrick had taken her out so far, and she doubted she'd have the circulation in her limbs to escape if she wanted to.

Hoot owls cried and the winds whistled a warning through the frosty treetops.

And, then all went still. Everything was frozen. The palpable feeling of being watched emerged in a circular format.

Derrick spoke at long last. "This can't go on, not for another day, not for another minute." He was calmer than Vera thought he would be, or at least his tone was calm and reserved. A sharp edge of energy was spiking though. His boundary, his demand, was definitely going somewhere, stretching, encompassing more than it had the day before and the day before that.

Vera gazed at him longingly in the low light. The rays of the dying sun were all but gone and the moon gave off a soft glow from behind a misty bit of cloud cover. The lunar orb weaved in and out of the nebulous veils like some form of exotic dancer, keeping a pace that neither of the mortals below seemed to recognize. Derrick was exceptional in the lunar radiance, and made to look completely unreal in the enchanted light. His long dark hair tousled by wind and by rage, his strong stature looming amid sharp shadows, the chiseled line of his jaw shaded with beard stubble and set with purpose. And more than all of that, there was the daring and unnatural green shade of his eyes. He pierced her with a fleeting glance and then took his attention away.

"You have a decision to make," he finally spoke again. "We both have decisions to make."

Vera was just about to respond when Derrick mounted the bike once more and took off, barely giving her enough notice to grip him. Her hands flew about his waist and she clung on tightly. He'd turned the bike around and from all indications was headed back to town. Vera hugged him; she hugged him tight and buried her face in the surface of his icy leather jacket. He was so cold, impossibly cold. Vera nuzzled up against him and sensed something else growing beneath the cool, hardened exterior. There was a hole and it went straight to the heart of him, deeper, to the soul of him. Some tumultuous sea sat there in the center. It was bashed about and there was screaming, silent and primal screaming. At Derrick's center, at the sea and seat of his soul, Vera found and recognized peculiar pain. She knew that pain. Mourning… and maybe something more…

Derrick parked his motorcycle along the curb in front of the Thompson house, in his usual space. The space was so frequently used that a small oil stain had developed on the concrete. He dismounted and Vera followed. She took a couple of steps away and towards her brother's house.

"I need to pick up a few things," she explained. "It won't take long."

"There's a discussion between us that needs to happen," Derrick insisted. When he spoke to her like that, with such strength and determination and keenness, she felt the way she did when she'd originally noticed him up on the porch, kicked back in a chair. It had been a late summer day and the sun set him ablaze when he'd joined her on the sidewalk. Tree roots twisted and turned up under her feet then and the world was coming apart, and she was lost, lost to him, lost for him. She'd found him magnetic and charismatic and everything else that made up the composite of irresistible. There'd been a dark, brooding melancholy she now understood to actually be masked anguish. He wasn't hiding it as well. He wasn't as deep or mysterious as he'd initially seemed, just tortured.

"I'll meet you over there. I just have to grab some of my stuff," she held her ground as best she could while taking another couple of steps away. Did she love him less now that he was more relatable, more anguished, more human? Or did she love him more? Vera wasn't even sure she loved him at all. She wanted him though, and maybe that was what mattered. Vera's body ached for him.

Derrick gave a single nod and strode up the steps, onto the darkened porch, and then inside Lillian's old home. Vera contemplated the outwardly dilapidated structure for a minute. It wouldn't be long before some of the elements began rotting the inside if measures weren't taken to prevent it. The gardens were gone. Was the house itself next? Slowly? Surely? As Vera continued to give the place a quick and sentimental survey, she noticed a new object in the auspices of the tiny front lawn, more like an obligatory patch of grass. It was a small, square sign pressed deeply into the cooling earth. Vera was too far away to read what it said, so she took a step forward and then another and another, until the blurry lines coalesced into words: 'Under Contract, S&N Development.'

The Thompson house was for sale. There was a potential buyer. It was a one-two punch of information slamming into Vera's brain. When she found her wits about her again, she dashed to her brother's house. She had to retrieve her things quickly. She had to get to Derrick and beg him to reconsider, plead with him not to sign anything, not to take an action that couldn't be undone. A development firm would more than likely destroy the house, tear it down and put up some modular monstrosity in its stead. Vera entered her brother's house, her current albeit little used home, in a state of panic and slammed right into Frank in the pitch black living room.

The dog yelped, skittered away, and started to pant in upset. Vera switched on the overhead lights.

Frank gazed at her with a mixture of adoration and disillusionment.

"Oh god!" she said just to get it out. He'd startled her a bit, but she was more pissed off at her foolishness for not turning the lights on right away. "Sorry, Frank. Poor baby," she cooed and clapped her hands, bringing the large dog with the lustrous black coat to her. Frank indulged her in appreciation and let her pet him to assuage her guilt. Vera kissed his muzzle and reminded him that he was a good boy. She patted his head and his back and then stood to full height for the more recent shock she was to endure.

The entire living room had changed. The furniture was rearranged and the drapes were a different color and fabric. The television set was gone and in its place was a forested mural and standing vase full of decorative feathers. The room was no longer sparse and functional. It was airy and easy. This was not her brother's house anymore, despite some of his stuff sitting in it. It was immediately apparent that this house was a home to John and Misty.

"What is going on here?" Vera breathed and looked to Frank as though he should answer.

Frank followed Vera into the first hallway that emptied out into the dining area and kitchen. More rearranging, except for the breakfast nook that went virtually untouched. The walls of the kitchen had been painted over and made to be sunshine yellow. There were herb bundles hanging on the walls and impressionistic pictures of wine and cheese and fruit. A few of Misty's garments, a sweater and a couple of scarves, were tossed over chairs. And as Vera peered down the second part of the hallway, she saw boxes at the end. She made her way towards her own room and switched on the hallway light fixture. Boxes with labels in Misty's own handwriting were taking up space in a back corner, waiting to be unpacked, whenever their owner was good and ready to do so.

It was quite obvious to Vera now. Misty lived there. Misty was living with her brother and no one had bothered to tell her, not in a text, a phone call, or in person. At that point in time, Vera would've accepted any of the communication mediums, but she had received none. She'd spent the whole day with Misty, and they'd started to make progress back across the strained divide that had cracked the length of their friendship, yet Misty said nothing about this gigantic development. Misty kept her out of the loop on purpose. As far as Vera was concerned, that was not the act of a friend, no matter what Vera herself had done lately. There was no justification Misty could give for this withholding.

In a state of growing upset, Vera went to her room alone. She heard Frank trot down the length of the hall after her door was shut, probably heading back to the living room for naptime on the sofa, awaiting his master's return. With the room fully lit and the ceiling fan whirling gently, Vera turned around in the mindset of efficiently packing. But, she was halted. She took a couple of paces and then stopped dead in her tracks. On her dresser, plain as day and plainer, was the doll. It sat there in a most innocuous manner, as though there were nothing remarkable about it, save the fact that it had neither visible eyes nor arms. It sat there as though it were harmless, a trinket, a grotesque piece of artwork and nothing more. It sat there as though it had never left, never accosted Vera for Elizabeth's sake in the upstairs hallway next door. It had situated itself rather disturbingly on top of Derrick's note from the morning, as if Vera had set it there, only she hadn't. And if she wished to retrieve the note, she'd have to touch the grotesque little creation. She'd have to do the one thing that had gotten her into this mess, if Elizabeth's explanation was to be believed.

Vera narrowed her gaze at the object. It had ahold of her; it was sabotaging her… or causing her to sabotage herself. She was clinging tighter and tighter to Derrick, tighter and tighter to the Thompson house with her emotionally charged, phantom limbs. Just because no one could see it in physical reality, didn't mean it wasn't happening, that they weren't there. Clutching. Gripping. Scraping. Vera was losing herself in the madness, in the connection, that was clear enough.

"Go on," Vera said very low, "move." She verbally prodded the doll.

The dark wooden figure sat motionless.

"Do something," Vera said a little louder.

It did nothing.

"Look at me! I know you can! Look at me! Look at me!" she screeched and shoved her face so near the surface of the hand-carved idol that she could smell the oaky aroma of the highly polished grain.

The doll did absolutely nothing.

"Why are you doing this?" she inquired, lowering her voice again.

"Because I am a terrible person," came Elizabeth's retort from directly behind her. It was meant to be candid and witty and horrible all at the same time, as it was meant to be the first time she'd spoken it, and the reply hit its marks... again.

Vera whirled about only to catch a flash of Elizabeth, a twinkling in the corner of her eye and the old woman in the white gown, with the undead vendetta born out of spite and pain, was gone.

"Time's almost out," Elizabeth's voice stayed... it whispered.

Vera wasted no more of her own time. She packed up a few necessary belongings in a bag as fast as she could. She had to get to Derrick.

As Vera made her way to the edge of the dining nook and start of the kitchen, she met John coming in the back side door. She met him as he met Frank. John patted the dog with loving care and then took a moment to let him out into the backyard before coming into the room again, before confronting Vera. He stopped and stared at her from across the table where the two of them had shared so many meals and childhood conspiracies.

"You look surprised to see me," Vera broke the tense silence between them.

John nodded. "To be quite frank, I am. I wasn't sure when to expect you to pop in again."

"I guess not... since you've decided to move Misty in here," Vera laid it out. She had to get to her point fast, reach some sort of resolution and get to Derrick's. If the resolution was only temporary, a patch for now, it would have to do. "I did stop by this morning, you know," she went on. Vera hadn't noticed all the changes then. It was early and dark and she'd been in a tremendous hurry, like now. But, now was when she did notice. This evening she flipped on the lights and took the newness in.

"Had you been here more, you would've noticed. This has been a work in progress since the end of October," he reported.

Thanksgiving, the harvest, it was fast approaching. Vera knew that much. She probably would've known more had she kept in touch with friends and family or even bothered to peek at her own cell phone, carefully tucked away in a coat pocket. End of October. She'd been neglecting her obligations for that long, and in some respects even longer. John gave her a distinct time frame to measure absences by; John was precise. He remembered all the details. He arranged them sequentially for her in a single sentence.

There was no way Vera was going to win a family battle with John, not in her current state of mind.

"How was your meeting this afternoon?" Vera switched tracks and attempted a mend. Perhaps that was only a temporary patch solution, too.

"Misty told you." It was more of a statement than a question.

Vera nodded. "Yes. Why didn't you?"

"You weren't here," he offered again. Logical. Linear. Cold. It was cold and calculated. The chill was what really bothered Vera about her brother's response. He could be all those other things on any given day and at any given moment, and it would be natural, but he was rarely if ever cool towards her. This was the same chill he'd displayed towards the slight memory of their father and the subject of their mother. This was the detachment he reserved for people who'd abandoned him.

"You could've called. There's been ice and bad weather… you could've called." Vera defended.

"You could've called, too," he reminded her. "A phone works both ways. Text. Email…"

Vera shook her head. "Let's not do this now."

"Ok. That's fine," John acquiesced. "I can see you have somewhere else to be," he eyed her bag. "But, we'll have to talk and soon."

"About what?" Vera asked.

"About our living arrangements. They're not going to work anymore," he said most succinctly.

Vera saw her brother, a man moving on with his life, and she saw that she'd been a flash in the pan. She'd come back from school and allowed herself to be welcomed in, only to find her tendencies had forced her out again. It was just like it had been when they were in high school, right after the terrible nightmare episodes concluded. She'd re-entered his world only to find he had no place for her. He had other things, pressing issues and engagements. It was just as it had been then… only, no, it was worse now. This time there was a relationship that also took precedence for him above Vera. This time there was Misty.

Vera shouldn't have stalled. She was very aware Derrick was waiting inside the Thompson house, his house, for her. She feared she'd cut him deep, too deep, by kissing Keith, by being caught kissing Keith. Vera felt she should go to Derrick straight away and have whatever discussion they were about to have, together, alone. She felt inclined to beg his forgiveness and put whatever embers she sensed slowly burning for Keith from her heart. She felt she might agree to put him from her mind, and if Derrick insisted further, from her life. They were going to have a discussion. And, it might be the last one, depending on how upset her explosive paramour turned out to be. He was reactionary, and she was the one bearing the brunt of those reactions. Up until the night that now held them both separately, she'd handled it all so well. But, life was unraveling fast, coming undone at the seams. The main problem was none of it was in her original plans. Vera's plans had been to come home, start up a coffeehouse with her supposed best friend, make decent money, have a relationship with her brother again, find someone safe for herself, and live happily and normally ever after. There was supposed to be structure. That was the ideal for which Vera had braced herself. That was what she'd intended to set up.

Fate had demolished it. Fate was what left her standing amid brown ivy tendrils, dead dandelions greens gone black and ashy, and fast frozen earth. Fate had turned her world and her intentions end over end and thrust her out into the night.

Vera left her brother's house, bag in hand, and went to stand alone in the weedy lot that had once been the spot of sumptuous gardens. She peered up at the mostly overcast sky, the graceful arc of the moon as it moved in and out of the veiling billows. She thought of how it would've looked had the oak tree not been cut down all those years ago. If her axis mundi had been there; it was the only father figure she'd ever really known and ever really loved, and she would've sought its quiet counsel. She would've leaned back against its creviced bark and waited for enlightenment, waited for peace, waited for possibilities to come forth. But her friend, her love, and her masculine connection were gone. It was all gone, save for the remains that had been carved into a hideous fiend to torment her. The irony of that aspect was not lost on Vera.

Vera understood her brother's internal workings well enough to know he would give her all of the reasonable time she needed to find another place and move out. The problem was, she was almost certain there was still no pay to draw for herself from the coffeehouse. She wasn't dating Lance anymore, and hadn't been in quite some time. When she thought back to him, she could barely remember the distinctive features of his face. He was becoming a blur, a mysterious phantom of the past with great height and blonde hair. She didn't have a firm commitment to or with Keith, and given the unfolding of events at the shop, she doubted any of that was on the horizon. No, she had no faith that Keith's proverbial ship would be there to save her. There was nowhere else for her to go. Nowhere but inside the Thompson house and hope that Derrick would take her in on a more permanent basis. But, she'd never had any idea what to expect from him moment to moment, and it was even worse now that she'd thrown a huge emotional monkey wrench into the mix.

Vera stood there in the frosty and frigid night. She stood in the back lot of the Thompson house until her extremities had gone almost completely numb. She usually felt so much. It was brief and blessed relief to feel practically nothing. And, it was then that the winds started to pick up. It was then that some invisible animal started to prowl around her, sticking close to the shadows.

There was nowhere else for Vera to go. There was nowhere else. The thought rolled around in her head. She was chanting it silently to herself. The words were echoing in each synaptic corridor of her brain.

"I have nowhere else to go," she finally said it out loud, speaking to the night and to the Fate that stalked her in it. "I-I just thought I would have more time…" she whined piteously.

It was then that she heard it. "We always think we will have more time… and then it runs out." The winds spoke to her.

Vera ran… out on her life and smack into the open maw of the Thompson house. The back door was open in expectation.

It was probably because Vera came in through the back door that she didn't notice right away. And, there was certainly more to take in. Surprises were in order. Shocks. But because of the area of entry, Vera just didn't see it coming. The few scant herbs were still hanging from the rafter beams in the kitchen and the dining room she walked through next appeared virtually untouched in the dusky glow. The grandfather clock winked at her with its metallic face as she strode by. In only one day, the world had changed. In a matter of mere hours, the foundation of her life had begun to crack and erode. It was when she discovered Derrick standing in the living room, staring out of one of the front windows, she also came upon another discovery. A good deal of the finer furnishings had been removed.

"What's going on here?" Vera blurted.

Derrick turned around slowly and took his time gauging the severity of her stunned expression. She was totally shocked. She was disarmed. She was left unbalanced and grappling. That made her practically helpless. What Derrick hadn't been prepared to cope with was how that helplessness would make him feel. He was so unused to dealing with internal explosions, any emotions raging other than anger and distain, that the quaint countenance of subtle harm threw him. He felt bad. He felt pity. Remorse. Derrick quickly attempted to wall back up. "What does he mean to you?" Derrick asked pointedly, ignoring her question to him.

Vera shook her head. "Where's the sofa and the chairs and —"

"What does Keith mean to you?" he overrode, remembering his promise, thinking on the sanctity of vows. Many people may have thought very little of him after getting to know him, his own family found no joy in his presence, but he had never broken a promise in his life. Derrick didn't want to disappoint or fail his grandmother. He took a step towards Vera, a powerful stride. It was enough so that his shadow cascaded over her face.

Vera glanced down at her feet and had a flurry of responses rush across her brain in a single second, from which she selected one. "He's confusing to me," she began. "He's a friend and a coworker… obviously."

Derrick had a scowl on his face, a brooding expression of disappointment tinged with regret. It made Vera wonder if he regretted everything he'd done with her, if he regretted getting involved with her or even knowing her. Maybe he wished he'd never said hello as she'd passed him by that summer evening. Was he sorry he'd brought her into this house? Was he shameful of the things they'd done, especially now that she'd proven herself unfaithful to him to some degree?

Vera was caught being unfaithful again. She'd been so with Lance when she'd taken up with Derrick, and she was doing the same thing to Derrick with Keith. If she'd found herself with Keith, could she be trusted to stay there and be honest and caring and filled to the brim with happy fidelity? Vera wanted to believe she was capable of bonding completely with someone, but she doubted it. She could cling tightly, but she could not commit fully. She could not bond and believe she wouldn't get hurt. The old wound was still there, the wound she'd carried all her life. It was the injury she shared with John, only he seemed to be healing, scarring over, and moving on. Vera was stuck. Vera was bleeding, bleeding to the point of hemorrhage.

"You have a decision to make," Derrick informed her and came in very close, so close she could smell his signature scent, the aroma of leather and oil and healthy flesh. There was also something woodsy about him this time, as though he'd wandered through a thick forest before coming home, which Vera knew he hadn't done.

"I do?" Vera chirped inquisitively, a quick and careful checking as Derrick slid his hands around her waist and pressed her to him. He rested his chin on top of her head in a guarding manner, and it was the closest thing to manly protection that Vera had known in a long time. It was overwhelmingly potent. Vera felt herself melt into him, going boneless, swaying back and forth as he rocked her and as she swooned. It was like being under mild sedation. Delightful. Unsafe. Unwise.

"Vera," he said her name in a low tone, but gingerly. It was the only gentleness she'd ever come across in the man. She hadn't been sure he was capable of it, actually. There was a longing and a regret and yet a strange determination wavering beneath the surface. It was as though Derrick were caught in a paradox, wanting and needing two mutually exclusive things. "Soon I will be clearing this place out. Everything will be sold. I'm getting rid of whatever I can and taking the cash." That was his admission and underneath it was a growl. Whether Derrick had growled or another entity near the two of them had done so, was unknown to Vera. Derrick had spoken a truth, that much was clear and hurtful. He was clearing out the house. The sign outside said that he was also selling it. Had that been all there was to it, Vera might have been able to eventually recover. If that were all Derrick had to say, she would've somehow been fine with it. But there was more. Derrick stopped himself short. He had a decision to make, too, but he hadn't come to it yet. And, a shadowed being in the room was stalking them both, stalking Vera mostly. Fate's primary target was locked in place, but Derrick's wavering dedication was beginning to grate. It was wearing Fate thin, and Derrick, too.

Vera buried her face in his chest and attempted to hold back the tears. She didn't want to look out at the room anymore. She didn't want to see the rest of the house and know what it had been and then imagine what it would be in only a few days. If Derrick was determined to clear it out, and from all appearances he was, then he'd have no trouble. The town was lousy with antique stores, and the women who owned them would fall under the spell of his charm. Vera fought to hold tears back, but they fell anyway.

She wept to the point where Derrick's shirt became sopping wet. Everything was spinning out of control. Were the seeds of Fate she'd sown with Elizabeth and that dreadful doll long ago finally about to bear poisonous fruit?

"You have a decision to make, Vera," he said again as she dug her fingers into the fabric of his shirt. "You can stay here and lose it all, lose me, too… or you can come with me."

There was sadness and there was hope. Vera heard it plain as day, and as soon as she gained some small measure of composure, she gazed up at Derrick through wet eyelashes.

"Please, come with me," Derrick said. It was the call of someone broken; someone tossed into an abyss and fragmented by the force. Vera couldn't know for sure if he were pleading with her or simply anyone who would answer, anyone who would make him feel whole, keep him from cracking further. Derrick, who had seemed so confident and strong and positive and rightful and willful, was cracking under a tremendous strain. The more he wore down Vera, it seemed the more he was worn, too. They were equally stressed by a force that felt entirely outside of themselves.

Derrick had planned to rip into Vera over her kiss with Keith. He'd meant to drag out the torment of the vacant room and the house clearing and the potential buyer that had put a sign up on the front lawn while they were away on his bike. Some new company with a handful of people in its employ would have the final say over the property Vera loved. It would've pleased his grandmother and eased her pain a great deal if he'd drug it all out. Transference. Misery did love company. And in doing that, he might have lightened his own burden, taken the edge off his own pain. He'd wanted to. A part of him still wanted to. But, it hadn't happened that way. Derrick wasn't able to let it unfold as he'd meant to, planned to, been told to. Something was wrong inside of him, just as something was wrong inside of the house, amid the grounds, anywhere and everywhere that Elizabeth stalked and touched. Derrick had been so full of plans; plans on behalf of the one person he'd thought truly understood and loved him. But, now he was not so confident in that arrangement. Now he was not as aligned with Elizabeth, not now that the threat of losing Vera was so real. For in all of his initial plotting, he'd never planned to fall in love with her.

Derrick had wanted to take from Vera, take until she had nothing left and then shatter her heart, the remnants of her world and her life. He'd brought her to that edge, just as he'd swore he would do, just as Elizabeth had cursed, exactly as the prowling Fate had urged. They were all so very close. Elizabeth seemed more alive after death as she viewed the proceedings and got her way. They were all in uncharted territory now, and who could say how or where it would end. Derrick thought he knew. He knew nothing. Interactions were changing. It may have been brought on by Vera's searching eyes and accepting heart. Perhaps he was helpless under the influence of her transforming appearance, her devastating reveals day after day as she flitted about in brilliant skirts and supple shirts and more vibrant colors than she'd donned from the beginning. It may have simply been because he was starting to believe she really loved him; she had the strength and determination to love him to hell and back… and he'd already drug her through the less intense parts of a personal underworld. She'd clung tightly, latched on. Derrick's heart was bleeding from the strain of serving two masters. His dark, wooden heart was cracked and weeping.

"Come with me," Derrick said again.

Vera picked up on the turmoil. After all, she had her own. Rolling around as though the time and tides were casting her about, as though the sliver of a moon outside held sway over her just as much as Derrick's hypnotic capacity, she knew only one thing. It was like the sight of land or a lifeline. Vera knew she could never make that kind of decision woefully under-informed.

"I-I need some time," she said weakly to Derrick as she semi-fought to emerge from the fog of his sedating effects and the pull of his luscious agony.

"Time is running out," he warned her. He reminded himself.

Vera had possession of the tiny key. The ancient journal was still under the pillow. "I know," she acknowledged. "It won't take me long, I swear."

❖

When Vera couldn't give him a straight answer immediately, Derrick left. But this time, he didn't saddle up on his motorcycle and ride into a foggy and moonlit night. No, this time he walked to the end of the block and vanished from sight. He hadn't said a word. He merely put on his coat and promptly walked out. Vera watched intently until the mists swallowed him whole and then she beat feet upstairs.

She made her way, key in hand, past each and every door, past all the tables and chairs and paintings of people long forgotten. She went directly to the master bedroom and entered. But as the door swung back and hit the wall with the force of her entry, she saw someone waiting in the room, she spotted Elizabeth in her milky white nightgown standing at the foot of the bed, daring her to come closer with icy eyes and pale skin and the knowledge of ages riding her.

Immediately beyond Elizabeth were the bed and the pillow and the jut of a corner of the diary peeking out. Vera could see the prize beyond the hurdle, the answers to everything she'd been simultaneously seeking and avoiding, but avoidance was not in her best interest any longer. She had to get at that book. She had to know the truth. Vera had a decision to make and the key to it in her quivering hand.

"You would dare to read my most private thoughts?" Elizabeth started in, the hint of a molten fury below her chilled surface was most threatening. "These thoughts were not left for your eyes to see. This book was not meant for you to find. Don't you dare!" she hissed. "Don't you dare!" A red, bloody sap began to form at the corner of Elizabeth's mouth, and it trickled only the slightest bit down her chin before coagulating.

"I need to know," Vera said, softer and more kindly than she'd actually intended. "I need to know what you've done to me, what you've done to yourself. I need to know if I can leave with Derrick —"

"Just leave!" Elizabeth shrieked. "Go! Go on! Get out!"

"I have to make certain of something. I have to know what Derrick might already know…" The words she said made little sense, carried little weight, and yet they were ironically profound. They were affecting Elizabeth significantly, and in doing so made Vera feel a bit stronger and more set in her course.

"Stop!" Elizabeth said and thrust the hand-carved doll out in front of her visage. The doll was dripping sap just as Elizabeth appeared to be doing. The doll's moves mimicked those of Elizabeth, as she started breathing heavier and heavier. "This doll has become yours. You touched it!" Her phrases were mere echoes of passages she'd spoken while she was alive. They may have been tethers to her previous existence now that she was dead. Elizabeth was not letting go.

Vera wasn't either, but she had no intention of breaching the plane Elizabeth hovered over, breaking the boundary guarded by the specter and the freaky wooden form. Vera stood there, watching. Waiting, waiting for something to shift.

"How long has it been?" A sweet and strong feminine voice emanated from behind Vera's back.

Vera whirled around to see Lillian standing there, proud and tall and draped in the supple fabrics she'd preferred in her lifetime. She wore a flowing red skirt and a sturdy black top. Her clothes were actually not that dissimilar from what Vera was wearing.

"How long has it been, sister?" Lillian spoke past Vera to Elizabeth.

Elizabeth's eyes darted back and forth between the two, from Lillian to Vera and then back again. "I don't recall. I can't remember," she snarled low and continued to hold the doll out, persisted in blocking the short distance to the bedside and the pillow and the book underneath.

"Too long," Lillian answered. "However long it's been, it's too long. I don't even remember how long we've been apart, how long it's been since we've spoken. Why has it taken death and extreme circumstance to bring us together again?" Lillian moved in front of Vera, and Vera had no reason not to trust her, have faith in whatever she was doing.

Vera wanted to wrap her arms around Lillian and have the two of them leave the room, move away from the horror that Elizabeth had become through the magnification of the death cycle, and the destruction she was set on inflicting. Vera opened her mouth as though to speak, but then caught a glimpse of Lillian's stern expression. Lillian did not wish to speak with her at the moment, and conveyed as much with a subtle glance over the shoulder. She wanted to talk to Elizabeth, her sister.

Elizabeth was weakening her position, thrown by the sudden manifestation of Lillian and her movement to the middle of the room. "You can't remember the love if you don't remember the pain," Lillian said to her own and one time flesh and blood. Then she looked back at Vera. "Either of you."

"What?" Vera had no idea what that meant for her, but before she could question it further, Lillian went on.

"You can't remember any of the blessings if you don't forget the curse," Lillian said barely above a whisper and took her sister by the wrists. She feared not the doll or Elizabeth's terrifying appearance or the manner in which her sister had positioned herself. "If you don't let her see that book of your own free will, then I will make it so," Lillian warned.

Elizabeth let loose a piteous yowl and pulled to escape Lillian's grasp. Lillian knocked the doll from Elizabeth and it clattered to the floor. The figurine writhed and wriggled in a most unnatural and ghastly fashion. And, when Vera tore her eyes from the doll, the doll that had lifted its invisible lids to reveal those insanely red ember eyes, she saw nothing more in front of her than a veil of swirling smoke. The room was full of it, and the smoke wrapped and rolled and attempted to envelop Vera before being blown by no winds at all back into the mirror that sat with the chest of drawers. The furniture rocked and the mirror pivoted. The room itself and then the house shook from an internal and ever-expanding thunderclap. The noise grew and grew; the thunder preceding the inevitable lightning Vera sensed crawling along the surface of her skin. It got so loud and intense that it drove Vera to her knees. She covered her ears and curled into a ball.

There was a brilliant flash of light, an interior display of a bolt, and then the thunder stopped. The smoke was gone. The room was silent. It stayed that way for quite some time before Vera summoned the courage to get to her feet. She stood motionless in the center of the room for a while, for so long that she'd almost convinced herself none of it could've possibly happened. It was more logical to assume she'd imagined it, that it was some sort of strange episode brought on by all the stress and sudden upheaval in her life, but she knew in the pit of her gut that wasn't the case. She had to stop living as though someone like John had all the answers. He had his answers, not hers. She had a sensitivity and had to start living as her own self. When Vera finally looked down and to her left, the doll was still on the floor, occupying the exact same spot it had from when Lillian knocked it out of her sister's grasp. The doll was no longer moving, but it was staring, staring at Vera with those same red eyes. Vera took it in. She stared back. She allowed the slow burning heat to cascade over her.

"Lillian?" Vera called out. "Lillian? Lillian, if you're there, please answer me."

Stone silence.

"Please! Lillian! Please, please answer me!" Vera screamed and heard only the echo of her own voice ringing back to her ears, as her words bounced off every wall in the house. Vera shut her eyes and listened.

Silence.

Vera tried to reach out and feel with whatever it was that resided in her, whatever it was that made her so sensitive and different and very much like Lillian.

Silence. Nothingness.

Elizabeth was definitely gone, and so was Lillian. And, Vera understood in the depths of her soul that wherever it was they'd gone off to, it was that place from which there was no returning.

Lillian had left the small and short path from the center of the bedroom to the book wide open for Vera. It was time for Vera to learn the truth.

At long last she crossed the length, took out the book, and with key already in hand, Vera unlocked the journal. She opened Elizabeth's diary.

It was hard for Vera to get her eyes to adjust initially. It may have been the sensation of burning embers heating her back as the doll continued to stare mercilessly. It may have been an innate reluctance on her part to not want to know everything, to fear the answers and to suddenly desire to delay acceptance of them. But, eventually, Vera's eyes did adjust. Inevitably, she took in the words on the page she'd opened to. She took in the account from Elizabeth's perspective of what had happened to her all those years ago.

There was a skewed narrative of what had happened, of the oak tree in the Thompson gardens and of the day it was chopped down, severed from the life it had possessed and the spirit of the land. There was an accounting of the moon and the doll; ebbings, flowings, comings, and goings. All of it was recorded in a heavy ink and a pristine hand. Every word was cold and crystal clear and calculating. It burned a thousand times hotter than any heat source Vera had ever experienced, so hot it burned cold and blistered Vera's mind; it seared her soul and left a permanent mark. There was mention of the magical working Elizabeth had performed; she'd worked it under moonlight in the gardens after the tree had been chopped down, with the remainder of the wood, with the heart of Vera's axis mundi. It was with a heart that had beaten its last in Elizabeth's hands and in front of Vera's eyes. The things kept bound in that book were memories Vera shared with Elizabeth; they were things Vera had lived and even dreamed. Dreamed. Everything changed the day Vera had ceased to dream. Vera's world certainly took an irrevocable twist then and there, a twist that just kept on turning as time passed, even if that had been the only perceivable and traceable way in which the world changed. It wasn't.

Vera flipped the book, back to the beginning. She wondered if Elizabeth had recorded what happened, what had passed between her and Lillian in a time before Vera drew her initial breath in this life. She flipped several pages and then discovered that the front of the book, perhaps a good quarter to half of what it had once contained was gone, ripped out, destroyed. There were no answers forthcoming for what had happened between Lillian and her sister. Vera could only hope that wherever the two of them were now, they had found their solutions, their reconciliation. Vera could only hope for peace. As for herself, in the present moment she was finding none.

Vera flipped the book again to find her place, the spot where she'd stopped reading, the space where curiosity had grabbed her and forced her to flip to the beginning. On and on the ravings went; it was a graphic account of hatred. It was a counting of perceived sins and flaws. It was the revelation that Elizabeth despised Vera so very much, and most of all because she reminded her of Lillian. In some way or in many ways, there was a striking similarity there that Vera had never pegged but Elizabeth did. She'd honed in on it like a shark smelling blood. Elizabeth hated Vera with all the fibers of her being that weren't busy despising her sister for some nameless wrong committed decades ago. But as Vera kept reading, the rage kept twisting until it had turned on itself, until Elizabeth realized her destructive desires for her own self. It was the lucidity of a wounded animal caught in a trap, and with nowhere else to go, nowhere else to take the pain, it was lashing out for relief. Even in death, Elizabeth had sought after that elusive relief.

Vera turned another page. A new handwriting showed itself then. The records from that point on were not Elizabeth's. There was a new and distinct handwriting in the journal, and it was a familiar scribbled scrawl. The notes Vera saw before her were not the work of a deranged old woman. They were Derrick's.

Vera dropped the book as though it had burned her, and it clattered to the floor. She heard a strange rush of breath from behind her and turned. There was no one there. Lillian wasn't next to her. Elizabeth wasn't almost upon her. And disturbingly enough, the doll was gone, too. It no longer lay on the floor eyeing her. It had vanished, removed itself from the situation. Vera bent low to look under the bed, to see if perhaps the horrid little thing had rolled under there, but nothing. She then allowed herself to retrieve the book she dropped. She forced herself to complete the mission she'd set out on, the mission Lillian had dispersed for. Vera owed it to herself, sure, but she owed completion and full disclosure of the truth to Lillian more.

Vera turned another page. Derrick's recorded revelations mimicked Elizabeth's in great and startling detail. Page after terrible page he went on and on, repeating her sentiments, echoing what it was that had driven her all those years. Page after insidious page he went on and on, and he had cursed Vera just as much in his own heart and in his own hand as Elizabeth had ever done. Only his hatred hurt more. It cut Vera in such a way that she felt certain wherever Elizabeth was, that sharp tragedy would bring her some measure of sweet, vindictive relief. If Elizabeth had wanted to torment her, then Derrick had succeeded on her behalf. Vera trembled. She quaked. She turned another page and then another. She looked and looked again. Vera could hardly believe her eyes and she could not protect her heart. She wasn't capable of that shielding. Derrick had hated her by proxy and had meant to damage her, to do what he had slowly been doing practically the whole time she'd known him.

Vera turned another page and the writings started to change. Derrick's drives weakened with every new turning, too, as though the weight of the extraneous arm of Fate was straining him. The tension was too much, even for someone as powerful as Derrick to bear. The tension grew until something in the ink broke. Something in Derrick broke. A page was ripped almost in half. Vera scanned the writings and markings, seeing the black and wooden-like heart of the man she clung so closely to breaking. He was crumbling from the inside, and that night, downstairs, it had started to show on the outside. He had cursed her from the beginning, but his journal entries ended on a desolate page and a different note: 'I think I love her.'

Chapter 11

Vera had to leave the house completely. Finding out what was in the ancient diary had only served to muddy the waters more. It cleared absolutely nothing up. It certainly hadn't helped her in making a decision. Seeing Lillian, feeling and being privy to Elizabeth's most private thoughts, knowing Derrick's terrifying span of emotions had escalated a call that had been howling beneath the external world's constant din. It was a call far below the mundane level. Vera had to get out of the house or be swallowed whole, offered up as some sort of sacrifice to Derrick's enveloping capacity and the memories of what once was.

She slipped the tiny diary key into the snug waistband of her skirt and stepped out into the night, onto the unhinged sidewalk, turning the corner of the block as Derrick had come around the other side. He hadn't seen her exiting, as he arrived. He stepped into a vacant house to find nothing amiss except the upheaval he'd eventually discovered in the master bedroom. The journal had been left wide open on the bed, blatant and grotesque. The doll Elizabeth had carved by hand for herself and for Vera lay next to it as though there were no danger in handling it, even dismissing or discarding it.

Derrick could see plainly enough that Vera had read all the way through to his final entry. Derrick could sense plainly enough that Vera would not be found anywhere in the house. She'd taken off. What he didn't know was whether or not she'd come back — this time.

Vera hadn't bothered to put on a coat before dashing out into the cold harvest evening. It felt like the end of times, as though nothing she did would've mattered anyway. She didn't have her phone and hadn't bothered calling for a ride. What good would that do, when one didn't even know where one was going? Vera walked and then jogged and then ran blindly in the direction that felt correct to her. Block after block, street after street, her body took her to a place her mind was not allowed to know. At long last she learned what she'd been running towards. As puffs of warm moist air hit the cold night breezes, as stars twinkled clearly in the sky once the fog began to dissipate, as barren trees reached out to scratch and claw and cling, Vera's feet hit the uneven surface of gravel and her ears perked at the sounds of drumming. There was soft light in the distance and wide-open fields holding a hovering dark. There was the sound of laughter and the spirit of dance. Up ahead was the Simms Farm. Waiting for her were the people who had beckoned from the drum circle.

By the time Vera reached the barn, her skin was flush and her arms and face were beyond chilled. Her crimson skirt had done very little to protect her from the elemental onslaught, and a few snowflakes once more hit the air and then matted her hair. She was slick and freezing and bedraggled when she joined the others in the glowing barn interior. The place had been set ablaze in the lantern light. And, the drumming didn't miss a beat upon her entrance. In fact, it was as though no one bothered to note that she was there.

Vera's eye scanned the room feverishly. She looked at face after familiar face around the circle. Magdalena and Casey were swaying in time to the beat, moving like the fluid spirals of a double helix, one dark and one light, one day and one night… and Vera was neither one but yet both of them. There was a definite connection forming, just from Vera being in close proximity once again with the two women. She could tell they knew she was there, yet no visible cues revealed such. Vera continued to eye the occupants and saw that both Misty and John were there as well. It was shocking to see John so at home and to realize that not only had someone given him a drum, but also he was playing it very well. He listened intently to the language of the other beats around him, to the musical conversation and responded appropriately, in kind. Misty did likewise, although perhaps not as meticulously as Vera's own brother. More easily recognizable faces made their way to the forefront of Vera's awareness, Keith's friends who had stayed on beyond the initial party at the farmhouse, a much smaller but more cohesive group. There was an artist sketching and a couple of nameless women dancing.

But, Keith was not among them. He was nowhere in sight.

Vera's bleary eyes finally managed to meet Isaac's. He had spotted her right off. He may have been the only other one, aside from Magdalena and Casey. Isaac kept on drumming as he sized her up in the moment, took in her tousled appearance and her far away gaze. She was breathing hard and shaking with cold, but a hot pulse beat about her veins, in defiance. Vera was a woman in a state of upheaval, a domesticated creature becoming feral through emotions and hidden memories she'd yet to decipher. Isaac kept time on his drum decked out in charms, more charms on it than when Vera had seen it last. He beckoned her without words to step into the timeless rhythm with him, to accept his lead, and to trust in the process and the path. Isaac held much knowledge, and Vera accepted in the span of one beat that he was there to guide her; he would never lead her astray.

Vera's breathing slowed as the two men who were both Isaac showed her that it was safe within the auspices of the barn and the circle, safe within his weathered and ever watchful sight. Isaac was a paradox of honest sentinels for her.

"I didn't expect you to be here," came callous words across the blissful abyss.

Vera was roused from her calm and forced back to a carefully checked and mutually agreed upon reality. She saw Misty standing next to her. Misty looked more like her own self but also not quite. Whatever she'd once had, but still lacked, continued to elude her. She managed to snag some of it, sure. There was more brightness and less hostility, less of a ragged edge, but all of what Misty had once been hadn't returned. Vera noticed straight off that Misty changed clothes from earlier in the day. She wore something more fitting to the occasion, an outfit meant to be alluring, meant to capture attention. Clad in panel after panel of shimmering materials spanning every color of the rainbow, Misty looked like some form of butterfly woman, half out of a cocoon.

"Where's your coat? You look like your freezing to death," Misty criticized. "Let me smooth out your hair," she said and began to fuss with Vera's battered locks.

Vera drew back and let her hands fly up in defense. "Stop. Just stop. I'm fine."

Misty wasn't sure how to respond to Vera's sudden insistence and pulled away several inches. "Ok. Have it your own way." A very heavy pause hung between them. Vera gazed into Misty's heaven blue eyes as Misty peered back into Vera's earthy brown peepers. "So, I suppose you've heard about the business deal going through…"

"What deal?" Vera asked.

"The merger. Apparently, that's what John was up to and why Keith—"

"Have you seen Keith?" Vera inquired without letting Misty finish, letting her eyes roam about the circle once more, just in case she'd missed him on the first pass.

Misty sighed. "No. No, I haven't. Listen, did either one of them tell you?"

Vera shook her head. "No," she was beginning to have to shout to be heard. The drums around them were growing so loud, insistent, maybe even trying to break them apart. Vera fought back and leaned in. "There are a lot of things I haven't been told about," she yelled. "You moved in!"

Misty tossed her curls back and forth with disapproval. "I don't want to discuss that right now. I'm trying to tell you something important about your brother," she returned in an elevated tone. "It turns out Keith has a lot of up front capital and John agreed to start the merger with renovations to the farmhouse—"

"I don't want to discuss this right now," Vera turned a version of Misty's words around at her. "I need to find Keith." She did. She needed to find him. Vera wasn't sure why, but she knew now that was the reason she'd ran to the farm all the way from the Thompson house. She ran in the cold and through the start of snows. She ran through the night and in the dead of a lingering fog that had lifted along the way. She needed more information; she sought clarity, and something primal within her that was waking, setting itself loose, knew that Keith was another key. The tiny key to the ancient journal could only provide so much insight. Derrick could only provide so much emotional longing to pull at her. Somehow and in some way, Vera understood Keith held the rest. That may have been why Derrick feared and hated him so much.

Vera left Misty standing there and made her way about the circle. Isaac had knowledge of Keith's whereabouts. Vera doubted very much if there was anything Isaac didn't know. She made her way over to him and watched as his eyes followed her every movement with a persistent guiding.

Vera signaled with her hand for Isaac to lean in as she came to his side.

He did so.

Vera placed a cold hand on his warm shoulder. "Where's Keith?" she said straight into his ear.

Isaac drew back and stared at her with brilliant and blazing black eyes. The fire from the lanterns was in them. Then he bent low to speak into her ear. "At the oak tree."

Vera was so cold, frozen through and through, that she'd stopped shivering by the time she went out behind the barn and reached the tree. Only a sliver of moonlight and a few of the brighter stars lit the way, but she found it without fail. She came upon it with without trying. Even with her becoming consistently more lethargic, she'd been able to spot the massive, spiraling oak. Vera struggled on up the grounds, earth covered in a layer of crunching acorns, until a friendly figure emerged from beneath barren boughs.

"Are you ok?" Keith asked, assessing her in the fragile moonlight. "Where's your coat?"

"I forgot to grab it. I left in such a hurry to get here…" Vera was having trouble concentrating as she spoke, but she understood in her core that she had to get the words out, had to relay her message, had to find out what was happening in her life and why Keith was so important to it all. Why had his kiss earlier rocked her entire world? Why had she instinctively fled the Thompson house to arrive on his grounds? "I had to see you."

"I'm glad you came. I'm really glad you're here now. I wanted to see you, too," he confessed and took another few steps forward. "Before you do anything or go anywhere, I need to talk to you. I have to be honest… completely honest." Keith came close enough so that she could easily see into his swirling gray and hazel eyes with no trouble at all. She discovered herself there and felt comforted, strangely contented. She sensed the emergence of suppressed memories, something familiar and wonderful and terrible all at once. It was so incredibly powerful that just before the recollections breached the surface of Vera's consciousness, she shoved them back down. Afraid. All that remained was the imprinted image of two people, bound by a single thread.

Vera pulled her arms tight about herself and let go of a heavy sigh; it was in response to the cold and the fear, a fear of remembering too suddenly and too much. "Who are you really?" It was better to bring the experience back around to words, make it something that could be verbally exchanged and quantifiable.

"What do you mean?" Keith asked, to be sure before he proceeded on.

Vera hesitated, shutting her eyes for an extended blink, and then slowly reopened them. She was going hypothermic, but she could not help persisting. "No one and nothing is who or what they originally seem… or seemed… to be…" she said, sounding totally illogical. Vera wasn't even sure her message made sense in the abstract. She tried again. "You formed some sort of merger, a new company with my brother. You have that kind of money, and yet you work at the coffeehouse? Why?" It was a better track. "What do you want? Who are you really?" she put it to him. "Up until today I thought I knew you."

Keith slid out of his woolen coat, checked with colors Vera could barely distinguish as the moon hid behind a cloud or a bit of mist or the remains of fog. It shrouded them in a delicate darkness. Keith wrapped his coat about Vera's tiny frame, concern plainly showing on his face. "It's sad every time this happens. It hurts every time you forget, but I want you to know before we go any further that I forgive you." And for the first time, Vera detected authentic anguish, in Keith's voice. Keith who always seemed to have it together, who was so kind and sweet and happy-go-lucky; good-natured Keith was fracturing, too. It wasn't a minor ache, an insignificant hurt. He was splintering along with Vera, just like Derrick. Only Vera could tell it was not for the same reasons, no matter how identical those reasons may appear to be at a passing glance.

"Forgive me?..." Vera wondered what on earth she could have done to harm someone as sturdy and positive as Keith. She'd never meant to. She cared for him more than she'd let on. She cared for him more than she'd allowed herself to realize. The surge of remembrance was pressing against the dam she'd built in her mind, in her soul.

Keith ran his hands along his shaved scalp, glanced down at the acorn-littered ground and then back up at her. "I guess the moment is here again, and we'll have to see how it plays out this time." Now it was Keith's turn to hesitate, to pause, to fear before he spoke. It was as if he'd made a wish before rolling the dice and then looked to Vera for some sign of assurance that everything would pop up all right.

The lines of worry in Keith's face and the fragility in his steely orbs made Vera quiver. Perhaps it was that she was warming up again, under his coat, under his gaze. Perhaps it was a ghost like Lillian or Elizabeth walking over her soon to be grave, if the vanishing doll they'd left behind had any influence. All Vera knew was that she wanted to smooth those lines and ease the ache she felt growing between them. She wanted it more than she longed for Derrick. "Keith…" she reached out a hand to him and watched as he forced himself to hold steady, to stay in place and not draw back and away. Vera placed a cool hand tenderly on the side of his face, feeling the stubble and the hurt there. He leaned into her palm and rested a bit before pressing on.

"Every lifetime is different," he began and kissed her open palm.

Vera brought her hand down to her side and gave him her full attention.

Keith continued. "There is no Fate, Vera," he said, tipping his hand even more, "none other than the Fates we make for ourselves. But, there are factors… agreements, choices, issues, and hard realities. We have to contend with those."

Vera didn't like how he was suddenly looping around things, dancing about the truths he held. "Answer my first question," she instructed, finding strength within herself as the blood began returning to her extremities. "Who are you really?"

"We've all met before. You, me, Isaac, Magdalena, Casey. The five of us have been friends, close friends, even family over and over and over again. I'm pretty sure we know Derrick, too, although not in the same way. And, that's something I can't seem to remember. It's also a feeling I can't seem to shake." Keith was trying to brace against a myriad of outcomes at the same time he was attempting to ease Vera into them.

"Who are you?" Vera asked again.

Keith gave her a painful sigh. He broke her heart right there on the spot. "I'm the owner of this farm and the associated estate, and better off financially that I'd let on. But, that's the surface answer and not what you really need to know. You need to know… I'm your soul mate."

Vera looked at him, gauged him, as they both were planted stone still right there under the amazing oak tree that had fallen asleep in the coming winter's cold. It slept and it dreamed and it probably remembered a great many important and incredible things. Vera slept, but she never dreamed, and she did not remember an ounce of the truth that she knew Keith was speaking to her. She studied him for any signs of deception. Her heart told her there was none. The drums that slowly amped up their vibrations from the barn seemed to confirm it as well.

Vera closed her eyes and shook her head, trying to get rid of a strange swimming sensation that crept up on her. Wave after wave of cresting emotions beat against her brain. "Why can't I remember?"

"You chose not to. In a moment of agony, immense pain… the moment I died, the moment I first had to leave you behind, you set in motion with that energy the wish to forget. You wanted to forget it all, so you would never have to feel such pain again. You worked a spell to forget the pain of losing me, but you can't forget the pain and not also forget the love, Vera."

It was as Lillian had told her. Beyond the veil, Lillian could see it. She'd known all along, either in life or in death, but she'd known long before Vera. But, now Vera was aware. Keith spoke the truth; Keith never lied. Vera wasn't sure he was capable of it.

"But, we're woven together," Keith went on. "And, so we both are spellbound to one another by the choices we've made. You don't have to endure the pain of remembering, but now I have to endure the pain of your forgetting. Life after life after life I endure it, Vera. That was your choice and my subsequent curse."

Vera understood what it meant to be cursed, and she shuddered to think for a fraction of a second that what Elizabeth had done to her she had done to Keith, inadvertently or not. It may not have been intentional and it may not have been in this lifetime, but she'd done it just the same. She and Elizabeth were indeed alike, as Elizabeth had told her all those years ago. She and Lillian and Elizabeth were so very similar in that perfect instance that all three may have been existing simultaneously through Vera as one. Vera had never felt so fragmented nor so whole.

"But, by choice you can break the curse, Vera," Keith pressed as hard as he dared, as much as he would allow himself. "Please, break the curse, Vera," he pleaded and took up her hands in his, their fingers interlocking.

And just like that, in a single touch and with a heart that had finally broken into bits so tiny they might never be sewn back together in full, her own heart, Vera remembered. A flood of awareness crashed into her brain, welling up from a more primitive place. The fluid of emotional release flooded every corridor and it was so much to take in, and none of it could be shut out any longer. The dam broke. The best Vera could do was close her eyes and let it overwhelm her, allow herself to feel, allow herself to realize that there was life and there was death, and both were equal parts of existence. There was manufactured Fate and there were her own decisions, and her whole life she'd been running away, tamping down, popping out of her shell only to slide back in again. Maybe she'd been running like that for eternity. It certainly felt like it. It definitely seemed plausible.

When she at long last became able, Vera wrapped her arms about Keith tightly and nuzzled her face into his chest, breathing in the scents of earth and oak and ecstasy. "Will you leave me again?" She recalled the torture of it and could barely stand up.

Keith gripped her tight and kissed the top of her head as he began rocking the two of them back and forth, from side to side. She'd come home to his arms in a way that Derrick had attempted to imitate for her. But, it had been a poor try, and Vera could see that clearly. "Someday. But, that doesn't really matter, Vera. For now, we both know that we'll always find our way home to each other," he reasoned with an unreasonable and unbelievable topic.

"Each lifetime seems so short when I'm with you and so long once you're gone…" Vera bemoaned what was likely to be the outcome once more, but she let loose a deep breath and let go of her desire to forget. "But, I'll remember you — always," she swore.

"We always think we'll have more time, and then it runs out… again and again," Keith counseled with words that used to be the winds', but now he claimed them for himself. Those words no longer seemed so threatening, so foreboding. "Let's make the most of what we do have." Keith reluctantly let loose of Vera, allowing her to fight and stand on her own, to bear up under the strain. He bent low to retrieve a single acorn from the frosty earth and slid it carefully into his pocket before clasping Vera's hand in his. "Come on," he said with a nod towards the farmhouse.

Instead of the drums calling to them, bidding them to come to the circle, as they'd done in the past, they pressed Keith and Vera in towards each other and away to the farmhouse. They pressed them on to make the most of what they had, then and there.

Keith led her into the vacant house, warmed by the low roar of an old furnace buried somewhere beneath the floorboards. He brought her up the stairs and straight away to the master bedchamber, the beautiful suite that had been conceived of purely as a labor of love. His grandparents had lived and loved there. Keith lived there, and he longed to bring love back into the equation. He desired to bring Vera back into his tapestry of existence, to weave her securely into the loom with that single and ever-enduring thread. He brought her meticulously to the center of the room and took the coat he'd given her away.

Keith took a few steps back then, far enough to truly admire her. She was draped precariously in weather worn fabrics and shivering with the slightest hint of a breeze, as it made its way through the room. Her hair was an utter disaster, flung this way and that and then gone limp with the moisture of a few snowflakes, but it suited the state of her life and made her vulnerable. Keith liked that. He enjoyed knowing she had nowhere else to run. She'd exhausted her options with false paths. Vera's eyes were red and watery and her face speckled with the remnants of sadness and love and great awareness. Vera still had secrets she was keeping from Keith. She had secrets about the doll and her own curse, and Derrick and the Thompson house, and about everything she'd ever really wanted for her personal sphere. She had waking dreams she'd yet to vocalize. And, Vera had never told him about her inability to dream while asleep, and what it would mean to her if one day she could regain that special gift.

"I need to tell you some things," Vera opened, when Keith had yet to speak a single syllable.

"No, you don't," Keith assured. "None of it matters, not now. Whatever's on your mind, tell me tomorrow or the next day or the day after that."

"And, what if we run out of time?" she prompted, calling to mind his utterings from beneath the spiral oak tree.

Keith gave her a smile, a smirk really. "Then I guess some things will always remain a mystery."

She grinned back. "I appreciate you being so accepting, but —"

"Don't," he stopped her, his voice a little louder than before. "Don't," he eased. "Just let me have this. Tonight. Let me have right now."

Vera nodded. She wanted it, but she wanted him to have it more. She'd have done anything for him then and there.

"You wanted to know who I really am, and I've told you. But, that's nothing compared to me actually showing you," he said sincerely. "Will you stay here with me tonight?"

Vera nodded again.

"Say it. I need you to say it. Say you'll stay," he prodded kindly. From the woman who up to this point had given him no vows, he needed that particular promise acknowledged.

"I'll stay," Vera released her highly charged response into the room, and the air felt as though it popped and sizzled around them both, a peculiar palpation of invisible lightning.

Keith reached out and touched her then, feeling elated with her promise not to leave, not to run off as she had a tendency to do, not to be taken hold of by a flight of fancy. Vera wasn't going anywhere. He ran his hands up and down, along her neck and torso, until they eventually settled at the bottom hem of her sweater. And in one bold move, Keith stripped the damp fabric from her body and let it drop to the floor.

Keith admired her even more then. Her slight frame and small, budding breasts were so tender and exquisite and required no support from an undergarment. He took in the sight of her glowing skin, as she stood there, topless. The only thing she wore above the waist was the glinting little white gold acorn that Isaac had given her, which Keith himself had placed on his grandmother's chain. It hung there still, the promise of potentials beckoning.

Vera shivered and drew him from his study of her. Keith had thought to undress her further, but decided to bring Vera into his arms for the time being and raise her temperature. He removed his own shirt so that their skin would press together, heat transferring from his body to hers, the beat of his heart signaling to her own to match it. His breath guiding hers in smooth inhales and exhales, as he wrapped her up tight and glided his hands along her back until the shivering stopped, until she was warmed through and through. Then Keith felt contented to begin again.

At the side of her daring crimson skirt gone cold and wet, Keith found a small zipper and worked it down so that the entire piece slipped off her hips. The skirt slid down her legs and pooled precariously about her feet, leaving her in nothing more than a simple pair of white silk panties. But as the fabric hit the floor, so too came the sound of a soft and subtle thud. Something else had dropped with it. Both Vera and Keith glanced down to see shining up at them, the tiny key. Vera knew that key. It belonged with the ancient journal, marked 'EMD,' that still sat wide open in the Thompson house. No doubt Derrick had returned by now and maybe even found it there and Vera long gone. What would he do? If she ever returned to him, what would he say? Did she have to give the key back?

"I feel so embarrassed," Vera whispered into Keith's ear. She felt flush for a thousand reasons.

"Why?" he breathed back.

It was a good question… so good that verbal answers were hard to come by. Vera forgot the key quickly, in a blink, but then had to contend with the entire scenario that was playing out. When Vera made love with Derrick, it was quick and fevered and in the dark. Everything moved so fast that Vera doubted Derrick saw her much at all. It was passionate and animalistic and so heady that anything and everything could get swept up and lost in the process. But, that's not how it was turning out with Keith. That was not where the night was headed. Even with Lance, everything had happened in the dark, in a shrouded shadow so that neither one of them had to focus on each other too much; it was more about the act, despite any caring that had resided between them. But, that's not how it was turning out with Keith. He wanted to see her, examine her, and understand her. He longed to have her bare before him in the chamber's elegant light. He would know her for who she was in every aspect. He might get to know her even better than she knew herself, and that just seemed dangerous and humiliating. What if he found something in her, or about her, he didn't like? Would he stop and turn her away? He hadn't in thousands upon thousands of years, numerous lifetimes. But, would he do so now?

"I-I've never… never once let anyone see me like this before," she finally answered.

"Yes, you have," he told her. "You just don't remember it."

Vera's hazy brown eyes met Keith's then and she tried to remember, she tried hard, but only a flash here and a still shot there came back. It was all snippets. Nothing cohesive. It was nothing like the sudden and overwhelming flood that had happened under the oak tree. Her brain had been awash then. The memories pooled in various places of her mind now, and she'd have to work to properly access them again in the days to come. But, at least they were set free.

"Tonight you will," he said with great confidence and leaned in to kiss her. His lips met hers in a light flutter at first and then slowly, inexorably, logistically moved to make the lock deeper and firmer. Vera felt his tongue dance along with hers, leading at the start but then guiding her to lead, to show him, to remind him as well who she was and to tell him who she could be. To communicate without words in that intimate instance, it was healing and it was madness. And, it set into motion some primal part of Vera so that she stood fast in her own strength once more.

Vera grew bolder and bolder along with the kiss, until she found her hands gliding along the strong and even planes of Keith's body, his torso and back first and then lower until her fingertips met with the edge of his blue jeans. She hesitated for only a moment, and Keith drew back a breath's width from her in anticipation, letting her see the play of emotion rush across his face, the blatant excitement at her drive to go further. Vera unbuttoned and unzipped him, pressing his pants down until they met with her skirt and the tiny, suddenly insignificant key on the floor.

Keith stepped out his shoes and then his pants, until he was naked in front of her. There was nothing between her gaze and his form; only he caught her looking away.

"Vera," he called her attention back to him, and she then gave him a fluttering glance. "Vera, it's all right," he said and stepped in even closer to her. It was immediately apparent that she didn't know how to respond with the lights on, with the ability to see everything put right in front of her, with hard reality merging shamelessly into something more magical. Keith decided to guide her with sensation and then visuals. He pressed his body up against hers lightly and let her hands find him again. He kissed her lips and her neck and nuzzled her lovingly as she explored, as she led the way, as she did what she longed to do. He could feel the smooth, cool surface of her silk panties rub up against the hardened length of him, and it was a most delightful torture. In all the centuries, perhaps even millennia, that they'd spent together, on and off, off and on, she hadn't lost her touch, her edge, her alluring and indulgent ways.

Vera's hands met with Keith's and she led him to the elastic edge of her undergarment, her only remaining stitch of clothing. He hooked his thumbs up under it, and Vera imagined him sliding them down and off of her in the same manner that he'd removed her other clothes. But, he didn't. In a split second, she heard a rip. It was the distinct tearing of fabric. She felt a pull and then the rush of air, as she stood completely naked next to Keith. He'd met his limit.

A tiny sigh escaped her lips then and Keith took it as his cue to lift her up. He swept her off her feet and deposited her on the bed not far from the center space they'd occupied. A curiously warm and dense blanket enveloped her from below and Keith positioned himself from above. He was perfect. He was made for her. How had she not seen that before? How had she not felt it the minute their paths crossed in this life? How could any working, any spell, performed be so strong as to blind her in such a way?

As Keith dipped his head low to kiss her once more, she spoke to him from a vacant heart waiting to be filled, from a brain full of memories finally let loose and waiting to be recalled, one at a time. "I'm so sorry for what I've done to you."

"Vera…" he was lost, without words to comfort or guide her. He could barely express his own feelings. All he had left was her name, a basic incantation. "Vera…"

She let her fingers play upon his lips until she found the will to speak again. "I love you, Keith. I do. I love you," She let herself go. "With all my heart."

He desired more from her. Keith was touched, but in the fraction of an instant, Vera could see he needed more.

"With all my soul," she affirmed for him, for herself. "I swear I won't ever, ever forget that."

When Vera woke, the crescent moon was still hanging low in the sky and the first rays of morning light were breaking over the farmland. Keith slept so peacefully, so soundly, and Vera could tell by the slight movements beneath his eyelids that he dreamed. She slid out of bed cautiously, not wanting to wake him, and went over to one of the windows. She needed to look out on the world now that everything for her had changed… yet again. Twisted. Turned.

Vera pulled back one of the gauzy draperies and stared at a day untouched and a land unencumbered. There was a sense of openness and newness, a curious calm that stretched for as far as the eye could see. The master bedroom's two main windows looked out over the main drive and the front two fields. To her right, Vera spotted the barn that had played host to the drum circle the night before. It appeared dark and empty. Everyone had left, took off when they were good and ready, and done so without bothering their host. Vera wasn't sure if she found that thoughtful, assuming he didn't want to be disturbed, or thoughtless… had they not assumed something could be wrong?... But, in a single sigh that fogged the window glass, it ceased to matter. Vera peered out and enjoyed the view as more and more morning light crept up over the horizon.

Vera was even able to see the top of the giant oak tree that was situated behind the barn. She leaned in towards the glass and had pressed herself up against it by the time she was able to make out the vague shape of the side of the tree. Half a trunk, expansive branches, and the twinkling top tiers that were coated in frost and light ice. It was a magnificent sight, a stunning tree. It was so like her axis mundi; it was strong and virile and masculine and protective. Vera continued to look for it and to pine for the connection she'd lost in her teenage years. Vera gazed at it for so long that the shape, the inherent structure of the spiraling tree, seemed to morph. It did not sleep, not in the harsh morning light. It changed until it presented as a large tree man. The oak resembled the tree man that had been chopped down in Vera's dream, a nightmare brought on by Elizabeth, the tree man that had been mutilated, dismembered. Vera blinked and it was gone. He was gone. There was only the oak tree as it usually appeared and nothing more; there was no man inside it, no man becoming it. The spiraling oak was not becoming a man either. The brother of the tree man from Vera's old dreams had vanished.

Vera released a shaky breath and told herself to look out again with logical eyes and a linear gaze. She told herself to see the world and the farm and the tree for what they really were. She dared herself to know the truth of it. And when she did so, she saw the tree looking back at her with soft, alluring, red ember eyes… many of them.

As hard as it was for Vera to come to terms with what she'd shared with Keith, with what had happened between them, between her and Lillian, her and Elizabeth, Elizabeth and Lillian… it was even more difficult to come to terms with the tree that had gazed back at her. She felt entirely too sane for what was happening. It was the same sanity that had been so much a part of her younger years, when Lillian had been there to guide her, assure her that magic was afoot and that intuition and imagination really did allow one to view the world as more than just what lay on the surface. Experience and exploration had been everything in those days. But, that confidence could be dangerous, just like the illusion of control, for it had led her down an insidious rabbit hole before. It might do the same now.

Keith kissed her goodbye as the sun straddled the line of the horizon, more above than below. He stood in the doorway of the front porch in jeans and a sweater, bracing himself against the cooled air that rushed around his face, swirling with the heat of his home at his back.

"We both should've been at the shop already," Vera said, trying to bring some of the mundane into the mix.

"Misty's there. I asked her to open up for me, for us, yesterday," Keith revealed. "She can handle it."

"When yesterday?" Vera put it to him, only half believing in his convenient story.

"When she got here for drum circle," he continued. "She seemed a little put off by it, but agreed anyway."

"And, why would you ask her preemptively like that?" Vera was ever the skeptic, at least a little bit, thanks to her brother's influence and the memories of nightmares long gone by.

Keith smiled at her as he stepped all the way through the wooden precipice to join her on the front porch. Keith left the door barely ajar behind him. "I knew you were coming Vera… Isaac knew, that is, and told me. But, I had an idea you might be staying, that you might choose to stay. And, I wanted to make the most of the time we had," he said and then kissed her slowly, letting his lips linger, building a blaze between them that might sustain. "Are you sure you don't want a ride back? It's really cold out here… and you're not wearing panties…"

Vera gazed at him for a prolonged moment, and with a blush, and then replied. "I'm sure. I've got a lot to think about on my way back into town."

Keith nodded his understanding. "I'll get over to the shop in a bit. It's one thing to ask Misty to open, and quite another to expect her to handle a Saturday morning rush."

"If there is one… Ok. I'll be in this afternoon," she informed. "And, there I go, slacking off again."

Keith grinned. "Well, I certainly won't hold it against you this time."

"No?" she questioned playfully.

"No. I'd much rather hold myself against you," he gave her a little wordplay and then wrapped his arms about her waist, pressing her small form into his, pressing her against the hard plane of his body so that she became pliant.

"Where's all this going?" Vera finally asked, queried directly once she'd found the courage to be so vulnerable and to stare up into his dazzling gray eyes, trimmed with an elegant hazel.

"Wherever you want it to go," he whispered and brought his mouth over hers. They stood there for so long that Vera started to shiver, both with the cold and with anticipation of what he might do to her next.

She eventually pulled back. "I've got to get going," she said with an embarrassed snicker. She was still in the weather worn clothes from last night, along with the woolen coat Keith insisted she borrow.

"All right," he said and turned her loose from his grasp. "See you at the shop." Keith watched as she walked down the gravel road to the edge of his property.

Vera turned and waved before she made her way towards the outskirts of town. She waved as she glanced back at the outline of the barn, the expansive oak's upper branches, the historic farmhouse, and the man who loved her more than anyone she'd ever known.

Keith waved also, wishing her well, suspecting where she'd stop off first.

Derrick spent most of the night outside. When he'd returned to the house, it was easy enough to put the pieces together. He'd found the journal and the doll. He'd felt his grandmother's absence and knew that she'd left him for good. He figured it was only reasonable, given what would be her obvious disappointment in him. Elizabeth had been the one person Derrick believed loved him for who and what he was, his whole and entire life. He and his grandmother had shared in their state of outcast together, making it a far less lonely territory, and now she was gone. She'd left his life without so much as a proper farewell, and he was set apart to contemplate what the best course of action would be. There was no one to staunch his internal wounds, as much as he thought Vera might try to help under the proper guidance. But, no, he had to attempt the mend himself. It could've gone better.

Derrick was sitting on the porch, hunkered low in the shade as the sun climbed higher and higher. He had no desire to warm himself in the encroaching daylight. He wanted his eyes shielded and his body chilled. He, so much like Vera only a few hours before, found comfort in feeling next to nothing. Derrick waited for her in the cold and stood up to full height as she strode past, his joints creaking with frost.

"Where are you going?" he asked and came forward into a shaft of hard sunlight at last. He stood on the edge of the porch, bracing himself for a blow that had yet to ever be delivered, by Vera.

Vera turned on her heels, looking less than startled. "Inside my brother's house for a hot shower and a change of clothes. I have to work today."

"You work every day," he challenged her priorities. As far as he was concerned, she owed him an answer above all else.

Vera peered up at Derrick, really taking the time to absorb who he was both visually and beyond the outward portrayal, not that there was much left of his once sturdy mask. But no matter what happened to him, he was still hypnotic. Underneath the layers and the locks and the walls and the motes he'd energetically built, he was still stunning, incredibly alluring. He was just as handsome as he'd ever been, only more fractured. He was changing, transforming, coming apart. Vera hoped that whatever happened, he would be put back together in some shape more deserving to house his elegant and battle-scarred soul. She looked into his unearthly green eyes and wanted for him all the things he'd been denied. She admired his long, dark hair and his pale skin gone downright pallid with the frigid temperatures. She envied his ability to wear such rebel clothing with no thought as to the message sent or the outcome brought back around. Then she saw something entirely new in the equation of the man; his hands were covered with the caked remnants of muddy earth. Derrick had been digging… and maybe also covering over. Derrick had done something, hidden something, buried something.

Vera reached into the hemline of her skirt and retrieved the key. She'd said she'd give him an answer. "Here," she announced and tossed him the key on the broken chain.

Derrick snatched the tiny trinket right out of the air. "You had no right to take it," he admonished, but carefully.

"You had no right to keep it from me," she said to the man she suddenly thought of as her former lover. "I think you should leave."

Derrick came down a single step. "I meant for it to happen, all of it. I won't apologize for that," he told her, wary and wearily.

Vera set her shoulders straight, despite the fact that she felt like curling up into a ball against the breeze that stirred between them. "I'd never expect you to."

"I'm still selling the house and everything in it," he went on and took another step down off the porch.

Vera nodded and swallowed a small lump that spontaneously emerged in her throat. "I know."

Derrick met her on the sidewalk. "Everything will be gone."

Vera smiled. In a rush, a memory of Lillian, a moment she shared with her dear, old friend, came back to her. It pressed itself into the forefront of her mind and wrapped her in a tender phantom embrace. "The house, it's not everything. The furnishings and the art and the books, those aren't everything. The gardens that I once loved and the memories contained in all these places, they aren't everything." Vera spoke with the commanding presence of Lillian herself; it was the same presence Elizabeth also had during the course of her life. "I can get over it."

Derrick merely considered her.

"Just… tell me one thing," Vera prompted. "Do you love me?"

It was Derrick's turn to try to fight off a growing lump in his throat with a fretful swallow. "Yes," he admitted, knowing it put him at an immediate disadvantage. "I'm your Fate, Vera," he enticed with a romantic edge. "Come with me."

"That you may be," she was willing to accept, "but no. I won't be going with you," she said in response to a flash of recall that snapped to attention in her brain. Keith had been right; they did know Derrick from some pinpoint in time, from some existence that had happened before. "Not this time." Vera had to let him go, and knowing that he loved her allowed her to do it with a measure of forgiveness that hadn't been possible at any other juncture. She was finally able to forgive him in the same way Keith was able to forgive her, only silently. Vera could not speak the words for fear they'd send the wrong intent in the message. No, she merely looked to him kindly but firmly. Steadfast in her resolve. Love had made the difference.

Chapter 12

It only took a week or two and Derrick managed to have the Thompson House cleared of what appeared to be all its belongings. The furniture, the fineries, anything and everything that could be pried loose and sold off, Derrick ripped out of there. Thanksgiving and what was left of the strangely cold harvest season passed Vera by in a parade of coffee drinks and drum circles and moonlit talks with Magdalena and Casey. There were also the glorious nights she spent with Keith at the farmhouse, falling asleep amid open fields, rustling tree branches in the distance, and starry skies.

The natural increase of declining cold, as winter blew its icy breath, slowed John's work down to a crawl, and one day Vera came back to his place to find him loading boxes into the bed of his truck.

"What are you up to? More home improvements?" Vera quizzed in the dreary gray light of early evening. It would be dark soon.

It was a reasonable assumption, given that John had taken to working on the inside of his own home some more with very little to do in outside restorations. "I'm packing up your stuff and hauling it out of here," he said to her flatly.

Vera was stunned. So, there was a limit to John's good graces and leniency towards her. True, he had warned her weeks ago, weeks that were stretching into months, that he needed her out. He needed his space, space to expand and then share with Misty. And, Vera had every intention of honoring that, but she'd become so honed in on herself and the evolutions in other areas of life, that she'd moved his request to the back burner. Faced with his movements now, she'd clearly seen that was a mistake. "Sorry," she said softly and cleared her throat. "I know I should've started the process sooner, but the truth is… the truth is… I don't have anywhere else to go," Vera revealed with a great degree of shame. There was still no decent amount of pay to draw from the coffeehouse for her own self, although she did manage to snag small amounts of cash here and there, with the stagnancy lifting and her attention returning.

John just shook his head. "Sure you do," he dismissed. "I'm hauling your stuff out to Keith's. He said he'd be happy to take you in, although goodness knows why. I warned him you were messy and flighty and prone to all kinds of moodiness," John said with dry humor. "So, the least you could do is put your purse in the truck, bundle up a little more, and help me unload this once we get there."

Vera couldn't help but smile, but she also narrowed her gaze reproachfully at her brother. "You and Keith seem to be conspiring an awful lot these days."

"How so?" John met her accusation. "Other than taking your things out there…"

"S&N Development," she said succinctly. "How could you two not tell me right up front you were planning that kind of partnership? And most of all, how could you not tell me you were buying the house next door?" It was another happy albeit hard instance to swallow. Keith and her brother were the proud new owners of the Thompson house, a property awaiting development in the spring season, no doubt. Vera worried what would become of it. Would they see fit to tear it down? Would they restore it to its previous level of grandeur? And, if they chose the latter, who would wind up living there? Vera still wasn't too keen on the idea of just anyone moving in, despite the fact that she'd told Derrick she could let it go.

John strode up to her, a cocky grin remaining plastered all over his face. "To be frank, we weren't sure the details would work out until we really sat down and went over the figures and the proposed agreements in black and white. It just so happens they did work out. And, now that we see more of you these days, perhaps you'll be privy to more information."

Vera rolled her eyes at her brother and nudged him in the ribs with her elbow. "Idiot," she said when there was nothing else left to say.

"Let's get you settled into your new place," John guided her right back to the task at hand.

Vera nodded and went around to the passenger side. She opened the door and tossed her purse inside. She was moving to her new home. "Let's."

❖

The spring season took a long time in coming. As far back as Vera could remember, winter had never stayed so long, or brought so much ice and snow to their little town. But even with the tempestuous weather and the days her business was forced to close, the coffeehouse started to flourish under Vera's blatant and nurturing attentiveness. By early April, red maples started to bloom, a whole month late. Vera could finally spot the wild onion and garlic greening in pastures and along the wood lines at the edge of the roadways in and out of town. Bluebirds eventually felt safe enough to nest, robins swooped through the fields and along the streets, and local bats left their hibernation dens to flit about dusky skies at long last. Dogwoods bloomed and willows started to look less skeletal. And, the townsfolk sloughed their heavy coats for light jackets on windy days. New life had returned after a hard winter drove everything and everyone inward and down. It was time for all to come out.

And it was on such a day in early April, as the sun was riding low in the west, that Keith told Vera he had a surprise for her. The greater truth was that he had many.

"I want you to see what your brother and I have done with the Thompson house," he said, as he broke trail out of the farmhouse and went casually over to his truck. Keith owned a pick-up that closely resembled John's, only it was older and had probably been one more thing he'd inherited, along with the farm and everything the estate contained.

Vera stopped dead in her tracks up on the wooden porch and didn't follow him down the steps. She knew the two of them had been busy restoring it, when they weren't focused on updates to Keith's farmhouse. Keith had been working less and less at the coffeehouse as spring took hold, as February gave indications that the weather was lessening, and despite the fact that their March had been a rough one. Keith had the farm and was a partner in John's business now. John had pressed for his company to get jobs done early, to work out in the uncooperative weather and whenever possible. And, Vera had been so busy at the coffeehouse, especially with staffing being light, that she'd allowed herself to be distracted by the workload. She hadn't wanted to think about what would happen once restorations to that grand old place were complete.

Keith turned and looked up at her when he realized she hadn't joined him near the vehicle. "What? What's wrong?"

Vera reflected upon that question. What could possibly be wrong? What could she find to complain about when so many people had been generous with her, and when she'd gotten so much of what she'd longed for at last? She had her business and a home with Keith. She had a functional relationship and a circle of friends who appeared to accept her for who and what she was, exactly and totally. She may not have fully repaired her state of affairs with Misty, and maybe she never would, but everything else had fallen into place under the pressure of a long winter's icy grip. Going in had made almost everything outside all right. So, Vera was left to wonder why the Thompson house and its Fate still had such a tight grip on her. The grip was harmless enough, but still so tight.

"Vera?" Keith checked again and made his way back up on the porch to stand beside her.

"I don't really want to see it," she said.

"Oh, come on. You pass by it now and then. It can't be that great a shock," he nudged.

That part was true enough. Every so often, Vera did pass by that poignant place to visit her brother and Frank and to hang out after work. Misty often seemed uncomfortable with it, but was wise enough not to create too much of a fuss. John liked restoring all things, even familial relationships, whenever he could. But on those occasions, Vera never paid too much attention to the Thompson house and the light in the sky was very low. Since the renovations began, she hadn't looked closely at it. She was afraid it would reveal too much about where the house was going, what they'd intended to do with it. Vera sighed. At least, they hadn't torn it down.

"It's just…" Vera stalled. "There are a lot of memories in there."

Keith nodded. "I know. And, most of them are good ones, right?"

Vera thought on it quickly. Her assessment didn't take long. "Right," she agreed. "Right." Aside from a few episodes on the timeline of her serpentine life, most of her memories and associations with the Thompson house had indeed been good ones.

"So, then come and see it. See all the work we've put into it," Keith encouraged and slid an arm in through one of hers so that they were wrapped together. "See it for what it's become."

Vera supposed she owed Keith and her brother that much. They'd always supported her in her work endeavors and various other pursuits. She really should see it through, be encouraging of them in their initial joint project, aside from the work to the farmhouse. Vera probably owed Lillian that much, as well. She should see what had finally become of the home her ancient friend had loved and then left behind.

"You owe yourself, Vera," Keith interrupted her thoughts. "You should see it through, for closure."

Vera walked down the steps and obligingly got in the truck. The entire short ride out to the house, Keith talked. He talked about the farm and continuing plans for the structures built on it. He talked about the coffeehouse and how happy he was that it was going so well. And, he talked about how very much he enjoyed working with John. Vera gazed out the window and listened and returned with the appropriate responses, but as they sped along all she could think about were the house and its Fate. What was to become of both those things? Could the doll really still be in there after the thorough restoration?

When they pulled up alongside the curb, Keith's truck covering the oil stain left by Derrick's motorbike, Vera thought about what had gone on in that house, not just the good but also the bad. Frightening things had occurred within the walls of the Thompson house and out in the back gardens and weedy lots. Erotic things had gone on in there also, between Derrick and Vera. As she stepped up onto the unhinged sidewalk, Vera thought of him, of Derrick, of the mesmerizing man that had taken from her to the point where there was nothing left, and then in that last moment between them, he'd attempted to give. Vera felt very sure that she'd never ever be able to forget him. There was no plausible way to do so.

Keith quickly joined her on the fracturing sidewalk, and together they peered up at the residence, tree roots easing up beneath their feet. It was no matter that the sun was setting, that they were losing the light of the day, for a stunning antique light fixture had been placed in the upper wooden overhang of the porch ceiling, and it was turned on. The front of the house was lit up and brilliantly displayed. Fine wood trim covered over in brand new paints met Vera. Dazzling whites, supple greens, and earthy browns were the main color palette. It felt sumptuous without being overdone. Every accent was lovingly created. Every touch was added with painful attention to detail. It was a seamless merger of both John and Keith's stylings, and it translated well into the work the contractors of S&N Development had carried out. Vera knew within the span of a single heartbeat that this was how Lillian had kept it in her prime.

"How's that for curb appeal?" Keith asked as he read her floored expression.

Vera merely gazed at him, tears welling up in her eyes. She wished Lillian could be there to see it, if only for a split second. But, Lillian was gone. In an inhale and an exhale, Vera was positive that Lillian was gone. Luckily enough, Elizabeth was, too. No doubt about it. The house was vacant in almost every sense, empty except for the memories.

Keith took her hand firmly in his. "Let's go in," he said and gave a gentle tug that led her up the steps and in through the front door. He flipped on the overhead lights for the living room's glory.

The soft, sand-colored carpeting was practically the same, only it was brand new. There were no wear marks, no matter how subtle. The tone however was an exact match to what had been there before, with only the slightest variation in texture. A delicate coat of fresh paint had been added, and a fabric similar to the original floral draperies had obviously been purchased and hung. The room was devoid of furniture, but bursting with refreshed potentials. Vera let her eyes and then her mind adjust. The integrity of the house from all initial inspections seemed to have remained intact.

As Vera took a few steps in and Keith let go of her, she also noticed something else. At the base of the staircase, there was the grandfather clock. She went straight over to it, moving as though she were bolting towards an old friend she hadn't seen in years. It was almost as good as seeing Lillian. She stared into the metallic face that winked at her with secrets and moments well kept. Vera wondered through her delight how it was that of all the original items in the house, it was the grandfather clock that had remained. With everything getting sold, how was it that this piece hadn't been? It was worth far more than all the other stuff combined, easily.

Derrick.

Vera's heart skipped a forlorn beat. "Was this here when you guys started the work?" she inquired, briefly glancing at Keith.

"Yeah," he admitted as he walked over to stand behind her. "We were very careful when we moved it to paint."

Derrick had left it. Had he left it for her? Vera wanted to think so.

"Was that the only thing left in here?" Vera continued her line of questioning, as she ran a hand reverently along the smooth and cool surface of the diligent timekeeper.

"No, there were scraps of fabric not worth saving, some dried herbs we had to throw out, and a statue of a dog that John decided to keep," Keith reported as he placed his hands atop her shoulders.

Vera knew the dog statue Keith was referring to; it was most assuredly the one she had encountered in the guest bedroom several months ago, the figure that had looked so much like Frank. Of course, John would want it. Naturally, he should have it. Lillian may have even meant it to be for him.

"I see," was all Vera had to respond with.

"Oh, and there was one other little thing that I thought you might like," Keith said. "Feel like coming upstairs?"

Vera peeked in at the dining room and also managed to see straight back to the kitchen. All empty. "Sure," she said and gave a faltering smile. Soon the house would be put up on the market again. Soon potential buyers would walk through it and fall in love and make offers. Soon it would be the property of someone Vera had never met. The Thompson house would belong to strangers. Vera's head and shoulders drooped as she followed Keith upstairs.

There were no portraits of people long forgotten in the hallway. No chairs and tables with small knick-knacks. There was nothing but a straight and blank shot back to several rooms and another fresh coat of neutral paint. Keith took Vera to what used to be the guest bedroom, a room ready for impressions, a room that had been devoid of any sort of judgment, perceived or otherwise. Not a stick of furniture or a scrap of fabric remained, not even curtains.

Keith walked over to the window ledge at the opposite side of the room and retrieved an object, which he then dutifully brought back to Vera. He opened his hand to show her another figurine that had also been left behind. It was the statue of a small squirrel holding an acorn, the piece Lillian had brought up in polite conversation from beyond the grave, the item Vera had very much admired, too. Derrick had taken so many things from the house. He'd even taken a piece of her heart that really could never belong to anyone else. Vera found she could silently admit that in the guest chamber and in the dwindling light. It was, after all, a room without judgment. She was able to admit it to herself and herself only, but the truth was there. Derrick had caused harm; he had taken. But, he had left what was important. Vera was suddenly very grateful to him, and that emotion stretched beyond the forgiveness she'd extended. She was able to actually be glad that he'd been a part of her life, no matter how brief or detrimental.

"It was Lillian's," Vera broke the heavy quiet. "I believe it was one of her favorite pieces. I've always liked this little figurine," Vera confessed, as Keith placed it in her hands.

"Do you want to see the rest of the house now?" Keith asked after giving her a moment of contemplation.

She looked up at him with bleary eyes. "I don't need to," she said, letting go. Letting go at long last and achieving what Lillian had wanted for her, what she needed for herself.

Keith swept her into his arms and simply held her, allowing her some time to feel, understand, and then categorize her emotions. He knew her. He knew she would need to do all those things… and more. Vera was someone who had to complete circles in her life, and that was why she fit so well into his. He adored her for that.

"You actually do need to," Keith spoke out into the room.

"Huh?" she said and wiped at the drying tears.

"You do need to see the rest of the house," he said to her as she exited his embrace.

Vera shook her head. "I really don't. I can tell that you and John have done amazing work here. This house is just as it was meant to be, and I have my memories. I'm content."

"You're also the new owner," Keith announced.

"What?!" Vera spat and almost dropped the tiny porcelain squirrel.

"You're the new owner. Don't you want to see all of your property?" Keith went on and kissed her lips that were slightly agape.

Vera could not speak. She had run out of words. She could barely even think.

"The surprises never end!" Keith said with as much showmanship as he'd ever displayed.

Vera walked through the Thompson house with Keith. She went through it room by room and didn't manage to see a thing. She was incapable of taking it in properly. Her brain was swimming in a turbulent chemical fog brought on by shock and awe and a torrent of emotional upheaval. She hadn't registered any bit of the reality until they exited for the gardens through the back door in the kitchen. And the first thing she saw there, what snapped her out of her stupor, was Isaac. He was standing in the center of fresh, raised garden beds, only a couple of which had started to sprout the miracle of unknown lush, green baby plants.

Isaac stood in a deep divot of earth, a scar for which Vera would never forget the injury. Her precious oak tree, her axis mundi had died there, had been ripped to pieces. The recollection still caused her an enormous bout of pain. But when she gazed at Isaac upon her approach, she once again saw not one man, but two. She clearly made out two distinct beings, two very similar and yet paradoxically different men. And as the last rays of light lit him from the side and behind, Vera recognized both of them. She saw her newly acknowledged friend, Isaac... and she also saw her beloved tree man. He'd found her. He'd come back to her. How had she not seen it before? Isaac and her axis mundi, the one she'd thought she'd lost connection with forever, were one and the same.

"Oh my god," Vera whispered, as she came within an arm's length of Isaac. She stood before him and reached out a hand to place it in the center of his chest.

Isaac let her.

Vera closed her eyes and felt. She waited for what she hoped would be there all on its own, and it was. The wooden beat of a rhythmic heart and the sensation beyond primary touch of warm, living tree bark. She listened to the sappy sounds that were heard without the aid of ears, the flow through his ethereal veins that revealed to her the entire truth of the matter. Vera knew then that when the tree man had died, his spirit went home to Isaac, like two halves of a whole coming together, like soul mates. That was why Isaac seemed so complete and so incredible in every instance. He was so knowing, so wise. Connected. Vera opened her eyes.

"Welcome home," Isaac said to her, as if nothing were amiss, as if the sensational were commonplace.

"I have one more surprise for you," Keith attempted to rouse her from her spiking euphoria. He clutched her hand and turned it palm side up, and in it he dropped the acorn he'd snatched from his own spiral oak the night Vera had finally come back to him.

Vera looked at the acorn and then to Keith in question.

"Your brother told me about the oak that was here when you were kids and how upset you were when they had to tear it down. It was just a short story he'd shared one day, not a big deal to him, however I thought —" Keith began.

But, Vera overrode him. And, she looked to Isaac when she spoke. "They didn't have to tear it down."

Isaac smiled tenderly at her, keeping her secret, his secret, something they shared with no one else. Vera felt mildly guilty, for it was just one more thing she kept from Keith, but it was a kind thing, a harmless secret. It was a mystery she deserved to have be hers and Isaac's, the tree man's, alone.

Keith gave a courteous nod. "Of course," he acquiesced. "But, let's set things right."

"Let's plant it," Isaac encouraged.

Vera knelt down with the acorn as Isaac moved from his spot on the wounded earth. And, Vera began digging, with her hands, just a small hole that would be a nice bed for a striving young tree. But when she started, she could not stop. Her original intention was overcome by something more, some force, some impulse that was greater. At about half a foot down in the soil, she felt a hard, smooth surface. It was warm and it moved slightly. Vera brushed away the dirt.

It was the doll, that twisted Fate. It stared up at her without eyes and with an expression that never changed, that couldn't change. Vera pulled back as if burned. The tiny monstrosity then looked at her but made no effort to do anything else. Vera peered back and after several moments gauged that it was incapable. It wasn't dead and yet it could do no further damage. It was done. It had run its course.

Isaac knelt down next to her. "Don't be afraid," he said low, as he stared at what was only the physical remains of one of his hearts.

Derrick. Images of him flooded into Vera's brain again, unbidden. She thought back to the last exchange they'd shared, to that cold morning and his pallid presence. She remembered his muddy hands. He'd buried the doll. He'd placed it here. But, why? To simply get rid of it? For her to later find it? For someone else to find and then have equally bad luck, if such a thing were even possible at this point? Did he think the doll would eventually unearth itself? Unlikely. Vera looked at the ugly little thing again. It was done. There was a swarm of questions buzzing, sure, and all of them stung more than a little. But, the doll was done. That Fate, which they'd had a hand in creating, was done. It had run its course.

"It was left with good intention," Isaac continued. "It belongs here. The doll is you." He spoke what were once Elizabeth's words. "You were the heart of that tree." He covered the doll back over with earth and let it rest. "Put the acorn over it," he instructed, with a hope and tenderness creeping into his eloquent voice, that rich baritone.

Vera did as she was told, and as she wanted to do. She set the acorn on the rich earth, and then she and Isaac covered it over with a light and loose blanket of soil, with new and fertile resources.

"I need it to heal," Isaac said so softly that he was positive only Vera had heard him. The last remnants of his dual heart, and he needed it to heal, to be reborn.

Vera understood. She gave a slow nod to show that she did. Of course, he needed it to heal. She thought of that aspect over and over and over again. She had to remind herself that it was more than a piece of random wood Elizabeth had carved into a supposed Fate. Before all of that and at its very center, that doll was Isaac's heart. Her Fate had been his in some way that was beyond her complete understanding, continuing to appear as a force outside of herself.

"It may not grow," Keith warned, speaking of the acorn. "But, we'll see." He was forever a voice of reason.

Vera stood up and brushed off her hands as best she could, with Isaac at her side, doing the same. It was then that the sound of dog tags jingling, followed by friendly, excited barking, reached her ears.

Her brother and Misty were out in the yard next door with Frank, running him around and tossing a ball that he happily chased.

"Hey!" Vera shouted and waved a hand.

Both John and Misty turned in unison, waved back, and started walking over, with Frank at their heels. Frank trotted along, ball in mouth, floppy lips bouncing in a playful display. He looked thrilled and ridiculous.

"Hey there!" Misty said as she came alongside Vera. "I see you are getting the tour of your new living space," she chirped.

"How long have you known?" Vera inquired lightly.

"Longer than you," Misty said with a wink, a nod towards her former self and the friendship the two women had once shared before some aspect of the bond went awry and shredded. "Look!" Misty exclaimed and thrust a hand in front of Vera's face.

In a couple of seconds, Vera's eyes adjusted to see that a shiny object caught glimmers of light at the end of her nose. She took Misty's hand in hers and brought it down a bit for better examination. It was a ring, a huge ring, an engagement ring! A band of gold encircled Misty's finger and atop sat a gigantic, brilliant diamond that shamelessly shimmered and silently spoke of how much the woman who wore it was adored.

"Shit!" The word flew from Vera's lips.

"Gee, thanks," Misty said and took her hand back.

"I mean, I'm just kind of in shock, is all…" Vera backpedaled. "When did he ask you?"

Misty beamed as she thought about it. "Last night, at dinner. It was so lovely," she reminisced by herself, swooning in a fantasyland Vera wasn't asked to be a part of anymore. There was a period of their past where Misty shared more, took her along for the ride. But, those days seemed to be behind them.

Vera made eye contact with her brother, a man who had helped with her business space and given her a home, someone who in one way or another had provided support her whole life. "Congratulations," she said sincerely.

John smiled at his sister. 'Thanks."

She returned the expression, making it mutual. Perhaps she'd given to him, too. Perhaps she'd given just as much but in different ways. Even so, John had been very good to her. "Thank you."

It was apparent then that Misty and Vera might be family one day soon, but they'd yet to really become friends again. Only time would tell if that was in the cards, if it would happen organically, healthfully. Deep down, Vera hoped so. She prayed it would happen before time ran out.

After the sun went down completely and the bugs began to bite, Keith suggested that everyone go inside. He led the way, followed closely by Vera and Isaac, and a little further back by Misty and John and even Frank, ball still in mouth. Vera wasn't sure why her brother and Misty went along, Frank at their heels, but she assumed they wanted to see the house, too… not that John hadn't seen plenty of it with all the restorative work. Who knew when it came to Misty?...

Vera didn't say anything. It didn't matter. She was going back inside, into the auspices of her own home, into the sanctity of the Thompson house, to be embraced by the memories and magic contained therein. It had meant so much over the years. She never, ever wanted to leave its confines again. Vera knew in her heart, in her soul that she would grow old there. One day she would die there. Maybe she would pass in the shade of an oak, in the heart of the gardens.

It was when Vera entered the darkened kitchen that she was met by a blinding burst of light and loud shouting.

"Surprise!" came the unified call of many people.

Surprise. That appeared to be the theme of the day.

Vera jumped back and smashed into Isaac, who carefully thrust her forward and well into the mix. As her eyes adjusted, she saw more people in her hearth space. There was Casey and Magdalena; they stood out among the crowd. In addition, there were the regular people from Keith's drum circle, many of whom Vera still couldn't name.

"What? What?" Vera couldn't form a more intricate question. She tried. She failed. "What?"

Casey bounced up and hugged her, then proceeded to drag her straight to the center of the room. "You are surprised, aren't you?"

"Does she not look it?" asked Magdalena in her rich and exotic accent.

Vera smiled at the both of them. "Yes, yes, I am! Many times over!" she exclaimed and gave in to the waves of feelings that crashed against her heart, the euphoria that flooded her brain against her own better judgment. Vera let herself be happy in the moment, contented in the space, grateful for all that she had. Vera let loose of any control along with the dangerous illusion of it.

"Happy Housewarming," Keith whispered into her ear and then kissed her cheek seductively, lingering longer than he normally would in a public setting.

Isaac came around to her next. "Welcome home," he said and kissed the backs of both of her hands, which were still smeared with fresh earth.

John and Misty took the time to hug Vera as well, and Vera was thankful for the affection, even if things continued to feel off with Misty. Vera prayed that the age-old adage was true, that time healed all wounds, including those afflicted without reason, those created by an unknown cause, at least unknown to one person.

The gathering spilled throughout the house, people milling about, wandering, taking in the grand structure that had been so carefully resurrected and preserved. People randomly asked Vera questions when they congratulated her, questions about how she would do up each room and what her plans were for the garden area. Would she fill the beds with herbs or flowers or vegetable crops? Vera answered as best she could, for she really hadn't gotten the chance to give it much thought. One thing was clear, however. Vera would make the Thompson house her own. Initially, when asked, she thought she would make each room what Lillian had made it originally. But then, she sensed Lillian wouldn't have wanted that. Lillian would not like her making a shrine to what was, living each day in a tomb that never changed. Lillian would've wanted Vera to bring light and life and unique interpretations back into the house. Lillian would have charged Vera to make the place her own home, her own way. And, Vera decided to do so.

After most of the swirling guests had left, Vera managed to snag a glass of wine for herself from the assorted libations that manifested in the kitchen. It was there, as she leaned back against a counter, that she saw Casey and Magdalena. They came through the dining room to join her there.

Casey looked bright as noonday in her tan sundress, and Magdalena was dazzlingly dark and draped in vibrant shades of blue. In her bright peasant top and daring layered skirt, Magdalena almost resembled a peacock. She even had her own version of a proud signature strut.

"I've been meaning to ask you two something."

"Yes?" they both prompted in unison.

Vera smiled at that. The connection they shared was endearing. "It's just something that's been rolling around in the back of my brain, and I know you've answered this before, but I sense there's more."

Magdalena looked to Casey. The two women shared a moment and then smiled in return.

"When we met for the first time at drum circle," Vera led in, "you two mentioned you were looking for a third. What does that really mean? And, don't give me your own version of a cord of three strands is not easily broken again. I don't believe that's the story in full," Vera cautioned in a friendly manner and took a healthy drink of her white wine. Refreshing.

"It means we've been looking..." Casey started but then stopped. She glanced at Magdalena.

"We have been looking, yes," Magdalena agreed and picked up the line of discussion, "but we have been waiting, too... for a third to emerge. We have been waiting for our third sister," Magdalena said with great finality.

Casey came over to Vera's side and wrapped an arm around her. "We've been waiting for you... to remember, to come back," she spoke so sweetly.

Vera set her wineglass down on the counter and held hands with both women then, sharing their space, all of them sharing the vital reverence of the hearth. "I guess I really have come home — finally."

Isaac was the last of the guests to leave, and Vera realized that to be fair, she didn't actually think of him as a guest. She'd downright told him as much.

"You're welcome here, anytime, whether I'm home or not. You're welcome in my house and my gardens," she said to him as he stood in the front doorway.

Isaac smiled down at her, the flickering flames of the ages kindled in his black irises. "Thank you," he said. "Good night to you both," he looked to Keith.

"Good night, Isaac," Keith said. "See you on Friday."

Vera closed the door behind her friend and tree man, and joined Keith for the rest of the cleanup. There wasn't much. A few beer cans, some plastic cups, and wineglasses Keith had raided from his own place to put in the sink.

After it was all done, Keith and Vera wandered back into the main room, the living room, where the lights were brightest and the space the greatest.

"We can come back in the morning and finish with the cleaning," Keith said as a cue for them to head out.

"I think I'll sleep here tonight," Vera suddenly said.

Keith laughed lightly. "There's no furniture."

Vera just looked at him blankly.

"Oh, come on. What? Are you going to sleep on the floor? With no pillow or blankets?" he continued.

Vera admitted the absurdity of her statement to herself, but didn't voice the thought out loud. Eventually, she sighed in resignation. "Oh, I guess you're right," she confessed. " I just really don't ever want to leave this place."

"You have the whole rest of your life to be here. In the next few weeks, we'll fill the house out with furnishings," Keith said pragmatically, sounding a bit like John. It was no wonder they worked so well together.

Vera snickered to herself about that, about how almost everyone around her was so pragmatic, so logical all the time.

Keith caught her little laugh. "What?"

Vera waved him off. "Oh, nothing. You're right. Let's head back to the farm for tonight."

Keith let out a sigh of his own. "Thank you. Gods, woman! I'm tired."

Vera snuggled up to him as he locked the front door and switched off the overhead lights. "It has been a busy day."

They made their way through the dining room and to the kitchen, shutting of lights as they went along. They went out the back door.

"Oh, here. This is yours now," Keith said and retrieved a shiny silver key from his pocket. "The locks are all new, too, and this key works on both the front and back doors. Your brother and I have spares," Keith informed and placed the cool metal into Vera's warm and expectant hand. She held the key, examined every facet and the shine of its newness.

Vera locked up her house. "Make one for Isaac, too," she said as they came down the steps and stood at the start of the gardens. She peered out to the open scar, the mark left by the magnificent axis mundi that once was and still remained, centered in Isaac and sleeping beneath an acorn.

"Ok," Keith said simply and took her hand in his. "Let's go. It's getting late."

And, it was. The moon, full and glorious in its milky white perfection, was riding high in the inky night sky. The stars twinkled in the heavens and spring peepers croaked to fill any void. She would have many, many nights like this in her future; season after season Vera would enjoy the wonders she'd been given.

Everything changed the day old Mrs. Thompson died, all those years ago. Vera's world certainly took an irrevocable twist then and there, a twist that just kept on turning as time passed, as the years melted away, even if that had been the only perceivable and traceable way in which the world changed. But, it wasn't. Things changed when Elizabeth arrived and then again after college and with Derrick. Derrick was one of the biggest twists of her life, and she would never come undone from that one. She'd be a shriveled old crone before the embers cooled in her core. Things changed when she'd made love to Keith, when she'd remembered who she was under the spiraling oak and who she belonged with, the people she belonged to. Things changed. Everything changed and all the time. Everything spiraled. Everything circled.

And that night, out at Keith's farmhouse, under the full moon and the star-littered sky, under the roof that was not her own but yet was a definite haven, Vera dreamed. She dreamed of the oak behind the barn, twisting up until it breached the ceiling of the sky and met new worlds and perpetual dawns. She dreamed of the acorn she'd planted with Isaac in the Thompson gardens, her gardens. She dreamed of it growing and twisting to full height and vigor, to a great stage of life and an unmatched degree of virility. It was the most majestic feature in the gardens, perhaps in the world. Her axis mundi, and her original understanding of it, had returned. She dreamed. She dreamed on and on, and it was glorious.

Vera dreamed, and as the tree grew unnaturally fast in her dreams, grew as a time lapse, it opened its eyes. It opened numerous red, ember, ethereal eyes. It spread its roots out as it reached its branches up. And from the sprawl of that oak came hundreds of thousands of other oaks, each with countless red ember eyes…